COLOMBIAN BETRAYAL

RANDALL KRZAK

Colombian Betrayal

A Bruce & Smith Thriller: Book 1

Copyright © 2020 Randall Krzak

ISBN-978-0-9789441-0-0

❀ Created with Vellum

To Sylvia, my true flower of Scotland,
And to our son Craig, of whom we're very proud.
There's no doubt I have the best family in the world.
Thank you for loving me.
I love you.

To Sarah,
Merry Christmas.
Hope you enjoy the story.
Best Regards,
25 DEC 2021

ACKNOWLEDGMENTS

Cover Design By: DarnGoodCovers.com

Colombian Betrayal would not be a reality without those who helped me along my journey including: Jenny Benfield, Richard Bishop, Steve Blake, Bobby R. Byrd, Oliver F. Chase, Wayne B. Chorney, Steve Denker, Rikon Gaites, Preston Holtry, Mark Iles, Mike Jackson, Michael Kent, Sylvia Krzak, James McLeod, Anastasia Mosher, M.D. Neu, Craig Palmer, Rachel Parsons, Jonathan Pongratz, Lynn Z. Puhle, Mike Rickerman, Vivienne Sang, B. William Slack, Les Stahl, Arthur Steele, Janis Stein, AJ Wallace, Gillian Watters, Rayner Jamie Ye, as well as other reviewers from The Next Big Writer and Scribophile. Many thanks!

Also a special thanks to Michael Maxwell and Blair Howard for their guidance as this novel came to fruition.

1

M edellín, Colombia
Spring 2004

THREE ARMORED Chevrolet Suburbans raced through the hacienda's open gates. Dust billowed in their wake as guards took up defensive positions on top of the high brick and concrete wall facing strategic areas of the driveway. Two unarmored SUVs escorted the procession. One raced ahead to take the lead while the other brought up the rear.

Seventy-year-old Jesús Pedro Zapata and his forty-five-year-old son, Oscar, relaxed in the middle vehicle. The Medellín Country Club's weekly buffet luncheon drew father, son, and Zapata's thirty-five-year-old daughter, Olivia, along with numerous local dignitaries and powerful landowners. On this rare occasion, Olivia missed the gathering due to a prior commitment in Panama City, where she and their lawyers sought to close a deal for the purchase of a sugar cane plantation.

As the convoy approached the road leading to the club, they slowed.

Zapata dropped the inner glass partition. "Why are we stopping? We'll be late."

"Sorry, Jefe." The chauffeur pointed through the windshield. "An accident or construction is blocking the way."

Ahead, yellow lights and trucks emblazoned with *Interconexión Eléctrica S.A.* blocked the road. A man dressed in white coveralls waved the convoy onto a side street.

The chauffeur stopped again. Additional vehicles impeded progress through the next intersection.

Before the convoy could reverse, more trucks cut off their escape.

Zapata spotted the movement and became suspicious. "*Hijueputa!* Get us out of here! Hurry, before it's too late!"

Men wearing blue coveralls jumped out of the blocking vehicles, aimed anti-tank weapons at the front and rear escort vehicles.

Passersby screamed and ran for any shelter they could find—the nearest trees and vehicles became temporary refuges.

The attackers fired their rocket-propelled grenades, and the escort vehicles soared into the air, plummeting back to earth as burning hulks. One of the SUVs flipped end over end before landing on top of a parked car. Thick, black smoke billowed upward as the stench filled the air. Shrapnel and smoldering pieces of metal from the destroyed vehicles littered the area.

Zapata's guards returned fire but were overwhelmed by the firepower of the attacking force.

One by one, the defenders succumbed to the withering fire when the remaining escort vehicles and two of the armored SUVs met the same fate. Gunfire waned, while moans from the injured and the crackling of burning vehicles grew in intensity. Random shots echoed throughout the area as the attackers rendered a coup de grâce to the few survivors.

The assailants approached Zapata's SUV through the thickening smoke. They lined up along the driver's side and glared at Zapata and his son.

Defiant stares greeted them.

Two men rushed away from the vehicle, shouldered their rocket-propelled grenades, and aimed.

Zapata's reign died as he and his son were immolated.

Francisco Tomas Kruz, Zapata's long-time friend and confidant, replaced the receiver without a word. He rubbed his hand through his dyed black hair as he strolled to the windows and gazed across the mountainous expanse. A smile flickered across his face, not reaching his cold, hazel eyes. *At last.*

He returned to his desk, lifted the phone, and placed a call. "This is Kruz. Give her the phone." He spoke for a moment.

Olivia screamed.

Moreno Hacienda
　　Barranquilla, Colombia
　　Present Day

Dawn broke with birds twittering outside Olivia's country estate. She opened blue-green eyes and focused on the view through the open window. Tinges of red and orange stretched across the horizon, seeking the deep blue heavens. More songbirds joined in, their melodious voices adding to the morning's chorus. Nearby, a rare Colombian screech owl hooted. Other birds shrieked, their wings beating the air as they scattered.

Olivia yawned and crawled out of bed. Twinges cascaded through her aching muscles caused by overexertion in yesterday's intense personal security training. *Time for some fresh air while it's quiet.* She slipped a purple velvet robe over her slender athletic body and pulled on matching slippers. Padding toward the balcony, she opened the doors and stepped outside. She gazed at the tranquil countryside and smiled.

Craack! Craack!

Bullets ricocheted off the stonework, missing her head by inches. She dropped to the floor amid a hail of flying rubble and dust. Hunched like a hermit crab, Olivia crawled inside and slammed the doors.

"*Madre de Dios!*"

Stomach lurching, chest heaving, she rolled across the floor to the bedside table. Her hands shaking, she grabbed the handle, opened the drawer, and removed her FN Five-SeveN handgun. She fumbled for a second magazine and stuffed it into a pocket on her robe. Keeping out of view, she crept back to the side of the balcony and slid down the wall.

She peered through a small opening, looking for signs of intruders.

Nothing. All seems normal.

Pushing through the doors, she dashed around the corner, squatted, and fired three times without aiming. An incoming round smashed into the wall in front of her. She leaned into the stone for cover as rough-edged shards whirled toward her face. Startled by the fast-approaching slivers, Olivia ducked and dropped the pistol. Blood trickled from a cut above her right eye. She sucked in her breath and wiped it away as anger replaced fear.

"*Alto.*" A man of medium height climbed over the railing from the patio. Piercing dark eyes shone beneath a mop of black hair as he plopped into a chair at the small bistro table, and helped himself to a glass of fresh-squeezed orange juice.

"*Diablo.*" Olivia spat the word as the man with the physique of a bodybuilder stood and helped her into the other chair. "Ramon, one day you'll cause my death. The training becomes more intense every day." She grabbed his goblet. "*Salud.*" She drained the glass.

"Doña Olivia, you hired me to provide protection. When I'm not here, you must do this for yourself and your family. Your enemies will give you no warning, which is why the lessons must become more realistic."

Olivia nodded. "*Sí*, you are correct. I want to live a long time and enjoy my fortune—unlike my father, brother, and first husband, who died before their time."

Ramon Cristobal Alvarez and Olivia Perfecta Moreno gazed at each other.

Bam! Bam!

Ramon rose. His movements panther-like, he approached the door. He turned the knob in minor increments while the thudding continued.

"Shhh." Someone outside the room cautioned and received a snigger in response.

Ramon yanked the door open. Caught off guard, two girls tumbled into the room. Laughing and giggling, they fell into a disheveled stack of limbs. He grabbed an arm of each child and helped them to their feet.

"Ramon, be careful! You'll wrinkle my pretty dress." Olivia's ten-year-old daughter, Maria, stomped her foot and straightened the folds of her pink frock.

"Maria, stop it." Silvina, her nine-year-old sister, dressed in blue, squirmed out of Ramon's clutches.

Together, the two girls darted across the Spanish tile, color-coordinated ribbons holding their long hair in place as they melted into Olivia's embrace for a much-needed hug.

Preferring the clothing of a tomboy, Olivia's darling, Silvina, fidgeted with her dress.

"Mamá, breakfast is ready. Papá says to come now, or you can't eat." Maria delivered the message in a serious tone, before bursting into infectious laughter.

Olivia smiled. "Sí. Let's not keep Papá waiting."

Ramon led Olivia and her daughters to the dining room, where Pedro Moreno sat reading a local newspaper. Once Olivia and the girls took their seats, Ramon headed to the kitchen. Breakfast remained a private affair, a chance for parents to interact with their children.

"Good morning, Pedro. Where's Alonzo?"

"Morning, dear. He called and said he'd be here—"

The door flew open, and Alonzo rushed into the room. Without uttering a word, he heaped a plate with beans, rice, and eggs from the buffet and joined the others. "Sorry I'm late. There was a union issue at the plant." He glanced at his mother, who gave him a knowing glance. "I must return after breakfast to ensure the problem remains resolved."

"Don't forget the party tonight," Olivia reminded him. "There will be ladies lined up to dance with you."

"How can I forget? You've reminded me every day since the staff hand-delivered the invitations."

"Only because our family's survival is at stake."

Alonzo frowned at his mother. "What if I don't find a suitable bride this time?"

"You must."

He sighed. "Sí, Mamá."

Olivia changed the subject. "Pedro, what are your plans for this morning?"

"I'm going horseback riding when we finish breakfast, and before lunch, Alonzo and I are playing tennis."

AFTER BREAKFAST, Pedro strolled from the dining room to the covered porch. Olivia allowed him one Cuban cigar per day, as long as he smoked outside. Before he sat, Ramon appeared.

"Tonight's party should be interesting." Pedro exhaled a column of smoke and glanced up at him. "The mayor, chief of police, and the local military commander are among those attending."

"Why were they invited?"

"Olivia wants legitimacy. This will be our first party since we moved here. Their attendance will demonstrate we are part of the community's elite. The wealthy and important will approach us, wanting their daughters to marry Alonzo."

Ramon nodded. "I understand, Pedro. My men and I will remain in the shadows, available if a situation arises. Please advise if you require anything else. Anything at all."

Pedro nodded, snuffed out his cigar, and strolled down the steps into the brilliant sunshine. He gazed around their new estate. A palatial mansion on 500 acres, the property boasted a six-stall stable, Olympic-size swimming pool, two all-weather tennis courts, and a helipad. A ten-foot concrete wall stood guard over five acres surrounding the house—home, at least for now.

He waited outside the stable for a saddled horse to be brought to him. This morning, Shadow, an all-black Arabian stallion, became the ride of choice. Pedro mounted and reined the horse toward the stone arch built into the perimeter wall. He put Shadow into a canter and traveled along one of the paths crisscrossing the estate.

Alonzo and his mother took their coffee to her office. They sat on matching easy chairs in front of her Italian oak desk. The cozy room was once the refuge of the previous owner. Its Brazilian cherrywood floor contrasted with the two walls lined with floor-to-ceiling oak bookcases.

A stack of hardwood in a stone fireplace waited to be ignited when the evening weather turned cool. The outer wall boasted glazed windows, with two sets of French doors opening onto the veranda. A massive portrait of her father seated on a brown quarter horse took center stage on the wall behind the desk.

"What happened at the plant, Alonzo? I thought you could manage without needing my intervention." Olivia leaned back in her chair and crossed her arms.

"Mamá, I thought when I finished university, I would run the legitimate businesses and let you know if I needed your help."

"You shall, but as my eldest, you must also learn about what provides us with real money."

"My MBA will help me run the shopping malls in Miami and Madrid, the restaurant chains in North America and Europe, and the hotels in the Caribbean. But, I understand nothing about the drug trade."

"I didn't either when I first started. Government troops killed your *abuelo* in Medellín, but before he died, he taught me both sides of the business. Now you must prepare in the event something happens to me."

"What about Pedro?"

"I married him for love." *Alonzo can't know the truth—I didn't really marry for love. I needed to replace his dead father, and Pedro was willing to raise someone else's son. It's unfortunate he ill-treated Alonzo when he was growing up. No wonder he hates Pedro. Still, Alonzo does well to cover up his feelings.* "He's useless in our business and wants no part."

Alonzo frowned. "Sí, Mamá."

"Tell me what happened at the plant this morning."

"Two of the guards grabbed a woman, pulled her into the bushes, and raped her. The woman's husband was unloading a truck when the attack occurred. When he intervened, the guards killed them." Alonzo's forehead puckered. "Although I abhor the use of violence, in this instance, we can't allow this behavior to go unpunished."

Olivia rubbed her hands through her long, violet-black hair.

"Tomorrow morning, find out the names of the two guards. Have them stripped and tied to poles outside the plant. Let them suffer overnight. The next day, assemble the workers. Make this a lesson to all. Render the same punishment to them as they bestowed upon the couple. This will send a clear warning."

Alonzo considered her comments for a moment. "Yes, Mamá." He grimaced. *When will she stop treating me like a child?*

THROUGHOUT THE AFTERNOON, guards searched the arriving trucks as they ferried the necessities for the Morenos' party. Additional security personnel poked through the flower arrangements, examined tables for hidden objects, and removed fine linens from their protective coverings to ensure nothing had been slipped between the folds.

As the day wore on, cleared caterers appeared, bringing their own special implements for creating sensational regional and local dishes for the buffet. The staggering menu included *Valluna* cutlets, *milanesa, arroz de lisa, mamona, lechona*, and tamales. Others brought cases of champagne, whiskey, vodka, and rum. In the corner of the mansion's ballroom, a twelve-piece orchestra worked through their repertoire, selecting pieces designed to awe their audience.

Everything and everyone was in position by seven thirty in the evening.

Eight p.m. Still no guests. Olivia's outward calm crumbled, and a frown replaced her smile. She paced back and forth from the entranceway to the ballroom, her grimace deepening with each circuit.

Eight fifteen. A taxi arrived—false alarm, a waiter late for work.

Eight thirty. Pedro strolled toward his over-anxious wife and smiled.

"A long string of fancy cars passed through the perimeter gate. Your guests are sticking to an old-fashioned tradition—arriving late." He sighed. *At last, they've arrived—for Olivia's sake.*

"As long as they come, that's the important thing. For Alonzo. And us."

Ricardo Natanael Vasco, the current mayor of Barranquilla, his wife, Camila, and daughter, Josephina entered first. Introductions ensued as Olivia, Pedro, and Alonzo created a short reception line. Ricardo and Camila joined them to welcome the rest of the guests.

The chief of police and the local military commander, their spouses and daughters, followed by a cluster of other local dignitaries, crossed the threshold and joined the festivities. The guests' bodyguards remained outside the house, augmenting those at the front and around the perimeter. By nine, everyone on the invitation list sipped champagne and chatted in small groups while the orchestra provided various classical and modern compositions.

Tall, with a well-toned body, black wavy hair, and chiseled features, Alonzo found himself the center of attention, each beauty vying for recognition. From their actions, every unattached woman hoped he would choose her.

Danced off his feet since he wouldn't decline any request, Alonzo sought one particular woman whenever possible throughout the evening. Gabriela Sofia, the graceful five-foot-ten-inch daughter of Colonel Bautista Enrique Santiago, military commander of the Atlántico department, captivated him. Chocolate hair with a natural curl fell in elegant locks around her perfectly-formed face and down her shoulders and back. There was a hypnotic quality to her deep brown eyes, framed with thick lashes.

Above the buzz of polite conversation, the clink of crystal, and subdued laughter, the orchestra's conductor proclaimed the final dance. Alonzo threaded through the tables. Hands grazing his arms, he dodged every grasp and made excuses to young women who tried to engage him in small talk. On the other side of the room, Gabriela stood talking with Josephina.

"*Señorita*, may I have the honor of the last dance?"

Gabriela gave a small curtsy. "Of course, *señor*. My pleasure."

Alonzo led her to the center of the dance floor and signaled the orchestra to play. As they danced, other couples joined them. Gabriela snuggled her head on Alonzo's shoulder, enjoying his closeness.

"May I call upon you next week?"

"You may, but first, you'll need *el coronel's* permission."

Alonzo laughed, twirling Gabriela in time with the music. "I thought so. Everything is arranged. I took the liberty of speaking with *el coronel* earlier this evening."

Cheeks reddening, Gabriela pulled Alonzo closer.

~

AFTER THE LAST GUEST DEPARTED, Olivia, Pedro, and Alonzo sauntered onto the veranda for a nightcap. While they sat sipping single malt whiskey, a myriad of night creatures serenaded them.

"So, Alonzo. What do you think about the lovely ladies who visited tonight?" Pedro drained his glass. "Did any stand out?"

"Pedro, it's not a cattle market," Alonzo grinned, glancing upwards. "But, one or two caught my attention."

"Make sure you marry for money and power. Love can wait."

Olivia rolled her eyes but held her tongue. *Sounds like his personal creed. What did I see in him? At least he gave me two beautiful daughters.*

Arm in arm, Pedro and Olivia ascended the grand staircase. Midway down the corridor, they kissed and separated, each going to their individual apartments.

After removing her makeup, Olivia shed her clothes and jewelry as she prepared for sleep. *Wonder if Gabriela is the right woman for Alonzo? He seemed to enjoy her company more than the others.*

She sat at her dressing table, am antique silver hairbrush in her hand. She began her nightly ritual of 100 strokes through her thick hair. *It's so hard to know who to trust.* She stared into the mirror, refusing to shed a tear. *I must be ruthless—as unforgiving and cold as my father and brother before someone murdered them.*

Finished, she climbed into bed and turned out the lights. *I hope I get a good night's sleep.*

Olivia tossed and turned for a long time. At last, sleep took her. Two hours into an uneasy slumber, she sensed someone's presence. Her eyes shot open, searching the darkness for any hint of an intruder. Her hand slid over to the nightstand as a voice distracted her.

"Olivia." The voice, distant, yet familiar, seemed to come from within.

"Yes, Papá?" Confused, she rubbed her eyes, unsure if she was awake or dreaming.

"You must build new alliances. Our business is suffering. Americans consume less product, and foreign competitors are encroaching upon our territories, stealing our fields and our workers. More security is required—tougher measures. You may not want to go to war, but a storm is on the horizon, my child, and the wind blows ill for those unprepared. Reach out to Días. He will help you."

The voice faded. Olivia waited, but she remained alone. *Did I imagine this?* She drifted off to sleep, a smile on her face. She understood her dead father's edict.

~

THE FOLLOWING MORNING, Olivia woke again to the hoot of the owl. She rushed to the balcony to find the bird's hiding place. Two shots rang out. Following her training, she crashed to the floor and squirmed back into the bedroom.

She grunted and laughed, thinking Ramon had upped the training. A moment later, a loud thump resounded against the door as Ramon forced his way inside, gun drawn.

"Olivia, this isn't training—it's real."

Ramon pushed aside a balcony door. He crawled outside, peeked between ornate pillars, and scanned the area for would-be assassins. After completing his sweep from the balcony, he returned inside.

"They're gone." He twirled his right index finger in the air several times. "Stay here. The guards will scour the full perimeter for those seeking to harm you, while I check on Pedro, Alonzo, and the girls."

Olivia nodded. Shaking, she wrapped her arms around herself.

Ramon walked to the door. Before he opened it—

A gunshot echoed in the corridor.

"*Madre de Dios!*" Ramon leaped toward Olivia, shoving her to the floor with one hand, a weapon in the other.

A high-pitched scream pierced the air, followed by a second.

Silence.

2

M oreno Hacienda
Barranquilla, Colombia

RAMON SNATCHED his radio from his belt. "Report!"

"Clear."

The hair on the back of Ramon's neck bristled. *Something's wrong.* All teams worked two-hour shifts, with two groups inside the house and four in the immediate grounds. German Shepherds, motion sensors, and fixed cameras augmented the teams. Six all-clear reports, yet an intruder had breached their defenses. *How?*

He frowned before turning to Olivia. "Jefe de la señora, lock the door behind me. Stay away from the windows." He held her chin for a moment. "Remember the protocols. No matter how much you want to leave the room, remain here and let me do my job."

"Sí, Ramon. Be careful." She grabbed his arm. "Check on my darlings."

Ramon nodded as he keyed his radio. "Inside teams, meet me at the grand staircase leading to the family quarters. Outside patrols move closer to the house."

Four guards waited for him when he descended the stairs—two men, two women.

"Did you hear a shot?"

They shook their heads.

"What about the screams?"

They mouthed, "No."

Ramon glared at them. "Where were you?"

Four pairs of eyes stared at the floor.

"Where?"

A young female guard pointed down the hall. "Taking a break in the kitchen."

"Everyone? I gave explicit orders—only one guard to take a break at a time."

Except for the female guard who had spoken, the others continued to focus on the tiled floor.

She raised her head, and her eyes flashed. "But—"

"I'll deal with you later." Ramon gritted his teeth. "Go upstairs. Remain in pairs and search every room. Now." *Incompetent loafers— can't trust them.*

Ramon followed them up the staircase and returned to Olivia's room.

"Jefe de la señora, let me in."

Silence.

Did the intruder get in her room? "Doña Olivia. Open the door, por favor." He heard the key turn in the latch and pushed past her.

She stared at him, eyes wide. "Are my daughters okay? What's happened?"

He placed a reassuring hand on her shoulder and gave a slight squeeze. "We're still checking, Olivia. So far, I'm not sure, but I vow to find out."

His radio crackled into life. "Ramon, please come into the hallway."

Olivia waved him away.

He left the room, noting the grim expressions and hardness in the guards' eyes. "What did you find?"

The group didn't speak as they turned and walked along the corridor, heels clicking on the terracotta floor tiles. They stopped at a black door—Pedro's room.

One of the guards inched the door open, and Ramon slid inside. Another guard stood next to where Pedro lay on the bed groaning. Blood spread across his face, the pillowcase, and splattered upon the blanket and the wall. Stench from the blood permeated the air.

Ramon held his breath and knelt to check for a pulse—*weak and irregular.* "Call for an ambulance—he's alive!" A quick examination revealed no other injuries.

Pedro struggled to sit. His face screwed in agony, he gasped and collapsed onto the sheets.

Ramon took in a sharp breath. *Unfortunately, he lives—but for how long?* He pointed to one of his men. "Stay with him. Did you find the girls—where are they?"

The guards exchanged glances but didn't speak. Ramon shoved them aside and rushed to Maria's room, cursing under his breath.

Yanking a pistol from its holster, he eased the unlocked door open. In the middle of the tile floor, a pool of blood formed a Rorschach pattern. He glanced around. *No Maria, no body. Where is she?*

As he scanned the room, a whimper emanated from one of the walk-in closets. Ramon motioned with his weapon for a guard waiting in the doorway to enter and approach the closet. In a position to respond to anyone hiding inside, Ramon gestured for the man to open the door.

A child curled in a ball lay on the floor. She raised her head and peered up at them. Tears running down her cheeks, bottom lip quivering, she shrank further into the clothes.

Ramon's eyes ran along the rack of clothes before kneeling. He spoke in a soft voice, "Maria, it's me, Ramon. You're safe now. Please, come out."

"I-I'm afraid."

"Maria, no one will hurt you. I won't allow any harm to come to you."

A tiny hand appeared, clasping the edge of the doorframe. From within, eyes filled with fright peered at Ramon.

"Ramon!" Maria jumped up and dove at him, grasping his legs as she burst into tears.

"Shhh. You're safe now." After hugging her, he examined her for injuries. Satisfied she wasn't physically injured, he patted her on the shoulder. "Tell me what happened."

"I-I heard a loud bang, like shooting but louder than Mamá's gun. The noise woke me. Someone stood in my room, staring at me. A man—he wore an evil mask. He held a coatimundi and slit its throat. I screamed, and he ran, taking the raccoon with him."

Ramon shook his head. *Perhaps a warning? For Olivia or maybe Pedro?*

Maria clutched his hand and whimpered.

"You're okay, Maria." He signaled to a female guard now standing in the doorway. "You've been very brave, but I want you to stay here. This woman will take good care of you while I check on Silvina." Ramon stroked her head after she released his hand. "Good girl." He rose and beckoned for the remaining guards to follow him.

"Señor." A guard pointed to the floor. Blood drops led from Maria's room along the hall.

They followed the trail to Silvina's door.

A hand on the doorknob, Ramon grimaced. *Let her be alive.* He turned the handle and eased the door open.

Inside, they found more blood on the floor. Silvina sat on her bed, a tennis racket balanced across her knees. She scooted off the bed and raced to Ramon when she spotted him.

"A bad man came into my room. He killed a coati and let the blood seep out before shoving it into a sack. I hit him with my racket. Twice. He yelled and ran out."

Ramon smiled at her courage and holstered his weapon as he hugged her. "You're fierce, little one. No wonder he left, who would want to fight you?" He released her. "What did he look like?"

"I don't know. He wore a mask, one from the Barranquilla Carnival, a red Diablo."

"You're okay now, Silvina. Will you stay with Maria and protect her? I must find Alonzo. Afterward, I'll take you to your mother."

The girls waited with their female guards, as Ramon and the remaining guard headed toward Alonzo's room.

As Ramon prepared to knock on Alonzo's door, a loud snore erupted. He tried the door—locked. Using his passkey, Ramon entered, his weapon drawn.

The room stank of liquor. Two empty bottles sat on the bedside table. Alonzo was sprawled on his bed in a drunken stupor. He emitted another deep-throated snore as Ramon checked him for injuries, while the guard ensured no intruder hid in a closet or the en suite bathroom.

Satisfied Alonzo remained unharmed and alone, Ramon and the guard returned to the hallway.

In the distance, multiple sirens split the air.

"At last, the policía and the ambulance." He turned to the guard. "Let them in. Take the emergency team to Pedro's room. Once they finish, instruct them to double-check the girls in case I missed anything. Put the policía in the library. Doña Olivia and I will join them in a few minutes and speak to el capitán."

The guard nodded and disappeared. Ramon returned to Olivia's room. He knocked—no answer. He knocked again.

Still no response.

Ramon turned the handle and pushed. As the door opened, he snaked inside.

Olivia sat on the bed, her pistol pointed at Ramon's face, her hands shaking.

"Jefa." He motioned with his hands to lower her weapon. "Olivia, the girls are safe. So is Alonzo. Someone hit Pedro over the head, but he's still alive. The doctor is with him."

The gun still pointed toward him, Ramon edged forward, taking small steps, so he didn't startle Olivia. He placed his hand over the pistol, forcing it lower, and slipped it from her fingers. After setting the safety, he shoved it in his waistband.

"Find who did this and make them pay." Her eyes flared. "Slow and painful."

"I will." *Must find someone to blame—but who?*

Once she composed herself, Ramon led her downstairs. As they stepped into the library, Barranquilla's police chief, Capitán Ernesto Juan Otelo, lurched forward.

"Señora, I'm sorry about this unfortunate incident. Unusual, but there are thugs in our city who might do you harm. I advised when you moved here to maintain a more robust security force. No matter how well-trained Ramon and his people are, his team should be three times bigger."

Olivia tilted her head and frowned at Ernesto's words. "Isn't this the job of the policía? How could you let this happen?"

Ernesto rubbed a hand over his hair and cinched his belt. "Señora—"

The door swung open, and the doctor escorted his patient into the room. A gauze bandage swathed most of Pedro's head, his natural tan pale on his bloodless face. He sank into an easy chair and closed his eyes.

"Señora, Pedro will be fine. His hard head sustained a small cut and bled a lot, but he shouldn't experience any permanent damage. I gave him medication to manage the pain. If he appears confused, slurs his speech, or complains of pressure in his head, call me right away. We will arrange a CAT scan to be sure as there might be a hidden contusion."

After the police and emergency team departed, Ramon instructed the butler to organize breakfast.

"Doña Olivia, after your family has eaten, I must speak with you. Alone."

"Where's Alonzo?" Olivia glanced around the room. "Is he okay?"

Ramon smirked. "He's fine—perhaps a bit too much to drink last night. He slept through the intrusion."

"Bring him here. I must take care of my family's needs. Afterward, we'll speak."

OLIVIA WAS HUNCHED over several documents when Ramon entered her office. She glanced at him and gave a half-smile. "I could use some wine, por favor." She held out her shaking hands.

Ramon nodded. He strolled to the bar in the corner and poured a glass of red wine. "Olivia, drink—it will calm you. I realize you wanted a low profile when we came to Barranquilla. Today's infiltration, firing shots, threatening the children—someone wanted to send a message you can't ignore."

She nodded before sipping her wine.

"Luck favored us today. Seems like someone wanted to scare you, or Pedro. If they had been determined, people would be missing or dead. It's clear your family isn't safe, and we must increase security."

"Sí." Olivia ran a finger around the rim of her glass. "Have you discovered who did this to us?" She raised a hand, gesturing for Ramon to continue.

"Not yet. I spoke with the policía chief. He will provide extra security for the main gate around the clock. This will free up teams I can use near the house."

"Sí, Ramon." She glared at him. "Do whatever is necessary. Hire more guards if you want. Find out who allowed intruders into my home—they must be punished. Now, I must prepare. This afternoon the business team will arrive for an important meeting. I want to meet with you again after they depart."

THEY HELD the meeting in the library. In addition to Olivia and Alonzo, the committee included accountants, lawyers, plant managers, a logistics expert, and one of her father's oldest friends.

Colorful bowls overflowing with fruit and pitchers of orange and guava juice adorned the polished oval oak table. Matching armless chairs held equal positions around the table. At each setting lay iPads, and for the computer-averse, pen and paper, even though everything would be confiscated after the meeting.

Olivia sat at the head of the table, Alonzo beside her, watching the men enter the room and take their seats. "My friends, thank you for joining us today. We must decide how to deal with our dwindling profits." She leaned on the table, her fingers tracing small circles on her forehead and temples, her eyes closed.

"The American market became more troublesome a couple of years ago. Each month we sell less product." Cesar Jorge Tabo, their accountant, handed blue folders around the table. "The same information is also contained on the iPads. The charts show our decline, almost twenty-five percent in the past year alone."

Francisco Tomas Kruz, once her father's closest friend, waved the folder without checking the details. "Why such a significant decrease?"

The logistics expert passed out new red binders filled with issues, causes, and potential solutions. "More competition, complicated transportation routes, and a switch to synthetic products are the primary reasons."

"Our processing costs are escalating. Security, chemicals, and labor all cost more and are now difficult to manage." Domingo Rey Vicente, the plant manager at Juradó, near the Panamanian border, glanced at the other plant managers for support. Heads nodded in agreement, but no one else dared to speak and incur Olivia's wrath.

"Yes. I'm experiencing the same problems, plus disciplinary issues," Alonzo added, supporting Domingo's comments. "Yesterday, I made an example of two guards who broke the rules. Their final punishment will occur this evening."

The other plant managers murmured confirmation, while Olivia permitted herself a slight smile. *My son is growing into a man.*

"New international currency and banking regulations create difficulties for cleansing our profits." Yago Miguel Fico, the accountant for the legal side of the family business, waved a hand in the air. "I'm attempting to purchase new enterprises, but in many countries, the authorities require proof about where the money originated. We're trying to purchase check-cashing facilities in America. However, these acquisitions are slow going, and the mafia outbids us all the time."

"Excuses! All I'm hearing are excuses." Olivia slammed her hand on the table. The sharp rap startled everyone as she jumped to her feet. "Must I do everything myself? Give me solutions—ideas on how to turn our business around."

"Olivia. Sit, por favor." Francisco used open hands, palms down to motion Olivia back to her seat. "Anger will not fix the problems. What would your father have done in this situation?"

She smiled. "He would have remained quiet, analyzed the situation, and put a comprehensive plan into action." She glanced at the ceiling. "Then he would shoot the next bastardo who made an excuse." One at a time, she focused on each face. "I need answers, not explanations."

"Exactly." Francisco swept his hand from left to right, encompassing the other board members. "Let your team help figure this out. Use their collective brainpower to resolve the dilemma."

She clenched her teeth before giving him a tight smile. "Señor Kruz—Francisco—you always understand the issues and reach to the heart of the matter. Thank you for your invaluable guidance."

Francisco tilted his head with a slight nod, acknowledging the rare praise she offered.

"The bad news is on the table. Anything positive to report?"

"Sí, Olivia." Yago stood, a regular practice for the committee when delivering good news. "We are receiving excellent profits from our malls and restaurants in America—up fifteen percent from last year. People have excess money to spend and are doing so. Occupancy is running high in our Caribbean hotels."

Everyone smiled at Yago's update as he sat back in his chair, rocking back on two legs.

"Sí, excellent news at last. Gracias, Yago. Anyone else?"

Alonzo, following Yago's lead, also stood while he spoke. "We can use whatever clean money we possess to improve our market share in these areas. The American economy is recovering, so we should buy now before the property market heats up, and prices increase."

He picked up his glass and sipped the guava juice before continuing. Every eye upon him, the executives waited to hear what he would say.

"I want to take advantage of the sluggish European economy and grab available hotels, restaurants, and high-end retail stores. The American dollar is gaining strength against the euro, and we must be in a position to harvest their money when they travel."

As Alonzo resumed his seat, a smattering of applause greeted his recommendations.

"Gracias, Alonzo. Work with our accountants and lawyers to determine the best options. Any other suggestions or comments?"

Beginning on her left, Olivia locked eyes with each board member. Some returned her gaze while several glanced away. No one spoke.

"We'll meet again in a week. Alonzo, Francisco, please remain."

The meeting at an end, when the last man filed out the door and closed it behind him, Olivia turned to Francisco. "Old friend, once again, you provide wise counsel. Gracias, for reminding me of my father. I always want to punish and move on without thinking of consequences."

"Like your father." Francisco hinted a smile. "You will learn as he did or meet the same fate."

"I will." Olivia faced her son. "Alonzo, I'm proud of you. Speaking before the board is difficult. You held your own. Continue working on our legitimate businesses and increase our profits while I try to improve the other areas."

"Sí, Mamá."

"Now, I must join my daughters. Francisco, please dine with us this evening."

"Gracias, Olivia. Another time. I met someone in the city, and she invited me to eat with her."

OLIVIA APPROACHED HER OFFICE. One of the servants held the door for her before pushing a cart loaded with delicacies into the room. Maria and Silvina spotted their mother, squealed, and pounced on her. Olivia fell to her knees, rolling across the floor with her daughters. Peals of laughter filled the room as Olivia tickled them. She kissed each one on the forehead and gestured to the food cart.

Out of breath, they climbed into their chairs. Olivia laughed as she pointed at an object. "Silvina, what is the tennis racket for?"

"If Diablo returns, I'll hit him again."

"And I'll scream, Mamá," Maria added, proud she could help.

Olivia gave both girls a big hug.

AFTER DINNER, Olivia kissed her young children goodnight. "Mamá is going to meet with Ramon now. He's placed a guard outside each of your rooms. I'll peek in before I go to bed."

"Sí, Mamá." Both girls hugged her and ran to Pedro, who led them out of the dining room and upstairs.

Olivia took her coffee onto the veranda. Ramon sat in a white wicker swing, waiting for her. She seated herself opposite him.

"Ramon, last night, my papá visited me." Olivia grasped Ramon's hand as she spoke. "In my dreams. Or perhaps it was my imagination, I'm not sure. Anyway, he explained a way forward if I'm brave enough to follow through."

He remained quiet, giving her time to decide.

"We must increase our sphere of influence, provide more security for our plants, and provide new methods to improve our growing, harvesting, and refining." Olivia turned away and gazed across the compound as if the answer lay beyond the lights from the house.

Her focus swung back to Ramon—her decision made.

"Arrange a meeting with Ramírez García Días."

Ramon's eyes widened, and he blinked. "Are you certain, Olivia? He's a dangerous man."

"We're in a dangerous business." Olivia stood in front of Ramon, pulled him to his feet, and wrapped her arms around his shoulders, drawing him close. "We must succeed for my family's future. They are my entire life." She sighed and stepped back. "We cannot have a deeper relationship as long as I'm married to Pedro."

Olivia kissed him goodnight before heading into the house.

Ramon grinned as he watched her go. "One day ... I'll rule this family—no one will stand in my way."

3

B arranquilla, Colombia
The Next Day

"Sí. Sí. Gracias."

Ramon closed his cell phone and shoved it in a pocket. He donned a double shoulder holster rig and grabbed his SIG Sauer P-226 pistols from a battered table in the cluttered security office. After shoving the guns in their holders, he slipped on his charcoal-gray jacket and strolled to the kitchen. The cook handed him a stainless steel travel mug filled with Sella Rojo coffee, and he continued his rounds within the house.

Giggles greeted him as he approached the dining room.

"Oh, Ramon, will you teach me to shoot?" Silvina maintained a straight face until Maria nudged her. Both girls burst into laughter.

"I'm glad you both recovered from yesterday's scare. Did you ask your mamá about learning to shoot?"

"Sí." Silvina pouted. "She said I must be older."

"Jefa is the boss. When she gives her permission, I'll teach you. Maria, what about you?"

She shook her head. "I don't want to learn. The noise scares me."

He chuckled and continued along the corridor. When Olivia called his name, he sipped his coffee and waited as she approached.

"Doña, everything is arranged. Días will arrive late this afternoon."

"Excellent. Alonzo will join us."

"As you wish."

"Don't let me keep you. I'm sure you're busy."

"Sí. I must still check on Pedro before I conduct my morning inspection of the guards. I believe he's having his daily cigar."

"Would it be possible to cancel today's training session?" Olivia yawned. "I was awake for hours after—"

"Sí. But for today only. Repetition is key to making your training become an unconscious response. Now, I must find Pedro."

Ramon caught a whiff of cigar smoke as he stepped onto the veranda.

Pedro sat at a bistro table reading *El Heraldo* as he puffed on his CAO Colombia Tinto cigar.

"Jefe, how is your head this morning?"

Pedro set the newspaper aside and knocked an inch of ash from his cigar into a container. "Buenos días, Ramon. My head is fine—a couple of cuts, a few stitches, but no permanent damage. Nothing on the x-rays and the doctor's pills handled the pain. I'm in excellent shape and will ride today since I missed my exercise yesterday."

"Do you want a guard to accompany you—just in case?"

Pedro shrugged. "No, *innecessario*. It would be a mistake." He patted his shoulder. "Besides, I'm prepared."

A FREE MORNING, Olivia met with the girls in the living room. Maria and Silvina curled up on each side of her on a plush sofa as she read from the fairy tale, "The Poor Old Lady." One of Olivia's favorite childhood treasures, Colombian poet Rafael Pombo wrote the story in 1854. Her mother had read Pombo's tale to her for years, and she never grew tired of the message.

"Mamá, why does the rich lady become poor?" Maria, hands clasped to either side of her face, waited for an answer.

Silvina smirked. "There must be a reason. Mamá will share when the time is right."

"Girls, let me continue, and what happens will be clear." Olivia finished the story and closed the book. "What did you learn?"

"I don't want to be poor," Maria wailed, her arms crossed.

"The lady became greedy. She never had enough." Silvina wore a satisfied grin as she rendered her opinion.

Squeezing her children closer, Olivia smiled at their comments.

"Maria, we won't be poor. But if we become greedy, bad things might happen. The moral of this story is material possessions don't make us rich."

"What does, Mamá?"

"What we do with our lives and the people we love."

RAMON RETURNED TO HIS OFFICE. Sipping on the remnants of his now-cold coffee, he gazed out the window and spotted Pedro strolling to the stables. *What's he up to?*

A few minutes later, Pedro led Charley, a strawberry roan Argentine Criollo, out of the building. After mounting, he put the horse into a slow trot along one of the outer riding paths.

Eyes pinned onto Pedro before he disappeared from sight, Ramon pulled a radio from his belt. "Humberto, he's heading your way. Follow him, but keep out of sight."

"Sí, Jefe."

Ramon returned to the security office and stretched a map of the estate across his desk. The hand-drawn diagram showed the large perimeter fence around the compound and the inner security barrier, buildings, and recreational facilities. He added six squares along the wall surrounding the hacienda to represent the new watchtowers under construction before he put his feet on the desk and leaned back in his chair. Satisfied with the changes, he gazed at the map and twirled the tips of his thick mustache.

He grabbed his coffee, took a swig, and grimaced as he swallowed the tepid, acidic brew. Ramon walked to the window and monitored the workers' progress as they ran concertina wire along the top of the parapet. *Should have been completed before we left Medellín and took over this estate.*

A call on the radio interrupted his hindsight musings.

"Ramon, Humberto here. Pedro is on his way back to the hacienda."

"Did he meet with anyone?"

"Sí. Two men. One tall, the other short. I recognize the short man, but don't remember his name."

"*Mierda!* How do you know him?"

"He's a member of Los Urabeños. I met him when I worked in Medellín."

"Gracias."

Ramon returned to his desk to contemplate this turn of events. *Why is Pedro meeting with a member of Los Urabeños? They wanted to take over Colombia's drug trade. What's he planning?*

ALONZO SET out on a personal mission as the other members of the family attended to their activities. Colonel Santiago had extended a luncheon invitation to him for an informal discussion in quiet surroundings.

A hazy day, the leaves on the trees ruffled in a slight breeze. *I hope Gabriela joins us for lunch. I'd like to see her again. There's something about her ....* He climbed into an armored, late model silver Mercedes S500 and drove out of the compound. *Don't want to be too early—it might appear I'm anxious. Does the colonel know about our family's business? Hope not.*

Alonzo arrived at Colonel Santiago's hacienda after a sedate drive through the rolling hills covered with mango, cashew, and lemon trees. Stepping out of his vehicle, he tugged on the cuffs of his shirt and ascended a broad staircase to the veranda and entrance of the imposing two-story hacienda. He checked the time on his Rolex. *Perfect—right on time.*

The door opened before he knocked. Expecting a servant, Alonzo took a step backward.

Colonel Santiago smiled. "Alonzo, please." He offered his hand and received a firm handshake in return. "Thank you for coming. Gabriela has babbled nonstop about you ever since the party."

"Thank you for the invitation, Colonel."

The men strolled into the dining room where Gabriela and her mother, Sofia, waited.

"Alonzo, I'm so glad you're here." Gabriela blushed.

"Señorita, my pleasure to be in your company once more." He bowed and kissed her hand. He repeated the greeting with Sofia.

Time sped by with light-hearted conversation and a simple but delicious meal of red snapper accompanied by green plantains, coconut rice, and a tomato salad.

"Alonzo, we enjoyed ourselves at your family's party." Sofia smiled. "We hope to extend the courtesy to you and your family soon."

"Gracias, señora." He glanced at Gabriela. "I'd like that."

The colonel pushed back his chair and stood. "I am afraid I must return to work. Thank you for a pleasant afternoon. You may call on Gabriela again."

Alonzo rose and shook hands with him. "Gracias, mi coronel. I shall do so soon."

"Do not take too long—I am afraid she will make our lives miserable."

Both men and Sofia laughed as Gabriela blushed.

After Santiago departed, Alonzo enjoyed a final coffee with the two women. Hearing the grandfather clock in the hallway announcing the time, he made his apologies.

"Ladies, I'm sorry, but I'll depart now. I must attend an important meeting in an hour. Thank you again."

Gabriela escorted Alonzo to the door. She gave him a peck on the cheek. "Call me. Soon."

A THREE-VEHICLE CONVOY approached the compound's outer gates a few minutes past four p.m. Ramon stood on the veranda, following the procession's approach. When the trucks stopped, he stepped down as armed men jumped from two troop carriers and created a cordon from the lead jeep to the veranda's steps.

A tall, emaciated man, wearing crossed bandoliers and brass-handled pistols over his black clothing, stepped from the vehicle. Hands on his hips, he stood waiting.

The visitor removed his sunglasses and pushed them into a shirt pocket. Ramon approached and extended his hand. Días glanced at Ramon's hand for a moment before shaking.

"Señor Días, welcome. I am Ramon Cristobal Alvarez, Señora Moreno's chief of security. She is waiting for you." He led Días inside the hacienda to Olivia's den. When they arrived, he knocked before opening the door.

Olivia stood as Días walked forward.

Ramon made the introductions. "Señora Moreno, may I introduce Ramírez García Días, our regional commander in *Fuerzas Armadas Revolucionarias de Colombia*."

"Welcome to my home, Señor Días. This is my son, Alonzo."

A member of Olivia's staff served refreshments as the four sat at a circular table placed in the room for the meeting.

"Señor Días, we require your assistance."

He smiled. "Señora, how may I help?"

She held his gaze, appearing cool and distant. "Call me Olivia, por favor. We require additional manpower to improve efficiency at our coca plants."

"How many men?"

Olivia glanced at Alonzo, motioning him to speak. "Alonzo is overseeing our modernization efforts."

He swallowed and cleared his throat. "Señor Días, we require two hundred men, split across our five processing plants."

Días laughed. "Be realistic. I do not have access to that many men to assist your drug trade."

"We are producing more product than your small plants." Alonzo stared at Días. "I researched your production processes, and you are in a position to assist us. We'll offer a five percent return for your help."

"Are you sampling your product or drinking too much?" Días tapped his fingers in a drum roll on the table and shook his head. "One hundred men for twenty-five percent."

"No, señor." Alonzo shook his head to emphasize his stance. "We will only provide you eight percent."

The two men continued to haggle over the number of men and the percentage until they reached an agreement.

"Señor Días, we accept your seventy-five men at fifteen percent. How soon before they join us?"

"Within forty-eight hours. Anything else?"

"Sí. We also require a better chemical supply chain to process our coca and poppy crops." Olivia wrinkled her brows. "But for two percent—no bargaining."

Días nodded. "Okay. We have sorted out the manpower and the percentages, I will also take an active role in running the operation." He stared at Olivia. "One other thing, señora. My men will report to me."

"No. You will be well compensated for your help, but I won't allow any interference." Olivia's eyes flashed with anger, her face reddening. *He's playing me for a fool—because I'm a woman. Should I try to charm him? No.* She stood, slamming her chair into the table. "How dare you come here and endeavor to take over my family's business when we ask for your help? No. Won't happen." *Why do men think I can't handle this? It's no longer a male-dominated world.*

"Señora, do you have the cojones to operate in this business?"

"Must I feed you your *las huevas* to prove myself?"

Días dropped a hand to his groin in a reflex action. "I am sorry if I offended you, señora. I meant no disrespect."

"While I remain here at the hacienda proving to the people of Barranquilla we are a welcome addition to their community, Alonzo is running the business. But don't underestimate us. We'll do whatever is necessary to ensure our family succeeds."

Días tipped his head to the side in approval.

"Señor Días, we're also dealing with several external issues which are hampering our business. Our transportation routes are becoming more complex, too. Can you suggest alternatives?"

Días pursed his lips. "We're allies, yes?"

Olivia and Alonzo nodded.

"Then, what affects your profit also affects mine." Días grinned, apparently pleased with himself. "I will do what I can. Other segments of FARC are negotiating a peace settlement with the government. However, there is another party who wants to expand its influence in South America. We might reach an agreement."

Olivia raised a brow but kept quiet.

"Excellent." Alonzo glanced at his watch and turned to his mother. "Jefa, I must return to the plant to oversee the final punishment."

Olivia cocked her head as Alonzo stood and offered his hand to Días. After releasing his grip, Días inquired about the problem.

"Two guards raped a woman before killing her and her husband. Hacked them to pieces with dull machetes."

"What is the final punishment?"

"The same will be done to them as a lesson to others."

Días gazed into Alonzo's eyes. "Who will carry out the punishment?"

Alonzo didn't flinch. "I will." He fixed a cold stare on Días. "Would you like to attend?"

"I think not." Días cocked his head before turning to Olivia. "I am glad we agree. Señora, if we are finished for this evening, I must return to my camp to begin the selection process."

"Gracias, Señor Días, for assisting us. I'm sure we'll meet again soon."

Ramon escorted Días back to his vehicle and watched the cavalcade until it had passed through the gates, before returning to Olivia's office.

She took no notice of him as he poured himself a drink and sat. "Is Alonzo going to carry out the punishment, or did he speak for Días' benefit?"

"We talked this afternoon." Olivia looked up from the papers in front of her. "He's of the opinion that to send the proper message, someone from the family must execute the men. I agreed." *Alonzo's reluctant to do this, but he must show strength. Perhaps I'm mistaken, but did I coddle him too much when he was a child?* She shook her head. *Why can't he be strong like me?*

ALONZO ARRIVED at the plant accompanied by a single guard, who doubled as his driver. Workers stepped aside and bowed as he strode across the compound.

Two naked men hung from x-shaped frames stretching their arms and legs as far apart as possible. Forbidden any food or drink and left to the elements for almost thirty-six hours, they were close to death.

Their heads on their chests flies covered their faces and torsos. Blood seeped down their arms as they attempted to pull free from their restraints. The overpowering stench of their urine and excrement pooled around them.

Alonzo covered his nose to ward off the foul air and turned to his driver. "Summon everyone. They must bear witness." He strolled to a nearby campstool and sat. Once the entire workforce gathered around Alonzo and the two men, he rose to his feet, a slight tremble in his hands. *I don't want to do this, but I must.*

"These men." He turned and glared at the prisoners as onlookers hissed. "These *cabrones* defiled one of our women, dishonored her husband. Not satisfied, they butchered them like sheep."

Alonzo turned in a circle, his gaze steady while he worked the crowd. He paused, glanced at the ground before picking up a machete leaning against his stool. He slid the blade over his palm, flipped it, and repeated the motion. *Am I strong enough to do this?*

"I've decided—punishment is demanded. They will receive the same treatment they gave to the couple."

"*Madre de Dios. Clemencia, por favor.*" Both men struggled against their bonds and begged for their lives.

Their pleas for mercy were ignored. People who knew the murdered couple hurled insults and rotten vegetables at them, calling for their execution. The crowd grew quiet, waiting for Alonzo's response.

"I will give you mercy. Unlike the dull blades used to kill our friends, I sharpened this one." Alonzo ran his forefinger down the blade, before rubbing the tip of his finger over his bottom lip. Ready, he raised the machete and veered toward the man on his right.

The crowd edged backward as scream after scream came from the prisoner, his eyes wide with fright.

Alonzo stopped in front of the man and glanced at the crowd. With a swift spin and a downward lunge, the man's left arm dropped onto the ground, a stream of blood spurted from the severed brachial artery.

Shrieks echoed across the compound. Birds burst into flight, but the crowd just stared, shocked at the vicious attack from their employer.

A horizontal swing of the machete silenced the man. Two hacks and his decapitated head joined the arm, followed by the torso.

Alonzo moved to the second man, who fainted. He motioned to one of the guards, who threw a bucket of water over the man.

After the man regained consciousness, Alonzo launched his attack, this time severing part of an arm. A single blow decapitated him, his remains joining those of his partner in crime.

Some women cried out at the onslaught. Several made the sign of the cross and knelt to pray. Others nodded in apparent approval and admiration of Alonzo's demonstration of authority.

Covered in blood, and tired from the physical and mental exertion, Alonzo placed the blade on his stool before issuing a proclamation. "For what those men did, their demise is just." He glanced around the crowd. "Next time, the punishment will be different—I'll use a chainsaw, starting with fingers and keep the offender alive as long as possible. Let this be a lesson—take heed. No second chances."

The crowd pulled back, fear etched across their faces.

He waved a hand. "Go—back to work."

Once the crowd dispersed, Alonzo turned to his driver. "Take some men and bury them—in an unmarked grave where they'll never be found."

Alone, the tension eased from Alonzo's body, and he stared at the blood-coated machete. *Madre de Dios! What have I done?*

4

CIA Directorate of Operations
Langley, Virginia

AJ BRUCE WEAVED through heavy traffic on the Capital Beltway. She alternated between leaning on the horn and cursing at slower motorists.

"Late again. I don't need this!" She slammed a hand on the steering wheel of her gunmetal gray Honda Pilot. "Boss is gonna kill me."

She slipped to the right around a banged-up clunker, her vehicle bouncing on the rough shoulder. AJ spotted her exit and sped along the edge of the freeway and flew down the ramp. She raced through a red light and whipped her vehicle toward the security checkpoint at the CIA facility in Langley, skidding to a halt at the end of a line of cars waiting for access.

"C'mon, c'mon!" AJ urged the cars in front to move faster. At last, her turn came. She flashed her badge at the sensor and shot past the barricade. She grabbed a pass from the console, flung the placard on the dash, jumped out of her car, and raced inside.

Once through the turnstile, she rushed to the elevator, the one-inch heels of her black leather shoes clicking on the tiled floor. Two minutes later, AJ waltzed into her section and made her way to the boss's office, stopping at a kiosk on the way for a cup of black coffee.

"AJ, so glad you could join us today." Robert Lintstone, head of the counter-terrorism division responsible for tracking terrorists in Latin America, sneered as he half-bowed and waved her to a seat. "What's your excuse this time?"

Prick. As if I'd tell him in front of others. He's always talking about the need to know. Staying out all night after the class reunion is my own business. Flicking her long, brown hair, AJ slid into a chair and glanced around the table. Four of her staff occupied seats, with empty coffee mugs in front of them. Within easy reach, notepads were covered with several lines of writing. *Damn! I'm really late—wonder what they already covered?* She tried to sneak a peek at the pad nearest her. The person smiled and turned it so she could read.

A stranger with black hair in a military cut, piercing green eyes, and olive complexion sat opposite her. Silver eagles of a full colonel adorned the epaulets of his uniform. His nametag read Smith.

Lintstone rubbed a hand through his thinning gray hair and cleared his throat. "There are indications the Islamic State is attempting to gain a foothold in our territory. They've already infiltrated a number of countries around the world. We're trying to ascertain the validity of the intel before we make a move."

"What's the source?" AJ scribbled on a notepad while her boss spoke.

"Two sensitive contacts, both unconfirmed. One reported Islamic State purchased an old freighter from an Iranian corporation through a cutout. They're using the Liberian-flagged ship as a floating command post. The other stated IS training camps are being set up in Colombia and Panama." He shook his head before peering at them through thick glasses. "It might be a smart move on their part since no one would believe they had willing conscripts in these countries."

Lintstone pounded a fist on his desk. The civilians flinched. "Dammit, people! We need collaborative intel. Fast! Someone check with NSA and Homeland Security. Find out if they can help. Call State as well, but I doubt they'll be of any use."

A tall, thin man with receding gray hair vaulted from his chair. "On it, sir." He hurried from the room before Lintstone added any further instructions.

"Contact the British and the Canadians, too. Perhaps they'll share with us, although there'll be a quid pro quo."

A bald man, on the heavy side, lumbered to his feet with the use of a cane. "Will do, chief."

"Don't offer any more than necessary."

"Yes, sir." The man limped through the doorway, banging the door shut behind him.

Lintstone glared at two women sitting at the end of the table. "Well, what are you waiting for? An invitation? Back to your computers and analyze. Contact NGA—see if the geospatial folks know more than they've shared. Find me something—anything to point us in the right direction."

The women nodded and left.

"What about us, boss?" AJ gestured toward the colonel to include him in her question.

"This is Colonel Javier Smith, First Special Forces Operational Detachment. He's here as an advisor. Colonel, meet AJ Bruce, my troubleshooter."

AJ gazed at the colonel. "So you're Delta Force?"

"Yes, but I'm not just here to advise." He glanced at Lintstone. "This will be my last time in the field before taking up a new assignment at the Pentagon. That's why I'm in uniform today. I met with my new commander earlier, and he's a stickler for proper military etiquette and attire. Didn't have time to change before this meeting."

Both stood and walked around the table to shake hands. The colonel dwarfed AJ's five-foot-ten-inch frame by six inches. AJ noted a thin scar running from his left ear to his chin. After a firm squeeze, both returned to their seats.

"You'll be working togeth—"

AJ pursed her lips. "Sir, I work alone." *Oh great. Just what I need— a special forces guerrilla tagging along. But, least he's cute.*

"Not this time. Orders from above."

"Don't worry, AJ, you won't slow me down." His bass voice resonating, Colonel Smith smiled.

"Excuse me, Colonel, I don't want you to be in my way." AJ crossed her arms. A frown etched her face.

"You two finished?" Lintstone glanced at both of them. "Good. You're working together—no debate."

"Yes, boss." AJ dragged the words out.

"Looking forward to it, sir."

Lintstone grabbed three folders from his desk. He handed one to each of them and opened the remaining file.

"Okay, imagery shows a Liberian-flagged freighter is docked in Port-au-Prince, Haiti. According to port authorities, they're dropping off a cargo of nuts, dried fruits, animal hides, and spices. The ship is scheduled for further stops in Colon, Panama, and Turbo, Colombia, before heading to a Saudi port."

AJ jotted notes in the folder. "What are they delivering in Panama and Colombia?"

"Unknown. The ship's supposed to be in Haiti for a couple more days. Talk with the analysts and make plans to fly to Haiti as soon as possible. Snoop around and find their manifests. Follow the ship to Panama and Colombia. We'll need eyes on the cargo, too."

Lintstone glanced at the wall clock. "Meet back here at four p.m. to go over any new information. Check out any intel the analysts uncover. They don't need to attend the meeting. You can give me the relevant information—if they have any."

JAVIER GAZED at the drab walls in the corridor, devoid of any color or pictures as they headed towards AJ's office. *Boring. With all the money*

the CIA receives, you'd think they'd brighten the place up. At least the Pentagon's halls have displays and photos.

"So, Colonel, shall we grab a coffee before we confer?"

"Please, call me Javier. At least in private."

"Okay, Javier, thanks." She gestured along the corridor. "An office down the hall always keeps a pot of 'Amor Perfecto' brewing. Beats the coffee in the cafeteria any day."

They grabbed their drinks and strode into AJ's office. She shared the space with her staff but had a coveted perk—a private room in the back, not a cubicle like her subordinates.

Javier glanced around the space—desk and chair, four-drawer safe, along with a small conference table and six chairs. A computer and three different-colored phones occupied the desk. A few framed certificates and diplomas, but no photographs or trinkets. *Efficient and impersonal. No family pictures—why not?* He examined a diploma from Georgetown University. *Masters from GU. Good looking and smart, too.*

"Cozy."

"Took years of hard work before I earned my own office. But right now, I spend more time overseas than here."

"I'm with you. Name a hotspot over the past fifteen years, and I've been involved. Want to slow down but still be active." He shook his head. "I'm not sure riding a desk in the Pentagon will be as exciting. But what else can a forty-five-year-old soldier do?"

AJ drained her cup. "I hear you. Just turned forty last year, so still a few years to go before I receive my retirement flag. I turned down my last promotion so I could still get out from behind a desk."

Javier glanced at her left hand. *No ring.* "Married?"

"Nah. Haven't found anyone who could put up with my regular global trips, never knowing when or if I'd return. How about you?"

"No. Same thing. It takes a special kind of person to hook up with someone like us. What's with your boss?" Javier glanced around. "Seems like a jerk."

"Lintstone?" AJ waved a hand in the air. "Most of the time he's harmless, although he does lie and backstab when it's to his advantage. Wanted to retire five years ago, but the stork brought an unexpected twin package when he turned thirty-eight. He's fifty-five now, but can't afford to retire with two kids heading to college in a year or so."

Javier chortled. "No wonder he's a grump."

"Yeah. Let's get to work. If you think he's a joy now, try showing up to a meeting without a plan. He'll have me stuck in headquarters for the remainder of my career."

AJ moved behind her desk, opened her email, and sent a note to her team: *You heard the boss. Let's meet at two p.m. to hash out our plan. The colonel and I are conferring but will need more intel.*

"Okay, the others will be here at two p.m. to provide us with any data they find. I'll send a note to Haiti telling them we're coming and arrange a meeting."

Javier nodded. "Good idea. Don't want to upset anyone by showing up unannounced. Receive more cooperation when we work together with those on the ground."

AJ typed a message and swung the screen for Javier to read.

To: COS Haiti

From: Western Hemisphere Affairs/Debutante

Will be in your AOR within forty-eight hours. Request meeting for myself plus one to discuss possibility of Liberian-flagged freighter being used to transport Islamic State personnel and/or their munitions to training camps in Panama and Colombia. Any local intel appreciated.

Javier studied her draft email. "Perhaps modify local to local/regional as they might possess additional data we can use. I assume the regional chiefs share knowledge on a regular basis."

"Agreed. I'll make the change." AJ's brown eyes appraised Javier. "For a soldier-type, you're alright."

"For a civvie, you're not bad, either."

AJ's team filed into her office at the designated time, arms loaded with maps, folders, and laptops.

"Whatcha got?" AJ gestured toward Phil. "You start."

"I-I spoke with a friend at NSA who monitors Saudi activities. He wouldn't confirm any link between the Saudis and Islamic State regarding training camps in this part of the world."

"Do you think he's holding back information?" The colonel rubbed his chin. "Or is it a case of he doesn't know anything useful?"

"He's been my friend for almost forty years, Colonel. I-I'm certain he'd tell me if he had something." Phil fidgeted in his seat as he wrung his hands and avoided eye contact.

"What about Homeland Security and State?" AJ typed a note for their meeting with Lintstone.

"Both requests for intel came up empty. If .... If anyone knows anything, they're not sharing."

"Thanks, Phil. Walter, any luck with the British and Canadians?" AJ turned her attention to a man wearing a blue button-down shirt and matching bow tie.

"The Canadians were unaware of the situation. The British believe they have a few pieces of data to share with us, but they want to finish their analysis first. Since this is about Islamic State, they didn't ask for anything in return."

"Understandable. They always play fair, but want to ensure their intel is above reproach before they pass it along."

"If you don't mind, AJ, I'll return to my cubicle in case they call."

"Okay, Walter, thanks. Makayla and MacKenzie, what has my favorite duo come up with?"

One of the twins raised her hand. AJ could never tell them apart, and they always dressed alike.

"Speak." *Damn! I sound like Lintstone. Better watch myself.*

"AJ, I'm Makayla. I had an interesting talk with Ike in his cubby-hole in the basement."

"Why does your lanyard indicate you're MacKenzie?"

Makayla glanced at her badge. "Oops." A sly grin crossed her face. "Must have picked up the wrong one this morning."

AJ shook her head. "So, who's Ike? Did I meet him before?" She rolled her eyes. *They'll provide their information when they're ready and not before.*

"Well, AJ," MacKenzie took over the conversation. "Ike runs the Maritime Shipping Office. Although, to be exact, he is the entire office. You should visit his space—it's filled with safes and lockable cabinets. He's crammed into an area not much bigger than ours."

AJ crossed her arms. "What did he say?"

"Oh. Didn't I mention what he found? Okay, a container ship named *Barwal* left Bandar Abbas thirty-five days ago. The ship stopped in Lattakia, Syria, for three days. No cargo unloaded, but they collected six containers."

Makayla glanced at her sister and picked up the report. "The *Barwal* sailed next to Benghazi, Libya. Two containers with unknown contents were dropped off, and four added."

"Get this." MacKenzie's face brightened with excitement. "Ike told us the shipping manifests for one of the containers loaded in Lattakia and another in Benghazi identified the contents as machine parts."

AJ nodded, making more notes.

"Bit of a dumb question, since machine parts could cover any number of things and uses, such as weapons and ammunition. Are there any specific parts mentioned on the manifests?" Javier frowned as he scratched above an ear. "What does the CIA want Special Operations to do? Snatch someone or blow something up? I need to know so I can plan our part of the mission—that's why I'm here. "

MacKenzie shook her head. "In the past, Ike tracked several shipments of machine parts to and from the top ten nefarious countries on our watch list. The manifests were false; the containers held weapons destined for terrorist training camps."

"Got it." Javier beamed as realization set in. "I doubt those countries would be exporting machinery given their current state of affairs."

"Wait, wait." Makayla nudged her sister and continued. "Four containers are headed for Panama and six for Colombia. Each location will be receiving one filled with 'machine parts.'"

The twenty-two-year-old twins performed a celebratory dance while seated, arms above their heads.

"Now I know why I don't invite you to meetings with Lintstone."

AJ smiled. *And they wonder why I keep turning down their requests for field positions. They act like cheerleaders and would draw too much attention to themselves if ever assigned overseas.* "Anything else?"

"No, boss lady," the twins sang as they left AJ's office, followed by Phil and Walter.

"What a team." Javier shook his head as he laughed.

"Phil and Walter are unpretentious and get the job done." AJ chuckled.

"The twins' shenanigans can be a bit much at times, but they always come through with relevant information. They're geniuses—graduated from Princeton at age seventeen with doctorate degrees in political science. Both speak Russian, Arabic, and multiple romance languages. The CIA hired them as soon as they graduated." AJ glanced at the clock and stood. "We better head for our meeting."

A few moments later, AJ brushed her shoulders and knocked on Lintstone's door.

Feet propped on the edge of his desk, a phone pressed to an ear, he motioned them toward chairs while he completed the call and hung up.

"Fill me in."

AJ nodded. "We've confirmed the sea route of a Liberian-flagged container ship called *Barwal*, the same freighter shown in the imagery you provided earlier. After leaving Haiti, it's scheduled to drop four containers in Colon and six in Turbo. According to the manifests, one for each location is identified as machine parts."

Lintstone laughed. "The terrorists still don't realize we've caught on to their euphemism for weapons. So what's your plan?"

"The colonel and I propose flying to Haiti tomorrow. We'll make arrangements to meet with the station chief, so we don't disrupt any of his operations. We hope to board the ship, plant trackers on the containers in question, and follow them to their final destination."

AJ paused. "We might require additional assistance to track them."

"Six additional people. Either from the colonel's group or some of your friends."

"Perfect, boss. We'll set up the usual contact arrangements. Anything else?"

"AJ, this is an off-the-books recon mission, nothing more—no kidnapping, no killing." Lintstone ground his teeth. "Am I clear? These countries are our friends."

"Yes, boss." *Like I go around killing everyone. Although I can think of a couple of people the world could do without.*

"Your mission is sanctioned." He waved a hand in dismissal.

After they left the office, Javier turned to AJ. "What did he mean about no killing or kidnapping?"

"Well, sometimes shit happens. I grabbed a person or two in the past and tapped some others." She shrugged. "No problemo—they got what they deserved."

5

M inistro Pistarini Airport
Buenos Aires, Argentina

ALBERTO CABRERA LOUNGED in the busy terminal at Ministro Pistarini Airport, Buenos Aires, and watched passengers pushing through the crowd as they headed to their gates or rushed into the scattered shops for last-minute items. He scratched his scraggly black beard and bided his time until his flight boarded, flicking through the pages of a magazine.

His plane had touched down in Madrid on a mild, spring day. Alberto left the plane tired and hungry but excited about his new adventure. *Am I ready to die for Allah? I think so.* After clearing customs, he spotted his contact holding a cardboard sign with his name and walked over. "I'm Señor Cabrera."

The man nodded and pointed toward the exit. Once outside, they headed to a beat-up white van at the rear of the parking lot.

The vehicle lurched forward as the man tried to reverse. After grinding the gears, he backed out of the parking spot, left the airport, and headed toward Bustarviego, an autonomous community outside Madrid.

"Give me your passport and ID. Forget Alberto. You're now Abdul Rahman."

Alberto handed over his Argentine passport. "Where are we going?"

"To the mountains. You'll join other faithful servants traveling to al-Raqqah. No more questions. You—"

A gong sounded over the loudspeakers, shaking Alberto from his reverie. A flight from London Heathrow had arrived. He picked up his bag and wandered over to a metal gate retracting into the ceiling, showing a cafeteria opening for business. He ordered an espresso and a muffin.

Leaning with his back against the counter, Alberto blew on the hot liquid and munched on the sweet roll as he continued to people-watch. *Wonder where everyone is heading? Business trips or vacations?*

Once his coffee cooled, he drank it and paid his bill. He joined the streams of passengers scurrying to lounges or heading to the exits, as a voice announced pre-boarding for the flight to Bogota: "All those with first-class tickets, anyone requiring assistance or traveling with small children may board at this time." He scurried forward.

One of the first passengers to board, Alberto presented his ticket, and an attendant escorted him to his seat—2A. After fighting with the overhead luggage bin, he punched his carry-on into the cabinet before sitting. He closed his eyes and relaxed, jumping when someone kicked his shoe.

A tall, brown-eyed, dark-haired man apologized for his clumsiness and climbed into the adjacent seat.

The men nodded at each other. Alberto proffered his magazine, with his ticket stub sticking out the top. The man returned the gesture with a newspaper.

They grinned.

"So, Michael, how was the flight from London?"

"Long, but the twenty-two-hour layover in Rome gave me a chance for some sightseeing." He leaned forward and whispered in

Arabic. "Good to see you, Abdul. Close call in Madrid last year, say what?"

"Yes, I was lucky to escape when the Spanish security forces broke into the warehouse and captured the others." He glanced around. "Call me Alberto here. We'll save Abdul and Mahmood for other missions."

"Gotcha." Michael tapped the side of his nose. "How many will we be recruiting this time?"

"None. We're to organize training facilities for up to fifty men."

"I don't understand anything about training. Why pick me?"

"I liked your style in al-Raqqah. You're dedicated to the cause, and with your European appearance and passport, you'll blend in and become invisible to the infidels who will only see their reflection."

"Understood." Michael switched back to English. "Gonna catch up on my sleep."

THEY TOUCHED down at Bogota's El Dorado International Airport on time, accompanied by puffs of white smoke as the tires accelerated to match the speed of the passenger aircraft.

Michael and Alberto cleared customs without difficulty and shifted their carry-on luggage to an empty baggage cart. They stepped through the barricades to the interior of the terminal where Alberto spotted their contact—a short, thin man in Western clothing and a Detroit Tigers baseball cap.

He nodded as the men took their luggage from the cart and walked past. In the parking lot they slowed down, waiting for the man Alberto knew as Pepe to catch up.

"*Hola, que pasa, amigos*?" Pepe waved them to a dark blue Toyota Land Cruiser parked at the curb.

"Hola. This is Michael." After tossing their luggage in the back, the two men shook hands, and then everyone climbed into the vehicle.

Pepe turned the ignition key, and the SUV shuddered before the engine belched a plume of black smoke. He grinned at the others and punched the pedal to the floor, flinging Alberto and Michael back in their seats before they had a chance to buckle up.

"Sorry. We're running late."

"I'd rather be late than end up dead." Michael shook his head. "Give us a little warning next time, okay? Whether we die from a heart attack or your driving, we'll still be dead."

Alberto chuckled while their driver chose not to respond.

An hour later, Pepe drove into a potholed parking lot at the rear of a seedy cantina, El Cerveza. He missed the larger holes, but it was still a bumpy ride. "Go inside. Señor Días is waiting for you. I'll be here when you finish your business."

Michael and Alberto grabbed their packs from the rear of the vehicle and marched toward the bar's entrance. A warped wooden door, once painted red, rested against the brick exterior, not fully closed.

Alberto slipped his hand into the space between the frame and the door and yanked. The door opened with a loud squeal as the rusted hinges gave way.

They stepped inside and waited for their vision to adjust to the dark interior. A myriad of faded advertising posters adorned nicotine-stained cinder block walls. A dozen rickety tables with mismatched chairs were strewn around the room.

A long bar, made from old planks laid across a wooden framework, ran the width of the cantina in the back of the single room. A large mirror marred by spidery cracks seemed appropriate for the once-proud watering hole. Two white-haired men sat on stools, glasses of beer by their elbows, debating the merits of a horse scheduled to run in an upcoming race.

Alberto and Michael stepped up to the bar and ordered beer. Without a word, the bartender grabbed two bottles of Cerveza Aguila from a cooler, popped the caps against the edge of the counter, and slid them across.

Michael glanced up and spotted two beady eyes staring back at him. A small rodent peered through a hole in a ceiling beam. "There's a rat up there." He pointed as the scavenger scooted away.

The bartender smiled. "Sí—that's Miguel. He cleans up after messy customers."

Michael paid for their drinks and shook his head.

"Alberto! Bring your friend."

He turned and spotted Días at a table with two empty chairs.

The men grabbed their drinks. "Señor Días, this is Michael. We trained together in al-Raqqah. Michael, this is Señor Ramírez García Días, a FARC regional commander."

The men shook hands, appraising each other.

"Welcome to Colombia, Michael. Since we are to be friends, call me Ramírez."

The three men hoisted their beers and drank a silent salute. They drained the bottles and slammed them on the table.

"Too many ears are listening here." Días pulled his phone from a pocket. "One more cerveza and Pepe will drive us to my Bogota home, so we might continue our discussion in private."

WHILE THE MEN drank inside the cantina, Pepe switched the Land Cruiser for a white Mercedes. He pitched the baseball cap and donned a chauffeur's hat. He answered his phone on the third ring. "Sí. The Mercedes."

After the men hopped in the car, Pepe careened through traffic, weaving in and out, honking his horn instead of using his brakes. He doubled back several times as he checked for surveillance. No obvious tail, but he changed directions once more, before heading to El Chico, one of the most desirable residential locations in the area.

"Don't bodyguards accompany you?" Alberto had joined Días in the back seat while Michael sat in front.

"Things are quiet now, so no need for additional personnel. Besides, Pepe and I are always armed."

Pepe pulled to a stop in front of a multi-storied apartment building. A red brick facade adorned the front of the structure while five steps led to a monoblock sidewalk lined with wax palm trees.

"Ah, here we are—one of my hideaways hidden throughout the city. Wait until you see the view—one of the best in Bogota."

Pepe left the car first, scanning the area for potential signs of trouble. His eyes roamed over the few pedestrians—a man walking his dog, an elderly lady pushing a stroller. Not finding anything out of the ordinary, he opened the door for Días.

"Let us go." Días hurried up the steps, followed by Alberto and Michael. On the approach to the entrance, an armed security guard recognized Días and buzzed the door.

Días led the others into one of the two elevators. Once the door closed, he inserted a blue plastic card into a slot on the control panel and pressed the button for the penthouse. The elevator accelerated upward and came to a smooth halt.

The doors opened inside the penthouse, revealing a massive living area with a commanding view of the city. Días allowed the men to gaze out the windows while he stepped behind a hand-carved bar.

"Gentlemen, I can offer you Tequila el Charro, various cervezas, or one of my favorites, Laphroaig Scotch. There is coffee if you do not want alcohol."

Alberto stepped back from the view. "Do you have Coke or Pepsi? I normally don't drink alcohol."

"But did you not have a cerveza in the bar?"

"Sí, for appearance because we were in a public setting. But I never drink alcohol in private."

"Understood. I'll get you a Coke."

"I can't get over this panorama. Stunning." Michael walked over to the bar. "Let me try the Laphroaig."

Días helped himself to a cerveza and directed the men to the seating area. Once everyone settled into the plush leather sofas, chitchat ceased.

"Alberto, when we met last month, you mentioned working as a recruiter for an organization wanting an out-of-the-way place to train new personnel."

"Sí. My—our organization has a special mission. We must convert everyone to the one true religion."

"Were you not raised Catholic?"

"Yes." Alberto raised a finger in the air. "But no longer. My new brothers call me Abdul."

"Why did you abandon the Catholic church?"

"My parents forced their religion on me." He shrugged. "As I grew older, I became disillusioned and looked elsewhere."

"I see." Días turned to Michael. "And what about you?"

"I grew up in a poor area. Everyone attended the Church of England, but I also became disenchanted with their teachings. I studied several religions until I settled on Islam. Now I go by Mahmood."

"If you do not mind, while you're in Colombia, I will keep referring to you as Alberto and Michael."

"No problem." Alberto pointed at Michael. "We use our original names for traveling—makes it easier to cross borders."

"During our training in al-Raqqah, our instructors singled us out," Michael paused before whispering. "As non-Arab members of the Islamic State, we're able to move about easier than our Middle Eastern brethren."

"What do you hope to achieve in Colombia?" Días switched his gaze between the two men.

"We want to establish a foothold so we can train recruits." Michael stroked his reddish-brown beard. "These men will be from various countries, mostly from the Middle East. Once they arrive in Colombia, I'll be their commander. Their training will be rigorous, and while all will not be suitable for the mission, their physical features will enable them to infiltrate into America with ease."

"We'll also provide training in Panama, perhaps at one of the old American bases." Alberto grinned. "Seems fitting to use what the Americanos discarded to prepare ourselves."

Días nodded. "What do you need from me?"

"A place to train away from prying eyes. Also, lodging and food." Alberto laughed. "But no pork."

"How many men?"

Michael took a sip of his scotch. "No more than fifty. Perhaps half that number—the rest will train in Panama."

Días pursed his lips, his head rocking forward. "I see." He drained his beer glass while eyeing the two men. "Okay, I can manage this. You will use one of the FARC training camps under my control. Food and lodging—no problem. What about weapons and ammunition? I can provide these—for a price."

Alberto and Michael glanced at each other before Alberto answered. "There is a Liberian-flagged ship in transit to Panama. The *Barwal* is carrying munitions—labeled as machine parts. One container will be offloaded in Colon, and the other here in Turbo."

"How will the men arrive?"

"A few are working on the ship. They'll disembark in Turbo. Others will arrive via two other ships, but most will fly in on several flights—pretending to be students."

"When will you require the camp?"

"In about two weeks." Alberto deferred to Michael, who gave a slight shrug and took over.

"What about payment? We can handle this via bearer bonds, diamonds, gold, or electronic transfer through a dummy corporation. Even bitcoin."

Días gave them an evil smile. "Money is not necessary. But, I will ask a favor in return for my help. Once your men are trained, I want their assistance in taking over a local drug cartel."

He paused before voicing his desire. "I also want them to capture or kill the cartel's leader: Olivia Perfecta Moreno."

6

M oreno Hacienda
Barranquilla, Colombia

ALONZO LET his breath ease out. His grip on the butt of the pistol firm, he raised the gun and concentrated on the front sight as he was instructed. He squeezed the trigger with the tip of his finger and fired at a paper silhouette. *Damn it, missed.* He repeated the process until the fifteen-round magazine was empty, all with the same results.

Shit. Why did I let Mamá *talk me into this? Why doesn't she listen? Did she suppose I would magically acquire this skill because she demands it? I'm so useless.*

Olivia stepped next to Alonzo and fired six rounds from her handgun in rapid succession. Four shots hit the target in the chest while the other two zipped through the head.

"Mamá, why must I learn to shoot?" He raised his arms skyward. "I'm no good at this. Besides, Ramon and the guards are here to protect us."

"Alonzo, you might be the brains in the family as far as business is concerned, but sometimes you're not too bright." Olivia reloaded and holstered her pistol and placed her hands on her hips. "Look what happened the other evening. How would you feel if the girls been kidnapped or killed because you didn't take your position in this family seriously? It was likely a warning, or there would have been more bloodshed, and that blood will be on your hands when they try again."

"You're right, Mamá." Alonzo dropped his chin to his chest. "I'm so useless with a pistol. Give me a shotgun. I know how to use one."

"Ramon will get one for you when he returns. But, any fool can use a shotgun. With a spray that wide, it's like swinging a broom. That's fine when they're standing away from you, but up close, useless. So, you must also carry a pistol." Olivia stared at her son. "To protect yourself and others."

"What about Pedro? If he's trained, we'll have plenty of firepower."

"He tried to learn before I met him." Olivia laughed. "He said he couldn't hit anything and would be more of a danger than a help. I agree with his assessment." Olivia clasped her son's shoulder. "I haven't given up on you yet, but enough training for today. I'll meet you in the office before breakfast."

When Alonzo entered Olivia's office an hour later, he found her reading the local newspaper. She handed him a glass of cold guanabana juice.

"Thanks, Mamá. You know how fond I am of this juice, although I'm always trying to decide which flavor stands out."

"I think today the flavor is more banana than lime or strawberry." Olivia took a sip and set her glass down. "How did the workers respond after you carried out the sentence?"

"They're scared. None would look at me, and they all kept their heads bowed as I passed." Alonzo drained his glass and helped himself to more juice from the iced pitcher. "I don't want them to be afraid."

"They are hired help, nothing more. Don't give in to your feelings. If they sense any weakness, they'll try to take advantage of you."

Olivia glared at Alonzo. "Fear is the best way to control them. They might hate you, but they'll do as ordered."

"Sí, Mamá, but is this the best way?"

"When I took over the business, I tried to be everyone's friend. A complete disaster. The workers opposed me at every step, rather than carrying out my instructions."

"What did you do?" Alonzo flexed his shooting hand, sore from gripping the pistol.

"I made an example of the one who ridiculed me the most. Tied him to a tree, stripped off his shirt, and lashed him until he collapsed." Olivia stared at her son. "My problems ceased."

Alonzo nodded. "So much for me to learn. Harvard Business School couldn't prepare me for this."

Olivia chuckled. "Life is a better teacher than books at times. You'll be fine." She stood. "Let's join the others for breakfast."

When they entered the dining room, Pedro, Maria, and Silvina were digging into their meal.

"Good morning, Mamá," the girls chimed. "We were so hungry we couldn't wait for you."

"Good morning, my darlings. It's okay to start without me." She hugged each girl. "As long as you leave something for me to eat."

Maria and Silvina giggled.

"Sorry, dear. I thought I should join them." Pedro set his fork down. "Remember, I'm going to Bogota this morning to take care of some old business."

"Sí, I remember. How long will you be away?"

"Perhaps three or four days. I'll call you if there's any change."

"Okay. I'll be able to catch up on paperwork and perhaps go shopping in Barranquilla."

"Pedro, would you like me to drop you at the airport?" Alonzo glanced at Olivia for approval. "I'll be driving right by on my way to the plant."

"Sí. Gracias."

~

ALONZO DROPPED Pedro off and continued on his way out of the city. Thirty minutes later, he left the busy highway and stayed on a faint track leading through fields toward a forest.

As the trail faded, three armed men stepped out from behind a long hedge of red and yellow *ixora coccinea* almost nine feet high. The barrel of an AK-47 held by a fourth person poked through the hedge.

A man motioned for the vehicle to stop. Alonzo came to a standstill and pressed a button to lower the tinted window.

"Hola, Jefe." A giant of a man, half a foot taller than Alonzo's six-foot-three-inch frame, waved the others back behind the hedge. He signaled for Alonzo to continue.

He drove along the path to a small green trailer, which he used as his office. Whenever he passed workers, they stepped aside, bowed, and waited for him to proceed. *Is it respect or fear making them bow? I feel like a fraud chasing Mamá's legacy.*

Alonzo parked the car next to the trailer. The distant clatter of their diesel generator disturbed the tranquil setting. He coughed and covered his mouth as a chemical smell wafted around him from a nearby building. After slapping dust from his clothing, he hurried inside the trailer, sat at a wooden desk, and began sifting through a stack of invoices and manifests.

PEDRO'S COPA AIRLINES flight touched down in Bogota on schedule. When he entered the terminal, his eyes lit up as he spotted a long-time friend waiting for him.

After handshakes and hugs, they left the building and climbed into a dark blue Land Cruiser. Ten minutes later, the vehicle stopped in front of a small, single-story building with a rusted sign advertising it as a café.

"Gracias, mi amigo." Pedro climbed out of the SUV as his friend drove away. With a final wave, he entered the café.

Inside, six rickety tables and chairs lined the walls on each side. A battered counter stood at the rear. Two commercial-sized coffee urns and a glass-covered container with pastries sat at one end. At the other end, a short man as old and shaky as the counter leaned over a newspaper, peering at the print.

Once Pedro approached, the man stood, pulling his right hand from underneath the counter. He smiled at Pedro and extended his hand.

"Hola, Diego. Nice to see you again." Pedro beamed.

"It's only been a week."

"Sí, but we're not getting any younger." Pedro leaned forward and whispered, "So, how's my favorite Urabeños lieutenant?"

"Same as always. Getting by. Shooting before someone shoots at me." Diego Fernando Sebastian, a senior leader in Los Urabeños, grinned as he poured two coffees. "One of these days, you must return to us."

"Sí, after we knock FARC out of the drug trade. Let them make peace with the government, but leave us the riches."

"How is Olivia's drug empire going? I heard she's been talking with Señor Días." Diego scratched an ear before slurping his coffee.

"I think she has a few difficulties. Olivia doesn't confide in me too much, but I overhear things. She thinks I'm disinterested, so she's turning to Alonzo."

"If only she knew the truth—that you're her biggest competitor!"

"She'll never find out. Why do you think I staged the break-in? Of course, the guy hit me harder than planned."

Diego broke into a fit of laughter and grabbed the counter with both hands to stop himself from falling. Wiping the tears from his eyes, he asked, "Who did you hire to handle the attack?"

"My brother, Edgar. He either got carried away or paid me back for some previous slight. Olivia still wants me to learn to shoot. I thought I had convinced her I was a rotten shot and might hurt someone."

"What? You're one of the best marksmen in Los Urabeños!"

"Sure, but I want to keep playing the bumbling husband to learn enough to take her down. In fact, I'm planning a little surprise." Pedro laughed. "She has no idea I want to take over her business—it's the real reason I married her."

FINISHED WITH HIS PAPERWORK, Alonzo left the trailer for some fresh air. He roamed around the camp, watching several workers exit from one of three old wooden barns nestled among the trees. Bandanas covered the lower part of their faces, giving them an outlaw appearance.

Away from the building, they yanked the bandanas away, revealing tears streaming from their faces. Several collapsed to the ground, gulping huge mouthfuls of fresh air.

Alonzo joined the workers, who staggered to their feet and tipped their heads as he approached.

"What happened?" Alonzo pointed to the barn.

"Jefe—" The foreman coughed. "One of the new men spilled some of the gasoline, ether, and sulphuric acid we use to process the coca. The fumes are making us sick. We can't breathe inside."

"Open the windows."

"We cannot, Jefe. They're nailed shut."

"On whose orders?"

"I—I'm not sure. This is the way, even at the other camps."

"I must find out why. Take a break and clean yourselves up. Find some fans to clear the air so you can go back to work."

"Sí, Jefe." The men bowed and scampered away.

Alonzo marched through the camp, his jaw clenched in determination as he examined the other refining buildings. Sheets of plywood covered every window, except one. A pale yellow plume of smoke drifted in the slight breeze from the open window.

As he walked closer, the stench made his eyes water and his throat constricted. Alonzo stumbled toward the center of the compound until a gust cleared the fumes away. He pulled an embroidered handkerchief from a pocket and dabbed at his eyes. *Carelessness, or is someone trying to kill us?*

Warning shouts rose from the entrance to the site. Whistles pierced the air. Gunshots erupted. Screams came from the hedge. Workers poured out of the buildings, running away.

Shocked by the unexpected activity, his heart rate accelerating, Alonzo froze.

"Jefe, you must come with me. At once! The federales are raiding!" A hunchbacked man shoved a pistol in Alonzo's hand, before grabbing his arm and tugged him into motion. "We must get you to safety."

They stumbled into the trees at a distant point from the commotion and stopped. Ahead of them, a ragged line of government troops, weapons poised, weaved their way forward.

In a show of misconceived courage, Alonzo raised his arm to shoulder level, pistol extended and stepped forward. *I must demonstrate my strength. I—*

The hunchbacked man clubbed Alonzo's gun. "Jefe, don't be a fool—they'll kill you."

Alonzo staggered at the unexpected attack from the worker and dropped the pistol.

Before he could recover, they were surrounded by soldiers, who aimed their weapons at Alonzo and the hunchbacked man.

"Alto! Down on your knees. Hands behind your back. Both of you! Now!"

Alonzo and his companion sank to their knees. Soldiers yanked on their arms, forcing their hands together while others clamped on handcuffs. Once secured, each man received a rifle butt to the back, knocking the wind out of them.

More troops piled into the compound, shooting several armed workers. Their bodies collapsed to the ground and lay still.

Those who put their hands in the air didn't escape punishment. Rifles, pistols, even a whip, were used to subdue them.

Three aging military transport vehicles pulled into the center of the grassy courtyard. One truck contained the bodies of four guards killed at the entrance. Additional bodies had been dumped in the back of the other two vehicles. Those captured were forced to climb over the bodies into the transports. Soldiers jumped up beside them.

Other soldiers set the buildings on fire. Red and orange flames reached for the sky as thick black smoke spiraled upward.

"What is the meaning of this intrusion? These are my people, and this is private—" A pistol slammed against the back of his head and silenced Alonzo's protest.

Two men tossed him into a truck. The remainder of the troops boarded the vehicles and soon departed, leaving behind death and destruction.

A MAN WATCHING the commotion from a distant ridge lowered his binoculars after they dragged Alonzo away. He chuckled as he picked up a backpack and disappeared into the brush.

"Olivia, this is only the beginning. Soon you'll beg for mercy."

7

Toussaint Louverture International Airport
Port-au-Prince, Haiti

AJ AND JAVIER exited the packed terminal at Haiti's Toussaint Louverture International Airport. Dressed in a white blouse and tan cargo pants, her eyes swept across the crowd, looking for anyone out of place. Standing next to her, Javier wore a blue sport shirt and tan Chinos. Both had backpacks thrown over their shoulders.

Horns blared as cars jockeyed for position, pigeons pecked at scattered food, people shouted—a regular occurrence at the busy facility. Passengers shoved past them to board a crowded bus as a battered white Chevrolet Suburban screeched to a halt at the curb.

"C'mon, hop in, campers," a man with a gray ponytail shouted out the open passenger window.

AJ turned to Javier. "Our ride," she whispered.

As soon as they climbed in, the driver tapped his cigar on the side of the car to knock the ash off and sped away in a cloud of smoke, tires squealing.

"Welcome to Haiti. I'm Tex." He blew the horn and swerved into oncoming traffic to pass a slow-moving bus. After cutting off the dilapidated public transport, he shoved a finger in the air. "*Salopri!*" He glanced at his passengers. "Can't stand these dumb drivers."

"Hey, Tex. What's the rush?" AJ stared bug-eyed at the oncoming traffic and tightened her grip on the back of Javier's seat as Tex squeezed between two three-ton trucks. *And people talk about my driving!*

"None, ma'am." He gazed in the rearview mirror at AJ, a confused expression on his face. "There's been a bunch of robberies and kidnappings when people leave the airport. No reason to tempt fate."

AJ chuckled. "Carry on. Who chose campers as our contact code?"

"Uh. I did. My favorite pastime." He waved his cigar in the air, sending a plume of smoke toward her. "Besides, can you imagine anyone here going camping?"

She opened the window and fanned the smoke. "I see your point. So, let's see how fast you can get us to the embassy."

Although a normal forty-minute drive from the airport to the American embassy, Tex slammed on the brakes twenty minutes later, the vehicle avoiding a collision with the embassy's twin wrought iron gates as they screeched to a halt. Once they opened, he eased forward. One guard examined everyone's identification while another used a mirror mounted on a telescopic pole to check the underside of the vehicle for explosives.

Tex, dressed in a multi-colored islander shirt and baggy cargo shorts, escorted AJ and Javier to the Marine checkpoint referred to as Post One. After examining their identification, the Marine on duty pressed a button, unlocking the bullet-resistant door, and allowed them access into the embassy. Portraits of the American and Haitian presidents, along with the current ambassador, lined the wall near a sweeping staircase covered with a vibrant red carpet.

At the top of the stairs, Tex unlocked a heavy metal door and held it open for the others. They entered and Tex led them to the third door on the right.

He stopped in front of the secretary's desk. "Is he in?" He nodded toward a closed door on the left.

"He'll be back soon." She glanced at AJ and Javier. "The chief's with the ambassador. Would you like some coffee, water, or a Coke while you wait?"

AJ shook her head. "Nothing for me, but thank you."

"Coffee, please. Black, no sugar." Javier stretched and yawned.

"When you finish with the chief, my office is two doors farther along the hallway on the right." Tex shook hands with AJ and Javier. "If I'm not back, grab a seat and wait—I won't be too far away."

"Thanks for the lift, Tex." AJ stifled a jaw-cracking yawn. "We'll catch up later."

The secretary poured a cup of coffee from a pot steeping on a warmer plate from a shelf behind her desk. As she handed it to Javier, a chime sounded. She shrugged and lifted a telephone receiver. After listening for a moment, she hung up and pointed at the inner door. "You may go in now. He's waiting for you. You can take your coffee with you."

They stepped through the door where a tall, muscular man stood, wearing a white short-sleeved shirt and dark slacks. Bright blue eyes stared at them. He extended his hand to AJ. "I'm Bill, the station chief. Welcome to Haiti. I'm sure you experienced an exciting ride from the airport. Tex enjoys giving his passengers a thrill."

"Has he considered stock car racing? He'd be good at it. Hi, I'm AJ Bruce." She shook his hand before gesturing toward her partner. "This is Colonel Javier Smith."

Bill laughed. "I think he'd end up crashing into spectators." After he shook hands with Javier, he motioned them to chairs around a small conference table. "So what can I do for you? Not often headquarters sends someone here without asking my permission first."

"We don't mean to intrude on your territory." Javier glanced at AJ. "We're tracking a Liberian-flagged cargo ship carrying weapons to terrorist training camps in Panama and Colombia."

Bill pursed his lips. "My people would have reported back if the ship came to Haiti."

"Yes, sir. In ordinary circumstances, I'm sure they would, but it's in the harbor right now, and your people are probably busy with more important tasks. We plan a clandestine approach to get on board, locate the cargo containers, and place trackers."

"Hmm. I see." Bill ran a hand over his bald head, his lips twisted to the side. "What do you need from me?" He glanced at AJ. "Your reputation is well-earned and respected. Otherwise, I'd throw you out of my office."

A hint of a smile creased AJ's face. "Sir, we wanted to explain why we've invaded your space. We'd also like to borrow a nondescript vehicle and perhaps a driver."

"I appreciate you taking the time to drop by and notify me." Bill chuckled. "Since you've met Tex, he can be your point of contact and driver. Try not to get caught—we won't confirm we know you."

AJ winced. "Thank you, Bill. We appreciate your help and loaning Tex to us. And don't worry, I've never been caught."

～

AJ AND JAVIER found Tex's office empty and made themselves comfortable in two mismatched armed chairs in front of the desk.

"I don't think Bill's too happy with us being here." Javier tilted his head back and forth, studying the ceiling as if he suspected there might be listening devices.

"We informed him about our mission before we departed." AJ shrugged. "Most station chiefs dislike encroachment on their territory, so his comments didn't bother me. I could tell you some stories—"

"Sorry, I stepped out." Tex entered the office and handed over cold Cokes, popping the top on his. "Been checking over the vehicle I requisitioned. Nondescript. Dented. Local plates. Should fit right in."

"Is there someplace we can crash for a few hours?" Javier nodded toward AJ. "I think we should rest before we head to the port."

"Sure, the embassy maintains a few Conex boxes set up for visitors—nothing fancy: bed, TV, fridge, shower, and toilet. Since the temperature ranges from warm to hot year-round, they're air-conditioned, too. We'll stop by the commissary so you can grab a few things."

After a quick trip for some provisions, Tex took them to their sleeping quarters. "What time do you want to meet this evening?"

"About nine p.m." AJ extended her hand. "Thanks for your help."

JAVIER AND AJ met under a covered walkway near their accommodations at the designated time.

Cigar smoke wafted through the air. Moments later Tex appeared, dressed in black and gray, a balaclava perched on his head, carrying three small pouches. "Sorry I'm late. Had to stop by the armory and pick up our weapons—SIG Sauer P226s." Tex handed each of them a pouch and kept one for himself. "C'mon, our transport awaits in the motor pool." He led them along the path to an area where a dozen vehicles sat. After he hit the key fob, the lights flashed on a silver four-door Nissan Frontier.

Javier gazed at their ride. "You weren't kidding about the SUV being dented. Even the roof."

"May not seem like much, but it blends in."

They climbed into their vehicle and departed from a side gate. Tex weaved his way through traffic, meandering along the crowded city streets. "We'll do a surveillance detection route before we head toward the port. Need to make sure we didn't pick up any unwanted company when we left the embassy."

AJ and Javier kept their eyes peeled for possible surveillance as Tex maneuvered around various types of transport: cars, trucks, graffiti-decorated buses, the Haitian version of a taxi, referred to as a 'tap-tap,' bicycles, and motorcycles.

Two hours later, Tex pulled over. "I think we're ready. The port's about a mile away. I'll drop you near the perimeter fence where the lights are burned out. The freighter you're after is moored on the far side away from us."

"How do we signal we're ready to return?" AJ glanced at Tex before scanning the port.

"I'll circle a few blocks and keep coming along this stretch until I find you."

AJ and Javier nodded.

"Ready ... go."

They bailed out of the vehicle in the sparse light as Tex slowed, weapon pouches dangled from a belt below their vests. A waterproof black bag containing a breathing apparatus and swim fins was secured to the back of their belts.

A spotlight flashed, momentarily catching them in its beam.

They rolled, came to their feet, and scurried to the ten-foot-high chain-link fence.

Javier knelt by the mesh while AJ grabbed wire cutters from her belt. She snipped through the rusted fence, creating a hole to slide through. After pushing the wire back in place, they hugged the ground while Javier used night vision goggles to scope out the ship.

Quiet, no guards in sight. Two lights onboard: one fore, one aft. No traffic on the street, they dashed to the ship's side. A metal gangplank led from the dock to the vessel toward the bow. Near the stern, the ship's accommodation ladder was lowered to form a second access point.

Weapons in hand, AJ and Javier stole up the stern walkway, their heads swiveling left to right.

Silent as a tomb.

Javier tapped AJ on the shoulder and pointed at a shadow in the moonlight.

A single guard, his AJ-47 balanced on his shoulder, approached the walkway.

AJ and Javier crouched behind a crate, hugging the side of the ship. She pulled out her pistol.

Footsteps receded as the guard continued on his patrol.

Javier tapper AJ's shoulder again and moved forward.

They stepped onto the deck. Several dim lights came from the left, where a three-story white superstructure with red and green trim held the bridge, radio room, crew quarters, and other facilities. To the right, winches and derricks towered over three sets of enormous hatch covers. Four twenty-foot containers were strapped to the deck near the bow, with two rows stacked on top.

AJ held a penlight over a scale drawing of the deck, locating stairs leading into the hold. She tapped Javier on the shoulder and pointed at the paper.

"The cargo hatches will expand enough to lower a twenty-foot container inside. We'll check the holds first. We're looking for two numbers: SYCO4603729 and LIPA0192837."

Javier nodded. "I'll remember psycho twenty-nine and lips thirty-seven."

AJ gave a soft chuckle. "Agreed. Let's find a way in."

They crept over to the superstructure, seeking an unlocked hatch. Javier found one and inched it forward. Empty, a pale light flickered against the far wall and two lockers. Inside, a companionway—perhaps their way to the cargo area. They headed down the metal stairs, turned right along the passageway, and approached a gunmetal gray door.

A small squeal came from the door as Javier opened it.

They froze.

AJ glanced behind them and between the rows of containers. She whispered, "Nobody here. Let's go."

He popped the lugs securing the door and eased it open. They stepped into the dark hold, Javier closing the door behind them. AJ snapped on her penlight, the red glow providing sufficient light to determine their destination.

Ahead and below a hatch cover, sat three rows of four steel containers. Javier scanned the hold and located a series of clipboards hanging on a pegboard.

"Psst, AJ." Javier held up a clipboard stuffed with papers. "Shipping manifests."

AJ dashed over and took the papers. Flipping from one to another, she glanced at the container numbers. She reached the last one and shook her head before going through them a second time.

"Damn. Nothing matches. Did someone make a mistake? I didn't find anything beginning with SYCO and LIPA followed by the numbers the office gave us. Will you check?"

AJ handed back the manifests to Javier, who repeated the process. "Nothing—wait a minute. What are the numbers again?"

"SYCO4603729 and LIPA0192837."

Javier rifled through the pages. "Got it, I think. Where were the containers loaded?"

"Six in Lattakia and four in Benghazi."

Javier nodded. "Destinations?"

"Colon and Turbo."

"Someone tried to be clever, but not smart enough. SYCO became LATU, and LIPA is now BECO. Wait a sec." Javier flipped through to the back of the clipboard, grabbed a blank manifest, and scribbled. "Yeah, they also switched the numbers. They shifted those associated with SYCO to BECO, but the last two digits are reversed. Same with LIPA."

With a smug grin on his face, Javier tapped his huge hand on the clipboard. He showed AJ the revised numbers: LATU0192873 and BECO4603792.

"Yep. Got them." AJ punched the air before doing a high five with Javier. "Now, all we need to do is locate the correct containers, place our trackers, and leave this tub."

Javier trained his penlight on the numbers while AJ made the comparisons.

"Found one— LATU0192873. The middle row, third from the end."

Javier fished in a vest pocket and pulled out two tracking devices. "See the oblong hole on the left at the bottom of the frame? I'll attach one inside. Should be a matching one on the opposite end."

"Better tag all the containers bound for Turbo—just in case the terrorists hid something else of interest in them. Same when we find the ones heading to Colon."

"Good idea." He pulled a Plumett NS50 Silent Launcher from a bag strapped to his chest. A faint hiss broke the silence as a climbing rope and grappling hook sailed upward.

Javier yanked on the line and the hook caught on the frame. He pulled himself up the rope until he reached the container. Fishing a tracker out of its pouch, he pulled the backing off and positioned the device. With a slight click, a magnet on the bottom of the tracker held it in place.

He located the others bound for Turbo and repeated the procedure. Finished, Javier recovered the hook and lowered it to AJ before climbing down.

She switched on a portable tracking unit. "Trackers are operational. Let's move."

A scan of the containers in hold two and three failed to identify the second one of interest.

AJ glanced at her watch. "We've been at this for over an hour. Tex will be wondering if something happened to us. Let's get a move on."

They found a door leading topside near the bow. When they reached the main deck, Javier inched the door open. He gave a thumbs-up signal to indicate the area was clear. They stepped outside, located the containers bound for Panama, and crept toward them, remaining in the darkest shadows.

The first numbers matched the revisions Javier worked out. He attached a tracker, and they snaked their way to the other end, placing three more.

A floodlight snapped on, catching AJ and Javier in its beam.

"Stop!" a voice shouted over a PA system in Spanish. The command was repeated in French, English, and Arabic.

AJ and Javier ignored the warning and raced to the side of the ship. Shots rang out as the clatter of feet pounding on the deck drew near.

A round seared Javier's upper left arm, blood seeping from the injury. "Go."

"What about sharks?"

"Too late to worry. Go!"

He stumbled and pushed AJ overboard. He followed. Four crewmembers skidded to a halt where they had jumped. Beams of light chased across the water's surface, seeking AJ and Javier. Gunshots cracked. Bullets zipped into the water as they dove below the surface.

8

B arranquilla Prison
Barranquilla, Colombia

THE LIGHT of dawn glimmered through barred windows. It bathed a pitiful creature curled into a ball on a dirty mattress, covered by a threadbare gray blanket. Clumps of aged straw held together by the sweat of countless residents served as a pillow. The stench of vomit and ammonia filled the air.

A rooster crowed once, twice, three times. The hapless inmate stirred, moaning as he pulled the blanket over his head as if it would reduce the racket.

Two guards marched between rows of cells, banging their batons against the bars, the rat-a-tats bouncing off the walls like firecrackers. "Wake up, you lazy peasants. Inspection time." One guard, a ragged red scar running from his right eye to his chin, stopped at Alonzo's cell. "Out of bed. This isn't a hotel. On your feet."

Aching from repeated blows to his lower back, hips, and legs during interrogation, Alonzo struggled to his feet in spite of fresh wounds. He limped to the cell door, gazing into the corridor. Other prisoners held out cups and small plates. He glanced around his cell. In the corner, a cracked enamel plate and dented tin cup. He bent over, a groan escaping from his lips, and picked them up.

Two inmates walked past each cell, one dropping a scoop of indescribable mash onto the plates while the other one splashed water into the cups.

"Hey, where's my fork, or a spoon?" Alonzo banged the cup against the bars, spilling water on his orange jumpsuit.

Several prisoners laughed. A server returned. "Where do you think you are, at home? This isn't a fancy restaurant, and your momma's not here. No utensils—eat with your fingers or like a dog. I don't care."

Alonzo sniffed at the small lump of gray mush on his plate and cringed. The sour smell caused his stomach to turn, and he stifled a gag. Dipping a reluctant finger into the mess, he gave it a tentative lick. "Yech. This swill isn't fit for swine. How do they expect us to eat this slop?"

The prisoner in the next cell laughed. "Señor, this is good stuff today. Most times, much worse. Shove your plate over—I'll eat it."

Without a word, Alonzo slid the plate toward the next cell and returned to his cot. He dozed again, tossing in fitful sleep.

A heavy thump on metal startled him. A broad-shouldered guard slammed the door with his fists. "About time you woke up, you filthy loser. Step forward and put your arms through the bars."

What's going on? Is my family in danger? Does anyone know what's happened? I need help. Alonzo groaned as he shifted his weight to ease the pain in his lower back and upper legs. *Why did they beat me? Don't they realize who I am?*

"Hurry up, or I'll give you more bruises."

Alonzo did as instructed. The guard slapped cuffs on him so he couldn't move and grinned at him. "You have a visitor. He'll be here soon." The guard chuckled as he walked away.

Perhaps Ramon? Pedro?

A scuffle broke out at the entrance to the cellblock. Shouts echoed over the usual clatter. Moments later, Colonel Santiago and three soldiers approached. Grim-faced, the colonel stared at Alonzo, not saying a word.

He hung his head. "Colonel—"

"Silence." The single word uttered by Colonel Santiago resounded throughout the cells. All conversations ceased. "Bring him." He walked away.

A guard unlocked Alonzo's cuffs. Two others entered the cell, grabbed him by the arms, and dragged him along the corridor, accompanied by jeers, boos, and whistles from the other inmates.

They stopped in front of an open door and shoved him into a shabby office. A dim light dangled from the ceiling. The once-cream walls were now a dingy indeterminate color.

Colonel Santiago sat in the sole chair in the room, behind a battered and bloodstained desk. His jaw clenched, he stared at Alonzo.

"Had it not been for my daughter, you would rot here." The colonel continued to glare at him. "I ignored the rumors about your family, but cannot believe your involvement in—in drug running."

Alonzo's heart sank as if it had turned to iron, and he swallowed. *I like Gabriela—a lot. What will she think if she finds out?* "Colonel Santiago—"

"Be quiet. Nothing you say will change my opinion of you. Since Gabriela professes her love for you, I will give you one chance. Leave the drug business or stay away from my daughter."

"Sí. I will do as you command." *Anything to get out of here. I'll deal with the colonel's options later—if he raises them again.*

"Should you break your promise and hurt Gabriela, I will shoot you myself." The colonel turned to the soldiers and nodded.

One soldier removed the cuffs while another opened the door and tossed in a bag of clothing.

The colonel stood. "Get dressed. I will escort you outside." He dropped his hand to his holstered pistol. "Do not force me to do anything I might enjoy."

After Alonzo had changed, Colonel Santiago and the soldiers

guided him from the building. The colonel pointed to a waiting taxi. "Your ride. Go straight home and consider your actions. I hope for your sake, you do not disappoint me."

WHEN ALONZO RETURNED to the hacienda, he found his mother in her office. She glared at him and slammed her hands on the desk before speaking.

"You—you. How could you allow yourself to be captured? Colonel Santiago called this morning to tell me what happened."

"I'm—I'm sorry, Mamá." Alonzo threw his hands in the air. "No one warned me about the raid." He unbuttoned his dirty and torn shirt and showed her his bruises.

Olivia stifled a gasp. "No excuse. You should always be prepared to depart on a moment's notice." She cuffed the side of his head. "Don't think you're getting off this easy. You should be ashamed— captured like a peasant. I don't have any idea what to do with you. You need more training, more backbone." *Just like his father—spineless when courage was needed. Alonzo must be stronger and show he's capable of being a leader.*

"Mamá, who was behind the attack? Someone tipped off the authorities. The site is small and well hidden."

"I don't know. Sometimes this happens. Maybe a worker became careless and opened his mouth where others could hear, or someone took advantage of government rewards for information." She frowned. "Perhaps, someone is trying to put us out of business."

"I wonder about Señor Días. We reached an agreement with him. Can he be trusted?" Alonzo's eyes narrowed to crinkled slits as he slapped a fist into his other hand. "Is he following another agenda, and using the cover of our partnership, taking the opportunity to catch us unaware?"

"It's a possibility. I also wonder about two other people."

"Who, Mamá? Should we deal with them now?"

"Not yet. My suspicions need to be checked out first. Ramon will take care of things. This is all new to you, but you must learn fast and heed any warnings." Olivia waved her hand, dismissing the conversation. "Have you talked with Pedro since your release?"

"No. Isn't he back yet? I thought he would return yesterday."

"I thought so, too. I hope he'll return tonight. I'm tied up with the mayor this afternoon. Ramon will accompany me." Olivia glanced at the wall clock. "Will you pick the girls up from school?"

"Sí, Mamá." Alonzo yawned.

"Bueno." She pinched her nose. "Take a shower—you stink. We'll talk again this evening."

ALONZO HEADED TO HIS ROOM. Alone, he sat on the edge of the bed. *Things are in a mess—I've let Mamá down.* He bent down and untied his shoes. *What should I do about Gabriela? Do I want to lose her?* He shook his head. *I'm acting like a teenager with his first crush.* He stripped off the clothes, which stank from his stay in prison, and took a long, hot shower.

After examining himself in the full-length mirror hanging on the bathroom door, he gasped. Dark bruises, scratches, and minor cuts adorned his once blemish-free body. He changed into fresh clothes and flopped onto the bed for a healing siesta. *I'm not cut out for this business. Unlike Mamá—she can be ruthless. How did I get into such a mess?*

After he woke, Alonzo glanced at the clock, and his eyes widened. "Maria and Silvina—I'm late! Mamá will be furious."

He raced from the hacienda, jumped in his Mercedes, and sped out the gates, a plume of dust marking his haste.

Alternating between a heavy foot on the accelerator and a hand jabbing at the horn, thirty minutes later, he approached the road leading to Colegio Nueva Barranquilla, the all-girls school his half-sisters attended.

Just after the turn, he slammed on his brakes.

Ahead, flashing lights from electric company vehicles reflected off parked cars. A tree wrapped in wires lay across the road. Several workers stood away from the tree, one waving his hands in the air as he gave instructions to the others.

"Damn!" Alonzo hammered on the steering wheel in frustration. "Of all the times for a delay!"

He waited a while before reversing his Mercedes. *Can't wait any longer.* Tires spinning, he headed back to the main road. Fifteen minutes later, Alonzo approached the school from the opposite direction. Once he presented his identification to the guards at the closed entrance, they confirmed he was on the access list and opened the gate, allowing him into the grounds.

Alonzo spun his tires, throwing gravel into the air as he hurried to the school's administration building where he expected the girls to be waiting.

A tall, thin man dressed in a blue suit and wearing a Panama hat, stood on the steps leading to a wide veranda.

"Hello, Señor Alvarez. Where are Maria and Silvina?" Alonzo stepped from his car and extended his hand to the school's principal. "I was running late, but I'm here to take them home."

"Buenos días, Señor Moreno. What do you mean? Your friends collected them after school finished—not fifteen minutes ago."

"My friends? I sent no one here." He glared at Alvarez and raised a fist. "Who were they?"

Señor Alvarez's complexion paled, his stance sagged. "But—but, Señor Moreno, they said you sent them. One of them was on the access list—a Señor Kruz. The other man was his driver. They knew the girls. Wait a minute—the girls spoke to them and laughed before climbing in the car."

"Wait! Are you sure it was Señor Kruz? What did they look like?"

"The driver was young, his face hidden by the chauffer's cap. The other was much older, with dyed hair—black. His eyes—dark brown, with a cold stare. This man spoke to Maria and Silvina before they entered the car, but I didn't hear what he said."

"Call the policía. Pronto! My sisters were kidnapped!" Alonzo grabbed his cell phone and called his mother—no answer. He tried again—the same result.

What's going on? First the raid, now the girls are missing. He slammed his fists on top of the car and grabbed his hair, pulling as tight as possible. *Mamá will kill me if I don't find them.*

The principal raced out of the building a few moments later, panting. "Señor Moreno. I'm so sorry. I'll hold the guard responsible. Wait! He said the older man spoke with a strange voice, almost like he had a lisp."

Alonzo glared at the principal before grabbing him by his arm. "Where are my sisters? Who took them?"

"Señor Moreno, the policía are on the way. They ask you to remain."

"No. I'm going home." Although he spoke in measured tones, his body shook with fury. "This wouldn't have happened if your people did their jobs. My mother must be informed. If the policía desire to question us, they can come to the hacienda."

Alonzo hopped in his car and sped toward the gate. The guards shoved it open, but Alonzo clipped the barrier. His car fishtailed out of the driveway, tires laying rubber as he headed home.

Mamá will be enraged. She'll blame me, rant about me not being responsible, and can't be trusted.

Alonzo beat on the steering wheel, blowing the horn at every car as he darted in and out of traffic, almost causing two accidents in his fury. Heart thumping as he sped along the highway, sweat ran over his scalp, down his brow, and into his eyes. His shirt stuck to his back, and his hands became clammy as he gripped the steering wheel tighter. He swallowed, trying to rid his mouth of a dry, sour taste. *How will I explain this? Why can't I do anything right?*

The gates to their compound open, Alonzo raced past the stunned guards as they saluted. He skidded to a stop in front of the hacienda as his mother and Ramon exited her car. "Mamá, something bad's happened ... Maria and Silvina ...." Alonzo struggled to breathe, tears forming in his eyes. "When—when I reached the school, they were gone."

Olivia staggered and grabbed Ramon's shoulder for support. "What do you mean gone? Where are they? Where are my precious girls?" Her face paled, and she squeezed her eyes shut. Quivering, she leaned against the vehicle. "We must find them. Now." Understanding sank in as she slumped against her son, beating on his chest. "They might be dead or worse—taken for the sex trade. I want my babies. Find them. Now!"

"Mamá, the policía will be here soon to talk with us. They'll know what to do." Alonzo glanced at the ground. "The principal said—"

"Said what?" She glared at Alonzo before turning to Ramon. "Deal with the policía. Alonzo and I will wait in the office. If this is a kidnapping, they might call, demanding a ransom. Find out what the policía can do before we take matters into our own hands." She pressed her fingers against her temples, wide-eyed, tears rolling down her face as she clenched her jaws. "No ransom will be paid—I want the bastardos who did this. I'll kill them!"

"Sí, Jefa—Olivia. I will come to you when there is more information." Ramon extracted his phone from his pocket and raced off.

Olivia and Alonzo hurried to her office, slamming the door behind them. Her face ashen, makeup streaked by tears, she threw herself into a chair, gasping for breath. "What is happening? First, the attack on the plant, now the girls are missing. Did you arrive at the school on time to collect them? Why did the school let them leave?"

"Mamá, I tried to tell you. The principal said it was Señor Kruz—"

She jumped to her feet and paced liked a trapped tiger, relentless. Her features became like ice. "No! I don't believe it. He's trying to cover up his incompetence."

Alonzo repeated the description provided by the principal.

"I only know one man who this might be." Olivia shook her head in disbelief. "But ... he wouldn't do this. He was my father's friend.

Francisco Kruz. It can't be him." She shook her head again. "But, he does have a speech impediment ...."

"I don't understand, Mamá. Where's Pedro? I still haven't seen him."

"He doesn't answer his phone. I have no idea where he is." Olivia poured a glass of whiskey, taking a gulp before offering one to Alonzo, who declined. "He thinks I don't know about the games he plays with that old group of men from Los Urabeños." She clicked her tongue. "He'll show up when he's ready—unless something has happened to him." *Should I worry about him, too?*

"Mamá, we must contact Señor Kruz. See what he says about Maria and Silvina. Perhaps he knows where Pedro went."

Olivia dialed Kruz's telephone number. No answer. She let the phone slip from her fingers, as seeping tears became a torrent. She fell to the floor, grabbing her chest as if in pain. "Oh, my babies. Someone must find them!"

Alonzo bent down, picked up the phone, and replaced the receiver in the cradle. He knelt beside his mother, trying to console her. His arms around her, they rocked, his shirt soaked from her heartbroken and terrified tears.

"You should have been waiting for them, Alonzo." She slammed her fists on his chest. "Your duty demanded this. I can't trust you— can't trust anyone!"

They descended into silence—waiting.

After what felt like several hours, the shrill ring of the phone shattered the quiet. Olivia picked up the instrument, putting it on speaker.

A raspy voice broke the silence and gave voice to her greatest fears. "Your daughters are safe. For now. Leave Barranquilla, and they will be unharmed. Otherwise ...."

"Noooo!"

9

The *Barwal*
Port-au-Prince, Haiti

AJ JUMPED into the bay from the *Barwal* and descended to the bottom. She stopped swimming and pulled flippers and a portable OPS Survival Egress Air system from the waterproof bag attached to her belt. After she donned the breathing system and began putting on the fins, she spotted an intermittent light coming toward her.

Her heart pounded, and her breathing labored. *Javier had been shot—where is he?* She drew her knife and swam toward the intruder.

The approaching adversary stopped, clicked on a small penlight, and aimed the beam at a hand.

AJ relaxed and smiled when the swimmer formed an okay circle with a thumb and forefinger. *Javier. Thank God, at last!*

She grasped Javier's right shoulder and pointed away from the ship. He nodded, motioning for AJ to lead. She took off in a slow swim, her movements mimicking those of a dolphin, not wanting to create any disturbance as they headed toward the surface.

Tᴇx ᴘᴀᴄᴇᴅ and stopped every twenty feet or so to scan the water with his night vision goggles.

Nothing. He glanced at his watch. *An hour late. Where the hell are they?* He retraced his steps. *I heard gunfire earlier, but it happens every night.* He frowned. *Might be a coincidence, but then again ....*

Reaching the end of the unlit parking lot near a scenic viewpoint, he stopped by a coin-operated tourist telescope set on a concrete observation deck adjacent to a wooden bench. After pulling binoculars from a pouch on his belt, he rested them on the telescope and used it to guide his movements. He trained the lens along the shore. *There! Climbing out of the water—two people.*

Tex hurried along a trail to the opposite end of the lot. He reached a clump of bushes growing at the top of a sand dune, directly above where he'd last seen AJ and Javier.

"Psst. AJ, Colonel. I'm here."

Bushes rustled as they pushed their way onto the path and waved.

Dressed in a dark shirt draping over his cargo pants, Tex pulled an unlit cigar from his pocket and shoved the chewed end into his mouth. "I circled as we planned, but I became worried when the rendezvous time passed an hour ago. So I switched to plan B and tried to find you." He squinted through the darkness at the colonel, trying to adjust his eyes. "Colonel, is that blood seeping down your arm?"

"Nothing to worry about. Only a graze."

"Never you mind. There's a small med kit in the car. We'll head back to the embassy, and I'll contact the nurse. You need to be checked over. Might be a scratch, but you swam in skanky water. Even sharks avoid the harbor, or so I've been told."

Tʜᴇʏ ᴡᴀɪᴛᴇᴅ outside a door labeled 'Nurse Practitioner – You're in My Hands Now.' Javier held several gauze pads against the long, shallow wound on his upper left arm while AJ and Tex stood on either side of him.

A short, rotund woman with spiky orange hair approached. "Tex, you better give me a good reason for waking me up in the middle of the night. This better not be another one of your practical jokes. If it is, you've had it." She unlocked the door and waved them inside.

"Would a bullet wound be enough reason, Ann? My friend got in the way of a stray shot."

"Let's take a look." She led them into the examination room and flicked a switch, bathing the room in intense light.

Ann donned nitrile gloves and checked over Javier's injury. "Hmm. Where I come from, this is a scratch. A few stitches, a tetanus shot, some antibiotics, and you should be fixed up."

Tex covered his mouth with a hand, and half turned toward the door. "I-I'll step outside. I've seen you work before, and you scare the bejesus out of me."

Everyone laughed as Tex and AJ went into the outer waiting area. Thirty minutes later, Javier and Ann joined them.

"I thought so—a minor scratch—but the arm will be tender for a few days. I'll give you some painkillers in case you need them, and you can be on your way. Try not to use that arm to do anything strenuous for a week, and you'll be fine."

"Thanks for patching me up." Javier shook her hand. "Anything I can send you from the States when I return?"

"Can't think of anything right now, but if something comes to mind, I'll pass the word." She gazed at Tex. "You, on the other hand, owe me. We'll discuss this later." After Ann had shooed them out of her office, Tex, Javier, and AJ stood in the corridor.

"Tex, I think we should call it a night. Okay to meet again in your office about 0900?" AJ turned to Javier. "Work for you?"

Javier nodded. "Yeah, we'll grab breakfast first and plan our next move."

～

AJ AND JAVIER walked into Tex's office at the agreed-upon time, carrying U.S. Embassy Haiti coffee mugs. Tex sat at his desk, legs propped on a corner, drinking from a Mad Hatter cup. He sat upright as AJ and Javier took their seats.

"The *Barwal* sailed this morning." Tex scanned a sheet of paper on his desk. "According to their departure paperwork, their next stop is Colon, Panama. They didn't waste any time leaving. A full day earlier than scheduled." He shook his head. "A bit unusual as the port schedules are usually adhered to, not to mention they rely on the tides."

"Perhaps we spooked them." AJ sipped from her mug and set the drink on a nearby table.

"Whatever the reason, we need to be positioned before they arrive." Javier turned to Tex. "Can you get us on flights right away?"

"Already done. You'll be in Panama City this evening and meet with Station Chief Richard Brown tomorrow at 0800." Tex paused for a moment. "I also arranged a motor pool car for your use after the meeting with him."

"Sounds like a plan." AJ rested her chin in her right hand. "However, I detect a 'but.'"

"Well, yeah. A big one. Brown has a reputation for being territorial toward outsiders, even if D.C. mandates their presence. If something goes wrong, he'll make sure he's clean, and any interlopers take the fall. You'll still need to meet with him, but be forewarned—he's an ass."

Javier waved a hand in the air to dismiss any concerns regarding Brown. "No problem, Tex—appreciate the warning. We've dealt with plenty of self-important people, and know how to handle them."

Tex glanced at the wall clock. "We'll head to the airport soon. Before we go, let me upload some maps to your phones. Oh, one other thing. You'll need to grab a taxi in Panama City to the embassy. No pickups like here."

An hour later, Tex pulled up to the terminal. "I'll let you both out here. Good luck." *I think you'll need all the help you can get.* He shook their hands as they exited the vehicle. Once they stepped away, Tex gave a final wave and departed, tires squealing.

AJ chuckled as she heard several car horns and shook her head at Tex cutting through traffic as he disappeared in the distance. "An interesting character—too bad he can't help us in Panama." She turned toward the terminal. "Let's go. Back to Miami. Tex booked us on a direct flight from there to Panama."

Their American Airlines flight touched down in light rain under gray skies at Tocumen International Airport outside Panama City as scheduled. They cleared customs and exited the terminal. Javier pulled two small roll-around suitcases while AJ carried their backpacks. They strolled to a nearby taxi rank and approached the first cab.

"Excuse me, would you take my husband and me to our hotel?" AJ stared at Javier as she squeezed his uninjured arm. "We got married this morning in Miami and came here for our honeymoon."

"Sí, señora. What is the name of your hotel?"

"I haven't the faintest idea. John, do you remember?"

"Why I sure do, pumpkin. The Hotel Coral Suites."

The driver opened the rear door for the newlyweds to enter. "An excellent hotel. The journey will take about thirty minutes. If you like, I can also show you the scenic route along the water. Perhaps an extra twenty minutes."

AJ glanced at her new husband and fluttered her eyelids. "What do you think, darling?"

"Let's go straight to the hotel, pumpkin. I'm bushed."

"No way!" AJ shook her head. "Not tonight!"

Javier laughed and helped her inside the taxi.

The vehicle pushed through the heavy evening traffic as the driver alternated between his horn and the brakes, following the pattern of other motorists. He stepped on the gas whenever a small opening appeared.

AJ snuggled into Javier. "Oh, darling, what a brilliant idea to surprise me with this trip." She glanced out the window. "Look at all the colorful signs inviting people inside. I want to do some shopping." *Should I really lay it on?*

She caught the driver watching in the rearview mirror, so she gave Javier a sloppy kiss on his cheek. "I thought we'd go to the Smokey Mountains or something. Why we didn't even have time to pack our bags."

"Sweetheart, we can always go to the mountains. This trip came up at the last moment, and I couldn't resist. You can buy whatever you need later." Javier returned AJ's kiss, causing the driver to swerve as a car stopped in front of them. "We'll fish on Gatun Lake, take a tour boat from one end of the canal to the other, and try our luck at the casino."

Once they arrived at the hotel, Javier paid the driver, giving him a generous tip to remember them by, and escorted his bride inside. Javier took care of the formalities at the check-in desk, while AJ headed to a small boutique she spotted as they entered.

When they were ready, bellboy led them to their suite, pushing a cart with AJ's various purchases and their luggage. After he unlocked the door, Javier scooped AJ in his arms, wincing from the effort, and carried her across the threshold.

Alone at last, secured in their room, he set AJ down, and they scrutinized their surroundings.

She tossed the bags on one of the king-sized beds. "I claim this one—closest to the bathroom." She raised her eyebrows at Javier. "I hope you don't snore."

"From time to time." Javier chuckled. "You can always crawl in next to me so you can nudge me without having to leave your bed." He patted the covers.

"I think our arrival charade in case anyone is watching us is over for now, darling." AJ laughed. "Don't think anyone will expect a new bride and groom to be here with an ulterior motive."

"Whatever you think is best, pumpkin. Didn't spot any tail." He grinned. "So, who gets the bathroom first?"

"Why, darling, haven't you learned anything? Ladies are always first."

THEY ENJOYED A CONTINENTAL BREAKFAST, checked out of the hotel, grabbed a taxi, and headed to the American embassy. After a glance at their passports by the Marine sergeant on duty, followed by completing entries on the visitors' log, they gained access to the chancery. By 0800, they sat across from a stern-faced secretary; glasses perched on the tip of her nose, brown hair in a severe bun.

"It is most irregular for people to drop in who weren't approved by Mr. Brown." Her words carried jagged edges designed to wound as if AJ and Javier had created a personal affront to her running of the office. "He won't be happy at all."

"Please tell Mr. Brown we're here. He's aware of our visit."

"Humph. No one notified me." The secretary picked up the phone and pushed a button. "Your unexpected guests are here."

She hung up, pushed her chair back, and stood. "Follow me." Back straight, arms swinging, she stalked to the wall at the end of the office. After knocking, she opened a door.

A balding, white-haired man sat behind a desk. Unlike the station chief in Haiti, he didn't rise to shake hands but pointed at two straight-back wooden chairs. "Sit."

AJ and Javier balanced on the hard seats and waited.

The man glared at them for several moments. "I don't understand why you think you can descend on my territory without my permission." His gaze rested on Javier and switched to AJ. "Well?"

"Mr. Brown, as you're aware, my boss—"

"Lady, I don't care who your boss thinks he is. He has no authority over what happens in Panama. That's my job."

"I understand, sir, b-but—"

"Don't stutter, get to the point. I won't waste all day on some wild guesswork by desk jockeys."

Javier sucked in a deep breath. "Mr. Brown, what AJ tried to say is we understand—"

"Listen, Colonel. I don't care who either of you are, nor do I give a damn about your mission."

"Whether you agree or not, we're here." Javier's face reddened as he glared at Brown. "Now, should we go outside, whip it out, and determine who can piss farthest? Win or lose, we're staying."

Brown gazed at Javier before bursting into laughter. "Colonel, you show a lot of guts coming in here and challenging me to a pissing contest. I like your style." Brown thumped his chest. "Most people grovel—I want to know what they're made of before I'll deal with them."

"Mr. Brown, AJ and I are tracking an arms shipment destined for a group of Islamic State terrorists. Some are to be offloaded in Colon, while others are destined for Colombia. We want to verify what they drop here—we attached trackers in Haiti."

"Call me Richard—never Dick. I hate Dick. Okay, you showed plenty of gumption, so I'll bend my own rules and help you as much as possible. But if you're caught, I've never met you."

"Understood, Richard. We'll need a car, a couple of weapons, and we'll be out of your way. The ship is supposed to dock in Colon tomorrow morning, so we'll head there today and settle in."

"No problem." Richard stood and shook their hands, ending the meeting. "Tell Priscilla, my secretary, that I approved what you require. She'll sort things out for you."

Leaving the office, AJ walked up to Priscilla's desk. "Richard said you would help us with a car, weapons, and a road map."

The secretary stared at them, her jaw dropping, a look of disbelief stretched across her face.

"If you don't believe me, check with Richard. We need these things within the next hour so we can begin our mission. We'll grab a coffee from the cafeteria and be back soon."

Priscilla nodded and picked up the phone.

AJ PAID for black coffees and two cheese Danishes, while Javier dashed to the men's room. He joined her a short time later at a small table in the corner of the cafeteria. A smile spread across AJ's face.

"What would you have done if he took you up your challenge to urinate?"

"Hosed him down."

They both laughed. AJ pulled the road map from a pocket in her cargo pants and spread it on the table. "Hmm. About sixty miles from here to Colon using the Panama-Colon Expressway. Figure ninety minutes for the trip."

"Perhaps more. Don't forget, we might pick up a tail or two." Javier drained the last of his coffee. "Want another?"

AJ shook her head and pushed her chair back from the table. "Okay, let's find our vehicle and be on the way. Who's driving?"

AJ smiled. "Who do you think?"

"Hope you're better than Tex."

A few minutes later, they checked over their Toyota Yaris and piled in, AJ behind the wheel.

Javier laughed. "I spoke with the mechanic while you collected our weapons. I thought the secretary tried to get back at us by reserving a family vehicle for us. He said the engine had been replaced with an eight-cylinder complete with an old supercharged carburetor—more suitable for chases and getaways."

"Hope the engine lives up to the billing. Buckle up, here we go!" AJ sped down the street, dodging a car door that opened in her path.

"Did you and Tex go to the same driving school?"

"Yep. How'd you know?"

Javier laughed as he shook his head.

AJ drove in a circuitous route through Panama City, doubling back several times. She scanned to the front and left of the vehicle, while Javier monitored the right and rear.

"No obvious baggage, AJ. Let's head to Colon."

Once on the expressway, AJ put her foot down and zoomed along the smooth road. Thick, lush trees hugged the shoulder, rushing past them in a blur. They continued north, with the dense forest giving way to copses and manicured farms. A slight breeze carried a hint of freshly-worked earth and luscious foliage.

Javier kept his mouth shut, and his eyes closed as AJ swerved from lane to lane to pass slower-moving vehicles.

Approaching the Panama Canal by Gatun, she pulled into a scenic viewpoint. "Your turn."

"What? Still about fifteen miles to go." Javier gazed at AJ. "Thought you wanted to drive the entire route."

"I did, but I'm not being fair to you. If things pan out in Colon, I'll be taking the car back to Panama City, leaving you on your own. Besides, I want a break."

"True. Okay, I'll take over."

After they had switched seats, Javier eased back onto the highway. He fell in behind a slow-moving bus and returned a wave from some of the passengers.

AJ drummed her fingers on the window ledge. "Uh, Javier, I thought you could drive. This—whatever you're doing—isn't driving. I think we're coasting."

Javier gave her a wicked grin and stomped on the gas. "Just having fun. I wondered how long it would take you to comment. Two minutes—not bad."

Before long, Javier screeched to a stop outside the Sand Diamond Hotel. They grabbed their belongings, and Javier tossed the keys to a valet. Check-in took moments, and a bellhop escorted them to the elevator and their room on the fifteenth floor, overlooking the harbor in the distance.

Javier tipped the bellboy and closed the door, turning back to the vista offered by the floor-to-ceiling windows. Multi-colored apartment buildings hugged one another, while closer to the port square and rectangle warehouses dominated the area. Various trees and shrubs fought for space, claiming open areas. "Perfect. If our calculations are correct, the *Barwal* should be in port soon." He pointed to the right. "There are several empty berths near an immense warehouse complex. She should go into one of them."

AJ used a pair of binoculars to zoom in on the area. "Plenty of activity—people are still wandering around the shops and restaurants. Why don't we hail a taxi and take a tour of the city? We can check out the Manzanillo port area at the same time."

FOUR HOURS LATER, Javier and AJ returned to their suite and ordered room service. Once their food was delivered, they sat at the small dining table near the windows.

"There she is—the *Barwal*—heading to a berth." Javier handed the binoculars to AJ. "The port is set up for twenty-four/seven operations, so the containers might be unloaded tonight."

AJ nodded. "We can monitor the action from here."

"I'll make my way to one of the vantage points we identified this afternoon. The trackers we planted will work for ten days before the batteries die. I should be able to pick them up on the meter and shadow them to their destination. In the meantime, you can spend the night here and head back to Panama City in the morning for your flight to Colombia."

"Okay, Javier. I'll check with the concierge in a few moments to confirm the availability of the rental car we requested." AJ turned back to the window. "So, why did you join the military?"

"There's been someone in my family serving our country since the Whiskey Rebellion in 1791." Javier shrugged. "Just seemed the right thing to do. Why the CIA?"

AJ laughed. "My family believes in government service, too. However, most have been involved in some capacity within the State Department. My father eventually became an ambassador."

"Anywhere exotic?"

"I guess, if you find Chad and Sudan on your bucket list."

They continued taking thirty-minute turns watching the *Barwal* for signs of activity. At midnight, AJ nudged Javier. "Psst. Wake up. Activity on the ship." She passed the glasses over. My rental is a white Hyundai, plate number CL1342—just in case."

He closed his eyes as he repeated the numbers. "Got it." Javier scanned the ship with the binoculars. "Hmm. I better go. Not many containers to be unloaded here. I'll head to VP-One now." He strolled into the bathroom to change, and reappeared a few minutes later, dressed in black from head to toe.

"Wish me luck."

"Vaya con Dios. Text me with any news."

Time passed without an update. After a long day, AJ put her head down on the table and closed her eyes. An hour later, her phone chimed—incoming text.

In play. Four batters stepped up to the plate, along with four coaches. All are singing—heading out.

"Yes." AJ pumped a fist in the air. Their planning paid off so far. All four containers they'd tagged for Colon came off the ship, were loaded on transports, and left the port with Javier in pursuit.

Eyes gritty from lack of sleep, Javier continued to monitor the movement of the containers away from the Canal Zone and into the interior. At 0600, he informed AJ he could no longer see the convoy.

After checking the meter was still registering the tracking devices, she ate an early breakfast and checked out of the hotel.

She raced along the highway back to Panama City and noticed a black van with tinted windows following and coming up fast. As she slowed down to let the vehicle pass, it slid in behind her. She sped up, and the van matched her speed.

AJ whipped around a small bus. The van followed, clipping the side of the bus. She increased her speed but couldn't shake her tail. In the rearview mirror, she spotted the silhouettes of two people inside the van. *Damn! What now?*

Her head jerked forward as the vehicle inched close. She shoved the pedal to the floor. "C'mon baby, let's move! Show me what you got!"

The vehicle rammed into the back of her car. "What the—?"

A second collision almost caused her to lose control. She pegged the gas pedal to the floor as the van slammed into her a third time.

AJ's car went into a spin, struck a rusted guardrail, and sailed into the air.

10

C ar Wreck
  Outside Colon, Panama

JAVIER SLAMMED the brakes and fishtailed as he rounded a corner on the narrow road leading toward Panama City. Ahead—blue and red flashing lights from two police cars blocking the way reflected off the trees and other vehicles. Nearby, an ambulance waited, the two-person crew leaning against the side of the vehicle. He inched forward as a line of cars and trucks squeezed past the scene, occupants gawking at the damaged car being winched up the hillside by a tow truck.

A police officer stopped the traffic as the back end of a white Hyundai came level with the road. Debris covered the license plate number, but the first two letters were clear: CL.

Javier swallowed and closed his eyes. *AJ's rental—same color and make of car. I'm sure that's the beginning of the license plate number she mentioned.* He opened his eyes and stared at the Hyundai.

The police officer blew a whistle, motioning for traffic to

continue.

Javier pulled onto the side of the road after he cleared the emergency vehicles. Jumping out, he rushed toward the damaged vehicle.

"Alto, señor." The police officer grabbed Javier's arm.

"My wife—that's her car." He took in a deep breath. "Is she—"

"Relax, señor. They found her outside the vehicle."

"Is she—"

The police officer smiled and waved in the direction of Colon. "She's alive. The first ambulance took her to the Manuel Amador Guerrero Hospital. Take Highway 3 toward Nuevo Cristobal and turn right on Calle 11."

"Thank you!" Javier shook his hand before rushing back to his Toyota Yaris, loaned by the embassy in Panama City. He sped past slower-moving traffic, blowing his horn as he approached intersections. *C'mon. Where's the hospital?*

He pulled a Y-turn and sped back to the last intersection. A sign bearing an H pointed to the left. He gunned the engine, narrowly missing an oncoming car, and raced along the street. *Get control—don't cause an accident. Just find AJ.* Skidding to a stop in front of the hospital, he grabbed his backpack, jumped from the car, and raced inside.

Out of breath, he spotted the sign for reception and dashed to the desk, sliding past a couple in his way. "Excuse me—my wife—an ambulance brought her."

A bored-looking nurse popped her gum. "Name?"

"Hers? Bruce. Mine's Smith."

"Why different names?"

"We just got married."

The nurse glanced up from the computer screen and smiled. "Fantástico! Room—" She counted on her fingers. "Five."

Javier glanced around.

"Señor." The nurse pointed at a sign. "There."

Javier hurried along the corridor, checking the room numbers. He paused in front of AJ's door and raised a hand to knock. *What if she's sleeping? I don't want to wake her.*

He turned the knob and peered around the door before entering. "Hey."

Dressed in a white hospital gown and snuggled under a pink blanket, AJ lay propped up in the bed, reading a magazine. A rectangular bandage hid part of her forehead. "Hey, yourself." She pointed to a chair. "Sit."

Javier gave a relieved laugh as he straddled the chair.

"When I saw the tow truck pulling your car up the hill, I thought—"

AJ smiled. "You thought what?"

"I'd have to train a new partner." He smiled and reached for her hand. "I'm glad you're still with us. What do the doctors say?"

"Nothing broken." She shrugged. "A splitting headache, though. They used a butterfly bandage to close the cut on my forehead. I was lucky—I spotted a van approaching from the rear and braced for impact. Next thing I knew, my car went over the edge. Bushes slowed the vehicle down, and I bailed out and tumbled away before it hit a tree, or I'd be in worse shape." She rubbed a patch of inflamed skin on her arm, covered with scratches and dark bruises.

"How'd you get the scratches?"

AJ laughed. "Would you believe they were caused by the paramedics hauling me up the hill on a stretcher? They pulled me through some thorny bushes. Anyway, the doctor ran several tests. The CAT scan didn't reveal any swelling, bleeding, or fractures of the skull, although the doctor thinks I might have a mild concussion. They want to keep me overnight for observation."

Javier nodded. "I'll stay with you. I don't think they'll throw me out since we're newlyweds."

"Don't get any ideas, buster." AJ's eyes shined bright. "Yes, you should stay. You need to fill me in on what happened at the—"

Someone knocked on the door.

Javier reached for his weapon, relaxing when a nurse entered with a tray with covered dishes and a cup filled with milk.

"Oh! I thought the lady was alone."

Javier stood and took the tray while the nurse adjusted AJ's bed. "I'm her husband."

"Oh, yes. The lady mentioned you would find her." She shook a finger. "Imagine going off sightseeing on your own."

"But—"

"You should have taken your beautiful wife with you."

AJ laughed as Javier dropped his head. "Don't worry, Juanita. He will be making amends—for a long time."

"Good." Juanita glared at Javier. "Serves him right." She patted AJ on the shoulder and left the room.

"Sorry, Javier. I didn't know what else to tell her." AJ struggled to keep a straight face. "It was worth it to see the expression on your face."

"Keep it up—paybacks are hell."

They both grinned.

AJ picked up a plate with an indescribable blob in the center and sniffed. "So, what happened at the port?"

"The vehicles transporting the four containers continued into the countryside for a few miles and stopped at a barricaded road." Javier frowned. "I couldn't drive any closer before armed guards moved the barrier, and the trucks disappeared behind some trees. I drove past as they replaced the blockade, and one of the guards waved an AK-47 at me, indicating I should keep going." He glanced around the room. "By the way, where's your weapon?"

"The ambulance crew brought my bag—my SIG is inside. The nurse put the bag in the cupboard. Should be safe there." AJ took a bite of her meal and grimaced before pushing the plate away. "I'm sure there's a joke about hospital food. Can't remember, but are they trying to poison their patients?"

Javier picked up a spoon and sampled the dish. He chewed for a moment before swallowing.

"Well?"

"Needs salt." He helped himself to more.

AJ yawned. "Enjoy. So what's the plan?"

"When I drove back to the port, the *Barwal* was underway. I pretended to be a nosy gringo—"

"You are a nosy gringo."

Both laughed.

"I asked someone where the ship was headed. The guy shrugged and glanced at a clipboard hanging on the wall of his shed."

"What did he say?"

"He didn't say anything, just looked away." Javier grinned. "As soon as he turned his back, I sidled closer for a look."

"Okay. You're forgiven for abandoning me. Did you find out the ship's next destination?"

He nodded. "Turbo."

"Yes!" AJ punched the air. "Ow!" She grimaced.

"I suggest we call in additional help. Recommend bringing some of my guys here while we head to Colombia as soon as you're released."

"Agreed." AJ yawned again. "I'm tired—gonna rest." She switched off the light above her bed.

"Sweet dreams." Javier settled back in his chair and pulled a tablet from his shoulder bag. The device contained government-contracted encryption. He used a special cable to connect the device to his satellite phone and composed a message.

To: *Jararaca*

From: *Cobra*

Mission progressing as planned. Request immediate dispatch of four-person team to take over surveillance duties as we continue following the Barwal.

Javier hit transmit and put away his SAT phone and iPad. He stepped to the window and tilted the blinds to block the late afternoon sun streaming in before returning to his seat.

He glanced at the now-sleeping AJ and smiled. *Am I falling for this woman? She looks like an angel—so beautiful when she's asleep, so sassy when she's awake. She's the first woman to grab my heart. Where will things go?* He shook his head. *Focus on the mission. Must find out who did this ... and eliminate them.* He pounded a fist into the palm of his other hand. *No matter who's responsible, they're toast.*

11

Port of Turbo
Turbo, Colombia

THE BLUE MERCEDES stopped at the port's entrance. Días lowered the rear window and handed the attendant a thick envelope. After glancing inside, the man smiled and pressed a button to lift the barricade. He waved as the vehicle passed.

Días shook his head and laughed. "Supposed to be the most secure port in Colombia, yet an envelope stuffed with cash allows access without questions."

Alberto's eyes shifted to Michael, sitting next to the driver. "Must make things easier for your ... uh, business."

"It does, and today it will make for a simple transfer of your containers from the *Barwal* to the trucks I provided."

The car halted near the berth where stevedores offloaded the ship's cargo. Shouts, whistles, and the noise from engines filled the warm air, which carried a hint of the sea and diesel.

Six unmarked semis waited for Michael and Alberto's containers.

One-by-one, a crane hoisted the heavy metal boxes from the ship and loaded them onto the flatbed trailers. After workers secured the final one, black plumes of exhaust erupted from the semis as the drivers formed a convoy heading for the port's exit.

Impatient, one of the drivers mashed on his horn several times as three men struggled with a forklift blocking their way. Swerving to avoid them, the first driver blew his horn again as he passed the struggling men. Each subsequent driver also sounded their horn before following the lead vehicle.

Alberto waved to disperse the smoke from the smoldering cigarette dangling from Días' lips. "Would you mind putting out your butt?"

Días chuckled. "I thought you enjoyed the aroma of smoke."

"Yes, when I blow something up or fire my weapons. But the stench of burning tobacco is something I've never enjoyed."

The window next to Días dropped, and he tossed out the remainder of his cigarette. He turned to Alberto and glared. "Better?"

"Yes. When will we reach your camp?"

"Soon." Días instructed the driver to follow the vehicles. "Our destination is about twenty-five kilometers from here. We will travel along the Pan-American Highway for most of the trip, before taking a road near the Paramillo National Park to the camp you will use."

"Excellent." Michael nodded. "Twenty of our associates will arrive this evening in Barranquilla on an Avianca flight from London while ten others will be on an internal flight from Bogota." He grinned.

"What is so amusing?" Días lifted an eyebrow at Michael.

"I believe this will be the most dangerous group of university students ever to visit your country." Michael made air quotes when he referred to the men as university students.

"One of my men will meet their flights and bring them to the camp on a bus. Just like students." Días raised his brows. "I assume you did not send boys to do men's work?"

Alberto glared at him. "All are experienced fighters. Many are mercenaries, vying for the highest payment, but they all witnessed combat in Iraq, Afghanistan, or Syria—some in all three countries."

"Their training should be simple if they are as good as you say." *And if they are not, they will be buried in a shallow grave.*

"Don't worry—they'll handle the training, and you can pick six of them to deal with your little problem. What did you call her?" Alberto snapped his fingers. "Oh, yes. That *puta,* Olivia."

After they passed the entrance to the national park, the driver followed the convoy from the highway onto a winding dirt road. He came to a halt, waiting for the billowing cloud of dust raised by the trucks to clear before continuing to the camp.

"Almost there. When we arrive, remain in the car until I signal." Días gave a slight nod to the driver watching in the rearview mirror. "Otherwise, my guards are instructed to shoot at any perceived threat."

The Mercedes stopped at a raised barricade. Armed men approached the vehicles and glanced inside. One tapped on the driver's window and motioned for him to continue. As soon as they passed, the barricade dropped into place with a loud clang.

Ahead, a two-story white hacienda with green shutters and trim, stood on the left while four barns faced the house from the opposite side of the compound. Guard towers straddled the walls in the corners, with armed guards facing outward. Additional guards stood on the veranda, AK-47s trained on the Mercedes.

"Welcome to one of my homes." Días opened his door. "I will let you know when it is safe to leave the vehicle."

Both Días and the driver exited the vehicle. After a signal from Días, the guards shifted their weapons away from the car. "Michael, Alberto, you may join me."

They left the Mercedes and followed their host up a short flight of steps onto the veranda. Días turned and pointed to one of the barns. "Your containers will be unloaded there, and when your men arrive, they will find the adjacent building will be their new home." He headed to the hacienda's entrance, the door held open by the driver. "Your rooms will be on the upper floor, down the hall from mine. Get acquainted with the hacienda and meet me later for dinner."

MICHAEL AND ALBERTO joined Días in the dining room as dusk settled. A guard stood at either end of the room, while a lone servant pulled chairs back for the men. After they sat, he offered them a glass of wine. Both shook their heads and requested water.

Alberto took a sip and waved a hand in the air. "I expected something more befitting your position. After we finished the tour your driver gave us, I realized this was not the case."

Días raised a brow. "You are correct." He waved a hand to encompass the compound. "This is a working camp, so no need to provide impressive furnishings and décor. Meals are simple affairs here, too. Tonight, we are having a chicken dish and local vegetables. Nothing fancy, but filling. Afterward, I suggest we inspect your cargo."

An hour later, the three men pushed back their chairs and headed to the storage barn. They entered through a side door and approached the row of six twenty-foot containers. LED light towers augmented the original fixtures suspended high above the floor. The bright beams cast shadows throughout the building.

Alberto pointed at a number on the last container: LATU0192873. "That one." He turned to Días. "Can someone cut the lock?"

"Of course." Días whistled and gave instructions when one of his men rushed to his side before turning to Alberto. "What is in the others?"

Alberto shrugged. "Have no idea. I was told several were being sent to help disguise ours."

Días' man stepped forward with a pair of bolt cutters. After a nod from Días, he gripped the lock with the cutters and squeezed. The shaft gave way under pressure and snapped. He set the tool on the floor and heaved on the rusty door of the shipping container.

Inside, massive wooden crates, stenciled with thick black letters identifying 'Machine Parts,' filled the front of the container.

Michael stepped forward and touched the first crate. "We surrounded the weapons and ammunition with boxes of junk." He laughed as he explained to Días. "We raided several recycling centers and collected as much metal as we felt we could pass off as parts, including vehicles, appliances—even some building supplies."

"All of the boxes have the same labels." Alberto pointed at a smaller one. "You can do as you like with the remnants, but the crates bearing letters A&M on the top are the important ones—for our training and eventual mission."

Días nodded. "I will have my men begin unloading." He pointed to an empty area behind him. "They will put your weapons over there."

Beep! Beep! Beep!

Días and the others rushed to the door.

Guards surrounded a bright yellow bus, weapons aimed at the windows. The door opened partway, but no one left the vehicle.

"Must be our men." Michael glanced at his watch. "Right on time."

Días waved a hand, and the door extended, allowing the passengers to disembark.

Bedraggled, unshaven men, most with black hair, dark skin, and humps on the bridge of their noses, climbed out of the bus, pushing and shoving one another and formed two ragged lines. Each carried a small backpack. All appeared to be in their twenties or early thirties. Many wore t-shirts supporting various American and European universities.

An armed guard led them toward the barn next to the storage facility.

Alberto joined them and spoke in Arabic. "Welcome! This is your home while we train. Follow directions from the guards. Fail to do so, and they will be forced to shoot you. For the sake of taking our fight to the infidel Americans, please do as instructed."

One of the new arrivals stopped and glared at Alberto's statement before shrugging his shoulders.

The thirty men filed inside the building. Bunk beds lined the walls. "There's plenty of room since no one will be joining us." Alberto gestured. "Showers and toilets are in the back. Food will be brought soon. Get a good rest as target practice will begin at dawn."

BIRDS SCREECHED and winged their way upward as the first blast of weapons fire echoed over the compound and shattered the morning's calm. Michael and Alberto lay on the ground facing pop-up targets, with fifteen men spread out to each side of them. Trees lined the sides of the range, with an earthen berm behind the targets.

Most of the men fired AK-47s, but the squad leaders used M4 and SA-80 assault rifles and ammunition stolen from various military base arsenals across Europe. Each man began with a stack of magazines, replacing the empty ones as if their lives depended upon it. Before long, Michael and Alberto's last shots faded away while the surrounding thirty men finished their practice.

The aroma of breakfast replaced the smell of discharged weapons. Días' men dragged out metal containers filled with scrambled eggs, fried potatoes, and bacon. The students filed past, filling plates. Most skipped the bacon, but a few glanced around before sneaking a piece or two.

Alberto and Michael joined Días at a folding table while the others found areas to sit on the ground under the trees.

Días shoveled food into his mouth, not bothering to swallow before speaking. "I have an unusual treat for your training."

"Your facilities are excellent, both for target shooting and the obstacle course." Michael smiled. "I assume you've held sufficient training sessions in the past."

Días nodded. "Yes, when FARC was busy fighting the government, we had plenty of recruits join us. Most of them learned their skills here." He pointed to his right. "My present to you."

A dozen guards led six men toward the table. Their arms were tied in front of them. Heads cast down, they bore numerous cuts and bruises.

He glared at them. "You know the punishment." Días turned to Michael and Alberto. "Government troops could have raided us at any time. These men betrayed me by sleeping on guard duty. They will help your men sharpen their skills."

Alberto rubbed his chin. "How?"

"Your men will face fierce opposition from the Norteamericanos. Why not train against real targets?"

"What do you propose?" Michael's eyes gleamed with excitement.

"I suggest you break your men into six groups." Días gestured to the distant hills. "Each of the prisoners will select a weapon or two from what I will provide. They shall be given a ten-minute head start. If they can reach the perimeter fence, they will live." He shrugged. "However, your teams will be free to hunt them down—and kill them."

12

M oreno Hacienda
Barranquilla, Colombia

ALONZO TOOK the phone from his mother. He picked up a decanter and poured a healthy splash of brandy into a glass. Putting an arm around her, he lifted the glass to her lips as she gulped until it was empty. She nodded, and he refilled it, watching her take tiny sips. The color returned to her face.

"Gracias, Alonzo." Olivia gave him a wan smile. "Dial Señor Kruz's number again. It's urgent we speak with him."

After doing as she instructed, Alonzo shook his head a few seconds later. "No answer."

"Try Pedro's phone."

Alonzo dialed but hung up when he heard laughter and voices in the hallway. He yanked the door open as Pedro raised his hand to knock. Francisco Kruz stood next to him.

Spotting Olivia's tear-streaked face, Pedro rushed to her side and knelt. "What's the matter, my dear?"

She grabbed his arm. "Where the hell have you been? And Señor Kruz, why did you arrive with my husband? We've been trying to reach both of you. Silvina and Maria—they've been kidnapped!"

Pedro ignored the question about his whereabouts. "What?" He jumped to his feet. "When? Who?"

"I-I went to the school to meet them." Alonzo shook a finger toward Kruz before crossing his arms over his chest. "The principal said the girls left—with him!"

Kruz stumbled into a wooden straight-back chair. "I did not arrive with Pedro—we happened to arrive at the hacienda in separate vehicles about the same time." He took a deep breath. "Olivia, Pedro. I do not know what kind of nonsense this is, but how could I take my godchildren away? You know me better than this." He rubbed his hands together as the muscles along his jaw tightened. "You must believe me—I had nothing to do with this!"

Pedro turned and glared at him. "You better not have." Face turning white, his eyes narrowed. He spoke in an ice-cold voice. "You'll be ... dead."

"Enough!" Olivia jumped to her feet. "Francisco, if you weren't there, why did the principal say you were?"

Kruz squinted in a furtive manner. "Perhaps someone impersonated me or wants you to think I'm involved?"

"Must have been a noteworthy performance." Alonzo rolled his eyes. "The principal insisted the girls talked with a man before hopping in the car."

Olivia stomped to her desk, picked up a paperweight in the shape of an angel, and slammed it down. "Arguing won't bring them back. But, why would the principal make such an accusation if it wasn't true?" Her eyes flitted from one face to another. "The voice on the phone said for us to leave Barranquilla, never to return, and they'll be returned unharmed." She pursed her lips. "Who did we offend? Is this about our business?"

"Olivia, someone must want to chase you from the cartel." Kruz rubbed his chin. "Will you leave?"

"No." She hesitated before shaking her head. "Never." She turned to Alonzo. "Get Ramon. We must find out who took my girls and get them back—at all costs. Someone will pay for this attack on my family!" She picked the paperweight back up and threw it across the room, narrowly missing Pedro's head. *If they've harmed my precious daughters, I'll hunt the bastardos down—and kill them.*

~

THIRTY MINUTES LATER, Alonzo returned to Olivia's office, followed by Ramon. Tension blanketed the room. Olivia's face depicted a crushing testament of a mother's love in turmoil, while Pedro and Kruz's hangdog expressions revealed their frustration as they avoided each other's eyes.

Ramon rushed forward and knelt. "Doña Olivia, my apologies for not taking better care of your children. Upon my life, I swear to you we will find them."

"This is all my fault." Alonzo sat in his chair, his elbows perched on his legs. his head cradled in his arms. "If I hadn't been detained by the federales during their raid, fallen asleep after my release, and been delayed by a downed tree across the road, I'd have been at the school on time."

Kruz glanced at Alonzo. "What happened at the plant?"

"Soldiers swept through the area, rounding everyone up. Several of our workers were killed." Alonzo stared at the floor. "They threw us in the cells. Colonel Santiago arranged for my release from the prison." *Should I tell them about his threat?* He shook his head. *They don't need to know—yet.*

"I returned to the hacienda, took a shower, and fell asleep. When I woke up, I rushed to the school, but the girls were gone."

"Hmm." Ramon paced the room. "Too many coincidences. Someone with connections and power set everything up. But who?"

Pedro beat a fingertip drumroll on the arm of his chair and stared at Olivia. "It might not be any of my business, my dear, but why shouldn't we leave Barranquilla and start over?"

She glared at her husband, her face contorted with rage. "You're right—it's none of your business." She gritted her teeth. "No one will make me leave. I owe it to my father's memory to be successful."

Alonzo closed his eyes. *At what cost? The lives of Maria and Silvina? Who's next?*

A slight noise came from outside the room. Moments later, a discrete knock sounded.

Olivia glanced at Ramon.

He pulled his pistol and stepped to the side of the door. He pushed down on the handle and thrust the door open, his weapon ready.

Two wide-eyed servants stood in the hallway.

Ramon motioned with his pistol for them to enter.

They nodded when they edged past Ramon, pushing two carts into the center of the room.

The taller one turned to Olivia and gave a slight bow. "Doña Olivia, you haven't eaten since this morning. You must maintain your strength."

"Gracias. You may leave. We'll serve ourselves later."

Both women backed away and darted out the door, pulling it closed with a soft click.

A delightful aroma of charbroiled chicken wafted through the room. No one approached the food as they waited for Olivia.

She stood and glanced at each individual in turn. "I can only think of one man who would be enough of a coward to do this." Olivia clenched her jaws. "If I'm correct, it will mean war. We won't run away."

"Who, Mamá?"

"From the day we arrived in Barranquilla, we've encroached on his territory. Despite his smiling ways and his agreement to help us, it must be Ramírez. García. Días."

THE ROOM WENT SILENT. Ramon glanced sideways at Pedro and Kruz.

Is she right? Will they keep quiet and let me handle things? He rubbed his abdomen as his stomach gurgled.

Olivia gave her first genuine smile since the news of her daughters' kidnapping. "I suppose we should see what the chef sent us. I can't listen to the groans coming from Ramon's stomach."

After they each placed small amounts of chicken, rice, and *mantecada*, a traditional corn cake, on their plates, they resumed their seats. Ramon scooped a mixture toward his mouth when the phone rang. He grabbed it, listened for a moment, before activating the speaker.

"Good evening." A synthesized voice echoed throughout the room. "I believe everyone is present— Señor Kruz, Pedro, Alonzo, and Ramon. Of course, la jefa de la señora is with you, too."

"Where are my children, you bastardo?" Olivia squeezed her fists into her lap, her face turning red. "How do you know who is here?"

The voice chuckled. "I have my ways, my dear." The sounds of fingers snapping popped through the speaker. "Almost forgot. There's someone who wants to speak with you."

Silence.

"Mamá? Are you there?"

"Silvina! Are you okay? Where's Maria?"

"Beside me, but she's too frightened to speak." Silvina lowered her voice. "The man—he's the one who came into the—"

The sounds of a struggle came through the speaker.

"Ow! You're hurting me."

The synthesized voice returned. "Remember—leave Barranquilla … or your children will die!"

13

M oreno Hacienda
Barranquilla, Colombia

OLIVIA PROWLED the corridors of the hacienda, her eyes bloodshot from the countless tears she had shed. She paused in front of the framed portraits of Maria and Silvina a local artist had painted the previous year.

"My darlings," she whispered. Using a forefinger, she traced their cheeks. "I miss you so much. Where are you? I hope you're unharmed."

She whirled toward the echo of footsteps along the hallway.

"Doña Olivia, you must rest." Ramon put his arms around her. "Don't worry, we'll find them. I promise." *Madre de Dios! What have those imbeciles done?*

Olivia drew Ramon close and kissed him on the cheek. "Gracias, my dear friend. I don't know what I'd do without you."

He released her, stepped back, and gazed into her eyes. "I'm at your service." *Who knows? Perhaps one day, we'll be closer than we are now.*

Ramon's phone rang. He glanced at the number. "Olivia, I must take this. I'll speak with you later." He turned and headed toward the security office.

The phone stopped ringing.

Ramon entered the office, closed the door, sat in his five-wheeled wooden chair, and dialed the missed number. "Días. What a surprise. What do you want?"

"Buenos días. I heard a nasty rumor last night, and I wanted to check with you."

Ramon pinched the bridge of his nose. "What rumor?"

"Late last night, someone commented about the disappearance of Olivia's daughters from their school." He clicked his tongue. "Horrible. Any idea who is behind their kidnapping?"

"Your communication system is excellent."

Días chuckled. "A man in my position needs such a system—just to survive in these dangerous times."

"Agreed. Otherwise, life might be very short." *What he's up to?*

"I was also informed of another tale from the grapevine." Días cleared his throat. "It seems someone believes I kidnapped the girls."

"What?" *Who's his source—someone in the household?* "I don't believe you would stoop so low." *Unless it was worth your time and effort—which it might be if you want to drive Olivia from Barranquilla.*

"This is the reason for my phone call. I must meet with Olivia and Alonzo to convey my sympathies and stress I had nothing to do with this—this situation."

Ramon glanced at the clock on his computer screen. "The family will be eating breakfast soon. Perhaps, mid-morning."

"Gracias."

Ramon flipped his phone shut and rubbed his chin. *Perhaps I can play this to my advantage.*

∾

THE DOORBELL RANG. One of the servants rushed to the door and yanked it open. Días stepped inside. The man gave a slight bow and gestured for him to proceed along a hallway to the right.

"Wait here, por favor." The servant indicated a chair with a wave of his arm and departed.

Días ignored the chair and wandered around the library, pausing to glance out the window. He spotted several armed guards in the distance. *Hmm. Not many guards. Two at the entrance where I entered and a few scattered around.*

The door opened, and Ramon entered. The men shook hands.

"Doña Olivia is waiting for you in her office. I warn you, don't provoke her—she's armed."

Días raised his hands. "I am unarmed. See for yourself. You may search me if you like." *They will not find the knife inside my belt or the one hidden in the heel of my shoe.*

"Won't be necessary." Ramon shook his head. "My pistol will be aimed at you the entire time we're in her presence. Make one move I don't like, and—" He made a pistol with his fingers and aimed at the FARC commander.

"Threats are childish." Días crossed his arms.

"Perhaps, but this isn't a threat. It's merely a reminder you are a guest here, not in charge." Ramon stood. "Time to meet with Doña Olivia."

They left the library and strolled toward Olivia's office. Ramon insisted Días walk in front of him as they left the library. They came to the office door, where Días stepped aside to allow Ramon to knock.

Olivia sat behind her desk, with Alonzo to one side, a shotgun balanced across his knees. Two guards stood in opposite corners, weapons in sight.

Días took the chair in front of the desk while Ramon sat next to her.

Olivia glared at her unwanted guest. "Where are my children?" She pounded her desk. "Where are Maria and Silvina? What did you do with them? I want them back!"

"Señora, you are mistaken. I did not take your girls, nor do I know where they are." Días tapped his foot on the floor. "Why would you think such a thing? We are partners, after all." *But I do not think we will be for much longer.*

"I'm aware of your desires to push me out and take control of the business." Olivia shook her head. "It won't happen as long as I lead this cartel."

Perhaps a change of leadership is needed—sooner rather than later? Días smirked. "I am not sure where you are getting your information, but it is incorrect. I have enough to worry about without trying to take over the Moreno Cartel." He leaned forward before standing.

Alonzo lifted the shotgun, using it to wave Días back in his seat.

"You must understand we survive in this lucrative business by being ruthless." Días crossed his arms and pursed his lips. "I am innocent of your false accusations. I do not make war on children. I never have and never will." *Well, perhaps when necessary to get what I want, but that was as a FARC commander, not a cartel leader—at least so far.*

"Why should we—I trust you? I'm sure you earned your reputation." She sighed. "I want my girls back. I don't care how, but they must be unharmed. Someone impersonated Señor Kruz and took them from their school. Someone organized this kidnapping—it wasn't done on a whim."

Días thrust his hands in the air. "To prove I am trustworthy, I will bolster your security until Maria and Silvina are recovered. No fee. I could also investigate further with my own resources if you like. Would I do this if I had taken them?"

"I don't trust you. You could be trying to hide your involvement." Olivia rolled her eyes. "You better find them—or else."

Días glanced at Ramon. "What is with all of the threats? I feel like I am unwanted in this hacienda."

Olivia shoved her chair back and stood, eyes burning with hatred. "Get out! Now!"

Alonzo jumped to his feet, pointing the shogun at Días, his finger tightening on the trigger.

Ramon pulled his second pistol from its holster. He motioned Días toward the door.

He grinned and addressed Olivia. "I shall keep Ramon informed of any information that I might come across." He tipped an imaginary hat. "I bid you a somewhat pleasant day, given the circumstances. You have my deepest condolences during this stressful time."

Días and Ramon left the room and headed outside. After shaking hands, Días climbed in his vehicle and waved for the driver to depart.

As his car left the compound, a smile caressed Días' cheeks. *Who is behind the kidnapping? An inside job, or is someone else making a move on the Moreno Cartel?* He shook his head. *Whoever it is, this is not good for business. I know just the person to speak to.*

THE THICK FOLIAGE from a copse of rosy trumpet trees hid a brown Jeep Cherokee. Inside, a man focused his binoculars on Días' vehicle. He watched the car grow smaller as it continued along the driveway from the hacienda toward the distant gate. He chuckled. *Perfect!*

14

Former FARC Training Facility
Outside Turbo, Colombia

MICHAEL STOOD under a canopy and blew a whistle. All training stopped. Six men jumped to their feet and hustled over. They formed a ragged semi-circle as Michael and Alberto looked each man in the face. Despite being in top physical condition, the men breathed heavily in the intense sunlight. Sweat stains dotted their clothing. One of them used the sleeve of his shirt to wipe the perspiration from his forehead.

"We have a challenge for your teams. After you empty your magazines at the stationary targets, reload." Michael gestured toward Días. "He's provided new targets for you. Not paper this time—live ones."

The team leaders glanced at one another. Most of their faces were devoid of expression, but two grinned. Each man nodded.

Michael motioned for them to join the other trainees before turning to Alberto. He spoke in a soft voice so Días couldn't hear him. "We must keep an eye on our benefactor. He may become an accidental liability. I overheard one of his men last night saying those who stand up to him end up in shallow graves."

"Agreed." Alberto shielded his brow from the intense sunlight. "I'm sure the men won't mind the new challenge, but what if one of us runs afoul of him?" He pursed his lips. "Will he do the same to us?"

"Remain alert and be prepared." Michael directed his gaze toward the firing line, where shooting tapered off as the men emptied and cleared their magazines.

SIX MEN STOOD IN A ROW, eyes wide with fear. A thick rope secured each man's hands.

Días walked in front of the men, staring into each face. "The rules of the hunt are simple." He pointed to a table holding a variety of implements designed to kill. "Each of you may take no more than two. You will be given a ten-minute head start." He gestured toward the distant mountains covered with trees at the lower elevations. Fences continued from the main compound, disappearing over the hills. "If you can evade the team giving chase and reach the outer boundary within forty-five minutes, you will be given a second chance to remain on the guard force."

"What about them?" One of the prisoners pointed at the first team. "Will they use the same weapons?"

"It is up to them. The hunters may use whatever they want, including knives, pistols, and rifles."

"What if they catch me before I reach the fence?"

Días stared at the man. "Death." He turned to Michael and Alberto. "Pick your first pursuit team. Their target will be this inquisitive prisoner."

The man sucked in his breath but didn't speak.

The team leader pulled a toothpick from his mouth. "What's your name?"

"N-Nicolas.Why?"

"So we know what to put on your marker."

The man's eyes seemed to pop out of his head as he realized what was at stake. "But ...."

Días gestured at the table. "Choose your weapons. Your ten-minute head start begins ...." He glanced at his watch. "Now."

The prisoner grabbed a machete, a bow, and a quiver filled with arrows. Without a backward glance, he stumbled forward, following an animal trail into the brush.

The others waited for the ten minutes to pass. Michael gestured toward the team leader. "Go."

The team leader gave a hand signal and stepped onto the same path used by their quarry. Four men followed, AK-47s at the ready.

NICOLAS HURRIED his pace as the ground became steeper. He paused behind an old *borrachero* tree. Realizing his temporary refuge was the source of 'The Devil's Breath,' also known as scopolamine, he held his breath and backpedaled.

He gazed at the leafy green canopy of yellow and white flowers. *Should I collect* some? *Rip up my shirt for a pouch and tie it on an arrow?* He shook his head. *Might end up like a zombie if I inhale the dust. They'd kill me for sure.*

After listening for sounds of pursuit, he meandered through the trees and thinning brush, desperate to reach the fence and freedom.

Craack!

A bullet ricocheted off a stone outcrop near his head. *Madre de Dios!* Adrenaline shooting through his system, the prisoner dropped the bow and arrow and lunged forward. Chest heaving, a moan escaped from his throat as the fence came into focus.

He skidded to a halt.

Two men appeared next to the fence, blocking his path to freedom, their AK-47s trained on his chest.

He raised the machete.

"*Aaaaah!*"

Nicolas rushed toward the nearest mercenary. He made it to within two steps of his target when the man fired a three-round burst into his chest.

The impact from the slugs shoved him backward. Arms flailing, he tumbled down the hill and collapsed.

The team leader approached. He aimed his M4 carbine at the lifeless body and gave a sharp kick to ensure their target was dead. Satisfied, he headed toward the camp, the others following.

The last man stopped by the body, picked up the machete, and slashed at the neck until the head separated. He grabbed it by the hair and joined the others.

Días, Michael, and Alberto sat under an umbrella at an outdoor table, seeking escape from the brilliant sunshine. They stopped talking when the first team approached.

"Job's done." The team leader motioned to the man carrying the bloody head. "Here's proof."

The man tossed the head on the ground near the table. Días' eyes lit up, while Michael and Alberto remained stoic.

"Excellent." Días pointed to a small enclosure. "The other prisoners are there. Toss the head inside. Perhaps it will give them an incentive to do a better job of evading the other teams." He turned to Michael. "Shall we wait about an hour before the next chase? Plenty of daylight left, and it is time for lunch."

THE NEXT PRISONER glanced at the various weapons and picked up a pistol. He checked to see if it was loaded.

Click.

He turned at the sound and found himself facing the team leader. Unwavering, the leader's rifle focused on the man's chest.

The prisoner grinned.

"Don't even think about it. You'll be dead before you aim that pistol at any of us." The leader gestured toward the hill. "Get moving."

The prisoner shrugged and tossed the pistol on the table. He departed after grabbing a knife and a machete. He sprinted through the shooting range, plowing his way through the undergrowth, not caring if he left a trail. *I'll show the others how to escape. All I need to do is run and keep running.*

The man weaved partway up the hill before beginning a series of zigzags, moving closer to a cliff edge. Despite erratic movement through the trees and doubling back on himself, the men tracking him had picked up his trail and encircled him.

He teetered on a massive boulder and peered down the embankment. *Could I jump and make it to one of the trees?* His legs weakened, and he gasped for breath. *Too far, but what choice do I have?*

"Ahem." The leader cleared his throat as his team pointed their weapons at the man.

The prisoner spun around to face his firing squad. Before they aimed, he spread his arms apart and flipped backward over the cliff.

He never uttered a word.

A dull thud indicated the prisoner had landed below.

The team leader glanced down at the sprawling body, blood spreading across the rocks. He yanked his cell phone from a pocket and took several photos to show Días and the others.

Three other prisoners met similar ends with varying degrees of bravery. Two jumped to their deaths while the third managed to climb to the top of the fence before bullets riddled his body.

At last, the final condemned man was brought to the table to choose his weapons. He fingered the remaining knives and one of the pistols before falling to his knees. "Please. Forgive me. My family— they won't survive without me."

Días kicked the man in the side. "Quit sniveling and take your punishment like a man. Grab a weapon and run."

Dejected, the man stood and walked away, his head hung low.

The last team leader glanced at his men. They each gave a slight nod before they strolled after their target.

With the slow pursuit, the prisoner approached the fence unharmed. He glanced around—no one. He placed a foot on the first plank and began to climb.

Snap!

His head jerked around at the sound of a branch breaking.

Five men stepped from the trees, their weapons by their sides.

The team leader stepped forward and motioned for the man to continue climbing.

"Why would you let me go?" He made the sign of the cross. "Are you Christians?"

"No. However, you were the only prisoner to mention a family. We do this for them, not you."

WHEN THE LAST team returned to the hacienda, Días glared at them. "We heard no shots. Where is the prisoner?"

The team leader shook his head. "He was too fast for us and was over the fence when we arrived." He shrugged. "You said any prisoner who made it over the barrier was free."

"I-I ...." Días' face turned purple with rage. "I wanted them all dead."

"You should have done your own dirty work." As one, the team turned and headed to their billeting.

Días slammed a fist on the table. "Michael, Alberto—these are your men. Control them."

Alberto grinned. "He's right—you said if anyone made it to the outer boundary, they would live."

"So, I lied." Días laughed.

Alberto ignored the comment and gestured at Michael. "I depart tomorrow for Panama to oversee the training there. Is there anything else you'd like to discuss before I leave?"

15

M anuel Amador Guerrero Hospital
Colon, Panama

As soon as the hospital doors swung inward, Javier pushed AJ's wheelchair into the afternoon sunshine. He opened the door of a white Hyundai minivan parked near the entrance and turned to assist her.

"I didn't need a wheelchair—I'm capable of walking." AJ grinned.

"Hospital's rules—all discharged patients must leave in a wheelchair. They don't want the liability if something happens." Javier opened the passenger door for her. "Besides, how often will I be able to push you around? At least you don't need crutches."

AJ climbed inside the vehicle. "Good points. Where to?" With careful movements, she eased back into the seat and strapped herself in.

Javier squeezed behind the wheel. "I rented a house on the outskirts of Colon." He started the engine, and they departed.

"What for? Aren't we heading to Colombia?"

"Patience." He took his eyes off the road and glanced at her. "While you lounged in a hospital bed catching up on your beauty sleep ...." He smiled. "I continued the mission. Yes, we're heading to Colombia, but I needed a base for the guys who arrived this morning from Bragg."

"What guys?"

"The ones I arranged to continue monitoring the facility where the containers were taken. We can't be here and in Colombia at the same time."

She tapped the side of her head and winced. "Duh."

"Well, that was brilliant." Javier smirked as he started the engine. "I proved my point without saying a word." He weaved the vehicle through several streets, and doubled back, checking for any signs of pursuit. Satisfied they hadn't picked up a tail, he turned onto a road leading out of the city. "A few minutes, and we'll be there."

AJ nodded as she stared out the window at the lush, thick trees.

Javier stopped in front of a black, wrought iron fence. A gardener rushed forward and opened the gates. With a wave, Javier continued into the compound, stopping behind two cars parked in front of a white, single-story dwelling, capped at each end by circular towers with golden parapets. Two smaller houses were nearby, both perched on stilts so residents could view the lake over the treetops.

AJ turned to Javier. "What's with the three houses? How much does this cost? We do have a budget, you know."

He laughed. "There are four houses—one in the back for the gardener and his wife, who does the cooking. He's also the night watchman. Everything costs less than two thousand dollars a month, including food and utilities. We're in the main house, while the guys are split between the smaller buildings." He opened the door. "C'mon, I'll show you around later. Let's meet the Snakes."

"Snakes?"

Javier chuckled. "Just wait."

She hooked her arm through Javier's as they stepped under a covered entranceway. Four ornate pillars supported the roof.

They walked into the living room. Several sofas and recliners filled the area, with a massive television mounted on one of the orange and yellow walls. A statue of a naked maiden holding a basket above her head stood in one corner.

"A bit vulgar, don't you think?" AJ wrinkled her nose.

Four men jumped to their feet. They stood to attention and saluted Javier.

He stifled a smile and returned their salute. "Knock it off, guys. Meet AJ. This is her show, and we're providing the support."

The men chuckled. They shook AJ's hand in turn, the last one grabbing her in a hug and lifting her off the floor.

"Down, Viper!" Javier motioned for the muscle-bound man to release her. "Sorry, AJ. He always does that—to guys, too."

"Aw, shucks. Can I help it if I'm friendly?" Viper chuckled.

She laughed.

"Meet the Snakes—from left to right: Viper, Mamba, Rattler, and Adder. They all speak Spanish, so they'll be able to assist with any interrogations."

AJ nodded. "The Snakes. Gotcha. Cool names." She glanced at Javier. "What's yours, and do I get one too?"

"Mine's Cobra. How about Taipan for you? Kills with a series of quick strikes."

"Perfect."

Viper ran his hand over his close-cropped blond hair. "We've been monitoring the trackers you placed on the containers—no change in location."

"Excellent. Is everyone ready to begin nighttime surveillance and check out the compound?"

"Hooah!" four voices responded.

"Relax, guys. No parade ground here. Take care of your personal needs. The first team begins coverage at 2000." Javier pointed at AJ. "We'll take the first watch until midnight. You guys sort out how you'll cover the next two shifts. Tomorrow we'll make an assessment and determine if we can reduce nighttime coverage to have someone monitor things during daylight hours."

A FEW MINUTES before their scheduled shift, Javier and AJ, both dressed from head to toe in black, hopped in one of the cars and departed. Moonlight and stars lit the sky, while a breeze tempered the humidity.

Approaching their destination, Javier switched off the lights and coasted past the entrance into a turnoff. They donned their NVGs, allowing their eyes to adjust to the murky green images. Afterward, they grabbed their backpacks and headed into the trees.

Without a sound, they crept up to a wire fence enclosing three sides of the compound, a brick wall fronting the road forming the fourth side.

AJ and Javier pushed back into the brush when they spotted two wavering lights approaching.

Two guards, both carrying flashlights, their weapons slung over their shoulders, passed without glancing in their direction.

After they disappeared, AJ waved a hand to fan her face and whispered, "Pot. They seem bored."

Javier nodded. "Makes our job easier. Let's go."

They climbed through the strands of the fence and slithered through the grass.

Nearing a barn with open doors, Javier raised a hand and signaled to stop. He pointed.

Inside, four trailers were crammed between wooden beams supporting the upper floor. A Conex box rested on each trailer.

"Looks like the seals are still in place on all but one of the containers." Javier pulled the tracking monitor from a pocket. "Appears the trackers are working fine. Let's head back to the perimeter and wait." He turned and weaved his way back, AJ following.

They settled into position, keeping an eye out for any roaming guards.

A roar shattered the evening, followed by the screaming of an animal in distress.

"Now what?" AJ glanced at Javier.

"Sounds like a jaguar found its dinner. If it has, it'll leave us alone."

"Excellent reason to keep alert—just in case there's another one."

The rest of their shift passed without any unusual events.

THE TWIN SNAKES, Mamba and Rattler, replaced Javier and AJ. After updating their replacements, the couple wormed away from the compound and returned to their vehicle.

"I'm hungry. Any grub at your villa?" AJ yawned.

"Plenty—I'll make you a sandwich and your favorite beverage—coffee." He put the vehicle in gear and coasted down the slight incline, lights off, before starting the engine.

"You do know how to wow a girl." AJ grinned as she used a hand to fan herself. "You'll be taking me dancing next."

Javier parked in front of the main house and glanced at her. "I'll have you know I'm an outstanding dancer. Wait until the mission is completed, and I'll show you." He struck a dancer's pose.

"Promises, promises." *Hmm. Not bad looking .... Good sense of humor ....*

After their late-night snack, they climbed upstairs to adjacent bedrooms, since Viper and Adder were camped out in front of the television, watching a pirated action movie.

THE TWINS NOTED the activity and location of every conceivable item or building they might require for future incursions into the terrorist compound. Viper and Adder relieved them and continued monitoring the site for any movements. Other than an occasional stroll past their location by two noisy guards, the time passed without incident.

Toward the middle of the last hour of their shift, the men jumped at the sound of a horn. They could monitor the gate from their location in the bushes. A blue and white pickup truck waited to enter.

Guards rushed to the entrance and swung the gate open. With tires spinning in the gravel, the truck shot forward into the compound.

Adder focused his telephoto lens on the passenger as he climbed out. "Who do we have here? Everyone's running around as if the boss had arrived." He took a series of photos.

"He appears to be South American—at least no apparent European features."

Viper nodded. "We'll stay a bit longer to see what happens. I'll slip back into the bushes and send Cobra a message."

Javier sipped his coffee, glanced at his phone, and read the incoming text: *New arrival—seems important based on activities. Will provide mug shot when we return—no app on this phone. Will stay in position longer to monitor the situation.*

He concurred and turned to AJ, who was typing on her iPad. When she finished, Javier nodded and sent a response: *Continue mission.*

"Wonder who arrived? Wish they had taken one of the SAT phones with them to send the photo right away." AJ drained the last of her coffee, reached for the carafe, and refilled both cups. "I received an update from MacKenzie. She says they've picked up chatter about a training camp in Colombia." She pursed her lips. "Wonder if this is related to the facility we're interested in or if it's something else?"

Javier shrugged. "If they can gather more intel, we should be able to check it out."

AJ's eyes widened as she reread MacKenzie's message. "There's an unclear reference to two young girls. Someone is speculating they were taken and sold into slavery." She shook her head. "After discussing the camp with the caller, the called party mentioned the girls—both men seemed pleased."

Heat flushed through Javier's body. He pounded a fist into the palm of his other hand. "Perverts—they need to be eradicated."

AJ nodded. "MacKenzie finished her note by saying Lintstone gave us the green light." Her eyes lit up with excitement. "We'll eliminate the kidnappers if they get in our way."

16

R ented Villa
     Colon, Panama

AFTER FINISHING THEIR SHIFT, Viper and Adder joined the others at the rented villa. Adder uploaded the photos from his camera, printed the best one of the new camp arrival, and passed it to AJ.

She studied it before handing the photo to Javier. "Doesn't look familiar. Perhaps a new player or someone we haven't heard about before?"

"Sorry you had to wait for our return for the snap." Adder rolled his shoulders and stretched his lips into a thin smile, one corner pulled down. "I forgot the SAT phone, so I used the camera with the telephoto lens because the piece of junk I took with me wouldn't connect with the network." He frowned. "Next time, I'll make sure I take what I need so I can upload any additional pictures and send them along ASAP."

"No worries, Adder." AJ smiled at his apparent discomfort. "For future surveillance missions, everyone will take what they need—

especially encrypted SAT phones and iPads." She glanced at Javier. "We'll make a list." *So much for assuming they know what they're doing. Of course, they're probably more comfortable blowing things up than doing surveillance missions.*

Someone tapped her shoulder. She turned.

"Señora, breakfast is ready." An elderly woman smiled and pointed toward the dining room.

"Gracias, Rosa." AJ returned her smile. "Grub's up guys—last one in helps Rosa with the dishes."

The others pushed past AJ and claimed seats before she uttered another word. She sat in her usual place at one end of the table. "What's for breakfast?" *As if I care. I only eat because there isn't a pill I can take.*

Javier passed her a loaded platter. "*Hojaldras, bollos, patacones*, and *carne salchicha guisada*."

"Hmm." AJ wrinkled her nose and pointed at what appeared to be a dumpling wrapped in a banana leaf. "What's that?"

"Bollos—one of my favorites. A bit of corn dough wrapped in the leaf and boiled. Goes well with the carne." He held a deep dish for her inspection.

"Is that a hot dog cut up and tossed in the stew?" She rolled her eyes.

Javier nodded. "The Panamanians call it a sausage. It's good for you." He laughed. "What about the hojaldras? The unsweetened dough is dried and also goes well with the carne."

"If the dough's hard enough, we could use it for ammo." AJ handed the dishes to Viper, who sat on her left. "I'll pass. I think I'll try some of the fried plantain and a coffee."

"Rosa made some *orejitas* to go with the coffee." Javier rubbed his stomach. "I love those sweet, buttery cookies."

"Yeah, right. I think you just like to eat. Hope the cookies don't ruin your figure." Her eyes sparkled as she struggled to contain herself. "Isn't there a saying about men and food?"

"Don't know about that." He patted his taut stomach. "But, we need to keep our engines stoked."

AJ chuckled and stood. "While everyone's eating, I'll check for any messages." Grabbing her coffee, she returned to the living room and switched on her iPad—one new message.

After responding to the update from MacKenzie, AJ closed her email and headed back to the dining room.

The cacophony of voices ebbed as all eyes fixed on her.

"New intel on three new players and one of the original ones." She glanced around the room to ensure they were alone. "Headquarters identified the original guy—a probable rogue FARC commander named Días. He mentioned a plot to remove the leader of an unnamed cartel." AJ pursed her lips. "He requested any information the others might hold regarding the kidnapping of two young girls. One was named Maria, but the other name was inaudible."

Viper wiped sauce from his face with a napkin. "Any location identified?"

AJ shook her head. "Not yet, but analysis is continuing. MacKenzie said she'd send any new intel as soon as it's verified."

"We still heading to Colombia?" Javier studied AJ's expression.

"Yes. I also requested additional support to meet us in Bogota. They'll be arriving this evening at about the same time we do."

"Anyone I've met?"

AJ laughed. "No, but you'll like them—all former special forces and part of my field team. Of course, they'll be using aliases."

Javier raised a brow but remained silent as he refilled AJ's coffee cup and passed a plate of cookies.

"When you two finish ... I checked the monitor—the four trackers are in the same locations as before." Adder snagged a cookie before the plate went the opposite direction around the table.

"Why don't you and Viper head back to the observation post and see if you can get additional photos." Javier stretched his arms above his head and yawned.

"Yes!" Adder pumped a fist in the air. "Action time!" He grabbed another cookie and followed Viper outside.

∼

Javier's men remained in the tree line, overlooking the compound. Viper scanned the area with his binoculars while Adder set up a black X64ACS directional microphone so they could listen to conversations. About the size of a standard laptop case, the unit came with long-life rechargeable batteries, lasting for up to twenty-two hours, and could pick up sounds at a distance surpassing 650 feet.

Adder plugged in his headset and aimed the device at a group of men standing near a house. He stifled a laugh and whispered, "Guys are guys all over the world. Talking about their conquests last night—each one trying to outdo the others."

"Someone just stepped onto the porch." Viper picked up the camera and took several snaps. "Same guy we saw last night. A shorter man is standing next to him, playing with his mustache."

"The guy with the biggest swagger said their boss arrived last night. Referred to him as Alberto." Adder adjusted the microphone so it focused on the porch. "Grab the other headset and listen."

Viper plugged in as Alberto spoke.

"The rest of the men will arrive this afternoon. All the weapons and ammunition we need are in one of the containers. We'll break the men into teams of five when they arrive—they'll remain in the same groups when they head north."

"When will they be informed of their targets?"

"Not until they're ready to cross the border from Mexico—don't want any leaks or anyone backing out."

Viper glanced at Adder. "You recording this?"

He nodded. "Yeah. Wish he'd give more details."

"I think we'll be hanging around longer." Viper gritted his teeth. "Perhaps we'll get the green light to take them out."

After the recon team returned and briefed the others, AJ sent a message to Washington.

To: Fortress
From: Hunter

Updated surveillance indicates new arrival is known as Alberto. Apparent attack being planned. Possible target: unspecified location, U.S. southern border area. Additional details will be provided when available.

She leaned back, tipping the front legs of her chair off the floor, and sipped her coffee. A few minutes later, her iPad pinged.

To: Hunter

From: Fortress

Your intel acknowledged. Use new resources to continue coverage. Green light is approved if/when target confirmed. Harry, Larry, and Samantha will arrive in Bogota this evening. They'll meet you at the usual place.

AJ smiled, dropped her chair back on four legs, and slid the iPad across the table. "Help is confirmed for Bogota."

Javier read the message, his brows rising. "Who are—"

"Part of my team. Don't mind their names—they're passionate and know their business—and aren't afraid of using permanent termination."

17

M ontearroyo Residential Complex
Bogota, Colombia

AN OLD MAN sat hunched over the table in the shadows at the bar in the villa's game room. He met his visitor's gaze as they sipped eight-year-old Ron Medellin Extra Añejo with a dash of Coke and a single ice cube.

Draining his glass, the middle-aged visitor smacked his lips. "Excellent rum."

The man tilted his head and crossed his arms. "I require your ... unique assistance."

"What do you need this time?" The visitor chuckled as he held out his glass for a refill. "Murder, smuggling, or kidnapping?"

After pouring new drinks, the man stared at the ceiling. "Your specialty—murder. But it must appear to be an accident. There is too much to lose if word spreads I'm behind this."

"How soon?"

The visitor leaned forward and spoke in hushed tones. "Within the month."

"My price is one million dollars—American." The guest poured Coke into his rum, using his finger to stir his drink. "No down payment from you, Don. I trust you." *At least when I'm in your presence.*

The man smirked as he slid a piece of paper across the table. "Make sure you do this in Barranquilla. I want to send an important message—don't mess around where you're not wanted."

"As you wish." The guest wiped a hand over his thinning black hair and glanced at the paper. "Do you want to—"

"Spare me the details—I don't care how you get rid of her—just do it."

The guest nodded and downed the remainder of his drink.

ALONZO DARTED down the steps and jumped into his Mercedes. He glanced around—no one appeared to be paying any attention to him. Leaving the compound, he drove to a cantina on the opposite side of Barranquilla and parked between two trucks at the rear of an adjacent parking lot.

After climbing out of his car, he glanced around. *Good, not a soul nearby.* He walked to the rear of the Mercedes. Perspiration appeared on his forehead and near his temples. He swallowed hard as his heart thumped. *I better go inside in case someone sees me.*

Before entering the cantina, he gave the area another check. *Can't see my car. Good.* As he reached for the door, a teenager of short stature grabbed the door and yanked it open, motioning him inside.

With a glimmer of a smile as thanks, Alonzo stepped into the cantina. He stopped in the dim light, waiting for his eyes to adjust.

Green neon signs over the bar advertised Cerveza Aguila, brewed in the city. Two men sat at a circular wooden table, watching a football match on a widescreen TV fastened to the graffiti-covered wall. They set their glasses down and stared at the intruder.

Both were mustachioed. One sported long, black hair. The other wore his silver hair cropped close to his skull.

When Alonzo approached, the silver-haired man gestured to an empty chair. "Join us. Would you like an Aguila?" Without waiting for a response, the man whistled and raised three fingers in the air.

A bartender rushed over with the requested beers and hurried back behind the bar, where he picked up a soiled rag and continued wiping dirty glasses.

"So." The man chugged his beer until little remained. "What do you want?"

Alonzo sipped from his drink. "Señor Gómez, I want—no, I need your help." He stared into the eyes of the man sitting across from him. "I intend to expand the Moreno holdings. We must do so or be run out of business." He shook his head. "That is unacceptable to both my mother and myself."

"Ah, yes." Gómez chuckled. "How is Senora Moreno? I heard the terrible news about her daughters."

Alonzo waved a hand in dismissal. "Under the circumstances, she's doing well, but it appears bad news spreads quickly."

"Does she know you're meeting with me?"

Alonzo slammed a fist on the table. "No! I am taking control of our operations. She'll be briefed if and when necessary."

The bartender yanked a shotgun from under the bar.

Gómez shook his head and waved the bartender away. "The young man is showing his cojones." He grinned. "What do you want from me?"

"I plan to move some of our product into Europe. I require an introduction to a few of your contacts."

"Hmm." He leaned forward. "What is there for me if I do this?"

Alonzo glanced at the black-haired man before responding. "What I tell you is between you and me—no one else."

Gómez nodded toward the bar.

His companion shoved his chair back and stomped away.

"You have my attention—don't waste my time."

"Señor, if you grant my request, I'm prepared to offer you twenty percent of the new business—providing you never speak to my mother about this."

"My business might suffer. To make it worth my while, I'll require forty percent."

Alonzo shook his head. "You're not the only Colombian with the necessary ties in Europe—twenty-five percent."

The man rubbed his chin and shook his head. "Thirty-five."

"My final offer—thirty percent. Not a penny more."

"Deal."

Alonzo grinned. *Just as I wanted.* They shook hands, and Alonzo stood to leave.

"One other thing." Gómez's dark eyes held Alonzo's gaze. "Check around and see what happens to people who try to betray me. A word to the wise—don't be foolish."

Alonzo nodded and left the cantina.

RAMON RAPPED on the door to Olivia's office and stepped inside. Shadows on the drawn curtains seemed alive as a tree outside one of the windows swayed in the light breeze. A single lamp cast an eerie glow across the room.

"Is there any news?" Olivia sat in one of the easy chairs, holding a glass filled with clear liquid. With a shaking hand, she swiped at her red, puffy eyes with a tissue. Tattered hair clung to her scalp. Despite being early afternoon, she was still dressed in her bedclothes, wracked with too much grief to bother changing.

"My informants are asking questions in Barranquilla, Bogota, Medellín, and the surrounding areas." He shook his head. "People know you're looking for Maria and Silvina, but so far, we have nothing to identify where they are or who kidnapped them."

Olivia sniffed. "Keep searching—someone must have the answers we need."

"Sí, Doña." Ramon's gaze dropped to the floor.

"What is it? What aren't you telling me?"

"There's—" Ramon locked his eyes on Olivia's. "A rumor—picked up by several of my men."

The muscles in her face tightened, and she slammed her glass on a table near her chair. "Tell me."

"Someone put a price on your head."

She gasped and closed her eyes. "Why? We've done no one any harm."

"Doña." Ramon shrugged. "You are a woman alone in a dangerous business. I can think of many cartel leaders who would want to take over your business. Everyone knows you can't be bought, so the only way to succeed would be to—eliminate you."

She sipped from a glass of wine on her desk and stared out a window.

The kidnapping has damaged her spirit. Will I be able to control her? "I doubled the guards as soon as I learned about the rumors. We must take every precaution to ensure your safety."

She turned her attention back to Ramon. "My life is meaningless without my daughters. Their recovery is our priority. Offer a greater reward for information leading to their return."

Ramon nodded. "Of course, Doña. How much?"

Olivia twisted her lips. "Increase the reward to five hundred thousand American dollars."

"At once." Ramon grimaced as he sat in a chair next to Olivia. "We must also consider your safety."

"Where's Alonzo? He should be here for this discussion."

Ramon waved a hand in the air. "Who knows? He said he was going to meet with Gabriela."

Olivia gave a half-smile. "They seem to get along well. I hope it lasts."

"Who understands what young people will do these days." He laughed. "Not like our generation." The muscles in Ramon's face tightened. "We must make plans for you. I have a friend—"

"I will remain here." Olivia clenched her hands. "No one will scare me away from my home."

"Doña. It is better for a strategic withdrawal while I determine the source of this death warrant. My friend has a small but well-fortified hacienda you may use."

Olivia sat motionless, staring at the ceiling. After several minutes had passed, she nodded. "Okay, I'll do what you suggest. Alonzo must be informed, but promise not to tell anyone else, not even Pedro."

"What should I say to Pedro if he asks where you are?"

"Tell him ... tell him I went away on family business. He appreciates it's in his best interest not to ask too many questions."

Ramon nodded. "As you wish." *Of course, for the right price, I could be persuaded to share this information. That would teach her to spurn my advances.* "When do you want to depart?"

"As soon as you make the arrangements." Olivia's eyes narrowed to crinkled slits. "Once you find out who wants me dead and who kidnapped my daughters, we'll deal with the issues. As the Americanos say, 'with extreme prejudice.'"

18

T errorist Compound
    Outside Colon, Panama

MAMBA AND RATTLER hid among the thick trees across from the brick wall fronting the terrorist compound. Two black and white panel trucks approached. After a brief halt, the vehicles entered.

"Big enough to carry the expected troops." Rattler snapped several photos of the vans, including close-ups of the license plates.

Mamba keyed his mic and whispered, "Two trucks inbound—could be the expected arrival."

"Move to secondary position. Viper out."

Mamba keyed his radio once to confirm the order.

Rattler and Mamba gathered their equipment and moved deeper into the tropical forest. On a parallel course to the road, they crouched, navigated into a ditch, and crawled through a heavy-duty culvert under the road. Designed to handle torrential downpours during the rainy season, the conduit provided a perfect means of converging on the compound without being spotted.

Fifteen minutes later, they climbed onto a rocky ridge over-looking their target. As with the surrounding area, a myriad of palm, jacaranda, and mahogany trees fought for space as they reached toward the sky.

Rattler took the first watch, focusing on a massive building where the two trucks were now parked.

Mamba contacted Viper, and once again whispered, "In position. Eyes on trucks. Appears to be around thirty men."

Viper keyed his radio to acknowledge but didn't speak as two guards approached their location.

Adder and Mamba slid back into a shallow depression under-neath the roots of a canopy tree. After the guards passed, they resumed their positions, with Viper aiming the directional micro-phone at the porch of the house.

The man they had identified as Alberto was joined by six of the new arrivals. Viper adjusted the microphone toward the discussion.

"Welcome. This will be your home while we prepare your teams for their movement into Norteamérica."

One of the new arrivals scratched his chin and gazed at Alberto. "We're ready now. When are we heading north?"

Alberto glared at the man. "Not until we say so. Michael is training the others at a Colombian compound. The two groups will move at different times but will join together in Mexico. Once you reach Múzquiz, you'll receive details regarding your targets."

The man nodded and spat a stream of tobacco juice onto the ground. "Suits me fine."

"Get your men settled and be prepared for target practice in an hour." Alberto turned and walked back inside the house.

Viper nudged Adder. "Back under the tree—we'll take a break until the shooting begins."

Adder smothered a yawn with a large hand. "Works for me. What about the other guys?"

"I'll tell them to stand down until the new arrivals begin their training. We'll check it out for a few minutes before returning to our quarters."

Viper, Adder, Mamba, and Rattler entered their rented compound. After piling out of the vehicles, they dashed inside to the dining room and found Rosa putting the finishing touches on a platter of sandwiches and pitchers of fruit juice.

They stood back as Rosa wiped her hands on her apron, surveyed her offerings, and smiled as she slipped out the door. It hadn't closed before Viper attacked a sandwich, taking a huge bite he could barely chew. "Since the new recruits, for want of a better word, have arrived, I think we should go back to shifts to monitor the situation—six hours on, six off. We're stretched kinda thin with just the four of us, but we'll make things work."

Mamba gulped some of his mango juice. "Did you pick up anything worthwhile with the microphone?"

Viper nodded. "Yeah. There's another group in Colombia being trained by someone named Michael."

"Sounds like he could be from an English-speaking country." Rattler finished his sandwich and belched. "Of course, it might be a cover name."

Viper pushed his plate aside and grabbed his iPad. Using two fingers, he began typing:

To: Jararaca, Cobra, Taipan

From: Viper

Local nest augmented by thirty new arrivals. Reference to trainer in Colombia named Michael. No further information available about him. Big Ears suggests the new recruits will be trained for unspecified attacks in North America, with an initial rendezvous point with the Colombian team of militants at Múzquiz, Mexico.

Please advise any change to operational parameters.

Viper hit send and turned to the others. "Anyone for coffee?"

Mamba raised his hand. "Three sugars. No milk."

Viper wandered to the warmer on the sideboard and poured two cups. After shoveling three heaping spoonfuls into one, he rejoined the others. He handed Mamba his cup and took a sip of his own before resuming his seat. "We'll begin our new shifts in three hours. Adder and I will take the—"

He glanced at his iPad. One incoming message:

To: *Jararaca, Viper*

From: *Cobra*

Intel acknowledged. Will see what rises to the surface regarding a terrorist named Michael. Continue your mission. Should the opportunity present itself, capture (alive) members of opposition for interrogation purposes. Go Snakes!

Viper chuckled after reading Javier's message. He gazed at the others, a slight smile creeping across his face. "Cobra says to grab one of the terrorists, but don't kill him—at least for now."

"Did he mean one of the guards, the trainers, or the new arrivals?" Rattler scratched at an insect bite on one of his muscular arms.

"Don't think the guards will have the info we want." Viper pursed his lips. "The new arrivals won't have all of the details yet." He glanced at each of the others. "Alberto would be my first choice, but perhaps one of the others who hang around him."

"Won't he become suspicious if someone disappears?"

Viper grinned. "One way to stir up a hornet's nest."

SOON AFTER DUSK SET, Viper and Adder crawled back into their observation post. A quick check of their hiding spot found no evidence anyone had discovered the site. While Adder activated the microphone, Viper scanned the area with his night vision goggles, taking care not to focus on any lights.

A male voice came through Adder's headset. "What should we do about insubordination? I don't like these guys coming here and acting like they own everything and telling us what to do."

The response was muffled. Adder adjusted the microphone as the first individual spoke again. "Very well. We'll be patient. But, if they keep defying my orders, I won't be responsible for my men's actions."

The voices faded as the individuals entered the house.

Adder aimed the microphone at several windows but didn't pick up any conversations.

The next three hours passed without anything of interest before Adder tuned in on a new conversation. "Enjoy your smoke, and see you in the morning."

Viper donned his goggles and searched for the smoker. He nudged Adder and pointed. "One person heading in our direction," he whispered. "He's got a cigarette in one hand and is poking around in the bushes by the wall."

"Should we take him down?"

"If he comes close, yes. Cobra gave us the green light, so let's take advantage." Adder monitored the green image strolling closer to their position. The smell of burning tobacco became prevalent.

"Now!"

The men jumped out and pounced on the unsuspecting smoker. Despite the man swinging his arms as if he was in a fight for his life, a swift kick from Adder to the man's right knee, followed by an uppercut to his chin, rendered him defenseless. Within moments, they secured their target and dragged him into the observation post.

Unconscious, but breathing, their captive lay still.

Adder held a Thorfire tactical penlight on the subject while Viper yanked a Panama hat from the man's head.

They both gasped.

"It's a woman!" Viper whispered and shook his head.

The woman's brown hair fell on either side of her face. A raised welt and a black bruise on the left side of her chin marred her otherwise unblemished skin.

Adder glanced at Viper. "Now, what do we do?"

"Take her with us. We'll find out what she knows."

"What then?"

Viper shrugged. "Another casualty of the war on drugs."

19

E l Dorado International Airport
Bogota, Colombia

HARRY, Larry, and Samantha left the arrivals area of El Dorado International Airport and headed to the taxi rank. Of similar height, with youthful appearances, they seemed to be university students, perhaps on vacation. Each carried a backpack slung over a shoulder. They walked past the first two vehicles, and climbed into the third one, with Harry sitting next to the driver.

Larry gave an address on the outskirts of the city.

The driver nodded, pulled into traffic, waved at the unflattering hand gestures from the cabbies his passengers had bypassed. They sped along Avenida El Dorado. To the accompaniment of blaring horns, the taxi made a sharp left near the American embassy and continued along Avenida Carrera 50 before turning right. Minutes later, the car screeched to a halt in front of what appeared to be a modest, three-level brick home. Several houses with lush, well-manicured lawns, dotted the area. Behind them, tree-covered hills reached toward the sky.

Harry paid the driver and turned, whistling. "Man, a fancy neighborhood and look at the view! Can't wait to limber up and stretch my legs." He gestured toward a sign pointing ahead. "Cool! A nature trail. Maybe I'll get some running in."

Samantha laughed. "AJ said the property has access to a pool, spa, and jacuzzi. I'm all for heading there and lounging for the rest of the day."

"I'm up for some tennis or basketball." Larry shook his head. "But, AJ didn't bring us here for a vacation. I'm sure we'll see some action before long."

As they approached the dark brown wooden door at the entrance, it swung inward. Framed in the doorway stood their boss, AJ. "About time, you three arrived. Did you get lost?" AJ's eyes twinkled. *I've known them for years, but they never seem to age. What's their secret?* "Come in and meet my new partner."

After introductions to Javier and a tour of the three-level, eight-bedroom property, they stepped onto the terrace at the back of the premises overlooking a wooded area. "You can relax for the remainder of the day, but first thing in the morning, our mission begins." AJ's gaze shifted from face to face.

"What's the target?" Samantha swatted at a mosquito buzzing around her.

"Intercepts reveal a tentative location for a terrorist training camp in Colombia. We need to check the accuracy of the information and ascertain how many people are there."

Javier nodded. "As AJ mentioned, we need to analyze the ground situation. My 'Snakes' are monitoring a different training camp—in Panama. We think the two groups might be working together and will be going after unspecified targets in the U.S."

"You have a couple of hours to relax and unwind before we start the meal." AJ nudged Javier. "He's a mean machine with the grill, so we're having baked potatoes, salad, and ribeye steaks."

AFTER DINNER, the five veterans relaxed around a fire pit, sipping on cold bottles from the Bogota Beer Company.

Javier drained his and reached inside a cooler for another. "Anyone else?"

"No thanks." Harry patted his stomach. "After that huge steak, I don't have much room left. I'll finish this one, have a shower, and call it a night."

Larry and Samantha seconded Harry's comments. Before long, the three disappeared inside, leaving AJ and Javier to enjoy the peaceful evening.

They lounged on a padded swing bench. AJ's head dropped to Javier's shoulder, and he put his arm around her. "If only this were how things were meant to be." She sighed, squeezed Javier's thigh, and stood. "I'm gonna inform Washington the three musketeers arrived. See you in the morning."

Javier nodded. "I'll finish my beer, and then I'll crash." After downing the remains of his drink, he walked to the low wall surrounding the property and stared into the thick trees. *What am I doing? We're on a mission, not a camping trip.* He shook his head. *Need to keep my mind on the job—not on AJ.*

ONCE THEY FINISHED BREAKFAST, Javier took the new arrivals to a locked room on the ground floor of the house. Using a keypad to unlock the door, he pushed it open and flicked on the lights.

Larry whistled. "Man! Are you ready for war or what?" He stepped inside and spun in a circle, taking in the racks and shelves of assault rifles, pistols, flash-bangs, and fragmentation grenades, as well as a variety of tactical communications equipment. He grabbed a Barrett M82 sniper rifle. "Mine." A smile spread across his face. "Reminds me of the mission to—"

"No, Larry. Even the boss isn't allowed to know about that one." Harry turned to Javier and shrugged. "Sorry, but you know the rules."

Javier laughed. "Understood. Load up—take what you want. Don't forget your ammunition." He pointed to another door. "In there."

Harry yanked an SA-80 assault rifle and a Mossberg 500 shotgun from the shelves and grinned. "I'm ready."

"What about transport?" Samantha lifted two SIG Sauer P226 pistols, picking up a double shoulder holster and a web belt. "I'll be driving these clowns, so I'll need a reliable vehicle."

Javier nodded. "In the garage. Your choice of an armored vehicle: Lexus LX 570, a Toyota Camry, or a Mercedes-Benz S-560. The Toyota Land Cruiser is mine." He gestured in the general direction of the front of the house. "The Ford Transit Cannabis van parked in the driveway is also armored—perfect for extractions."

Harry shook his head. "Did you win the lottery? Who's paying for the toys?"

Javier chuckled. "AJ scrounged up a few things, and my organization chipped in, too." He glanced at his watch. "You have thirty minutes to grab your gear and stow it in one of the vehicles. AJ's checking on the latest intel and will give us a briefing before we deploy." *They're like children in a candy store. Hope they're as good as AJ says.*

After securing their equipment, Harry, Larry, and Samantha joined AJ and Javier in what was once the studio, but now housed a tactical command center. Maps of various Latin American countries covered the walls. Three computer terminals sat on desks along the back of the room. Two plasma screens centered above the desks showed CNN and *Nuestra Tele Noticias 24 Horas* (NTN 24). A rectangular table in the center of the room held a mock-up of the suspected terrorist training camp. In a corner, a commercial-sized coffee pot and a battered fridge provided refreshments.

"Where'd the intel come from for making the mock-up?" Samantha gestured toward the table.

"MacKenzie worked her magic with the satellite guys. We were lucky—one was positioned over the general area when she put in the request, so it didn't take much maneuvering." AJ pulled up a chair to the table. "Grab yourself a coffee, and we'll begin. There's bottled water in the fridge if you'd prefer."

Javier brought two cups, putting one in front of AJ and sat down. The others filled mugs and joined them.

AJ took a sip of the black liquid and smacked her lips. "Colombian coffee—perfect." She pointed at the mock-up. "This'll be your target. Reconnoiter, collect photos of anyone who appears to be a major player, but remain hidden. There should be around thirty or so bad guys training here, so look after yourselves."

"How far from here?" Samantha gazed at a road map with two large red tags attached.

"The camp is outside Turbo. It's four hundred seventy miles from here. Averaging fifty miles per hour, it'll take about ten hours." AJ handed Samantha a map. "A suggested route is marked for you. The lower tag is where we're at now, and the upper one is Turbo. I recommend you leave in the morning so you can get in position before dark."

Samantha pursed her lips while Harry and Larry nodded as they continued examining the mock-up.

"What are you and the colonel going to do?" Harry scratched the side of his face. "Are you coming with us?"

"The plan was for us to meet you there." AJ glanced at Javier. "However, this morning I received new intel. The source is so sensitive I had to beg to be allowed to share the data with you."

Javier shook his head. "Why the games from your headquarters? This is how good folks get killed—not sharing vital intel."

"I agree, which is why I kept pushing." AJ swallowed. "According to an unnamed but very reliable source, someone is planning to use the terrorists to deal with a private grudge." She stared into the distance.

Javier twirled a finger in a circle to encourage her to keep speaking.

"We learned earlier about two young girls being kidnapped a few days ago. Well, if the source is correct, a contract was issued for the elimination of a cartel leader—a woman." AJ pursed her lips. "We only know of one person fitting these criteria—Olivia Perfecta Moreno, the head of the Barranquilla Cartel."

"Who is the source?" Harry stared at AJ. "Don't you think we should know?"

AJ shook her head. "I've been instructed not to share the name of the source with anyone. Suffice to say, someone in Olivia's organization might be playing both sides. Javier and I plan to meet with her and find out what she knows about a rogue FARC commander named Días."

Javier twisted in his chair so he faced AJ. "What if she won't talk with us?"

"We'll improvise."

He nodded. "Isn't Días believed to be hosting the Turbo training facility?"

"Yes. We might have to refer to his connection with Olivia to push for our meeting. Our orders are to extricate her and learn as much as we can about the connection between the terrorists and Días while the others are scouting out the camp in Turbo."

"Then what?"

"If Días is helping the terrorists with their training and access into the United States, we've been given the green light—terminate."

20

M oreno Hacienda
Barranquilla, Colombia

FRUSTRATED, Olivia frowned at Ramon and rose to her feet. She paced the room, clenching and unclenching her fists. Pausing to look out a window, she raised a hand to her forehead and rubbed her fingers in a small circle to release some of the tension.

"Doña, what do you want me to do?" Ramon stepped forward and placed a hand on Olivia's shoulder. "You'll be safer at my friend's hacienda while we deal with this crisis."

She turned and gave him a half-smile, her voice devoid of emotion. "I will go there. Once Alonzo returns, we'll decide what else we should do. In the meantime, reach out to your contacts about Maria and Silvina. Do whatever is necessary." Her body stiffened as she screwed up her face. "Double the reward."

Ramon nodded. "At once." He gazed at Olivia's face. "Try to rest. You must be at your best—for your family's sake."

She nodded as she headed for the door. "I'm going to my room.

Call me as soon as Alonzo arrives." *We must get to the bottom of this mess. One way or another—no matter who stands in our way.* She shook her head. *I must be strong—for my darlings, even though I'm so confused, I can't think straight.*

Olivia walked into her office and headed to the bar. She poured a large gin and sat behind her desk. She rubbed her temples before downing the drink and pouring a second one. *No one must know how frantic I am—especially Alonzo and Ramon.* She leaned back in her chair. *First, my father and brother are killed. Now my angels are kidnapped, and I'm threatened. When will it end?*

She tossed a suitcase on the bed and began selecting items to take with her. Olivia held up an A-line linen knee-length dress. *In case I need to look nice. Everything else to allow movement—better to wear if there's danger and we must flee.* She smiled. *I'll pack my stiletto and pistol in their hidden compartments, too.*

TWO HOURS LATER, Alonzo eased his Mercedes to a halt in front of the hacienda. He smiled as he climbed out of the car and, scurrying up the stairs, entered the foyer.

On his way to the kitchen, Ramon stepped out of the security office and blocked his path. "Ah. You're back. You seem pleased with yourself."

Alonzo nodded. "I had an enjoyable afternoon with Gabriela. One of my best days in a long time." His grin faded. "Any news about Maria and Silvina?"

"I hate to ruin your day." Ramon frowned. "Your mother is ...."

"What, Ramon?" The smile left Alonzo's face. "What's wrong with her? Wait, is this about Maria and Silvina?"

Ramon shook his head in slow motion. "Even worse than their kidnapping—someone put a price on her head."

Alonzo's face paled. "What? Who?" He leaned against the wall for support. "We must do something!" *What's happening to my family? First, my sisters—now this!* He turned and punched the wall.

"I've arranged for her to move to a secret location, just waiting for her final approval. You're the only one who knows this. Tell no one else."

"When? My mother's safety is at stake. She can't delay."

"She knows that, and will make a final decision soon."

"Should I..." Alonzo tried not to panic. "Should I come with you?"

"No. You must remain here. If anyone's watching the property, it'll appear natural to see you here, and no one should be suspicious. Another thing, your mother insisted Pedro not be told."

"What if he asks me?" Alonzo rubbed a hand on his left shoulder. "What should I tell him?"

"Relax, Alonzo. Tell him your mother went away on family business. He'll understand. She's done this before."

"We should inform Colonel Santiago. He'll provide protection."

"No!" Ramon grabbed Alonzo by the shoulders and shook him. "We can't trust anyone. My people are investigating. As soon as we uncover who is behind the threat to Olivia, they'll be dealt with. Go about your business as normal."

When Alonzo entered his mother's sanctuary, she was already behind her desk, with Ramon sitting on the other side. Both wore somber expressions. He rushed forward.

Olivia raised an open hand, palm outward, toward a chair between two side tables. "Sit. This is a dire situation, but no worse than my father used to experience." A glimmer of a smile creased her face. "With Ramon's help, we'll make it through this."

"Why isn't Pedro here to help? He should be." Alonzo slammed his fist on the table next to his chair. "Mamá, you seem too calm. I'd be ripping my hair out and screaming if I were in your shoes. What are you planning?"

"It's probably better not having Pedro here. My emotions have been all over the place: fear, hurt, anger, terror, and rage. My fear is for my poor darlings—what must they be going through?" Olivia shook her head. "All I feel right now is rage—against the bastardos holding Maria and Silvina. If I could get my hands on the kidnappers, I'd rip them apart and stamp on the pieces." Her face turned crimson with fury. "Mark my words—someone will die."

Alonzo's eyes flicked toward Ramon before settling back on his mother. "What about this death threat?" *Ay dio mio! Did I somehow trigger something when I went behind her back to discuss expansion?*

Ramon filled three glasses with whiskey and handed them around before resuming his seat.

Olivia took a sip and set the glass on her desk. "I'm drinking too much, but the shock of what's happened is too much to bear. We need to eat, too. Shouldn't drink on an empty stomach." She grimaced. "I'm a woman in a male-dominated business. Threats are a cost of doing business in the drug trade. We can't ignore them, but we cannot allow them to dictate how we function either."

Ramon frowned. "If I may interject, Doña. You've made as many enemies as your father, perhaps even more." He cleared his throat. "You must continue to project strength, or you will be ...." He glanced at the ceiling. "You'll be redundant, and in this business, those who are unnecessary are killed—no long-term retirement plan."

Olivia chuckled. "Trust you, Ramon, to put things in perspective." She turned to Alonzo. "Ramon suggests a ... strategic withdrawal to a secluded location. I agree with his plan. You'll take control of the business until everything is back to normal."

Alonzo nodded. "Of course, Mamá. When will you depart?"

Olivia glanced at Ramon, eyebrows raised. "I'm ready now. I couldn't rest, so I packed a few things I might need for an indefinite time away."

Ramon nodded and jumped to his feet. "Thirty minutes. I'll let my friend know we're on our way—he doesn't like unannounced visitors."

Olivia and Alonzo stood. She approached her son, hugged him, and whispered, "Be strong, my angel. We'll weather this attack on our family—somehow."

"Sí, Mamá."

As they left her hacienda behind, Olivia thought about her father. *He dealt with similar death threats—at least before someone caught up to him. He tried to shield me from the business, but it didn't work.* She shook her head, leaned against the door jam, and closed her eyes.

Three hours later, Ramon's armored Toyota Land Cruiser climbed through the forest-covered hills and stopped in front of twelve-foot high gates. Concertina wire draped the upper levels of the concrete wall, where armed guards patrolled. A covered shelter sat on either side. Two guards stepped out of each one, along with two growling Anatolian Shepherd dogs.

One of the men recognized Ramon and raised a radio to his lips. "Open the gates. El jefe's guests have arrived."

The doors swung inward. Once open, the same man motioned for Ramon to proceed. The guards converged on the open gates, turning to face outward in case of any threat.

As soon as the vehicle entered the compound, the gates closed with a clang. Ramon pulled up to the main house, similar in appearance to the Moreno hacienda.

A white-haired, wizened man dressed in a white shirt, blue tie, and a dark suit waited for them on the verandah. Armed guards stood on either side of him, both holding the leads of German Shepherds.

Ramon and Olivia exited the Land Cruiser and ascended the stairs, stopping in front of their host.

"Señora Moreno, welcome to my home. I am Matias Zapata, a distant cousin of your father. We met many years ago when you were still a child. Ramon told me about your ... difficulties." He waved a hand encompassing the compound. "You'll be safe here. I have fifty armed men and a dozen attack dogs for our protection."

"Gracias, Señor Zapata. I'll try to stay out of your way."

Zapata smiled. "My wife died two years ago—it'll be a change to have such a beautiful woman in my home once again. A woman as lovely as you couldn't possibly be in the way. Please, stay as long as you wish."

Olivia twisted her head to the side and gave a small nod. "Once I determine who kidnapped my children and threatened my life, I'll deal with them."

Zapata gestured for Olivia and Ramon to follow him inside. "I remember your father and brother." He shook his head. "Such a tragedy to lose them in their prime of life. You won't remember, but I recall bouncing you on my knee when you were young." He smiled at the memory. "I will provide any assistance you require to rescue your children. If necessary, I pledge you my life."

21

U nknown Compound
    Somewhere in Colombia

TINY FISTS BANGED on the wooden door while hard shoes whacked the bottom. "Let us out! Open the door and I'll—"

"Silvina, please stop." Maria sat on the bed, watching her sister's antics. "Remember what happened last time?"

"The coati man came in, and I kicked him in the shins." Silvina grinned.

"Sí, and he threw you across the room."

"True, but he was limping when he left." Silvina ran and jumped on the bed. "I'm bored. There's nothing to do." She waved her hands in the air. "He brought us coloring books and crayons!" She crossed her arms. "As if! I'm almost nine, and you'll be eleven soon."

"He promised to bring some DVDs and a DVD player, too."

Silvina rolled her eyes. "Why doesn't he just return us to Mamá? Sooner or later, she'll find us—and he'll be sorry!" She slid off the bed and went to the window. "Too dark outside. I can't see anything."

"At least Valentina opened the shutters outside so we can look out during the day." Maria's stomach growled. "I'm hungry. I hope someone brings us something to eat before I starve. Like hamburgers from Hamburguesas El Corral."

"Ugh." Silvina turned to Maria and stuck a finger in her throat. "Last time they were cold. Anyway, too much beef isn't healthy—Mamá says so."

"You complained, but you ate two of them." Maria's brows knitted into a frown.

"That's all they brought, and I was hungry." Silvina stuck out her tongue. "I'd rather eat vegetables."

"Are you trying to make me sick? Why—"

Silvina stomped her feet in a mild temper tantrum as something bumped against the door. "Shush."

A key jiggled in the lock, and the bolt slid back with a loud snick. Someone pushed against the door, and it squeaked as it opened. A man wearing a balaclava entered, followed by a woman in her early twenties with long, black hair. Once inside, he shoved the door closed.

He gestured for the woman to place the package she carried on the dresser next to the television. He turned to the girls. "Time for dinner—whether you enjoy it or not makes no difference to me. If you don't eat, you'll go hungry until tomorrow morning."

"When will you let us go home?" Silvina glared at him. "You've kept us here for ages." She stuck her nose in the air. "Free us, and I'll ask Mamá not to kill you."

The man raised a hand and stepped forward. "Quiet! It's your fault I locked you in this room. You shouldn't have tried to escape."

"What do you expect? You didn't ask us if we wanted to come here." Silvina pointed to Maria. "My sister is afraid of you—but I'm not."

"Sí. I remember when I was in your hacienda, and I hit me with your tennis racket. Very courageous, but not too smart."

Silvina stuck out her tongue. "Smarter than you. Bet you didn't even finish elementary school."

The man shook his head in exasperation, his chin jutting out. "Do you have an answer for everything?"

"That's what my mamá and my teachers say." Silvina glanced at the young woman who smiled. "What if I promise to be good? I'm bored. Do you know what they say about people who are bored?"

"No. What do they say?"

"We can get sick. That means you'll have more problems with us."

He frowned. "I suppose if you behave this evening, perhaps we might come to some sort of arrangement." He pointed at the woman. "I'll discuss this with my daughter, Valentina. Can you ride a horse?"

Silvina laughed. "Know how to ride horses? We both have our own and go riding almost every day."

"In that case, I might let Valentina take you riding tomorrow." He rocked back and forth on his heels. "Of course, armed guards will accompany you. There'll be a penalty if you try to escape."

"What's the penalty?"

He drew an imaginary knife across his throat.

AFTER THE MAN and Valentina left the room, Maria scooted off the bed and rushed to the bag. "From Hamburguesas El Corral." She opened it and smiled. "Hamburgers!"

Silvina smacked her forehead. "Not again. We're gonna turn into cows." Fists on her hips, she leaned forward. "Moooooo."

"Quit complaining. At least they're feeding us."

Silvina nodded. "I guess. Toss me one. What did they bring to drink?"

Maria rummaged in the bag. "Water and *Manzana Postobón*."

"Good. I hope it's apple flavor."

"You're in luck." Maria pulled out two containers. "Apple!"

After they finished eating, they took turns using the attached bathroom and knelt by the bed. They bowed their heads and prayed.

Silvina finished her prayers with, "Dear Lord, please protect Mamá, Papá, and Alonzo. Also, do something about the coati man so we can return home. Amen." She glanced at Maria. *Or let us escape so Mamá can find us.*

THE NEXT MORNING, Valentina unlocked the door and entered. She smiled at the girls. "I convinced my father to let you join me on a ride this morning." She looked over the top of her sunglasses. "You must promise to be on your best behavior."

Maria nodded while Silvina stuck a hand behind her back and crossed her fingers. "I promise. Just get us out of this room."

A few minutes later, they approached a red wooden barn where three men each held the reins of a horse.

Silvina glanced at Valentina, a questioning expression on her face.

"Our guards, but don't worry. My father is very protective and never lets me ride alone. At least two of his men always accompany me." She climbed into her saddle and waited for the others.

When they were ready, the guards mounted their own horses. One of them led the way out of the compound and along a trail through the forest. Valentina took her position behind the leading guard, with another behind her. Maria and Silvina came next, followed by the remaining guard.

The occasional birdcall and the creaking of leather saddles were the only sounds as they weaved among the trees. A warm breeze tempered the sticky air as intermittent clouds floated past in a deep blue sky.

"Aaaaah!"

Maria's horse reared as she screamed.

Ahead on the path, a snake, with black, white, and orange bands, sunned itself.

Valentina grabbed the reins of Maria's horse, while one of the guards rushed forward. He pulled out a weapon and fired.

"Let's keep moving." Valentina led the way, each horse giving the dead snake a wide berth.

Silvina urged her horse forward, and she rode next to Maria. "You've seen ground snakes before."

"I know, but I didn't expect one here."

Silvina glanced around. "Maria, we're outdoors—they can be anywhere."

They continued along the path in silence.

Before long, a distant rumble disturbed their quiet trek.

Valentina reined in her horse and waited for Maria and Silvina to join her. "We'll stop soon. Hear the noise like thunder? A waterfall and rapids are not far away. Soon we'll be able to see into the valley— it's awesome!"

The girls grinned.

"Let's go!" Valentina turned her horse toward the trail. "About fifteen minutes, and we'll be there."

As they approached the falls, the forest thinned out, leaving an overgrown meadow. The lead guard continued through the field, stopping when he neared a hitching post.

"My parents liked to come here and had the rail installed so the horses won't wander in search of greener grass." Valentina shook her head and gestured toward the rushing water cascading from above. "Didn't I tell you this place was fantastic? Check out the view—I wish the hacienda overlooked this area instead of being stuck in the woods."

Maria rubbed her hands on the ill-fitting jeans they gave her to wear. "Where's your mother?"

"She died." Valentina glanced downward. "Some type of cancer, I think. One day she seemed fine and the next—gone."

"We're so sorry." Silvina and Maria chimed.

Valentina shrugged. "The doctors didn't know what to do. I don't remember what they called her illness, except they kept saying stage four." She glanced at the guard who had finished securing their horses to the rail.

He nodded, whistled, and pointed. The remaining guards took up positions away from the water, scanning the trees for any intruders.

Valentina and the girls dismounted and picked their way through the rocky area next to the ravine where the crashing water threw up plumes of mist.

Maria stepped closer and pointed to a small rainbow above the rocks.

Valentina reached for her arm. "Be careful—you don't want to fall in."

Maria pulled back, her feet slipping on the wet grass.

Valentina tried to grab her without success.

"Maria, no!" Silvina reached for her sister's outstretched hand but missed.

"Aaaaah!"

Eyes wide, Maria toppled from the cliff.

"No!" Silvina peered over the edge, watching Maria struggling to keep her head above the raging water.

22

Temporary Command Center
Colon, Panama

AFTER GIVING instructions to the Snakes to capture someone if possible, AJ and Javier departed. Adder and Viper moved into the main house, freeing up one of the smaller buildings for use as a temporary detention center.

Viper threw his backpack on the bed vacated by AJ, while down the hall Adder did the same in Javier's former quarters. "Whaddya think?" Viper raised his voice to be heard two rooms away.

"Nice," Adder shouted back.

"I'm going to check on our guest."

"Have fun, but beware of nasty things in small packages."

Viper laughed, left the house, and walked across the grass to relieve Mamba. "How're things?"

Mamba finished chewing his tobacco and released a stream of brown juices over the edge of the porch. "Pretty quiet. There was some banging a while ago, but I reckon our prisoner must have given up."

"I thought she was tied to her chair." Viper climbed the porch steps and joined his friend. "How'd she break loose?"

"She kept yelling she needed the toilet." Mamba shook his head. "Made so much noise I couldn't sleep, so I went inside, pistol drawn, to see what was going on."

"So, what happened?"

"She took one look at my SIG Sauer and called it a toy." He grinned. "Once I pulled out my KA-BAR D2 knife and approached her chair, she shut up. I locked the bedroom door where we're keeping her before I cut her loose. After she did her business in the en-suite, I tied her hands back together but left her legs free. No place for her to run, anyhow, since the windows are boarded up."

Viper nodded. "Okay, we better go talk with her. She's had a couple of days on her own in the dark to contemplate her situation. Too bad we had to subdue her when she approached our listening post." He glanced at the red streaks down one of his arms. "She fought like a lioness protecting her cubs."

Mamba laughed. "Good thing she didn't bite you when she tried —you might have needed one of those tetanus or rabies shots. You owe me for clocking her one before she chewed you up."

"I'll buy you a bottle of whiskey. We better get started." Viper motioned for Mamba to lead the way.

When they approached the bedroom, the woman yelled. "Let me out of here. You can't hold me here forever. I'll kill you!"

Viper glanced at Mamba. "Doesn't appear solitude has softened her attitude, does it?"

"Be ready for an outburst when we enter." Mamba chuckled. "Protect your eyes as she'll try to gouge them out." He inserted a key into the brass Master Lock, securing the door with a heavy-duty hasp. He removed the padlock. "Ready?"

Viper nodded. "Showtime."

They eased the door open and crept into the room.

Mamba turned on the light.

Sprawled across the unmade bed, their captive glared at them, her eyes blinking against the sudden harsh light. "About time. Are you guys deaf? I've been yelling for hours." With her hands tied, she struggled into a sitting position and held her arms out. "Release me."

Viper took a step forward. "Miss, we found you in a terrorist training camp. Before we can let you go, you must answer a few questions. If your responses check out, we'll set you free." *Maybe. Some day. Or perhaps not.*

"Humph! You think you're tough. You're nothing but a coward. Cut my hands free, and I'll let you die with dignity." She flicked her long, brown hair with her head, her eyes glistening with anger.

Mamba grabbed her by the arm and tossed her into the chair. He yanked out his knife and waved it in front of her face. "Behave, bitch."

She turned toward him and spat on his shoes. "Another dickless wonder. It takes two of you to question little ol' me?" She laughed.

He leaned forward, anger etched across his face. "Shouldn't have done that." His hand unwavering, the blade inched closer and closer. He dragged the butt of the knife across her ear.

"Ahem." Viper gestured toward the woman Mamba seemed intent upon impaling on his KA-BAR. "We need answers, not a body to dispose of."

Mamba nodded. He stepped back with reluctance, sheathed his knife, and crossed his arms.

Viper directed his attention to the woman. "First, what's your name?"

"What's yours? What about your friend?"

"I'm called Viper, and he's Mamba. Now, what's your name?"

The woman laughed. "Yeah, that fits. You're both a couple of snakes." She tossed her head to settle her hair into place. "I'm Blanca."

"What's your last name, Blanca? Where are you from? Why are you at a terrorist training camp?"

Blanca rolled her eyes. "Since you insist on answers, my last name is Días. My brother, Ramírez García Días, is a former FARC commander. I'm here at his request. Obviously, you don't understand who he is. If you know what's good for you and your 'friends,' you better release me and run for your lives."

As she lunged from the chair, Mamba grabbed her in a lightning move and slammed her back on the seat. "Stay. Seated." He waved his knife and glared at her.

Viper caught his attention and jerked his head toward the door. In the corridor, he whispered, "What do you think?"

"I think she's playing us. Her answers are too pat."

Viper nodded. "I agree. Something isn't right."

"Here's a thought." Mamba rubbed his chin. "What if they knew we were watching them, and they sent her to grab our attention so we'd leave them alone?"

"Hmm. It's possible, but they don't have any idea what we might do to her."

"What if they don't care? Perhaps she's no more than a means to an end."

Viper pursed his lips. "Turn off the light, and we'll leave her alone for tonight. Don't give her any food. We'll come back in the morning. In the meantime, let's do some checking on what she told us."

~

To: Jararaca, Cobra, Taipan

From: Viper

Began interrogation of our captive. Claims her name is Blanca and says she's the sister of the former FARC commander we're already aware of. She's purported to be in Panama at his request. Please advise.

Viper closed his iPad and joined the others for a quick meal. Afterward, they turned on the television and chuckled at the rookie moves made by the heroes in an action-adventure film dubbed in Spanish.

Mamba passed a beer to each of the others and grabbed a seat, joining in the camaraderie. "Think we should check on our prisoner?"

"Naw." Viper took a swig of his beer. "She's not going anywhere. We'll take a look later."

THE FOLLOWING MORNING, Viper logged back into his iPad. One new message waited for him.

To: Viper

From: Jararaca, Cobra, Taipan

Intel confirms Días has a sister named Blanca, about twenty-five-years-old. Colombian authorities want her for the murder of three police officials in Bogota. She shot one, knifed another, and killed the third with a garrote. Consider her a lethal combatant and don't take any chances. Quiz her on the role of the trainees to see if it matches our info.

Should she be unresponsive, request her immediate extraction, and continue monitoring the camp.

Viper whistled to get the attention of the other snakes. Once they crowded around, he filled them in on the response from Javier. "I suggest we keep monitoring activities from the listening post." He glanced at Adder and Rattler. "Mamba and I'll head there while you two take a crack at Blanca."

The men nodded.

"The gloves are off, but don't be extreme. We'll shake her for whatever we can obtain."

"What if we don't get anything else from her?"

"Use your judgment—Don't kill her, but convince her you will."

ADDER AND RATTLER entered the bedroom where Blanca sat in the dark. After one of them flipped on the lights, Blanca raised her hands to shield her eyes from the intense glow. She staggered from the bed and collapsed on the chair.

After Adder cut her loose and returned to the doorway, Rattler handed her a small plate of fruit and a bottle of water.

Blanca sucked the juice of the oranges and tore into the pineapple. "'Bout time you fed me. I'm starving." She glanced at the new arrivals. "Are you snakes, too?" She laughed.

Adder uncrossed his arms and pulled out his SIG Sauer. "Deadly, so no more games. We've confirmed your identity, but don't buy the bit about you being at the training camp for your brother." He holstered his weapon and smacked his open hands together, causing her to jump. "Isn't it true you're here to evade imprisonment back in Colombia for murder?"

She shrugged. "My brother wanted me out of Colombia for my safety and thought Panama would be a better place."

"Give us all the information you know about the training camp. What's their mission? What's the timeframe? How many men? What about logistics?"

"If I tell you what I know and my brother finds out, I'll be dead."

"Not our problem."

Blanca glared at Adder as she threw the empty plate at him. "If you make one mistake, I'll kill you and spit on your grave."

Rattler grabbed her arm and twisted it behind her until she cried out. "Shut up! I haven't started yet. Now, answer my friend's questions. What do you know about the camp?"

"You saw the camp—can't you figure it out? Or, are you both stupid gringos?"

Rattler twisted her arm a second time.

"Ow!" She yanked her arm free but remained on the chair, rubbing her elbow. "Bastardo!"

Rattler pushed her against the backrest and yanked zip ties from his pocket. He lashed her hands together. Reaching into another pocket, he pulled a set of handcuffs out and used them to secure one of her wrists to an arm on the chair. He grabbed her hair and forced her head back. "Speak."

"You fight like a girl." She spat at him again. "My brothers are tougher than you."

He wiped it off his shirt and grinned. "So you want things rough? We can play that game." A sudden backhand sent her backward in the chair, a trickle of blood appearing at a corner of her mouth.

"Enough!" Adder stepped forward. "What are those men training for?"

Blanca's eyes almost closed. "To kill the likes of you."

"When? Where?"

"Not soon enough." She laughed. "When I'm free, I'll join them. American cities will burn. Your women and children will cry for you."

"Yeah, yeah. Listen, sweetheart." Rattler gazed at the forlorn figure as she struggled to extract herself from the cuff. "It's not our policy to kill without provocation, but what we will do might make you wish we did." He sighed. "You're going to take a one-way trip. A place where you'll be secured, and they're gonna throw away the key."

"I'm not afraid." She gave them a bloodstained smile.

"You might not be afraid of us, but you'll talk. Wait until Taipan meets with you. No one evades her questions." He gave a chilling laugh. "No one."

23

AJ's Safehouse
Bogota, Colombia

HARRY KEPT WALKING around the table, his eyes fixated on the primitive model of their target. He scratched his head and glanced at AJ while pointing at the cardboard, paper, and scrap wood mock-up. "How do you know the layout of the compound?"

AJ nodded. "A valid question. We had voice identification of individuals discussing the camp—not its specific location, but in generalities, such as the layout of their tents in relation to the main building and the small river in their valley. The analysts did a bit of homework and found a nearby cell tower—a fixed location for both inbound and outbound calls. Their boss pulled some strings and had one of the satellites zoom in on the area. The photo guys analyzed the results and sent us a diagram." She gestured toward Javier. "He was like a child in a sandbox building this thing."

Javier chuckled. "Reminds me of building forts and castles with Lego when I was a kid."

Everyone laughed.

Harry smiled and gave the mock-up a final glance. "Guess we're a go. Time to rock 'n roll!"

"Just remember—keep outta sight." AJ glanced at each face. "Once we finish our new mission, we'll join you."

Javier raised a hand. "Things just got more interesting. Seems the person the Snakes grabbed in Panama is the sister of FARC commander Días. She's a killer—wanted for the murders of three officials."

AJ snapped her fingers. "Perhaps this is something we can use to persuade Olivia to work with us. I'm sure the Colombian government would be very interested in her dealings with Días. We could threaten to expose her interaction with murderers—both Días and his sister." She turned to Harry, Larry, and Samantha. "If there's nothing further, keep your heads down. Contact us when you're in position."

Chairs scraped on the floor as everyone stood and shook hands before the three operatives departed.

Left on their own, AJ placed a hand on Javier's shoulder. "Guess it's just us. We'd better get moving, too."

He took her hand in his and gazed into her eyes. "Whaddya have in mind?"

AJ smiled and pulled her hand back. "Down, boy."

"Got it—mission first, gentle persuasion logged for later."

Samantha climbed behind the wheel of the black and white Ford Transit Cannabis van and waited for Harry and Larry to join her. Several minutes passed. *Wonder what's keeping them? Time's a-wasting!*

"Sorry for the delay." Harry held up two plastic shopping bags, the strap of a black gun case over his shoulder. "Food and water for the trip, so unless necessary, we won't need to stop anywhere along the way where someone might take notice of foreigners."

Larry held up his bags and grinned before climbing in the back of the van. The smell of cooked chicken and beef wafted throughout the vehicle.

Men and their stomachs. "Good thinking. Let's roll." Once Harry and Larry stowed their gear, Samantha fired up the engine and headed out of the suburban area.

Before long, she merged onto the Bogota-Medellín highway. Towns and farms gave way to rolling hills as they overtook slow-moving trucks loaded with a variety of goods destined for the local markets. The countryside passed in a pattern of forest and compact fields of coffee beans, cassava, and sorghum.

Harry kept tuning the radio, searching for a decent station. After a while, he became bored with pushing the antiquated radio's buttons. With a grimace, he settled for a soft pop station, nodding to the music while tapping his leg.

Samantha glanced at him and smiled. "Just like old times, huh? Nothing much changes when you're driving through a target country en route to your mission."

"Got that right, although the terrain can vary." He glanced out the window. "Of course, things can become busy real quick."

"Uh-huh."

A low snore came from the back seat as if someone were cutting logs.

Harry glanced over his shoulder and grinned. "Sleeping Beauty is hard at it." He reached back and shoved Larry's knee. "Wake up!"

The snoring morphed into grunts and groans. "Are we there yet?" Larry rubbed his eyes. "You ruined my research."

Harry glanced at Samantha, who was shaking her head. "Research? What were you searching for?"

"I was on a beach, minding my own business when a blonde and a redhead approached—"

Samantha and Harry laughed.

She glanced in the rearview mirror. "Yeah, right. Some research."

"Hey! I have to do something to recharge my batteries while waiting for our mission to begin."

Harry rolled his eyes. "You've been asleep for almost six hours."

He stared at the map on his lap. "Shouldn't be long before we're in the outskirts of Medellín."

"I'll need to stop for fuel before we detour around the city." Samantha yanked the wheel, avoiding an animal trying to cross the road. "Our fuel consumption increased more than I expected once we started going through the mountains." *I need to pee, too, and I'm not going to stop by the road like Harry and Larry and let my ass hang out.*

Thirty minutes later, Harry pointed to a billboard. "Truck stop ahead—about three miles."

"Great." Samantha urged the van faster along the twisting and winding road, despite a surge in traffic heading toward the city. She followed a loaded truck off the highway. When it veered to the left to enter the parking area, Samantha headed to the fuel pumps.

She stopped at an empty pump. "Fill it up. And be careful. It wasn't long ago gang members from Los Urabeños killed a couple of truckers near here." She jumped out and called over her shoulder, "Be right back."

When she returned, Samantha found the van locked and unattended. A whistle from behind caused her to spin around.

Harry waved for her to join him.

They edged around the corner of the building. He pointed to a copse of trees. "Over there."

Larry stepped from behind a tree as they approached. "Your warning about being careful paid off." He nodded toward the tree. "Come meet our new friend. He thought he'd try to rob us—picked the wrong people."

A young man sat on the ground, his hands tied behind him. He stank.

Samantha wrinkled her nose at the offending odor. "What happened?"

Harry laughed. "He held up a puny pocket knife and demanded money, or he would kill us. Larry pulled out his blade from a sheath, and the guy soiled himself."

Larry stood over their hapless assailant. "He offered to guide us around Medellín if we don't kill him or turn him over to the authorities."

"No thanks." Samantha shook her head. "He's not getting in our vehicle with his stench. Besides, we know the way thanks to AJ's directions. Cut him loose, and let's go."

Harry raised a hand. "Wait. Better to knock him out before cutting him loose. In case he's connected to anyone we don't want knowing where we're going, if he's taking an enforced nap, he won't know which way we went."

Samantha nodded. "Good point. Take care of it."

EVERY ROUTE CARRIED the threat of additional gang members or other criminals detaining travelers in some way, so the occupants remained on alert. The rest of the trip passed without incident.

Four hours after leaving Medellín, they passed a sign indicating the national park was ahead. Samantha turned onto a narrow winding road as dusk descended. "Took a lot longer than AJ's guesstimate of ten hours." She glanced at her watch. "Closer to fourteen. I'm glad you guys spelled me behind the wheel a couple of times, or I'd be exhausted." She pointed toward the trees. "The compound should be about a mile from us."

Ten minutes later, they stopped in an area AJ had marked on the map. Harry pointed out the window. "Should be a few hundred yards."

They climbed out of the van, stretching their limbs to loosen stiff muscles. Expecting sporadic lighting around the camp under a moonless evening, the three operatives donned their NVGs and grabbed their backpacks and weapons. They crept through the foliage until they reached a small clearing surrounded by Ceroxylon palm trees overlooking the compound.

Samantha focused first on the large house before shifting to each of the four barns in turn. *All dark.* "Shit." She turned to Harry and

Larry. "Check things out. I don't like it—the place appears abandoned."

They nodded, dropped their packs, and squirmed forward.

Samantha paced in the clearing, waiting for their return. As a sliver of moon rose, she turned when a branch snapped. She yanked a pistol from its holster.

Harry and Larry appeared, with a gagged and bound man between them. They let the guy fall on the ground.

Larry shook his head. "This is the cook and the compound caretaker. He said everyone else left a couple of hours ago. No one told him where they were going."

"Damn! What are we supposed to do with him?" Instructed to send text or email updates only unless there was an emergency, Samantha punched two digits on her phone's keypad as she continued to monitor the camp.

AJ answered on the second ring. "What's up? What's happening—everyone okay?"

"There's no one here! The training camp's been abandoned!"

AJ gasped. "Verify—perhaps they're all inside."

"Negative. We already infiltrated the camp. Not a soul to be found. We're too late."

"What? Tell me it isn't so!"

"Sorry, AJ. What's the plan?"

"Remain in position until I get back to you."

AJ broke the connection and turned to Javier. "You're not going to believe this!"

"What's up? I can tell from your expression something's not right."

"I'll say. The terrorists are gone!"

24

M oreno Hacienda
Barranquilla, Colombia

ALONZO SAT at Olivia's desk and sipped an espresso. Dark shadows under his eyes and lips set in a grim line, he gazed around the room. *Who's behind the disruptions to our family? I now understand what Mamá meant when she told me long ago everyone wants to knock down the person on top of the pyramid and take over.*

He finished his coffee and pushed the cup aside, putting his arms together on the desk and resting his head on the makeshift pillow. Before long, he dozed off.

Alonzo awoke with a start. Looking out the window, he noticed the bright sunshine and clear blue skies had been replaced by dusk's violet and red hues. He stretched his arms above his head and yawned. *Without the laughter of Maria and Silvina, the house is like a tomb.* He pushed back the chair and left his mother's office.

Ding. Ding. Ding. ....

Alonzo counted the chimes of the old clock, which had belonged to his grandfather, echoing in the hallway. *Eight p.m. No wonder I'm hungry.* He placed a hand over his grumbling stomach. *I hope the cook left something for me.* He hurried along the corridor and stepped into the kitchen. A man sat at the table, sipping from a tall glass, his back to the door.

The man turned and smiled.

Alonzo halted. "Pedro! When did you return?"

"Hello, Alonzo. I arrived about fifteen minutes ago and came into the kitchen for some orange juice. Where is everyone?"

Alonzo grabbed a chair across from Pedro. "Uh, Mamá had some family business to take care of."

"Where?"

"She didn't mention where she was going but said she'd return in a couple of days." *Why all the questions? He's never cared before about what Mamá was doing and was never there for me when I was growing up. I never liked him from the start, and now I detest him.* Not wanting to meet Pedro's gaze when he asked further questions, Alonzo went to a cupboard, pulled out a glass, opened the fridge door, and poured some mango juice. He took a sip before returning to his seat. "I think Ramon went with her."

"Hmm." Pedro scratched his scraggly beard. "She's never at home when she should be."

Alonzo stifled a snort. *What a joke. How would he know? He's never here, either.* "You should be sympathetic—she's distraught over Maria and Silvina."

Pedro nodded. "We're all stressed over their disappearance. But her place is here. She should be monitoring the search efforts."

Bastardo! "What about you?" Alonzo pursed his lips. "They're your children, too." *And my halfsisters.* "Where have you been?"

"You may not be my son, but you'll show me the proper respect." Pedro slammed a fist on the table. "And what I do when I'm away is none of your business."

Alonzo jumped to his feet, placed both hands on the table, and leaned toward Pedro. "Respect is something to earn—you haven't come close to earning any from me."

Anger inflamed Pedro's face as he lunged toward Alonzo. "Someone needs to teach you a lesson—and I'm just the person to do it since your mother and her pet monkey, Ramon, aren't here."

Alonzo scooted back and laughed. "Old man, you're so far out of shape, your shadow could outrun you." He yanked a pistol from the small of his back. "Back off, or you won't like the consequences."

"From you?" Pedro sneered. "I've watched you shooting at targets during your training sessions. Maria and Silvina can shoot better than you. At least Silvina does."

"I can't miss from this range. Are you sure you want to take a chance?"

Pedro raised his hands and backed away.

Alonzo waved the pistol toward the door. "I suggest you leave the hacienda—now! Go back to your decrepit friends from Los Urabeños and tell them your stories. It's all you're good for."

"You forget your place. This is my home, too. So, you better sleep with one eye open." Pedro glared at him before turning and leaving the kitchen.

Alone, Alonzo's spirits sagged. *Great. Another issue to resolve—as if I don't have enough to worry about. I shouldn't have challenged him, but Mamá's let him get away with too much.* He shook his head. *Now my appetite's gone, too.* He headed upstairs to his room, keeping an eye out for his latest enemy.

Safe in his private area, Alonzo threw the three deadbolts to secure the door. He headed into his small sitting area, pulled out his phone, and punched in a series of numbers, long-committed to memory. He listened to several rings before someone answered.

"Hello. You have reached the American Embassy in Bogota. How may I direct your call?"

~

PEDRO STORMED out of the house, cursing as he went. *Hijueputa! How can that son of a bitch treat me like this—in my own home! I should have taught him better manners when he was growing up.* He climbed into his brown Jeep Cherokee, slammed the door, and gunned the engine, speeding toward the compound's exit.

The guards swung the gates open for the approaching SUV, jumping out of the way of the fishtailing vehicle.

On the highway, Pedro grinned as he thumbed open his cell-phone. "I'll be there in about an hour. Contact the others." He terminated the call and pushed a CD into the slot on the dash. He tapped his leg in time with the Colombian folk rhythms. The hilly, forested countryside gave way to urban areas as he sped toward his destination.

Pedro slowed as he entered Malambo. He weaved his way through the narrow streets before stopping opposite Mario de Moya's cantina. He killed the engine, jumped out of the SUV, and jiggled across the road to the beat of music blaring through several loudspeakers. Once inside, Pedro let his eyes adjust to the dim light before nodding at the bartender and heading to a private room in the rear.

Heads turned as he took his seat at the table. Several individuals acknowledged his arrival by raising their beer bottles in his direction.

He glanced around the table at the eight men. *All here. Time to take control of the group.* "Enough talking. We want back in the drug business, and I know how to make it happen."

One of the men, white-haired with a chunk missing from his left ear lobe, raised a hand. "We enjoy the stories from our youth. Why should we give them up?"

Pedro shrugged. "My stepson, Alonzo, called us decrepit and lost in our past, with no way forward." He slammed an open hand on the table. "I say no more. We'll write new stories, which will become legends. Now is the time to strike."

"How?"

"My wife is shirking her responsibilities as a cartel leader. Her—our children are consuming her time. It's time for someone new to lead the Barranquilla Cartel—me." He gazed at each individual in turn. "With your help, of course."

"We offer our commiserations over the kidnapping of your girls."

The white-haired man nudged the bald guy next to him, who appeared to be sleeping.

Pedro chuckled and tapped his nose. "I've always known who took them and where they're being held. That's my little secret—to teach that bitch of a wife nothing is forever."

Everyone glanced at one another but remained silent at Pedro's announcement.

"So, are you with me? Shall our forgotten band of Los Urabeños compadres show the others, the young men who changed their name to *Clan del Golfo*, that we aren't just old men living in the past?"

Filled with the false courage of alcohol, one of the men jumped to his feet, followed by the others. They broke into a chant, "Los Urabeños! Los Urabeños!"

Pedro grinned and raised his hands for silence. After the men resumed their seats, he nodded. "We shall teach Clan del Golfo what it means to be feared. Blood will run in the streets if it means we achieve our objectives." He pursed his lips.

"What do you need from us?"

"Changes are already underway. I contacted one of Olivia's family friends going back to before her father was killed. At my request, he put a contract out on her, so I know Olivia's in hiding, even though Alonzo said she's away on family business."

The white-haired man nodded. "What should we do first?"

"One more person is standing in my way of taking over the cartel and returning us to our former glory. He must be eliminated."

"Who is it?"

"Who else?" Pedro smirked. "My good-for-nothing pampered stepson, Alonzo. It's time to be rid of him."

25

AJ's Safehouse
Bogota, Colombia

THE KNUCKLES of AJ's hand grew white as she attempted to crush her cellphone. She gritted her teeth as she threw the phone across the room. *Damn! Nothing's going right with this mission.*

"What's up?" Javier asked. "Who just crapped in your coffee?" He smirked.

She dropped into the chair across the table from Javier and slammed her hand down. The slap echoed like a shot. "The camp outside Turbo is empty!"

"What?" He jumped to his feet. "Everyone?"

AJ's eyes rolled skyward. "Sit down, you big oaf. Samantha said a cook, who also functions as a caretaker, was the only person they found. She said there were others who didn't leave, but they couldn't find anyone else."

Javier rubbed the stubble on his chin. "How long ago did they depart?"

"A couple of hours before the team arrived." She grabbed her backpack and pulled out her iPad. "Better let the folks back home know. They'll need to hustle to find them before it's too late."

To: Fortress

From: Hunter

Turbo compound empty. Personnel departed in two buses. Destination unknown. Request immediate assistance in locating targets.

She hit send and leaned back in the chair. "MacKenzie will get the ball rolling. In the meantime, we'd better start working on our own objective."

"How we getting there?"

AJ gave him a look as if he'd lost his mind. "Airplane—it takes over fifteen hours to drive. Samantha and the others needed to take an arsenal with them, which is why they drove. We'll be traveling light, so we'll take a commercial flight and rent a vehicle from Barranquilla Airport." She opened her iPad again. "I'll check on flights."

"Want more coffee?" Javier went to the counter where a warming plate kept the coffee hot. "It'll help us think while we deal with this setback."

"Always." She held up her empty cup. "Better put on a new pot. I think that was the one I made several hours ago. It'll be like tar."

"Gotcha."

They concentrated on their tasks without talking.

Javier finished first and poured two cups. He set one in front of AJ. "Here ya go. Just as you like it—hot, strong, and black."

She nodded. "Thanks." She took a sip. "Perfect. There's only one flight for the remainder of the day to Barranquilla. We'll need to be at the airport around 1900. The plane's scheduled to land at 2215, too late to go visiting, so I booked us into the Dann Carlton Hotel."

Javier tested his coffee. "Sounds good to me. When will we hit Olivia's hacienda?"

"Tomorrow morning."

〜

THEY DOZED on the flight from Bogotá to Barranquilla. After picking up their Nissan Qashqai from the rental agency, AJ drove while Javier served as navigator. Weaving through the moderate evening traffic, she pulled into the hotel's parking lot twenty-five minutes later.

At the check-in desk, Javier took the lead. "Good evening, we have a room booked for three nights—Mr. and Mrs. Smith. I requested the top floor with a sea view."

The clerk scanned his computer and nodded. "Yes, sir. I found your reservation. One moment please." He whispered to another employee. "All of our standard rooms on the top floor are filled, sir, but there is still one grand suite remaining. Since it's so late, we'll let you have it at the price you were quoted when you made your reservation."

Javier smiled. "Thank you." He smothered a yawn with a large hand. "Excuse me. Been a long day."

"The restaurants are closed now, but you can order something from room service. The menu will be on one of the tables in your suite. Just dial the operator when you're ready to order." The clerk passed over two keycards and leaned over the counter. "Do you require assistance with your luggage?"

Javier glanced at their two backpacks and laughed. "No, we can handle it."

"As you wish. The elevators are over there." The clerk pointed to a small alcove on the other side of reception. "Enjoy your stay."

They took the elevator to the top floor and located their room without any difficulty. Once inside, AJ scanned the suite. "Uh-huh. One bed. Flip for it?"

Javier laughed. "It's big enough for three."

AJ's face froze into a thoughtful pose with a prominent frown telegraphing her feelings about sharing a bed.

His face reddened. "Fine. You take the bed, and I'll grab the couch." *Oh, well. No harm in trying.*

She chuckled. "Great minds think alike." AJ tossed her backpack and carry-on case on the bed. "I feel naked without my SIG."

Javier nodded. "Know what you mean, but no way we could bring them on the flight. If we had driven, we'd—"

"We'd still be on the road. No worries. I know someone who'll provide what we need without asking questions." She yanked her iPad out and logged on. "Better check if MacKenzie has an update for us." One new message waited.

To: Hunter

From: Fortress

Unable to determine whereabouts at this time. Special assistance requested to locate missing travelers. Hope to provide an update soon.

AJ turned the device so Javier could read the message.

"Special assistance?"

She nodded. "MacKenzie and the others will contact the various intel agencies—both ours and the 'Five Eyes.' They already have at least one phone number associated with the group, so they'll be scanning any calls and running some data mining programs to isolate any locations. All we can do is wait."

Javier grimaced as he paced. "Waiting sucks. It requires the one quality I don't possess. Patience." He stopped near AJ. "Guess I'll take a shower and call it a night—unless you want the bathroom first."

"I thought the army was all about hurrying up and waiting." AJ waved a hand in the air. "Go for it. You need your beauty sleep." She laughed at the sudden lift of his eyebrows and gaping mouth as he searched for a comeback.

EARLY THE NEXT MORNING, AJ sent a text message to a local contact. After Javier returned from working out in the hotel's gym, she showed him the response. "We better get moving. No time for some breakfast before we head to our rendezvous point." She pointed to herself. "I know the area, so I'll drive."

Javier shrugged. "Fine with me."

Twenty minutes later, AJ parked on the street across from Venezuela Park. They hopped out of the car, scooted across the road in front of a slow-moving bus, and strolled along a tree-lined path with benches staged about every fifty feet.

AJ carried a small shopping bag in her left hand. She touched Javier's shoulder and gestured. "Over to the right. Beyond the outdoor physical fitness equipment."

Javier peered in the direction AJ wanted. "You mean the picnic area?"

"Yeah. Our contact should be at one of the tables in the back."

They trotted along the path until they approached the designated spot. At the rear, a skinny man wearing a baseball cap scanned the area and nodded when he saw them.

AJ and Javier joined the man at his invitation.

Once they sat, he pointed to a cooler on the seat beside him. "Time for a sandwich and a soft drink." He handed out some of the food and Cokes.

As AJ munched away, she slid the bag across the table.

The man pulled it onto his lap and peeked inside. A smile lit his face as he shoved the bag into a pocket. "What you asked for is in the cooler under a layer of sandwiches. Two SIG Sauers, four magazines for each weapon, and plenty of ammunition."

"Thanks." AJ put an arm around Javier as a couple approached. She whispered in his ear, "When we stand, shake his hand and take the basket. We'll head to the SUV and be on our way."

Javier nodded.

The man stood, followed by AJ and Javier. As their contact walked away, AJ picked up the food wrappers and empty bottles while Javier grabbed the container.

Depositing the trash in a receptacle near the exit to the park, AJ crossed the street and unlocked the Nissan. They hopped inside.

After shutting the front passenger door, Javier lowered the basket below the window and pulled out one of the weapons and two magazines. He checked the magazines were loaded and slid them into AJ's waiting hands.

She inserted one of the magazines into her new weapon, shoved the SIG into a holster on the belt of her tan cargo pants, started the car, and merged into traffic. "Next stop is Olivia's hacienda. Shouldn't take long to get there."

Javier pulled a shoulder holster out of his backpack and strapped it on. After loading his weapon, he tucked it into the holster, which was covered by a billowing shirt. He sighed in contentment.

AJ followed the streets out of the city, gaining speed as the traffic thinned. Forty-five minutes later, the vehicle slid to a halt.

A waist-high barricade blocked their access to the hacienda.

"Do they really think their barrier will stop anyone who wants to enter?" AJ kept the engine running and glanced around.

"Perhaps not." Javier gestured. "However, those six men armed with AK-47s might be more of a threat. Let me talk to them." He rolled his window down as one of the men approached.

Two others followed their leader, spreading out behind him while the remaining three pointed their weapons toward the vehicle.

Javier spoke in Spanish. "We are here to meet with Señora Moreno."

The guard shook his head. "No one here." He waved them away. "Go."

"When will she return? It's urgent we speak with her."

"I know not when they will return." He raised his weapon and pointed at the front of the vehicle. The others followed suit. "Leave now—unless you want to die today."

"Could we wait in case she returns soon?"

The guard pointed his weapon at Javier's face. "Go! Now! Last warning!"

26

Unknown Compound
Somewhere in Colombia

VALENTINA RAISED her hands as if to cover her eyes. They froze at her temples, her face a mask of horror. She screamed, "No!"

Maria flailed her arms in the water as she fought against the current. She bobbed to the surface before a surging eddy swamped her, and she disappeared into the maelstrom.

Silvina shoved the stunned woman out of her way and jumped into the raging torrent after her sister. Caught in the grasp of the swirling current, she struggled to keep her head clear. Snagging a breath whenever possible, she tried to fight against the relentless onslaught as rushing water propelled her forward.

It seemed like the world had slowed, and time was screeching to a stop, but only seconds passed before the rapids calmed. Battered and shaken, Silvina gulped in air. Gathering her strength, she swam to the bank before realizing how shallow the water was. She stood and pushed strands of dripping hair from her face, gazed around. A small patch of red caught her attention. *Oh, no! Maria! She was wearing a red top.*

"Maria! Maria! I'm coming!"

Exhausted, Silvina struggled against the current. Her vision obscured by brimming tears, she stumbled and fell into the water. She struggled to her feet and, spitting out the brackish taste of the river, tried to reach the sandbar where Maria lay, before falling over a submerged rock. The effort to rise too much, Silvina continued to crawl forward through the shallows.

Perched on an exposed sandbar, Maria lay on her back, not moving.

Silvina reached her sister and gazed at her face. "Maria." She shook her sister's shoulder. "Maria."

No response.

She struggled to turn Maria onto her side. Moments after she changed Maria's position, her body jerked. She coughed, water spewed from her mouth.

Silvina grabbed her sister in her arms. "Maria! I thought I had lost you."

"What .... What happened?"

Silvina helped Maria into a sitting position. "You fell in the water. I jumped in to save you."

Maria touched her sister's face. "You're so brave—I swim better than you."

"I know. Stupid, but it was a reflex action." Silvina laughed. "At least we're alive. How did you fall in?"

Maria glanced at her sister. "I can't always let you be the fearless one, and I thought we needed to escape. I knew if I jumped in, you'd come after me." She shrugged. "It worked." She raised her arms. "Come here. You might younger, but I'd be lost without you."

"What are sisters for?" Silvina slid into Maria's arms for a quick hug before glancing around. "We'd better run. They'll be searching for us."

∾

VALENTINA TURNED and screeched at the guards. "Don't just stand there—go after them." She pointed at the nearest man. "*El stupidos!* Jump in and follow them."

"I ... I can't ...." He dropped his head.

"What?" She placed her hands on her hips and stomped her feet in the grass. "I don't care if you can't swim. Someone is going to follow them while the rest of you search along the bank."

"I can swim." The youngest guard smirked while he handed his weapon to one of the others. "Meet you downriver." He jumped off the bank. Moments later, he tumbled into the raging water, before disappearing.

The two remaining men scurried along the embankment, weaving through the trees and undergrowth. One let out a strangled scream after tripping over a hidden log.

Valentina shook her head. She watched them until they were no longer in sight.

SILVINA PULLED Maria to her feet. Together they waded into the shallows, struggling to remain upright as they stumbled over slippery rocks.

At last, they staggered onto a small sandy beach. Exhausted from their ordeal, they collapsed in the sun-warmed sand.

"Two minutes, Maria. No longer."

Maria gulped air as if she couldn't suck enough into her lungs. "I'm so tired."

"We can rest after we get away." Silvina stood and held a hand out to her sister. "C'mon, let's go."

Grabbing hold of bushes and vines, they hauled themselves through the foliage to the top of the bluff.

"Which way?" Maria turned to the left.

"No, silly. We need to follow the river away from the falls. Go right." Silvina turned and squeezed between two trees. "There's a game trail. If Ramon were here, he'd be able to tell us what kind of animals use the path."

"Uh-huh. As long as they can't eat us, I don't care."

"Hurry up, Maria. Stop being such a—girl." Silvina rolled her eyes. "Remember what Ramon taught us—if we ever become lost, follow a river until we find help."

"Oh!" Maria frowned and shook her hands. "Just because you're a tomboy, you think you have all the answers. I'll have you know—" She screamed. "Look! In the trees. A snake!"

Silvina glanced at the branch, which had caught Maria's attention, and laughed. "Maria, that's not a snake—only a thick vine. Let's go."

"I thought it was alive!" Maria trembled as they pushed forward. "I hate snakes."

Fifteen minutes later, the trees and undergrowth thinned as the trail widened.

"Look, Maria. Told ya! We'll make better time in the meadow. Race—"

Craack!

Both girls spun toward the sound.

"Where do you think you're going?" Two guards approached, weapons leveled at the girls. "Little *putas!* You've angered Valentina and made fools of us. You'll pay for your stupidity, she will see to that."

Maria and Silvina raised their hands.

The older guard used the barrel of his AK-47 to point them back along the path. "Don't try anything. Valentina said to bring you back, but she didn't say we couldn't teach you a lesson." He leered at them and licked his lips.

AFTER TYING the girls together with nylon rope, the men half-walked, half-dragged Maria and Silvina back to the waterfall. Valentina sat on her horse, a hint of anger clouding her face. "After all I've done for you …. Made sure you had decent food, were kept together—even this trip outside the house. What do I receive for my generosity?" She glanced upward. "Nothing but grief, even though I show you nothing but kindness. Untie them."

After they were untied, Silvina stepped forward. "Hey, lady. We didn't ask your father to kidnap us."

"He's not my fa—I mean, I wasn't involved."

Silvina laughed. "I didn't think he was your father. Even as young as I am, I have eyes and can see how he looks at you. A proper father wouldn't do that."

Valentina gestured toward the horses. "Climb on. If you don't, the guards will help you—and tie you in place."

"Shouldn't we wait for Oscar to return?" The older guard pointed to a riderless horse. "We didn't see him."

"Who cares?" Valentina shrugged. "No one pushed him into the water. He can find his own way back. Bring his horse."

ONCE THE GIRLS were secured in the room used as their temporary prison, Valentina sought out the man responsible for kidnapping them. She found him outside, smoking a cigar and gazing into the distance.

He turned to her, his face expressionless. "Well, did you learn anything useful?"

Valentina placed a hand on his arm. "Sorry. Pretending to be your daughter didn't work. What now?"

He headed inside the hacienda. "I'll think of something. Let's check on our young visitors."

Before Valentina unlocked the bedroom door, the man pulled a balaclava over his head and nodded.

They stepped inside.

Maria leaned against the bed's headboard, her face tear-streaked.

Silvina sat on a chair, defiance etched upon her young features, her fists clenched in anger.

"I guess our plan to get you to reveal more about your family to Valentina failed." He shook his head. "Never mind—she's not my daughter, but my niece."

"Mamá told me never to use this word again." Silvina jumped to her feet. "But, you're a bastardo!"

The man laughed before yanking the balaclava from his head.

Silvina and Maria's eyes widened. "You!"

"Yes." He grinned. "Since you now know who I am, what should we do with you? Do you think your mother will pay a ransom? I don't think so—the cost would finish her and your family." He yanked a machete from a sheath on his belt and stepped toward the girls.

Shrieks filled the air as Silvina lunged for the bed and held Maria.

The man grabbed one of Maria's legs. "Come here. Your mother will do as I command once she receives my message."

Silvina kicked at the man's arm with her free leg, while Maria tugged on Silvina's waist.

"It's time for you to die!"

27

Moreno Hacienda
Barranquilla, Colombia

AJ BACKED AWAY from the gate at Olivia's compound and executed a three-point turn, tires spinning, as she sped along the access road. She pounded a hand on the steering wheel. "Damn! Our luck's getting worse. So much for our intel!"

"Relax. Everything will come out in the wash."

AJ glanced at Javier and laughed, her tension easing. "So, when's wash day?"

He shrugged. "Could be today, might be tomorrow. Since we didn't have breakfast, I suggest we find the nearest cafe and load up on grub while you check for any new info from MacKenzie."

"I knew there was a reason I let you join this mission." She reached over and squeezed his hand. "You're always so laid-back." *And kinda cute, too.*

"Yep, that's me—an excellent counter to your feisty manner." He nudged her shoulder with a fist. "We're a perfect team."

She smiled. "Yes, we are." *I hope we become closer, too. I'm getting used to his company.*

Once they approached Barranquilla, the fourth largest city in Colombia, it didn't take long before a billboard caught Javier's attention. "Make a right at the traffic light."

"Why? Something the matter?"

"We just passed a sign for *Restaurante Donde Mamá*. Any restaurant called Mamá is worth checking out."

AJ laughed. "Okay, big boy. Hold on." She yanked the wheel and made a sharp turn before bringing the vehicle to a sudden halt. She pointed. "Here we are."

The building was painted in peach, blue, and white. Decorative security bars crisscrossed the windows and the door. Inside, vivid blue pillars and orange plant containers contrasted with the black and white checkered tile floor. Plants and colored lights hung from the rafters.

They found an empty table toward the rear of the restaurant. After ordering breakfast, AJ powered up her iPad. "An update from MacKenzie." She whistled as she read.

Javier noted the expression change on AJ's face, from puzzlement to delight. "Anything worthwhile?"

She nodded. "Give me a sec—almost finished." In a couple of minutes, she typed a brief message, closed her iPad, and resumed eating.

"Well? Gonna keep me in suspense?"

AJ grinned, shifting her gaze to people seated around them. "I'll fill you in later. But we've caught a break."

Once they finished breakfast and Javier paid, they scurried back to the vehicle.

AJ started the engine and maneuvered their SUV to an empty area in the parking lot. She pulled out a roadmap from the driver's door to appear as a tourist gaining their bearings. "Here's the scoop. MacKenzie says someone in the Intel Community collected locational data for Olivia's phone and picked up a call. Based on the conversation, she was speaking with a son named Alonzo and telling him not to worry about her. She was being treated like a house guest rather than a prisoner, and said things would work out."

Javier thrust a fist into the air. "At last! Where are we heading?"

"Not so fast. There was also a call between Días and Olivia's security chief, Ramon. They couldn't establish a fix on the phone Días was using, but Ramon's was co-located with Olivia's." She flashed a toothy grin. "They're outside Sincelejo, about three hours from here."

"Should we arrange back-up?"

"Negative—taken care of. Remember I had Harry, Larry, and Samantha remain in place in Turbo? After I read MacKenzie's email, I sent something to Samantha. They're packing up in Turbo and will rendezvous with us in Sincelejo, which is about thirty minutes from the rolling hills where Olivia is located. They'll need at least four hours to join us, so there's no rush."

"Outfrickin' standing."

"We better top up the fuel and hit the road. Check the route on your iPad."

"Not the map? I found Sincelejo on it." Javier glanced at her. "You trust me to find the way?"

"The map was for pretending we were loco tourists in case anyone was watching." AJ laughed. "Besides, I forgave you for getting us lost in Panama. Also, GPS is built into the device."

"I can't help it if I'm all thumbs on this thing."

"Can you say, 'I'm technically challenged?'"

"Nope."

They chuckled as AJ pulled out of the parking lot in search of a gas station. While AJ took care of the fuel, Javier struggled with his iPad.

She finished paying and hopped back in the vehicle. "Well? Did you find the road?"

"Yep." Javier beamed. "All we need to do is find signs for the Caribbean Transverse—National Route 90."

AJ yanked the wheel and fishtailed around a corner.

"What's up?"

She gestured back to the intersection. "As you spoke, we came upon a sign pointing us in this direction."

"Look—Sincelejo is two hundred thirty-eight kilometers."

"Saw it." AJ ground her teeth and flashed her lights before blowing the horn at a slow-moving vehicle straddling the two lanes, making it difficult to pass. After the truck moved over, she gunned the engine and accelerated past, narrowly missing an oncoming car. She returned the rude gesture she received from the car's driver.

"Did MacKenzie mention if they have any new satellite photos of the area where Olivia is located?"

"Not yet. It can take time to have a satellite repositioned. She put in a request, but for now, we're on our own."

As the miles passed on the smooth road, both remained quiet, although from time to time, Javier hummed an unrecognizable tune.

AJ slammed on the brakes, putting the vehicle into a controlled slide, coming to a sideways stop across the road.

Javier's head shunted toward the windshield. He frowned and scrutinized the surroundings. "Good thing I was wearing a seatbelt. What happened?"

She glanced out the side window. "Some raccoon-type of animal was taking a shortcut across the highway. Didn't want to hit it." The coast clear, she resumed her speed.

"Where I come from, you don't cause an accident to save wildlife."

"We ain't there, now are we? Get over it."

Both laughed as they kept a watch for further animal incursions into their path.

As the terrain increased in elevation, the straightaways became shorter, and the road snaked along the edge of valleys, with severe drop-offs. Stunted trees grew wherever possible.

Javier gestured to the latest distance sign. "Fifteen clicks." He shifted in his seat. "Be glad to get out and stretch."

"You and me, both."

"Hey! The road number changed—we're on 25SC!"

AJ shook her head. "You have nothing over Sherlock Holmes. The road number changed when we came through the last village, about twenty kilometers ago."

"Oh." The sides of Javier's mouth turned down. "Guess I better get my head in the game."

"Excellent idea." AJ smiled out of the corner of her mouth. *He seems distracted by something. Hmm, I wonder. Could it be me? Nah—he's a professional. He knows how to compartmentalize his life. He just sucks at directions. No wonder he drops in by parachute.*

She slowed the SUV as they entered Sincelejo, the commercial center for the agricultural region, and headed toward the city center. Stopping across from the St. Francis of Assisi Cathedral, she killed the engine.

A van located about a hundred yards past the church flashed its lights.

Moments later, AJ's phone rang. "Hello?"

"The stooges await your command."

AJ laughed. "Okay, let's roll. Want to be in position before dark."

The two vehicles headed out of the city on a winding road into the forest-covered hills. Thirty minutes later, they passed a turn-off.

AJ slowed and pointed. "Up ahead—a cell tower."

Javier nodded. "As you drove past that narrow access road, I spotted tall gates embedded in a concrete wall. Appeared to be concertina wire strung along the top. I also saw two armed guards watching us."

"We better keep moving before they become curious."

A mile along the road, AJ found an area underneath several trees big enough to park both vehicles.

Javier and AJ stepped out of their vehicle and headed to the cargo area, joined by Harry, Larry, and Samantha.

"Let's do this." AJ turned to Samantha. "We have pistols but need something heavier."

"No worries. We've plenty in the hidden cargo area in the van."

Once the five armed themselves, they donned their body armor and comms gear. AJ reached back in the SUV and pulled a tranquilizer gun from a small box.

"Expecting trouble?" Javier pointed at the weapon.

AJ shook her head as she shoved the weapon in her belt. "Contingency planning—in case we need to silence dogs—or guards."

"Good idea. Makes sense."

After making adjustments and strapping on night vision goggles, Javier took point, heading through the trees in the general direction of the compound.

The others followed in single file, with Samantha as their rear guard.

After reaching a break in the trees at the edge of a ravine, AJ whispered to the others, "Javier and I'll monitor the compound from here. You three work your way to the other side. We want to locate Olivia and rescue her."

Harry nodded and glanced at the others. "What are the rules of engagement?"

AJ pursed her lips. "For now, no contact—do not engage anyone unless fired upon first. If that happens, the gloves are off. The ROEs will change once we identify where Olivia is being kept. Sound off when you're in position."

Harry, Larry, and Samantha nodded, and headed along the ridge-line, keeping close to the ground.

Javier scanned the compound with a pair of Bestguarder NG-900 night vision binoculars. "I want to work closer. We're at the edge of the maximum infrared distance. I can spot various guards, but need to move another fifty yards down the rim to identify people passing by windows inside the house."

"We'll both go." She set off down the hill without waiting for Javier. She stopped at a closed gate in a wall surrounding the house. She gave a shove.

Unlocked.

As she pushed it wide enough to squeeze through, a rusty hinge squealed. She ducked into the shadows, checking whether anyone had heard the noise.

A slight rustling came from behind.

Slightly limping, Javier joined her.

AJ grabbed his arm. "'Bout time you made it." She gestured at his leg. "What happened?"

"Nothing to worry about—just twisted my ankle as I chased after you. Are you part gazelle?"

AJ gave a slight chuckle. "I wondered what kept you."

He snickered and handed her an M-4 carbine. "I policed the area first—you left this behind."

"Oops." She pulled the binoculars from him and focused on the house. "Damn! Can't see anyone."

"Perhaps they moved into another room."

Noise crackled in AJ's ear, and she raised a finger to silence Javier. "Repeat, Samantha." AJ raised three fingers to let Javier know Samantha was on channel three.

He switched to the correct channel as Samantha gave a SITREP. "Larry says he's spotted our target. She's in a room on the far side of the house away from you."

"Positive ID?" AJ grinned.

"Affirmative. Harry pulled up the photo you sent us earlier, and they both agree it's Olivia."

AJ and Javier did a fist bump before she issued instructions. "Remain in position and keep contact on target whenever possible. Anyone with her?"

"Negative. She appears to be in a bedroom on the second floor and able to move around without restraint."

"We're on our way."

THIRTY MINUTES LATER, the five operatives huddled behind a stone outbuilding on the compound. They checked for exterior alarms. Finding none, Harry cut a path through the concertina wire, and they climbed onto the wall.

"Harry, Larry, and Samantha, you remain here. Suggest remaining on the wall in case the gate Javier and I came through can't be used as an exit point."

"Roger, boss," Samantha whispered.

Moving one at a time, AJ and Javier jumped from the wall and scampered forward in a crouch, rendezvousing behind a copse of trees.

Javier glanced to his left.

A shadow leaped toward him.

He tumbled with the impact from one hundred and fifty pounds of animal.

AJ pulled a tranquilizer gun from her belt and fired.

Once. Twice. Three times.

At last, the enormous beast dropped to the ground.

Javier slid from underneath. He adjusted his NVGs, knelt, and examined the animal. He turned to the others and whispered, "Anatolian Shepherd Dog. No need for conventional alarms when the grounds are protected by one of these." He stood. "Still alive, but will sleep for some time." He glanced at the resting dog. "I love animals, but not when they attack me. Sent my heart racing."

"No wonder we didn't spot any guards outside." AJ touched his arm. "Are you okay? You're sweating."

He wiped the perspiration from his forehead with the back of an arm. "A few scratches but nothing serious."

She nodded. "Spread out and check for any entrance points on this side of the house. Let's find our target before any more of these dogs appear or guards come looking for their rover." She rushed forward, not stopping until she reached the edge of the house.

Moments later, Javier joined her. He pointed to her right. "Outside stairs—leading to a terrace. Might be an access point?"

She nodded and keyed her comms gear. "Identified possible way inside. Close on the exterior wall of the building and wait for my signal."

Click. Click. Click.

Satisfied the others were aware, AJ edged toward the steps and began climbing.

Javier followed, his head swiveling back and forth as he checked for guards.

Nothing.

At the top of the stairs, a door to the left.

AJ tried the handle—unlocked.

She motioned to Javier, who stepped forward and squeezed inside as AJ held the door open. She followed, closing the door with a soft click.

Their NVGs bathed everything in green. They were in a corridor, a plush carpet stretching the length of the hallway. Side tables underneath large portraits dotted the area.

They crept down the hall.

Chirp. Chirp. Chirp.

"Geckos," Javier whispered. He bumped one of the tables.

AJ's hand shot out and caught a teetering vase before it fell to the floor. "Take a clumsy pill this morning?"

"Oops. Good catch."

Javier hugged the left wall while AJ did the same on the right. They crept toward the first door on the left.

Locked.

AJ pulled out her lock picks. Within seconds, she smiled as she pushed the door inward. They removed their NVGs.

Someone sat in a chair reading.

Javier crawled forward while AJ covered him.

He raised four fingers, dropping each one to indicate when he would move. After making a fist, he jumped to his feet, his right arm snaking around a woman's head, his hand covering her mouth to prevent any screams.

AJ stepped in front of the chair. "Olivia?"

The woman nodded.

"We're here to rescue you. If my friend removes his hand, will you promise to remain quiet?"

Olivia nodded.

Javier dropped his hand, ready to replace it at a moment's notice.

Olivia jumped to her feet and studied their faces.

AJ took one of her arms and Javier the other.

"Are you CIA? Aren't you the ones who put a contract out on me? That's what Ramon, my security chief, said. Don't kill me—I have useful information."

28

American Embassy
Bogota, Colombia

GRAVEL CRUNCHED under Alonzo's boots as a Colombian security guard escorted him from the American embassy to his car. Glaring at the guard, he keyed the fob to open his door, yanked the handle, and eased into the driver's seat.

Alonzo started the engine and weaved through the vehicles parked near the building until he reached the exit. As soon as the guards lifted the barrier, he gunned the engine and shot in front of an approaching vehicle. Horns blared, but he didn't slow down until he reached a quiet stretch of road where he pulled over.

"*Mierda!*" Alonzo thumped his fists on the steering wheel. "A waste of time. Why wouldn't that pompous son of a bitch listen to me?" He smacked the window before spotting an opening in traffic and resuming his journey. *What should I do now? I thought the Americanos would help me—what a joke. The official just laughed when I told him I graduated from Harvard. He didn't care about my family employing hundreds of Americanos.*

Alonzo ran his hands through his hair. *Mamá said to find help, but from whom?* He snapped his fingers and smiled. "I know just the person."

AFTER RETURNING TO THE HACIENDA, Alonzo showered and changed clothes. He stood in front of a full-length mirror. Hair still damp from his shower, he ran his gaze over the dark suit and white shirt he'd changed into. *Not bad. But will my professional appearance make any difference? I'll soon find out.* He saluted his reflection, smiled, and left the room.

Forty-five minutes later, he stopped in front of the imposing two-story home of Colonel Santiago and climbed out of his Mercedes. *Remain calm. Don't appear desperate.*

With unhurried steps, Alonzo mounted the broad staircase to the front door. After adjusting his sleeves, he gulped and pressed the bell. *If the colonel answers, he'll either slam the door in my face or shoot me. A risk I must take—for my family.*

He pushed the doorbell.

The resultant chimes echoed in the distance.

Footsteps.

Alonzo braced himself.

The door opened. A man taller than Alonzo peered at him. "Sí?"

"Coronel Santiago, por favor."

The butler shut the door in Alonzo's face with a click.

Alonzo turned and gazed across the broad vista, taking in the well-manicured gardens and shrubs. In the distance, the hint of mountains seemed to lean against the horizon.

Moments later, the door opened, and the servant beckoned Alonzo inside. "*La biblioteca.*" After shutting the door behind Alonzo, the butler gestured toward the marble-floored corridor. They marched past family portraits adorning both walls. The butler stopped at a closed door, knocked once, and opened it, standing aside for Alonzo to enter.

Colonel Santiago sat on a green upholstered sofa. Behind him, the national flag of Colombia, adorned with several bullet holes, stretched across the wall.

The colonel motioned for Alonzo to sit on a sofa opposite him. "Coffee, water, or whiskey?"

Alonzo shook his head.

With a wave of his hand, the colonel dismissed the servant. "So, here you are at last." He glanced at the well-groomed Alonzo. "I admit you are dressed much better than when I freed you from Barranquilla prison. I see your bruises and scratches have healed, too."

Alonzo turned red from his neck to his cheeks. He swallowed to moisten his mouth. "Yes, Colonel. Not one of my best days." He grimaced. "May I come straight to the point, sir?"

Santiago inclined his head.

"There's a problem I'm unable to deal with on my own." He shook his head. "Colonel, I'm at my wit's end. I'm in need of your help—I've no one else who might be able to sort out my problems."

"Would this have anything to do with your trip to Europe?" The colonel rubbed his chin. "My sources inform me you are trying to expand into the European drug trade." He speared Alonzo with eyes like daggers. "I told you if you ever wanted to visit with Gabriela again, you must leave the drug trade forever—even if it means leaving your family."

"But .... But, Colonel, my trip to Europe was to try to find someone to aid my family in their expansion into the service industry while I assume full control of the legitimate family businesses—our malls and restaurants in America and our Caribbean hotels. It wasn't about drugs." *Well, it was, but I'm going to stay away from that part of the family business.*

"Hmm. If what you say is true, I could accept your proposal." He crossed his arms. "Is there someone who can corroborate this?"

Alonzo nodded. "His contact information is at the hacienda, but I can have him call you."

The colonel waved a hand in the air as if dismissing Alonzo's offer. "So, what help can I provide?"

"My family's in danger. Maria and Silvina were kidnapped—we don't know where they are or who is behind this. There's been no ransom demand. Also, someone put out a contract on Mamá—she's in hiding."

"I suggest contacting the American embassy for assistance. You were the top student in your class at one of their most prestigious universities. It seems to me after all the money you spent on your education in America, one of their officials might lend you a hand. I believe your businesses there also provide many jobs."

Alonzo shook his head. "I tried, thinking the same as you. Some counselor laughed when I presented my case. I even offered everything I knew about the family's drug business and various connections, but he said I would need to speak with one of the Drug Enforcement Agency's representatives." He frowned as his shoulders slumped. "But, they were too busy to meet with me. Something to do with a scandal over one of their agents providing classified information to narcos. He told me to come back in a month."

The colonel shrugged. "Why am I not surprised? The Americans talk about eradicating the influx of drugs into their country but do not appear to be doing everything they could. What about their CIA? They have several people at the embassy."

"I asked about the CIA as well. All the man would do is take my name and telephone number. He said he would give it to the appropriate person." He gazed into the colonel's face. "What action do you recommend I take?"

"Return to your hacienda and wait for a call. It might take a few days, but I will see what I can uncover. Once we have some details, we can make plans to recover your sisters and stop the contract on your mother."

Alonzo felt his shoulders relax for the first time in days. "Thank you, Colonel. Before I depart, there is a rather important question I wish to ask."

"Oh?" The colonel remained stoic. "Would this have something to do with my daughter by any chance?"

A puzzled expression etched across Alonzo's face. "How did you know, sir?"

The colonel tapped the side of his nose. "I might not look it now, but I was young once."

Alonzo laughed." Yes, sir. It might be premature to ask, but I was wondering what your thoughts might be on me proposing to Gabriela?"

The colonel chuckled. "Yes, it is a bit premature. If you can prove to my satisfaction you are leaving the drug trade and sticking to the legitimate enterprises you mentioned, I would not object. However, I am not sure what Gabriela would think. I am sure you realize she is very strong-willed."

"Yes, she is. Despite all the beautiful women at Mamá's party, once I laid eyes on Gabriela, I didn't care about any of the others."

"My warning remains—leave the drugs behind. Otherwise, you will be sorry." The colonel stood. "I must return to my office. Gabriela is in the hacienda. Wait here. I will inform her you would like to speak with her."

"Thank you, Colonel."

THE DOOR BURST OPEN. Gabriela, dressed in a bright yellow skirt with a matching round-necked blouse, rushed into the library. "Oh, Alonzo! I've missed you so much. Why didn't you come to see me?" She darted into his open arms.

"Sorry, my dear. Too much work requiring my attention. Plus, there were some family issues I needed to sort out."

They kissed before taking a seat on the sofa.

"Papá told me you were very busy. He said he's providing you some guidance about dealing with the local community."

"Yes." He placed a hand on her partially bared shoulder. "Someone kidnapped my sisters—stepsisters. My—"

"Oh! How horrible!" Gabriela's hands shot up to her cheeks. "Papá will know what to do—he always does."

"I hope so. Even worse, someone wants my mother ... wants her dead."

She gasped and grabbed Alonzo's hands. "No wonder you couldn't visit me. The rumors must be true."

"What rumors?"

She shook her head as she stroked his face. "Don't think for one minute I haven't heard about the Barranquilla Cartel—run by your mother."

Alonzo blushed. "You are aware of the truth about my family and are still willing to meet with me?"

She nodded. "For now. But, you must do as el coronel commands."

"I want to spend my life with you."

Gabriela laughed. "First things first. Promise me you'll leave the drug business. I love you, but I don't want to be a young widow."

He reached over and kissed her on the cheek. "I promise. It won't be easy, but one day ... perhaps one day you'll marry me."

Her eyes sparkled. "Sí." *One day—soon. I hope.*

29

rmed Compound
Near Sincelejo, Colombia

JAVIER RESTRAINED Olivia's arms as AJ grabbed a shoulder and tugged her toward the door. "You can share your information later. Right now, we need to get out of here before someone realizes we're breaking you out of this place."

Olivia continued to resist as she tried to find a means to escape. "I'll scream for help."

"Try it. You'll be in the line of fire if anyone enters." AJ eased the door open and glanced in each direction along the corridor. "It's clear. C'mon."

"How do I know you won't kill me?" Olivia shook her head as she pulled away. "Ramon said I'd be safe here."

"Lady, do as she says." Javier released his grip. "Otherwise, I'll toss you over my shoulder and carry you."

Eyebrows raised, Olivia glared at him. "You wouldn't dare."

"Enough! We're the good guys and here to rescue you. You must trust us." AJ pointed toward the corridor. "We depart—now. Otherwise, my friend will do as he says. We don't have all night. Never know when a guard will make an unexpected appearance. If we have to shoot our way out, we will, and you could catch a stray bullet."

"Very well. Follow me." Olivia turned and headed to the window.

"Where are you going?" AJ shook her head.

"The hacienda's owner wants me to remain inside at all times, but I would go crazy here if I didn't leave the building from time to time. Ramon taught me to know my surroundings in case I need to escape. There's a rose trellis outside my window. You and I won't have any problem." She glanced at Javier and rocked her hand back and forth. "Him? He might be too heavy."

"Wait! Let me check first." AJ rushed to the window and pulled a curtain aside.

A full moon provided sufficient lighting to show two shapes moving along the grass toward the house. They stopped, and moments later, two brief lights flared. The pungent smell of marijuana and tobacco drifted toward the open window.

AJ dropped the curtain. "Two guards—stopped for a cigarette break. We'll go as soon as they leave. I'll lead the way." She turned to Olivia. "Do you have a bag? Take anything important with you. Don't worry about clothes or toiletries—we can buy you new ones."

Olivia rushed to the closet and grabbed a large handbag. "All set— I'm always prepared, thanks to Ramon's guidance. They didn't search my bag when we arrived, and there's a pistol hidden in the false bottom. A stiletto, too." She took two steps and stopped. "Wait! Where's Ramon?"

"We don't know. Except for the guards, the house is empty. We'll try to find him later. You're our priority."

Javier raised his brows before peeking through the curtains. "Coast is clear. Let's move." He shoved the curtains aside and opened the window before helping AJ onto the ledge.

"Got it." AJ used the trellis like a ladder and reached the ground in moments. She crouched next to the building, her SIG Sauer in hand.

"C'mon, lady. Your turn." Javier offered a hand to Olivia.

She accepted his offer, and within no time, she squatted beside AJ.

Javier placed one foot on the top horizontal bar of the trellis. He bounced on the wooden frame, trying to gauge if it would hold his weight. *Hope this is stronger than it appears. I want a controlled descent, not a—*

As he shifted his other foot onto the frame, his first one slid off. Off-balance, he struggled to secure a hold.

"Hurry up," AJ whispered.

He grunted. "I'm doing my best." Javier stopped his haphazard slide, thorns tearing long scratches on both of his arms. "Be right there."

When he shifted his weight to step down to the next horizontal crosspiece, he felt it loosen.

Craack!

As the broken wood gave way, Javier launched himself away from the trellis, completing a tuck and roll as he landed next to the women.

"Well done, Tarzan. Graceful like an elephant." AJ chuckled. "Unless the guards are dead, they'll be investigating."

"Where are the dogs?" Javier donned his NVGs and scanned the area. "Don't need another run-in with one of those wandering around."

"Just the one so far, but it should still be under the effect of the tranquilizer. We better dash for the wall. Keep Olivia between us."

"Go. I'll cover."

AJ and Olivia took off in a crouch, eating up the distance between the hacienda and the wall.

Three yards away, Olivia froze. "My bag!"

"Javier has it. Move!"

Blam! Blam!

Echoes from the shots rolled over the compound.

"Alto! Alto!"

"Hurry, guys!" Harry shouted from the top of the wall. "They're getting closer. Catch!"

AJ reached the wall before Javier and grabbed the knotted rope lowered by one of their support team. "You first, Olivia. More friends are on the wall." She turned and fired at a guard sneaking around the corner of a wooden shed. "Hurry!"

A bulky shadow appeared.

AJ aimed.

"Psst. It's me."

Recognizing Javier's voice, AJ climbed up the rope as gunfire intensified from the scattered guard force converging on their position.

Return fire from atop the wall kept the guards at bay, but they continued shooting.

"Ow! Damn!" Javier clutched his left forearm.

"Incoming!" Harry jumped down from the wall. He gestured to Javier. "Climb! I'll keep them pinned down."

Trying to minimize the use of his left arm, Javier hoisted himself up the rope. Before he reached the top of the wall, Larry leaned over and gave him a supportive tug. "Gotcha."

Moments later, Harry scampered over the wall.

"Are you alright, Javier?" AJ glanced at his arm.

"Yeah. Just knicked me. The thorns on the roses caused most of the damage. Let's get out of here before the guards organize themselves."

The five operatives and Olivia dropped down the other side of the wall and disappeared into the trees. AJ and Javier held onto Olivia's arms, and they pushed through the underbrush.

Shouts and sporadic gunfire continued as Samantha led the group up the hill, with Harry acting as rearguard.

Thirty minutes later, they climbed out of the ravine near their vehicles.

AJ opened one of the rear doors. "Olivia, you'll ride with Javier, Samantha, and me. The others will stay behind. Samantha, after we clear the area, check Javier's wound and patch him up if needed."

"Will do."

"Why aren't they coming with us?" Olivia climbed inside, followed by AJ.

"They'll watch for any pursuit."

"If there is, what will happen?"

"They'll deal with it."

"Where are we going?"

"Questions, questions." AJ chuckled. "We'll take you to a safe place."

"Wait! What about my girls? Some … somebody took them."

"We know. Don't worry, we're working on it."

"How will you find them?"

AJ shook her head. "Never mind—we have our methods."

Samantha climbed behind the wheel, while Javier rode shotgun.

AJ pulled out her encrypted iPad, checked the time, and sent an urgent message.

To: Fortress

From: Hunter

Package collected. En route to airport near subject's home. Request urgent transportation for four passengers from this airport or another viable location. Our ETA approximately four hours. Please acknowledge.

AJ glanced up. "Samantha, head to the coast and work your way north. We should have our destination confirmed soon." She kept her iPad open on her lap.

Except for an occasional sniffle from Olivia or a cough from Javier, little sound was heard as Samantha turned onto National Route 90.

AJ passed water bottles around. A ping signaled an incoming message.

To: Hunter

From: Fortress

Subject's airport will work. Cessna in the air now and will be on the ground before you arrive. Head to 'staff only' vehicular gate where a local contact will meet you. Identify yourself as Hunter, and the response will be Prey."

"Yes!" AJ thrust a hand toward the vehicle's roof and grinned. "Our destination is Barranquilla Airport."

At the mention of Barranquilla, a barely audible gasp escaped from Olivia before she regained her composure.

SAMANTHA STOPPED the SUV at the specified gate. Two men approached, one holding a clipboard. She lowered the window a couple of inches.

AJ and Javier faced the approaching men, their weapons held out of sight.

The man without the clipboard pointed. "Passengers park on the other side of the airport. This entrance is for airport personnel and aircrews."

"We're at the correct gate." Samantha gave the men a tentative smile. "I'm Hunter."

The man with the clipboard laughed. "Yeah, and I'm your prey." He turned to the gate guard. "They're expected. Please open the gate."

After they pulled inside the airport, and the gate was locked, 'Prey' climbed into the backseat next to AJ. "Two minutes, and we'll be at the plane."

As they rounded a corner of the terminal, AJ spotted a white Cessna Citation CJ1 with blue and red stripes. "Our ride?"

The man nodded. "After you board, I'll take care of your vehicle. Over the weekend, I'll return it to your safe house in Bogota."

AJ shook hands with him as the others climbed the steps and entered the cabin. Once she boarded, AJ knocked on the door to the cockpit and stepped inside. "Everyone's aboard. Let's take off before the authorities get suspicious."

The pilot and co-pilot nodded and resumed their departure preparations.

AJ joined the others and strapped herself into the seat closest to the door.

Moments later, the Cessna began moving and trundled toward the runway.

"This is your captain speaking. Please buckle your seatbelts and prepare for takeoff. The freedom bird is ready to fly."

Everyone sank back in his or her seats as the plane completed its taxi, and the pilot increased power.

Olivia glanced out the window, watching Barranquilla disappear in the distance as the aircraft increased speed and gained altitude. "Where are you taking me?"

AJ smiled. "Somewhere safe. Guantanamo Bay—Gitmo."

30

L a Cantina Maria
  Panama City, Panama

IN THE DARKENED rear of the cantina, Alberto sat at a round table covered with cigarette burns and gouges. Music wafted from the speakers positioned in each of the room's corners. A television above the bar replayed Panama's recent soccer match. A few of the customers cheered or whistled when the home team scored a goal.

He sipped his Coke while he people-watched. Draining the final dregs from his glass, he set it on a coaster and glanced at the clock over the exit. *Eleven a.m. He should be expecting my call.*

Alberto tugged his cell phone from his shirt pocket. After thumbing through his contact list, he hit the desired number.

On the sixth ring, someone answered. "Aló?"

"Michael, it's me—Alberto."

"As-salaam-alaikum."

Alberto glanced at the nearby tables—no one within earshot. "Wa-alaikum-salaam. Good to hear your voice, my brother."

"Same here, Alberto. How did the training go?"

"The teams were so eager, we finished early. They're on their way north as we speak."

"Understood. My teams are also headed north, although we did have a problem with one of the team leaders after you left. He was the one who was lenient with the live target when he should have been ruthless."

"What happened?"

"Días took care of him." Michael laughed.

"Doesn't his early departure leave the team a man short?"

"No. One of the men working for Días joined us."

Alberto scanned the room again. Everyone still engrossed in the game, he whispered, "Allahu akbar!"

Michael repeated the phrase. "Soon, we will strike. My teams will depart in the morning. Tomorrow afternoon, I'll fly to Mexico City. When will you arrive?"

"I'll be there tomorrow evening."

"See you at the airport, my brother."

"As Allah wills."

MacKenzie stared at the computer screen in her cubicle, surrounded by piles of documents. She swallowed a bite of her ham and cheese sandwich and grabbed the ringing telephone. "Seventy-five, fifty-four. MacKenzie speaking."

"Hey, Mac. Bob here from NSA. Got something you'll want."

"Hi, Bob. What's it gonna cost me?"

"I'm still waiting for you to agree to go to a baseball game with me." He chuckled. "I guess I can only hope. In the meantime, remember the terrorist trainer you're interested in—a guy named Michael?"

"If what you possess proves golden, I'll agree to the game, but nothing else."

"You drive a hard bargain. Okay, an hour ago, Michael received a call from someone named Alberto. Most of the conversation was in English, but they did use a couple of Arabic phrases. Turns out a couple of years ago, we lost track of a terrorist named Abdul Rahman. Two cell phone numbers were associated with him, but no activity for months."

"Why should this interest me?"

"Rahman is also known as Alberto Cabrera. We—I—think Alberto is his real name, and Rahman was the alias he used in the Middle East."

"So, this Alberto contacted Michael." MacKenzie leaned back in her chair, balancing it on two legs. "Anything noteworthy in their conversation?"

"Yes. The gist is the teams are heading north. Michael and Alberto are supposed to meet in Mexico City tomorrow night."

"Yes!" She brought the chair down on all four legs with a loud bang.

"Hello. Are you there? I heard a crash."

"Still here. Just brought my chair back to earth. This is fantastic news! Keep me posted."

"Okay. How about a game this weekend at Camden Yards?"

"Who's playing?"

"Orioles against the Tigers. Seats on the third-base side behind the dugout."

Damn! "Okay, Bob. I'll go. Send me an email later with the details."

"Will do."

MacKenzie hung up and hit a button on the intercom. "Makayla, drop whatever you're doing and come here."

Moments later, Makayla pushed the door open to AJ's office and smirked. "Does the boss know you've taken root in here?"

"If you don't tell her, she'll never find out." MacKenzie snickered. "Want to go to a baseball game this weekend?"

"Sure. Who with? Not you—you hate the game."

"Remember that cute guy, Bob, who has the hots for me—you —whatever?"

"Yeah. So?"

"I just agreed to go to a game. Please go—he won't be able to tell the difference."

"What's in it for me?"

MacKenzie laughed. "I know where you live—and I'll make your life miserable."

"We're roomies—you always make my life a misery. Yeah, I'll go. Is that all?"

MacKenzie rolled her eyes. "The terrorist called Michael will be in Mexico City tomorrow night. He's meeting with another thug. They've launched teams north. I better inform AJ so she can decide how we proceed."

"Yes!" They fist-bumped. "Any idea of a target?"

MacKenzie shook her head. "Not yet. Bob will call if they pick up any additional information. Why don't you grab us a coffee—the good stuff—my treat. I'll send a note now to AJ."

To: Hunter

From: Fortress

Target named Michael will be in Mexico City tomorrow night. He's joining someone referred to as Alberto. Details to follow.

They revealed their teams are proceeding north. No destination identified.

Should we arrange coverage with the station? Please advise.

THE PLANE CONTINUED its journey through the clear and calm skies. Javier loosened his seat belt and shook AJ's shoulder. "Psst. Wake up. Your iPad vibrated."

AJ shook her head, twisted the cap off a bottle of water, and quenched her thirst. "Why didn't you check—could be important."

"Uh ... it slid under you. Didn't think you wanted me rooting around while you were asleep."

AJ laughed. "I wasn't asleep, just thinking. Let's see what's up." She accessed her email and read the message from MacKenzie.

"Things are heating up. We need to deal with Olivia when we land, but someone needs to head to Mexico City."

"What about Harry and Larry?" Samantha stretched and yawned. "They'll be anxious for more action."

AJ nodded. "Excellent idea." She typed a response.

To: Harry, Larry, Fortress

From: Hunter

Many thanks for update. Don't wake up anyone at the station. We'll keep this among friends. Harry and Larry, stop twiddling your thumbs and get to Mexico City Airport ASAP. Photos required of bad guys mentioned in email chain. Determine who they meet. Any details regarding the teams they trained are of utmost importance.

Should the opportunity arise, capture and interrogate individuals. Gloves are off. Use whatever means necessary to disrupt their mission. Termination approved if deemed prudent.

AJ glanced at her watch. "Another thirty minutes or so before we begin our descent."

Javier gestured toward the sleeping Olivia and whispered, "What are we doing taking her to Gitmo? I didn't realize there are females imprisoned in the facility."

"There aren't. We'll put her in protective custody, but not with the terrorists in the detention center. We've done this before. Best I could come up with for now."

Javier shook his head. "I dunno."

"Relax." AJ smiled. "She'll be fine at Penny Lane."

"What's that?"

"A small facility we use on the island. The site is officially closed, but we still use it for occasional off-the-record meetings. All the comforts of home—kitchen facilities, showers, televisions, and real beds."

"What if something goes wrong or she escapes?"

AJ chuckled. "Where can she go? If she managed to get out of the building, the guards would find her. She'll be fitted with an ankle alarm bracelet. She won't be confined twenty-four seven but will only be allowed out under escort with two female guards." She gazed into Javier's eyes. "Should she escape, the guards know what to do."

bandoned Hacienda
Somewhere in Colombia

MARIA REELED under the backhanded slap from their captor, sending her crashing to the floor. Blood spurted from her lip as Silvina rushed to her sister's side.

The assailant pulled a serrated knife from his belt and stretched toward them. Light gleamed along the seven-inch blade.

"No!" Valentina grabbed a lamp from the dresser and smashed him on the back of his head.

Thump!

She hit him a second time before tossing the lamp onto the bed.

He crumpled onto the carpet as Maria and Silvina scooted away, crouching against the wall, as they tried to make themselves as small as possible. They held each other as they sobbed, tears streaming down their cheeks.

Silvina forked her fingers through Maria's hair, trying to calm her.

Valentina kicked the man in the ribs—he didn't move. *I hope I killed him after what he tried to do to me. He'd have raped me if I hadn't threatened to cut his penis off when he's asleep. If it weren't for the girls, he'd be dead.*

She stomped on his knife hand and yanked the blade away.

"Is he dead?" Silvina rose, helping Maria to her feet.

"I don't think so." Valentina knelt beside the unmoving body and checked for a pulse. "He's still alive, but has a very weak pulse." She pointed to the dresser. "Check inside the drawers and find something we can use to tie him up."

Silvina and Maria rushed to the unit and yanked open the top two drawers.

Maria held up two black, red, and yellow striped ties. "Ugh! Ugly. Will these do?"

"Bring them here, and we'll find out. Silvina, help me roll him over."

Together Valentina and Silvina turned the man onto his side, allowing his head to bounce on the floor.

Valentina used the ties to secure his wrists, looping the ends through his belt. She tightened them until she knotted the pieces together. "Grab something to shove in his mouth. We don't want him yelling for help."

Silvina snatched a pair of white socks from a drawer and pulled them apart. "How about one of these?"

"Perfect." Valentina forced the sock into the man's mouth.

"But our captor is Uncle Edgar." An anguished expression crossed Maria's face as she clasped her hands. "What if he can't breathe?"

I don't care if he suffocates. He got what he deserved. "I pretended to be his daughter, hoping you might tell me more details about your family. It didn't work. I'm sorry, but he forced me to help him." Valentina shook her head. "I don't remember my father—he left when I was younger than you." She searched through the man's pockets and extracted a key. "We'll lock him in here."

After shutting and securing the door, Valentina and the two girls rushed along the corridor and down the stairs. "We're safe for now. He sent the guards away earlier." She hugged each girl.

"Gracias, Valentina," both girls said. They squeezed her arms.

"Let's find something to drink to calm you." She led them into the kitchen. Maria and Silvina sat at the table while Valentina opened the fridge. *Need to keep their minds off what's happened.* "You have a choice—I can make some warm milk, or there's juice. My mama always gave me warm milk when I was upset. Sometimes, she added some cocoa."

Silvina's hand shot in the air. "Juice!"

Maria frowned. "Silvina, Mamá says we must drink plenty of milk each day, so we make strong bones, and they don't become bitter."

Valentina laughed. "I think your Mamá meant so the bones don't become brittle."

"Oh. I thought they were the same." Maria pouted.

"In that case, I'll have juice, por favor." Silvina smirked. "Mamá says brittle bones is an old person's disease—plenty of time to drink milk when we grow up. We're still young."

"I dunno, Silvina." Maria crossed her arms. "I'll tell Mamá." She turned to Valentina. "Cold milk, por favor. With cocoa."

"Oh, Maria! Quit being so ... so practical." Silvina rolled her eyes.

After pouring their beverages and a glass of milk for herself, Valentina grabbed one of the mismatched chairs and joined them at the scarred wooden table. *They're scared—who wouldn't be? Hopefully, the drinks will keep their mind off what happened.* "We must decide what to do—where to go."

Tears began streaming down Maria's face again. "Why did Uncle Edgar take us away from Mamá? Won't Papá be angry with him?"

"When Mamá and Papá find us, we'll tell them Uncle Edgar took us from school but didn't take us home." Silvina reached out and patted Maria's arm. "They'll call the policía, and he'll be taken away."

"Can't we call the policía now?" Maria glanced at Valentina. "Isn't there a phone?"

Valentina shook her head. "No house phone and your Uncle Edgar took my cell phone." She smiled as she stood. "Come—we'll look in his room. Perhaps, we'll find my phone or his—I know he made several calls since we've been here, although I couldn't hear the conversations."

The girls followed her out of the kitchen and to a room at the back of the house. Valentina tried the handle—locked. "We'll have to go near the room where he kept you. I think he left a bunch of keys on the table in the hallway."

Maria shuddered. "I won't go back there. What if he gets loose and hurts us?"

"Wait here with your sister. I'll check."

IN THE CALM EVENING, the rumble of an approaching vehicle could be heard. Tires crunched on the gravel outside the house. The engine cut out, a door slammed, and footsteps neared the front of the building.

Silvina dashed to the window and pulled a curtain aside. "Wait for Valentina to return. Don't open the door."

Maria grabbed the drape from Silvina and glanced outside. "But it's Papá! He's found us!"

Before Silvina could grab her older sister, Maria unlocked the door and yanked it open. "Papá! Papá! I knew you'd come for us." She rubbed her tear-stained eyes.

Pedro put his arms around his daughter. "Of course! No one could keep me from you. As soon as I was aware you were missing, I began looking all over Colombia for you and Silvina. You're safe now—I'll protect you."

Silvina stepped forward into Pedro's embrace. "Where's Mamá?"

Pedro shook his head. "Waiting at home for you." He glanced around. "Aren't you going to invite me inside? I could use a drink of water."

Maria took Pedro by the hand. "This way, Papá." She led him into the kitchen and pointed at the table. "Sit down, Papá, and I'll get you a drink."

"Are you girls alone? Who brought you to this abandoned hacienda?"

"Uncle Edgar." Silvina slid into a chair next to her father. "He's kept us locked up most of the time—he's a bad man."

"Where is he now?"

Silvina smiled. "He's tied up in the room where he kept us. Valentina knocked him out with a lamp."

Thump. Thump.

Crash.

Pedro looked up at the ceiling. "We better go see what's happening—sounds like a fight."

They rushed up the stairs. Silvina pushed past Pedro.

"Alto, little one. I know you're brave, but let me go first."

Silvina shook her head as she shoved open the bedroom door.

Inside, Valentina stood over a dazed Edgar, the remains of another lamp in her hands. Her breathing ragged, a crazed expression etched her features. "He got loose! The ties must have stretched."

"Valentina! Enough! Put down the lamp." Pedro grabbed her arm with one hand and yanked a pistol from a coat pocket with the other.

She tossed the lamp on the floor and turned her glazed eyes toward his voice. "Who are you?"

"I'm Pedro, your father. Don't you remember me? What are you doing here?"

She stared at his face before pointing at Edgar. "You look like him." Tears dotted Valentina's cheeks as she clenched her fists. "Why do you care why I'm here? You left me—and Mamá—when we needed you."

"I haven't seen you in years, but a friend managed to take photos of you from time to time. I hated to leave you behind, but your mother gave me no choice. It was to leave both of you behind, or she would turn me in to the authorities."

"I don't believe you." Valentina's eyes grew wide as she took a step back. "What did you do?" Tears began trickling down her cheeks.

"I killed someone—one of your mother's lovers." Pedro pointed his weapon back at Edgar. "What's one more?" He pulled the trigger. "No one steals my girls!"

Maria, Silvina, and Valentina screamed as the round entered Edgar's forehead. His head jerked, and his body slumped, twitching once before remaining still.

Pedro swung toward the girls, the weapon aimed in their direction. "Tell me where Olivia is hiding. She's not at the hacienda." He grinned, the glow from a ceiling light catching a gold-capped tooth. "Who's next?"

Valentina pushed Maria and Silvina behind her. "You'll have to kill me first. Leave them alone—they're innocent." She lunged at Pedro, her eyes burning with hatred.

"Stay back!" Pedro aimed his pistol at Valentina's chest. "I'm warning you—for the last time. Stop now, or I'll shoot!"

32

Temporary Command Center
Outside Colon, Panama

A SHORT WHISTLE pierced the air and drew the attention of the Snakes. When they crowded around, Adder gestured towards his iPad. "The vehicles we're tracking are leaving the compound. Someone better go back to the listening post to find out what's happening."

Mamba jumped to his feet. "On my way." He rushed out of the building, followed by Rattler.

Adder glanced at Viper. "Time for a serious talk with Blanca. She knows what's going on."

"What if she won't tell us anything? Or worse, gives us false information to lead us on a goose chase?"

"If we don't have any success, we'll turn her over to the local CIA boys. AJ gave me a contact number." Adder grimaced. "So much for this being a cushy assignment—looks like we're behind the eight ball." An email, which had been forwarded by Javier earlier in the day, caught his eye. "Damn! I hate failure. According to intel, our targets abandoned their compound, and are heading north. No known destination, but their trainer is proceeding to Mexico City."

"As soon as Mamba and Rattler provide a SITREP, we'll decide on our next move. In the meantime, let's keep our date."

BLANCA LAY SPRAWLED across the bed when Viper and Adder entered the room. She sat up and glared at them. "So, snakes, where have you been? A person could die of boredom waiting for you to come back." *At least they're cute, although I won't be able to sweet-talk my way out of here.*

Adder loosened the bindings securing her hands and thrust a bottle of water at her.

She twisted the cap off and tipped the bottle back, taking huge gulps. When the last drop was gone, she glanced around for somewhere to put the empty bottle, and finally decided to let it drop to the floor. "So, what's up?"

Viper crossed his arms. "It's time for you to—"

He yanked a vibrating phone out of his pocket and hit a couple of buttons as he stepped into the hallway. "Talk to me."

"Rattler and I checked out the compound. Everyone's gone. Gimme a minute."

Viper heard Mamba and Rattler speaking in the background, but couldn't understand any of their conversation.

Mamba's voice came through the phone. "Sorry about that. We're on our way back and came across an old man on a burro. Rattler spoke with him. He said while leading his animal along the highway about an hour ago, two buses almost ran them down."

"Did he know where the buses went?" Viper pursed his lips.

"All he knew was they were heading inland away from Colon."

"Understood. Return ASAP, and we'll sort out what to do next." Viper cut the connection and dropped the phone in his pocket. He returned to the room and glared at Blanca. "Where are the buses going?"

"What time is it?"

"Why? What does it matter?" Viper glanced at the large face on his watch and turned his wrist so she could see it.

Blanca gave him a lackluster smile and raised her bound hands. "They should be at Panama City Tocumen Airport now. The men are taking a chartered flight."

"Where?"

Blanca shrugged. "Why should I tell you?" *I can always lie. Before they find out, I'll be gone.*

Adder pulled out his blade and stepped closer. "If you don't tell us everything you know, and right now, I'll skin you."

"You wouldn't dare. Your government won't let you, and I know my rights."

"Yeah. The right to die if you continue withholding information."

"Big man. You're pretty brave—at the moment. Let me loose, and I'll teach you a lesson."

Click.

Viper aimed his SIG Sauer at Blanca's face. "You have until the count of three to enlighten us. One. Two. Three." He pulled the trigger, the round whizzing by her head and into the wall.

Blanca jumped but remained silent.

Viper aimed at her right knee.

"Wait!" She raised her arms. "Do you have a pen and paper?"

"Why?"

"There's a number you need to call." Her gaze shifted from Viper to Adder. "Please." She licked her lips.

Viper gestured to Adder, who left the room, returning a couple of minutes later. Still holding his knife, he handed her the pen and paper with his free hand.

Blanca scribbled a series of numbers on the paper and held it out.

Viper snatched the offering. He rubbed the barrel of his weapon against the side of his head as he examined the note. "Colombian phone number. Who is it?"

Blanca swallowed before her mouth gaped open. "My—my handler at the American embassy in Bogota. He works for the DEA. I've been providing him information for years regarding what I learned from my brother about the drug cartels."

"You're evading my question." Viper waved his pistol in her face. "Where is the chartered plane going?"

"Promise to call my handler?"

Viper hesitated before nodding. "I'll talk to him, but I'm not promising anything. However, your information better check out."

"Guadalajara."

"Mexico?"

She nodded.

Viper turned to Adder. "Keep an eye on her. I need to send a message to Cobra and Taipan."

VIPER WENT INTO THE KITCHEN, sat at the table, and opened his iPad. *My fault our targets scattered. Coverage of the camp should have been tighter.* "Damn!" He slammed a fist on the table before he began typing.

To: Cobra, Jacaranda

From: Viper

Targets flew the coop. Captive, who says she's a DEA snitch, revealed the destination is Guadalajara, Mexico, via chartered aircraft. Recommend we turn her over to available contact in Panama City and follow. Please advise.

Viper listened as a vehicle approached the house, followed by footsteps dashing up the stairs. He pulled out his weapon and moved beyond direct line of the entrance.

The door popped open.

Viper relaxed and returned to his seat.

Mamba and Rattler joined Viper. "Sorry, boss. They got away." Mamba pointed at Viper's iPad. "Any orders?"

"Just waiting for a response. Shouldn't take long as they'll be landing in Gitmo soon."

Ping.

Viper pulled up the incoming message.

To: Viper, Jacaranda, Fortress, Taipan

From: Cobra

All Snakes proceed Guadalajara posthaste. Onsite contact will meet you at airport with updated intel and new weapons upon arrival. Turn captive over to local CIA office before departure.

Viper turned the device around for Mamba and Rattler to read. He stood and rushed into the bedroom. "Secure her and call the number AJ gave you. We're dumping her and heading to Mexico."

"Wait!" Blanca jerked her head back and forth. "You promised to call my contact in Colombia."

"Not my problem. I'm following orders." He glanced at Adder. "Be prepared to depart in fifteen minutes."

AFTER HANDING Blanca off to the local CIA contact in Colon, the four men climbed into their vehicle with Adder behind the wheel. "Next stop, Tocumen Airport." Viper grimaced as he tried to type on his iPad while they rocketed along the highway.

"Do we have tickets?" Mamba yawned as he gazed at the lush green scenery, interspersed with occasional fields of corn and banana trees.

"Working on it." Viper's hands flew across the keypad. "Yes!" He punched a fist in the air. "Yes! I upgraded us to business class, so we were able to get on the next flight. Economy was filled."

Rattler shook his head. "Aren't we supposed to travel economy?"

"Yes, but Javier said to hurry, so I made a command decision."

An hour later, Adder slammed on the brakes and skidded to a halt outside the airport. "Get my boarding pass. I'll drop the car off in the nearest parking lot."

After the others hoisted their packs and dashed into the terminal,

Adder headed for a short-term lot. "C'mon, c'mon." He raced down one line of vehicles and up the next. In the third row, he found an empty slot. After hooking his bag, he locked the car and hotfooted to the building. Once he cleared customs, he hurried to the gate, arriving as the others began boarding.

"About time, Adder." Viper grinned. "Let's get on board—drinks are on me."

"Uh, aren't they free in business?"

"Yeah, but I bought the tickets."

The others laughed as someone slapped Viper on the back.

THE AIRCRAFT BOUNCED along the taxiways and took its position on the runway. Moments later, the pilot engaged the engines, and speeding down the asphalt strip, they soared into the air.

Viper sipped on the free champagne before raising his glass. "Here's to the next part of the mission." He closed his eyes. *No failure this time. Let's hope we catch the bastards before it's too late.*

33

P enny Lane
Guantanamo Bay, Cuba

AJ TIGHTENED her seatbelt as the sleek Cessna Citation CJ1 knifed through the clouds hovering over Guantanamo Bay NAS Airport. Once on the ground, the aircraft taxied toward the terminal as directed by the flashing lights of a 'Follow Me' truck. The vehicle led them to an area away from the building, where the pilot cut the engines.

Olivia pressed her face against the window, watching as armed guards took up positions around the plane. She turned to AJ. "Why the guards? You told me I wasn't under arrest."

"Don't worry. This is standard procedure when this aircraft arrives. Not everyone brought here is a friend or someone who needs help. Many are terrorists." AJ smiled. "We'll take good care of you, and no one will be able to reach you here." *I hope. Never had someone worth so much money visiting Penny Lane. Will someone try to bribe the guards?*

The lone cabin crewmember opened the hatch after ground staff pounded on the door. He secured the panel and motioned for AJ, Samantha, and Olivia to depart.

"What about him?" Olivia gestured toward Javier, who stopped at the doorway. "Isn't he coming with us?"

"No. He has another mission. Samantha, please escort Olivia to our vehicle. I'll be there in a moment." She turned to Javier. "Be careful. Things are moving forward at a fast clip."

"Aw shucks. Nothing will happen to me. Besides, I'll have four Snakes to protect me."

AJ gave a soft chuckle, leaned forward, and gave him a peck on the cheek.

Javier blushed. "I may never wash my face again. I'll remember your touch forever."

Her face lit up with a wide smile and sparkling eyes. "Take care of yourself. See you soon." AJ turned and dashed down the steps, pausing to glance back at Javier before she slid into the rear passenger door of an armored Mercedes SUV.

He gave a brief wave as the crewmember closed the hatch.

"Let's head to Penny Lane." She leaned back in her seat.

The chauffeur nodded at AJ as he waited for the Cessna to taxi out of the area and back toward the flight line. The guards followed the Mercedes in a second vehicle.

"AJ, will you show me around the base?" Olivia nodded toward a squat brownish building on their right. "Is that where we're going?"

"No to your first question. There are prisoners here who would riot if they saw such an attractive woman." She laughed. "I know from experience. Since you're so beautiful, no tour for you."

"How long will it take to get to this Penny Lane you mentioned?"

"A few minutes. It's several hundred yards from the prison's administrative offices. That's the building you pointed at earlier."

Olivia nodded. "I wish Maria and Silvina were with me."

"Don't worry, we'll find them. I have my best people working on it right now."

The vehicles passed a ridge covered with thick scrub and cacti and turned onto a dirt road.

"Almost there, Olivia."

The convoy drove through two fences topped with concertina wire. The guard shacks were empty, and the barriers raised—a testament to times in the past when Penny Lane was an active facility.

The vehicles pulled between two rows of four small cottages and stopped.

One of the female security officers jumped out of the chase vehicle, rushed forward, and opened Olivia's door. Samantha and AJ climbed out and joined them.

"Where will I live?" Olivia glanced at the drab single-story buildings and frowned.

"Not up to the standards of your hacienda, but it'll do for the short term." AJ pointed at one of the cottages in the right-hand row. "You'll be in the second one from the left. The security officers will be in the first one, and Samantha and I will be in the one on the other side of you."

"Will I be able to go for a walk?"

AJ shook her head. "Not on your own. Procedures call for you to have protection at all times, but of course, you can ask them to walk with you. When inside, don't try to leave. Sensors on the door and windows will alert everyone to a possible intrusion, and the response will be immediate." She gazed at Olivia. "And deadly."

Olivia sighed. "Seems like a prison—without the bars."

"The same processes used to keep people in are just as effective when reversed to protect you from people who want to do you harm. Once we recover your children and the threats to you are removed, you'll be free to return to Barranquilla. Of course, the DEA and others will want to speak with you."

Olivia rolled her eyes. "Of course."

"Let's check out your new home." AJ motioned for Olivia to walk in front of her, while Samantha brought up the rear. After digging the keys out of a pocket, AJ handed them to Olivia. "I'll let you do the honors."

"Where did you get the keys?"

AJ laughed. "I have a master key for all of the cottages, but the driver handed me a set for you before we got out of the car."

"Oh." She took the keys from AJ and unlocked the door.

They stepped inside.

Olivia turned in a circle, glancing at the brown upholstered sofa and chairs facing a large screen television mounted on the wall. "Who did the decor? They should be shot." She crossed her arms and screwed her lips into a grimace. "I suppose this is how the peasants live."

AJ and Samantha laughed. "No peasants here, just the low bid winner for a government contract. At least it's clean and doesn't leak when it rains." AJ gestured toward the TV. "You'll receive several Spanish channels through a satellite connection."

Olivia pointed to three doors. "What's behind them?"

"The one on the left is your bedroom. The middle is the bathroom, and the one on the right is your kitchen. The fridge and cupboards are stocked with basic supplies. Make a list of what you'd like, and we'll provide those."

Olivia opened the middle door and peeked inside. "No bathtub. At least there's a shower. I'm dying for one. Do you mind?"

"Go ahead. We'll amuse ourselves while you freshen up." AJ sat on the sofa and pulled out her iPad. "Might as well find out if there are any updates."

"I'll check the other rooms to make sure everything is secure." Samantha disappeared into the kitchen.

AJ found a message from Javier saying he'd be joining the Snakes in two hours in Guadalajara and that he missed her.

She smiled as she typed a brief response. *I miss you, too. We make a good team.* AJ leaned back on the sofa. *Wonder if things will go any further?* She shook her head. *I'm acting like he's the first male to pay me any attention, although most stay away when they learn what I do for a living. Plenty of time in the future to worry about things developing with Javier—if they do. The mission comes first.*

AJ opened a second email, this one from MacKenzie.

To: Hunter

From: Fortress

Be advised intel picked up a conversation between Días and someone named Pedro. Días inquired about Maria and Silvina, to which Pedro responded they were fine, and he was with the girls. He stated they'd remain in position for at least the next two days. Coordinates of nearest cell tower attached.

"Yes!" AJ punched the air. "Hey, Samantha, come here."

Samantha rushed into the room, her pistol drawn. "What's up?"

"Read."

Samantha's eyes widened as she read the short message. "Are we going after them?"

"You bet. Let the security officers know we'll be leaving ASAP and request additional coverage until we return."

"On it."

AJ heard the bathroom door open, and she looked up, a grin on her face.

Olivia approached, dressed in a fluffy pink robe and matching slippers, using a towel to dry the ends of her hair. "I feel much better. Thank you."

"You're welcome." AJ gestured to a chair. "Please sit. There is something I need to mention to you."

"What is it?"

"We just found out where Maria and Silvina are being held. Do the names Días and Pedro mean anything to you?"

Anger flashed in Olivia's eyes. Her body stiffening with rage, she leaned forward. "Pedro is my good-for-nothing husband—I don't know where he is. I hope he rots in hell. Días is a FARC commander trying to take over my business. Both are bastardos and deserve to die."

A knock on the door made AJ jump to her feet. She rushed to stand in front of Olivia and motioned for Samantha toward the door.

Samantha checked the peephole and yanked the door open.

Three female security officers walked in, each dressed in black uniforms with holsters attached to web belts.

AJ faced Olivia. "These officers will remain with you until Samantha and I return. Nothing to fear—they're trustworthy and won't take bribes from anyone, so you're safe with them."

"Where are you going?"

"After your daughters." She stared into Olivia's eyes. "I'll bring them home."

34

P enny Lane
        Guantanamo Bay, Cuba

FLIPPING HER PHONE CLOSED, AJ nodded toward the others. "We'll be departing in about two hours. We're in luck—there's an inbound plane which can take us back to Colombia."

"I'm going, too." Olivia crossed her arms and stared at AJ. "You can't stop me."

"Ain't happening, lady." AJ shook her head. "No way. Out of the question. There's still the contract out for your death. Besides, this is what I do, and I don't want you in the way." AJ gave a slight smile. "Don't worry. Samantha and I will recover your daughters for you. That's a promise." *Although I'm not sure when you'll see them.*

Olivia sighed. "What about Pedro?"

"What would you like us to do with him? He appears to be the one behind the kidnapping of Maria and Silvina."

Her face reddened. Olivia gritted her teeth and clenched her fists. "Our marriage was over long ago. Do what you want with him. Cut off his cojones with a rusty blade and feed them to the pigs while he watches." An evil grin washed over her face. "You can kill him for all I care—just make him suffer."

AJ nodded. "As soon as we free your girls, I'll instruct your guards to let you know they're safe. We'll decide later what to do with Pedro. However, if he resists while were freeing Maria and Silvina, all bets are off."

"Gracias—and good hunting." She removed a charm bracelet from her wrist. "Maria and Silvina gave me this last Christmas. Please show this to them, and they will know they are safe with you. If I can't accompany you, at least take my prayers for a safe mission. I don't care who gets in your way, but bring them back to me."

AJ tilted her head as she strolled to the door.

After they left Olivia's new home, AJ pulled Samantha aside. "As soon as we arrive in Barranquilla, we'll head into the mountains. One of our contacts will provide transportation. He'll also be an extra gun if the situation warrants, but I want to recover the girls without any bloodshed—if possible."

"How many perps do you think we'll be up against?" Samantha pointed at an approaching vehicle. "Our ride?"

"Yeah. The driver will take us to the runway so we can board as soon as the aircraft lands." AJ adjusted the straps of her backpack, so it rode higher on her back. "Other than Pedro, there's no telling how many we'll face. Best to be prepared, so I requested back-up SIG Sauers, extra ammo, and a few flashbangs. A couple of M4s, too."

"Better include NVGs, an emergency medical kit, and zip ties."

"Great idea."

THE GULFSTREAM G650 touched down at Barranquilla Airport. As soon as the aircraft reached its designated parking slot, a black Denali SUV with tinted windows pulled alongside. The man previously identified as Prey jumped out of the vehicle and approached the plane as the stairs opened and locked into position. He dashed inside. "Hey, Hunter. Welcome back. Let's not dally. They're going to move the plane into a hangar for maintenance." He gave AJ a knowing glance. "If we're quick, this'll be our ride out."

AJ and Samantha shook his hand before picking up their packs.

"The items you requested are in the SUV. Should take about an hour to get in position."

AJ nodded. "You're going with us?"

"Yeah." He chuckled. "I'm due some time off, and figured this was the best time to take it." Grabbing their bags, he led the way to the vehicle.

AJ climbed in the front passenger seat while Samantha sat in the back.

"There are two boxes in the back with your stuff. I'll pull into a truck stop on the way so we can prepare. Don't want to do it here— too many watchful eyes."

After leaving the airport, Prey sped along a near-empty street, taking a right at the first traffic light. Leaving the commercial area behind, the streets were now lined with a variety of single homes and three-story apartment buildings. Minutes later, the vehicle merged with traffic onto a twisting road heading in the direction of Baranoa.

The three operatives settled into a comfortable silence. Before long, light snoring could be heard from the back seat.

Prey glanced in the rearview mirror. "Your partner's asleep."

AJ gave a soft chuckle. "Youngsters—can't keep up with their elders."

They passed a sign indicating three kilometers to Baranoa. "We'll be at the truck stop in a couple of minutes. Better wake her."

AJ reached back and grabbed Samantha's leg. "Nap time's over."

"Huh?" Samantha yawned and stretched. "You ruined an exciting dream—now I won't know how it ends."

Prey turned on his blinker and followed the signs for their destination. He slid to a halt at the pumps. "I'll fill up now—just in case. Would one of you grab some coffee? Afterward, I'll pull behind the cargo vehicles, and we'll prepare."

"I'll go. Need to stretch my legs." Samantha hopped out of the SUV and dashed inside.

When Samantha returned, she was carrying a large paper bag. "Coffee, Cokes, pastries, and bananas. Name your poison." She pulled out a Coke and a pastry and set them on the seat next to her.

Prey and AJ opted for a coffee.

"Let's do this." AJ gestured to Prey. "Find a sheltered spot for us to get ready."

He nodded and pulled away from the pumps, angling for the area where long-distance drivers parked while they ate and slept.

Satisfied they were blocked from anyone's view and the nearby vehicles were empty or the occupants were in the back sleeping, the three climbed out of the SUV and headed to the rear.

Prey opened the latch and gestured at their cargo. "Weapons and ammo are in the left box. Everything else is in the right one. The backpack's mine, and so is the tennis bag."

AJ laughed. "Don't think there'll be time for tennis."

"True. But we might want the breaching gun hidden inside."

AJ pulled out web belts with holsters and ammo pouches attached and passed them to the others. Buckling on her own, she reached back into the box and grabbed two SIG Sauers, followed by several magazines.

Samantha handed out NVGs, zip ties, and flashbangs. "Almost forgot." She reached back into the package and yanked out three D80 military knives.

After arming themselves, they hopped back in the SUV. Prey eased out of the parking lot and onto the highway. "Another twenty clicks, and we'll veer onto a trail near Arroyo Grande."

"Gotcha. MacKenzie said there should be a cell tower by the river, which is where Pedro's phone registered." AJ frowned. "I hope the kids are still in the area." *And alive.*

The road narrowed as they approached a single-lane bridge over the river. On the left, a cell tower dominated the landscape, while on the right, a faint trail disappeared into the flora.

Prey pulled onto the path and maneuvered through the thickening bushes.

AJ pointed to the right. "Park over there. We don't want the noise of the vehicle to alert anyone. We'll hoof it from here."

They scurried along the trail, coming to a path leading away from the water and stopped.

"Listen." AJ swiped her hair behind her ear, holding her hand cupped under it. "Sounds like a waterfall or some rapids. Let's check out this path."

As dusk descended, they crept through the foliage. In front of them, a two-story hacienda was tucked among the trees. Dim light escaped from a window on the upper floor. They crept forward.

"No vehicles. Samantha, head around back—check for access. Prey, do the same on the right." AJ gestured in the directions she wanted them to go. "We'll meet back here."

Samantha and Prey nodded. They slithered toward their destinations.

AJ scanned the front of the house. *Don't see anyone. Except for the light, it appears abandoned.* She scampered up four steps and tried the door.

Locked.

AJ pulled a fiber optic cable from a pouch and slid it under the door. *No one—empty room ahead. A door to the left, one to the right.*

She returned to her initial position as Samantha and Prey returned.

"There's a back door, but it doesn't appear anyone's used it recently. A heavy trunk is blocking access." Samantha stifled a sneeze. "Sorry. Must be allergic to something."

"I glanced in a window and spotted a guard." Prey gestured toward the house. "He was lounging in a chair, smoking a cigarette."

"There might be more, but we'll have to chance it. Let's move."

Weapons drawn, they inched up the stairs.

Prey readied the breaching gun and glanced at AJ.

"No—we need to be quiet. Use your lock picks." She took a deep breath to relax. Ready, she nodded at Prey.

Samantha, Prey, and AJ crept back to the door. While Prey worked on the lock, Samantha and AJ monitored the area for activity.

Snick.

Prey nudged the door, and it swung inward.

They rushed inside as a guard appeared, his AK-47 level with his waist. He swung his weapon toward them.

Thunk!

A knife thudded into his chest, and he collapsed to the floor without firing a shot. Blood pumped out of his body onto the floor.

AJ checked for a pulse and shook her head. She gestured for the others to spread out.

Samantha yanked her knife from the dead guard, wiped the blade on his body, and headed through an archway.

Moments later, Prey and Samantha returned. Both gave a thumbs-down signal.

AJ turned and headed upstairs, the others following in single file.

She glanced to her right.

A single door.

AJ tried the handle, and the door swung inward.

A toilet.

They headed past the stairs to the opposite end of the house. Three doors, with a glimmer of light showing under the edge of the middle one.

Samantha turned the knob and pushed inside.

A shadow rushed toward her when she entered. As a machete arced toward Samantha's back, AJ leveled her SIG and fired.

The man collapsed to the floor, a hole through his heart. He twitched once and remained still.

On the bed, two figures squirmed, tied together, with tape across their mouths. Their eyes were wide with fright.

A second guard stood next to the girls with his weapon pointed them. "Leave or I'll kill them."

Without hesitation, AJ leveled her pistol and blasted a hole in his forehead. His head snapped back as blood and brain matter decorated the wall behind him.

AJ rushed forward and checked for a pulse. *Good. Met his maker.*

While Prey stood guard at the entrance to the room, AJ and Samantha pulled their knives and cut through the ropes binding the girls.

AJ teased the ends of the tape before giving a quick yank.

"Ow!" The girl rubbed her lips where the tape had been. "I'm Silvina." She pointed at her sister. "That's Maria. Did Mamá send you?"

"Yes, dear." AJ pulled Olivia's bracelet from her pocket. "She gave me this to show you we're the good guys."

Tears staining their cheeks, Maria and Silvina reached out and touched the bracelet.

Silvina smiled. "It's Mamá's. We gave this to her for Christmas."

"Yes, she told me." AJ glanced around. "Where's your father —Pedro?"

Silvina shrugged. "He left and took Valentina with him."

"Who's Valentina?"

"Papá said she was his daughter, too."

AJ frowned but held her tongue. *What's going on? Olivia never mentioned another daughter. From a previous marriage?*

Meanwhile, Samantha held Maria close, the young girl's chest heaving with sobs.

"Come, girls. We'll get you out of here and someplace safe." AJ wiped a tear from her eye. *They must live in some world where this doesn't seem to phase them. Poor girls.*

Maria snuggled into Samantha. "Are you taking us to Mamá?"

AJ wrapped an arm around Silvina's shoulders and led her out of the room. "Not yet. We're going to America."

35

I nternational Flight
Between Colombia and the U.S.

AJ GLANCED at the seats where Silvina and Maria were curled up, fast asleep. *One day, perhaps I'll have some kids. If I do, I hope they're like Silvina. She reminds me of myself when I was her age. Sassy. Bold. Courageous. Bet she loves being challenged.* AJ smiled before returning her attention to an email from MacKenzie.

To: Hunter

From: Fortress

Congrats on recovery. Collection officials will meet plane upon arrival in El Paso before your departure to Mexico.

AJ acknowledged the message, closed her iPad, and shut her eyes. *A couple of hours before touchdown. Enough time for a decent power nap.*

Samantha nudged AJ and whispered, "Aren't they cute? Too bad we have to give them back."

AJ yawned and nodded. "Yes. But things can change." She wiggled her eyebrows with a cagey grin before closing her eyes again, thinking of Javier. *When this is over, what will happen? Is there anything between us, or is it just my imagination?*

The aircraft continued its journey to the northeast. With little cloud cover and wind, the flight remained turbulence-free.

The next thing AJ knew, she heard a ping before the pilot came on the intercom. "Fasten your seatbelts, please. We're approaching the coast, and it'll be a bit bumpy for the remainder of the trip as there's a storm front between us and our destination."

Startled from her nap, AJ sat upright, always ready. She unbuckled her belt and stepped over to Maria and Silvina. Neither stirred during the pilot's announcement, so she gave each a slight nudge until they came to.

They both jumped at her touch. Maria gasped, while Silvina came up with a fist, determination etched across her young face.

"Whoa! Just wanted to make sure you're buckled in. There'll be some bumps—turbulence. After what you've been through, I didn't want you to worry."

"We're okay, but thank you." Silvina smiled and grasped Maria's hand. "We've flown before."

THE GULFSTREAM TOUCHED down about an hour later and taxied to a quiet area of the airport. A white Ford Crown Victoria with a broad green diagonal stripe on the door waited for them. Leaning against the vehicle were two women, both dressed in civilian clothes.

AJ led Maria and Silvina down the stairs toward the vehicle and introduced the girls.

"Where are we going?" Silvina glanced around, eyes wide.

"Where's Mamá?" Maria squeezed Silvina's arm. "I want to see her."

"Your mother is safe. We'll reunite you with her as soon as I take care of some urgent business. It might take a few days, but these women will look after you."

"We'll have a great time, girls." A tall, willowy brunette spoke to them in broken Spanish. "My name's Michelle, but you can call me Mickie."

"Maria and I both speak English. Will it be easier for you?"

Mickie smiled and nodded.

"Are you hungry? We can eat whatever you want. Afterward, we'll watch a Disney movie."

"What's your name?" Silvina glanced at the short woman with blonde hair. "Do you have a nickname, too?"

The woman laughed. "Please call me Andi. My real name is Andromeda."

Silvina frowned. "You have a funny name. What kind of name is that?"

Andi winked at Silvina. "My parents liked astronomy and named me after a galaxy." She darted around the vehicle to the driver's door. "Hop in and away we'll go."

Before jumping in the car, Maria and Silvina hugged AJ and Samantha.

"We'll be back for you before you know it." AJ shut the door after the girls and waved as the Border Patrol vehicle departed. She continued to watch the car until it turned out of sight.

"Back on board, boss." Samantha gestured toward the plane. "Business awaits."

"Let's do this." *I hate leaving the girls here, but no choice. Hope I see them again.*

～

WHEN AJ DISEMBARKED IN MONCLOVA, Javier rushed forward, enveloping her in a bear hug and lifting her off the ground. "Glad you made it!" He held her close and squeezed.

"Put me down, you big oaf!" AJ chuckled as Javier released her. "I guess you missed me, huh?"

"You bet." He glanced at Samantha. "Welcome to Monclova. The Snakes will meet us on the highway—didn't want too many gringos meeting your plane."

Samantha stepped forward and hugged Javier. "Where are Harry and Larry?"

"They're still in Mexico City." Javier rubbed his thickening beard. "Should be hearing from them soon."

AJ reached out and rubbed his beard. "Looking good. Who's it for?"

"Thought it'd hide some of my handsome features so no one would remember me." He laughed. "C'mon, the vehicle's this way." He led her around the side of the terminal building, through a security gate, and stopped by a four-door silver Nissan D22 pickup. Javier opened the front passenger door and the one behind. "Your chariot awaits, my ladies."

"Thank you, kind sir." AJ and Samantha laughed and climbed inside.

After leaving the airport, Javier sped along the highway, passing an identical vehicle parked on the side of the road. "Just passed the Snakes. They'll follow, checking for any surveillance, and will join us at a cantina a couple of miles ahead."

AJ and Javier entered the red, green, and white-painted building. After their eyes adjusted to the dim light, they found an empty table in a corner and sat.

Moments later, the door swung open. Four men entered and went to the bar. Once they received their drinks, they headed out a side door.

Javier stood and gestured. "Let's go."

AJ and Javier joined the Snakes at a circular table in the walled courtyard. Two massive sun umbrellas, emblazoned with Dos Equis Lager logos, provided shelter from the blistering sunshine.

After greeting the team, AJ glanced at Javier. "What's the plan now?"

"We're staying at a family-run hotel not far from Highway 57. It's in a quiet neighborhood with easy access for our continued journey."

"The coast is clear." Mamba drained the last of his beer. "Didn't spot anyone following you from the airport."

Javier nodded. "Drink up, and let's head out."

Twenty minutes later, they pulled into the parking lot of the two-story mustard and white Hotel Capital and drove around to the rear of the building. Javier reversed into a slot with a tall, whitewashed wall behind them. "Already have the keys. They had plenty of rooms, so instead of doubling up, we each get our own." He grinned. "Yours is next to mine—there's a connecting door between us."

AJ rolled her eyes. "Down boy. The door will stay closed between us. I've done a lot of traveling and need to catch up on my beauty sleep."

Javier twisted his face into a deep frown before grabbing her bag. "No harm in hinting. You better place a chair under the doorknob, or who knows what will happen? It'll take more than a closed door to keep me away."

She gave him a girly laugh and patted her SIG. "Oh yeah, you sure you wanna do that?"

They both laughed.

"The rooms are plain but comfortable. We found a restaurant nearby if you're hungry." Javier unlocked her door and handed her the key. "Catch up later."

"Thanks, Javier. I'm going to shower and see if there's any new intel from MacKenzie before crashing."

After taking a hot shower, AJ slipped on a white hotel robe before logging onto her iPad.

To: Hunter

From: Fortress

Updated info. According to sensitive sources, targets are converging on Santa Rosa de Múzquiz. Your contact is Captain Hernández from the XI Military Region based in Torreón. His unit is in the Múzquiz area on drug interdiction duties. He'll provide additional weapons and combat troops if the situation warrants.

AJ acknowledged the message, shutdown her iPad, and switched out the lights.

∾

CRAACK! Pop! Bang!

Staccato bursts of automatic weapons, interspersed with shots fired from handguns, jolted AJ awake. Grabbing her SIG Sauer, she scooted onto the floor and rolled toward the door. She edged it open and peered along the corridor.

Nothing.

Someone grabbed her from behind.

"Get down!" Javier yanked her back into her room.

"Who's shooting?"

"Doesn't involve us." Javier gestured in the direction of the continuing gunfire. "Across the street. As far as I can make out, the authorities raided a house, resulting in a firefight. The Snakes are monitoring the situation, but we need to be ready to depart in case the situation deteriorates." He held a hand over an earbud. "Please repeat."

After listening, Javier confirmed the message and turned back to AJ. "Mamba says we need to move. The firefight appears to be spreading this way."

"Gimme a minute—I need some clothes."

"Hurry up!"

AJ yanked on her top and jeans, sliding her feet into her shoes. She grabbed her backpack. "Ready when you are." She took a deep breath. "Let's do it."

Javier rushed out of the room, followed by AJ. They turned right and scampered to the exit. "Ready? Keep low." He shoved the door's crash bar and darted outside in a crouch.

AJ followed, her head moving left and right as she scanned for targets.

When they reached their vehicle, she reached for the passenger door.

Zing!

AJ clutched the side of her head. Knees buckling, she slumped to the ground.

Behind the steering wheel, Javier's jaw dropped. "No!"

36

P enny Lane
Guantanamo Bay, Cuba

IN THE ADJACENT COTTAGE, the security technician yanked off her headphones and turned to her partner, a squat, bald man named Henry. "Miss High and Mighty is at it again. Wants to kill her husband, someone named Días, and an unspecified terrorist commander."

Henry laughed. "Same threats as before. Do you think she knows we're recording her?"

"Not a chance. You should have seen her coming out of the bathroom butt naked and prancing around in front of the TV. She has no idea she's being monitored."

"Unless she's an exhibitionist." He pouted. "Too bad I missed the show."

Martha rolled her eyes. "You get worse every day."

"What can I say?" He shrugged. "At first, I got a kick out of guessing what she might break next, but she doesn't even rant anymore. It's become boring. When we first started our surveillance, her tirades were interesting. But, since she stopped kicking the furniture and throwing cushions and pillows at the walls, I feel neglected." He sniffed." She just doesn't appreciate all this undivided attention we've given her."

"How about a bit of sympathy for her?" Martha shook her head. "Put yourself in her shoes. How would you like it if someone kidnapped your children, only to find out your spouse was behind the plot? No wonder she wants revenge."

"Hmm. Suppose you're right." He glanced at the monitor and yawned. "She's back in bed."

"Good." She checked the time on the wall clock. "Our relief will be here soon. Busy day tomorrow. Some big shot from D.C. is coming to interview her."

"Perhaps there'll be something worthwhile to watch."

"You might want to spend the rest of your career in this dead-end job, but I have plans." Martha glanced at the ceiling. "The word is no audio or video recordings are to be made while the visitor is here. We can resume after he departs."

TWO GUARDS ESCORTED a stooped man with thinning gray hair wearing John Lennon glasses and dressed in a dark blue three-piece suit to Olivia's cottage. A guard unlocked the door and stepped inside. He shut the door while the remaining guard stayed with the visitor.

Moments later, he returned and motioned for the visitor to enter.

The guest walked into the cottage and glanced around before taking a chair across from where Olivia perched on the brown upholstered sofa.

She held his gaze without making a sound. Olivia glowered at the visitor and rolled her eyes.

He looked away first. *Bitch! Thinks she's better than me.*

"Who are you, and what do you want?" Olivia crossed her arms and legs, continuing to stare at him. "Doesn't anyone believe in making appointments, or am I under arrest without any rights?"

He cleared his throat. "I'm Robert Lintstone. You're here because of my people. I want to understand why we should continue to protect you. At this time, you're not under arrest but in protective custody."

"A woman named AJ brought me here. She didn't say what agency she works for, but I assume it's the CIA? Does she work for you?"

Lintstone nodded. "AJ brought you here. She's one of my best people." *Even if she does take matters into her own hands without consultation far too often.* "She said there's a contract on you and someone kidnapped your children."

Olivia jabbed the air with a finger. "Yes, my *bastardo* husband took my children. I want you to kill him or bring him here, and I'll do it myself."

He examined the fingernails on one of his hands as he chuckled. "My dear, we don't kill people." *At least we won't admit it to people who don't need to know.*

She raised her brows. "I don't believe you—I've heard the stories. In any event, I can pay—I have lots of money. Plenty of people, too, if you can identify who issued the contract."

"We're bound by laws and rules of engagement." Lintstone shook his head. "It would be illegal for me to take money from you, even if we could bend the ROE to assist you."

"What does that mean? In my world, ROE means return on equity."

He laughed. "You make it sound like you're a legitimate business-woman. ROE means rules of engagement."

"Well, I won't tell anyone if you bend them." She leaned forward, her light blue blouse billowing open to show ample cleavage. "What can I offer, which might be of interest to you, so you'll let me go?"

His eyes betrayed his lust before he regained his composure. "Hmm." He rubbed his chin with a thumb and index finger, as he appeared to contemplate a response. "I want access to Latin American terrorist organizations which pose a clear and present danger to my country."

Olivia sat back and adjusted her clothing. "How would I do that?"

"Use your money and people." Lintstone leaned back in his chair. "I don't care about groups like FARC. They are has-beens trying to become legitimate. I need details about al-Qaeda and ISIS trying to gain a foothold in South America in preparation for infiltrating the U.S." *This could get me promoted into the senior ranks—and set me up for a soft landing when I finally retire.* "Also, you mentioned money. I can't take it from you as an agency representative, but if you were to gift it to me privately, I could forget its origin. Say, five million dollars." *A better insurance policy than being promoted. I've earned it for putting up with decades of bureaucracy and incompetence.*

"The money means nothing to me. Get the contract on me canceled." Olivia snapped her fingers. "I read stories about the CIA's involvement in the drug trade in Southeast Asia and Afghanistan. I want access to the fields and protection of my opium business."

I knew I should have stayed behind my desk. Been too long since I was in the field and dealt with criminal elements. "That's a bit much, don't you think?"

Olivia shrugged. "I have what you want, and you can give me what I need. What's the problem?"

Only a long-term stay at Leavenworth or worse. "If I agree to this, none of it's going down on paper."

"Do you think I'm stupid? As my father used to say, 'The best deals are made between people with nothing to lose and everything to gain.' He also said, 'Never admit to anything in writing—it'll come back to haunt you.'"

Lintstone nodded. "A wise man. What happened to him?"

"He broke his own rules—and died."

"We'll keep this agreement between us." *I can always arrange an accident if things get out of hand.*

"There'll be too much information to commit to memory." Olivia glanced toward the laptop sitting on a nearby table. "Perhaps I'll put some details on a USB drive, but there'll be no admission about the origin of this information. How do I get it to you? I watch the movies and know you use what's called dead guys for this."

Lintstone laughed. "I believe you mean dead drops. I'll give this some thought."

"How long will you keep me here? When will my children join me? I want to return to Colombia."

"One thing at a time." He raised his hands. "This agreement will be our secret, so you'll remain here until our arrangement is established." Lintstone's beady eyes focused on her. "No one—I repeat—no one must know about this."

"What about AJ?"

He slammed a fist into an open palm. "Especially not her. Better for both of us to work together in a deniable manner." *You can be dealt with if necessary, without anyone finding out about my involvement.*

"Not a problem—I'm used to handling important deals by myself without any interference."

Perfect. Easier to close the door if things turn sour. He stood. "I'll return in a few days, and we'll have a longer chat." Lintstone gave her a look from head to toe. "Is there anything else you need?"

"Just a USB drive. And some decent wine—none of the cheap stuff they've been giving me. Perhaps, a few bottles of French wine, such as Domaine de la Romanee Conti. Or if that's too expensive for you, how about Petrus?"

"I'll see what I can arrange. I'll be in touch." He tapped the side of his nose. "Remember, this stays between us."

AFTER LEAVING OLIVIA'S COTTAGE, Lintstone glanced in both directions before heading to the adjacent building. He rapped on the door.

Henry checked the peephole before throwing the deadbolts.

Lintstone pushed past, stopping in the middle of the room. "I want today's audio and video recordings."

"But, sir. We followed your instructions—no recording while you were here." Martha raised her hands in supplication. "There's nothing to give you."

"Remove the disks or drives—whatever you use—and I'll take them anyway." He glared at Martha and Henry in turn. "If I find you did make a recording—this'll be your last assignment for the government. Do I make myself clear?"

They nodded.

"Good. It's best for your careers to forget you ever met me."

37

H otel Capital
Monclova, Mexico

JAVIER JUMPED out of the Nissan and raced to AJ's side while firing his SIG Sauer in the direction of the gunfire. He slid to the ground between her and the shooters, cradling her in his arms. Glancing at her head, his heart sank when he saw all the blood. *Don't leave me!*

Mamba joined him. "Put her in the pickup. The others will cover us."

They lifted AJ's limp body and placed her in the truck's cargo area. Javier climbed in beside her, reloaded his weapon before holding her again. "Let's move it."

Mamba nodded, tossed Javier's backpack to him, and hopped behind the wheel. With tires smoking on the concrete, he sped out of the lot, almost colliding with an approaching police vehicle. Fishtailing, he zoomed down the street. He yelled out the window. "I remember the sign for the hospital. No more than ten minutes from here."

Javier examined AJ's head wound. *Deep graze.* He pulled a sterile bandage from his bag and wrapped the wound. A single tear trickled down his face as he stroked her cheek. *Hang on, AJ, please, hang on!*

Mamba slammed on the brakes, sliding to a stop at Hospital Saint Marie under a covered area marked 'EMERGENCIA.'

An orderly leaning against the wall smoking watched Javier and Mamba lift the unconscious AJ from the back of the pickup and rushed to help.

Mamba pushed the man away as Javier cradled AJ in his arms and dashed toward the entrance. "Find help. Pronto!"

The orderly ran inside, yelling for assistance.

Two nurses and another orderly pushing a gurney rushed to help.

After Javier placed AJ on the stretcher, the senior nurse took one glance at their patient and yelled in English and Spanish, "Emergencia!" They stormed down the corridor, where a doctor waited by an examination room, shouting orders to the medical staff.

Javier and Mamba attempted to follow, but the attendant barred their way.

He pointed to the waiting room and spoke in passable English, "Wait, please. Someone give update soon."

JAVIER KEPT GLANCING at the wall clock in the waiting area as he walked a hole in the tile floor. He remained stoic, although his pacing belied his concern. *What's taking them?*

Mamba placed a hand on his shoulder. "Hang in there, boss. I'll find some coffee."

When he returned, he handed Javier a plastic cup. "It's lukewarm, but that's all I could find. At least it has caffeine. Any word?"

Javier took a sip and grimaced. "Nothing—it's been over two hours. What's taking so long? Is something wrong?" *I can't lose her now!*

"I don't know. But, as the saying goes, 'No news is good news.'"

"Yeah."

Another hour passed. A doctor, several blood splatters on his green scrubs, joined Javier and Mamba.

"How is she, Doctor?" Javier searched the doctor's face, his eyes widening with hope.

"She lost much blood but was lucky. Two bullets grazed the left side of her head but didn't penetrate the skull. We cleaned her wounds, stitched two flaps of skin, and put her on an IV drip with painkillers and antibiotics."

"Will she be okay?"

The doctor held a hand in a horizontal position and tilted it back and forth. "I hope so. We ran many tests, which took much time. No fracture but perhaps concussion. We see how she is in the morning."

"Can we see her?"

The doctor nodded. "Soon. A nurse will take you to the woman's room. She might sleep."

"Thank you. Do whatever is necessary to help her. She's my ... wife." *Please, God! Don't take her from me!*

"Of course." The doctor shook their hands and departed.

Fifteen minutes later, a nurse approached. "One person may go."

Mamba glanced at Javier. "Go, man. I'll wait here for the other Snakes."

He followed the nurse without a word. She stopped in front of a closed door and turned to Javier. She put a finger to her lips and motioned for him to follow. "She sleeping. I put chair by the bed for you. Are you *familia*?"

Javier nodded. "Husband. Just got married." *Who knows? Perhaps, one day for real.*

The nurse opened the door wide enough for Javier to slip inside. A soft light emanated from a fixture above the bed. Medical equipment beeped on occasion when it checked AJ's vital signs. Her head swathed in bandages, she appeared to be asleep or unconscious.

Javier sat in the chair. His eyes moist, he took her hand. "Don't leave me. I—I can't live without you."

No response.

With her hand in his, he closed his eyes. The mechanical sounds of the equipment lulled him into a restless sleep.

LIGHT FILTERED THROUGH THE BLINDS, casting shadows across the bed. AJ's eyes popped open. *Where am I?* She glanced at her left arm and spotted the IV line. She looked to the other side and smiled.

Javier sat in a chair, his head tilted back, a light snore emanating from his open lips. He held her hand in his massive paw.

AJ gave a slight squeeze.

Javier's eyes opened, and he gazed into AJ's face. "Hey."

"Hey yourself," she whispered. "What happened?" She swallowed. "My throat's dry, and the side of my head aches."

Javier poured a glass of water from the pitcher on a roll around cart and handed it to her. "When we tried to leave the hotel, you caught two rounds before we got away. You're in a local hospital." He gestured toward the door. "Mamba popped his head in an hour ago, and said the rest of the Snakes and Samantha are in the waiting room."

"What about the mission?" She took a sip from the glass.

"I—I needed to know you were okay before we headed to Santa Rosa."

"How. Sweet." AJ's eyes fluttered before remaining open.

Javier blushed. "Yes. Well, ..."

"My head hurts." She gave his hand another squeeze. "I'll be okay. You better continue the job."

He nodded. "Samantha will remain here while the Snakes and I meet with Captain Hernández and plan our attack. She sent an update to MacKenzie."

"Go get 'em, tiger."

He stood, leaned over, and let his lips brush hers. "I'll be back for you."

AJ smiled as her eyes closed once again.

JAVIER JOINED the Snakes and Samantha in the waiting room. "Time to rock and roll. Samantha, I told AJ you'd stay with her."

"Agreed. Good luck, guys, and kick some ass!"

The team headed to their vehicles. Javier joined Mamba in the silver Nissan pickup. The other three climbed into the blue one and followed.

"Let's get a little payback for AJ!" Javier squeezed his hands into tight fists. *No one better stand in my way.*

"We'll be in Santa Rosa in about two hours. Our contact will join us near the city, and he'll take us to his camp."

AFTER AN UNEVENTFUL DRIVE through several villages scattered along Mexican Highway 57 and Coahuila State Road 22, they passed a sign indicating five kilometers to Santa Rosa de Múzquiz.

"Keep your eyes peeled. There should be a turnoff in a few hundred meters." Javier glanced at a message on his iPad from MacKenzie. "It's behind a tall hedgerow."

"I see it." Mamba gave his left indicator a quick flick to let the trailing vehicle know they were turning onto a side road.

The two-vehicle convoy stopped beside a Mexican Army Humvee painted in green, black, and brown. A tall, slender man with black hair and mustache and a swarthy complexion climbed out of the vehicle and motioned for Mamba to stop.

Javier hopped out and approached. "Hola, Captain Hernández. I'm Colonel Smith." He held out his hand.

The captain saluted before shaking hands. "Welcome to the Múzquiz area. We are honored to assist in your efforts against the foreign terrorists who invaded our country. My men and I are at your service."

"Thank you, Captain. Sorry for being late. One of our people was caught in a firefight in Monclova between members of a drug cartel and the authorities."

Hernández nodded. "I am aware of your situation. Someone named MacKenzie contacted the *Centro de Investigación y Seguridad Nacional*—our intelligence people and the information was passed to my commander. The authorities you mentioned are part of my unit, and they updated me. I assigned two men to provide external security at the hospital as long as your injured companion is there."

"Thank you." Javier gave a tight smile.

"We have taken photos of the terrorist camp." He gestured toward Santa Rosa. "They are in a valley with high cliffs on one side and a lower hill on the other side covered with stunted trees and brush. About fifteen kilometers from us."

"I'd like to get eyes on the area if I may, Captain."

"Of course. We will stop at my encampment. My men built a small replica of the target for you and your men to examine."

"How many men can you spare for the attack?"

Hernández rubbed his chin. "I command a reinforced company assigned in the area for drug interdiction duties. My colonel ordered me to provide as many men as you need, along with any weapons and equipment you might require."

"Perfect. Shall we go examine your model?"

HERNÁNDEZ ESCORTED Javier and the Snakes into a large command tent. Two *soldados* jumped to attention as they entered.

The captain returned the privates' salutes and motioned for Javier and the others toward the center of the enclosed area, where a sheet of plywood mounted on sawhorses supported a primitive model. He pointed to the display. "Nothing fancy, but this will give you an idea of our objective."

Adder rubbed a hand over his head. "Some rocks and trees for them to hide behind, but those tents won't protect them."

"Be like a turkey shoot." Rattler turned and spit tobacco juice on the ground. He glanced at the captain. "Sorry, forgot where I was."

Hernández waved a hand to dismiss Rattler. "I like your term turkey shoot. We will make it so."

"Turkey shoots can still be dangerous, so let's not get overconfident." Javier turned to Hernández. "Captain, there are likely forty to sixty terrorists in the camp. I think two or three to one odds would work. If you could provide at least fifteen men who are expert marksmen, we should be able to achieve our mission." Javier scanned the model once more. "I'd like direct eyes on this."

The captain nodded. "I have such men—I will also participate. We need to teach these *cabrones* a lesson. If you come with me, we will pay a visit to the area."

Thirty minutes later, Javier and Hernández climbed out of a Jeep and followed a trail up the hill adjacent to the valley. When asked who made the trail, Hernández shrugged. "Many wild animals in this area. Could be dogs, wolves, or pronghorn antelope." He grinned. "But, I think this one was made by drug or people smugglers."

After reaching the crest, the men crawled to a vantage point nestled among the low scrub. Javier scanned the camp with binoculars. "They appear overconfident, with only one guard at each end of their encampment." He pulled his gaze from the terrorist camp and focused on Captain Hernández. "We attack at 0300."

A FEW MINUTES before Javier's planned attack time, twenty-two men climbed through the brush and formed two-man teams along the ridge. Wearing NVGs and tactical comms gear, they were armed with M4 and FX-05 assault rifles, they focused on targets within their designated killing zones. Fingers poised along their triggers, they waited for the command.

"Fire," Javier whispered, with Hernández repeating the command in Spanish to his men.

Tracers lit the sky, and gunfire shattered the stillness as the murderous onslaught slammed into the camp, shredding tents and bodies. Smoke and the stench of weapons fire wafted over the valley but did nothing to hide the screams of injured men. Few terrorists returned fire before they succumbed. Voices in different languages cried out in surrender.

"Cease-fire," Javier ordered, once again repeated by Hernández.

One-by-one, the attacking force stopped shooting.

Viper rushed up to Javier. He released a sigh as he glanced around, weapon at the ready. "Adders's been injured."

"How bad?"

"A through and through in his right calf. Mamba is treating him now, along with one of the Mexican medics. Lots of blood, but the bullet went through the fleshy part. Serious, but not life-threatening, although he won't be dancing any time soon."

"Okay, keep me informed." A discussion behind him caused Javier to turn.

"Captain Hernández stepped forward and saluted. "Colonel, I have just been informed we have casualties—one dead and three wounded. The injured will live."

Javier nodded. "Do what you need to do, so your men are safe."

"At once, Colonel. Gracias." The captain issued instructions to two subordinates standing next to him.

Javier surveyed the attack site. *We're lucky with our casualties— could have been much worse.*

As silence returned to the valley, the distinct sounds of two vehicles fleeing the area echoed off the cliffs. Javier turned to Hernández. "How did they escape?" He gestured toward the sound of the fleeing vehicles.

The captain yanked a radio from his belt and requested information. After receiving a response, he turned to Javier. "I am sorry. The way was blocked, but those escaping rammed through the barricade. My men said one of the terrorists' vehicles is damaged."

"Captain, I suggest rounding up your men and taking charge of the camp before any remaining terrorists can rearm and organize resistance. Don't kill them—capture them if possible. They might know something we can use."

"At once." He gave the order to his men. "What happens now?"

"If you and your team will secure the area, we'll go after the escapees."

"Will you capture them and bring them back for justice?"

Javier placed a hand on the captain's shoulder. "Up to them. If they surrender, we'll bring them back for interrogation. Otherwise, they'll die."

38

C IA Headquarters
Langley, Virginia

AFTER RETURNING to his office at CIA Headquarters, Lintstone yanked his chair back from the desk and flopped onto the custom-made orthopedic cushion. Sighing with relief, he grabbed his phone and dialed a number long committed to memory.

With no answer after five rings, he began to replace the receiver when he heard someone clear his throat. Lintstone brought the phone back to his ear. "About time, you answered. Party too much last night?"

The man at the distant end coughed. "No. I caught a cold and stayed late in bed. What are you calling for? I told you the last time we spoke before I graduated from Harvard, I wouldn't betray anyone to help your career."

Lintstone squeezed the handset, his knuckles turning white. "Listen, Alonzo. I own you—you'll do as I say or I'll release the photos I've kept for a rainy day."

Alonzo laughed. "After all this time, no one will believe the photos are of me. Besides, I believed she was of legal age."

"Perhaps in your country but not here in the U.S. The statute of limitations in Massachusetts hasn't expired yet, so a district attorney could still charge you with statutory rape. But, I know someone with connections in the local DA's office."

"What do you want?" Alonzo sighed.

"Nothing much. I met with your mother yest—"

"Is she okay? Where is she? Tell me!"

"Do as I say, and I'll arrange for you to meet with her at a location of your choosing. In answer to your questions, yes, she's okay. For now, her whereabouts will remain my secret."

"You bastard! If I do what you want, then you'll give me the photos—and any digital copies."

Lintstone glanced at the ceiling and chuckled. "I suppose anything's possible." He sat upright in his chair. "Here's what you must do for her. You will use a significant portion of your inheritance to spread rumors. They will tell a story of betrayal against your mother by a former FARC commander named Días and her head of security, Ramon Alvarez. They are conspiring to have her killed."

"What? Impossible—Ramon wouldn't do anything to harm her."

"Doesn't matter whether it's true or not. I want this done. I'll be informed when you've achieved this task. Colombian authorities under our control will pass the information along."

"And if I don't?"

Lintstone snickered. "In addition to supplying the photos to local law enforcement agencies, I'll announce the capture of your mother as the head of a Colombian drug cartel. She'll rot in jail."

"Why you! You're an evil asshole. I'll do—"

"Be quiet! You'll do as I instruct." Lintstone tapped his fingers on the receiver. "Something else to consider in case you're thinking of defying me. There will be severe consequences."

Alonzo's breathing came through the handset in heavy bursts. "What?"

"My people are holding your stepsisters. Would be easy to turn them over to Homeland Security as illegal immigrants. Who knows what might happen to them? Are you aware of the cages, no toothbrushes, and zero health care? There are rumors of young girls being raped in custody, too."

"You bastard! I'll kill you!"

"Many have tried, but I'm still here. I'll give you seventy-two hours to spread the word. I'd get busy if I were you." Lintstone disconnected the call. He reached into the bottom drawer of his desk and pulled out a flask and a tumbler. Pouring two fingers of Jack Daniels into the glass, he downed it. He leaned back in his chair, hands behind his head, feet propped on the corner of his desk. *All good plans come together. Olivia will be parting with a large chunk of her money soon, and I'll be the sole recipient.*

ALONZO TOSSED his cellphone on the bedside table and struggled to an upright position. *Drank too much cerveza last night. I should know better.* Pushing himself off the bed, he staggered into the bathroom and turned on the shower.

Finished with his ablutions, he dressed in a blue short-sleeved shirt and brown Chinos and made his way to the kitchen. A pot of fresh-roasted coffee on a warming plate, he filled a cup and popped a couple of aspirin, swallowing them while sipping his drink. Footfalls echoed on the wooden floor as he sauntered along the hallway and out of the house. After draining his cup, Alonzo strolled out to his Mercedes, climbed in, and drove away, a cloud of dust billowed behind him. *I hope the colonel can help. I don't know where else to turn.*

Thirty minutes later, the stoic butler escorted him to Colonel Santiago's den.

Alonzo nodded when asked if he wanted something to drink. "Coffee, por favor."

The butler turned to Colonel Santiago, who waved him out of the room. "So, Alonzo. On the phone you mentioned there was an urgent matter to discuss." He glanced at his watch. "I can give you some time, but I must depart within the hour for an appointment with the governor of Atlántico."

"Thank you for meeting with me, Colonel." Alonzo swallowed. "There are many things I want to raise with you, not the least of which is Gabriela. However, before I can talk about her in any detail, I require your advice on a different matter—one related to my family."

The colonel's eyes focused on Alonzo while he tapped a finger on his desk. "Go ahead."

"I—I don't know what to do. I have no experience in these matters. The CIA took Mamá into protective custody. Pedro indicated he was behind the kidnapping of his own daughters—he's threatened to kill me. Now, the CIA wants me to spread rumors about Mamá's security chief, Ramon, and Días, the—"

Colonel Santiago held up a hand. "I am familiar with Días and his lofty goals. The government has made peace with FARC, and he hopes to be a politician one day. How things change." Santiago shook his head. "For years we have tried to put him in prison, but someone kept tipping him off about planned raids. Perhaps ...." He gazed out the window for a moment. "Perhaps, one day, he will receive the justice he deserves."

The door opened and the butler pushed in a cart with coffee and pastries. After serving the men, the butler departed.

Santiago sipped his coffee. "Rumors are circulating about Ramon and his high-handed security measures, but given the circumstances embroiling Colombia for decades, he has not been alone in trying to safeguard those requiring protection—even if many are criminals."

Alonzo nodded.

"I am also acquainted with the whispers about Pedro and have been for a long time. He is a has-been from the Los Urabeños trying to reclaim his youth. Hiding his daughters and claiming someone kidnaped them might be his undoing." Santiago held Alonzo's gaze. "He is scheduled for an accident."

"What?" He swallowed, trying to moisten his dry throat.

"Nothing to worry about. This is one of the topics I will be discussing during my appointment." He wrinkled his forehead. "Now, why is the CIA holding your mamá? I am aware of the contract put out on her. One of my sources provided this information a couple of days ago."

"I'm not sure how she ended up in their clutches. The man who contacted me threatened to expose a ... problem I had when at Harvard."

Santiago chuckled. "Yes, I am familiar with, eh ... the situation."

"How did you find out?" Alonzo clenched his jaw raised his brows.

"Alonzo, when you became interested in Gabriela, I had your background torn apart. I understand what happened and do not hold it against you—we all make mistakes when we are young. However, as I said before, you must renounce the drug trade and become an honest businessman."

"Once Mamá, Maria, and Silvina are safe, I plan to return to the United States and run our legitimate businesses there—shopping malls and restaurants. I want them to come with me—Gabriela, too, if she'll agree."

Santiago finished his coffee. "An excellent proposal. While my wife and I would miss having Gabriela near us, she would be much safer." He stood. "I must go now. Come back tomorrow evening and join us for dinner. Once the women have left us, we will smoke cigars, drink brandy, and discuss the best way to spread stories about Ramon and Días. Perhaps pit them against each other."

39

U nnamed Valley
    Outside Monclova, Mexico

"Hurry!" A blood-spattered terrorist aimed his AK-47 out the window of the speeding vehicle, emptying the clip despite no apparent sign of pursuit. "Hurry! Don't lose sight of our other truck. They know the route to take us to the others."

Ebrahim nodded, as he pressed harder on the accelerator, the pickup fishtailed when he swerved onto the end of the dirt road. He glanced into the rearview mirror but couldn't see anything but a cloud of dust. "I know the way, too. We're supposed to meet Michael outside Ciudad Acuña. There's a warehouse on the new wind farm where we'll join him to make our final plans before crossing the border."

"How come you know so much?" The terrorist glanced over his shoulder at the remaining two men, both injured in their earlier encounter. One nursed a bullet graze on his right arm. The other mumbled, his glassy eyes opening and closing as he stared into nowhere. The stain on his left hip continued to increase as he lost blood. Neither man appeared interested in the conversation in the front seat.

"Don't forget, I was one of the team leaders during training—but you belonged to another team. Michael briefed all the leaders about the mission, including our final destination. Once both teams are together, we'll strike."

"So? Where will we avenge our brethren?"

The driver grinned. "I shall lead the attack on the Alamo in San Antonio while others will hit commercial targets such as Market Square and the Rivercenter Mall. We'll leave the warehouse during the early morning hours so we can be in position when the decadent people begin shopping. The destruction of the Alamo will be a symbolic strike against this shrine of American aggression."

MICHAEL DROVE into the Acuña wind farm support depot. Numerous trucks and machinery dotted the area in front of various metal buildings housing workers and for storing construction materials. He stopped the Toyota Land Cruiser in front of a prefab warehouse he and Alberto rented for their staging area. "At last, we're here. It won't be long before we strike fear in the hearts of the Americans."

Alberto yanked a bandanna from his pocket and dabbed at the perspiration dotting his forehead. "Our teams should start their insertions the day after tomorrow. Are you sure their documents are in order?"

"Yes. We paid thousands of dollars to have a team of forgers in Europe create the necessary documents. The passports, ID cards, and driver's credentials should stand up to any scrutiny—many will have documentation showing they live across the border but are helping to construct the Mexican wind farm."

The door to the warehouse opened. Two armed guards stepped outside, waving for Michael to enter. After he pulled inside, the door slid shut with a clang.

Michael and Alberto climbed out of the Toyota and followed the guards to a raised platform. Dozens of chairs faced the stage, but over half remained empty.

Ebrahim embraced them and swung a hand to encompass the seating area. "We lost many men in a fight with the Mexican Army near Múzquiz."

A frown etched Michael's face. "How many survived?"

"I'm not sure." Ebrahim shook his head. "Eight of us made it here a couple of hours ago, but two of them were injured in the fight. A few others escaped, but I'm not sure how many."

"If the injured can't be treated, you know what to do. No witnesses. They can't be left behind to reveal our mission." Alberto glanced at his watch. "Those who flew into Mexico City from Saudi Arabia should arrive soon." He turned to Michael. "Will the ten of us and the twenty additional freedom fighters be enough?"

"I'll take care of the injured. If they survive, it is Allah's will. In any event, we will have enough to carry out our mission."

～

A ONCE-YELLOW BUS covered with travel stickers raised a cloud of dust as it sped along the road toward Acuña. The driver kept checking the mirrors for any signs of someone following them. *I should be with my family instead of driving these crazed people across Mexico. I'll be glad to get rid of them.* He slammed on the brakes, causing several occupants to slide out of their seats. Backing up, he made a left at the small sign for the Acuña wind farm. The dust cloud increased as the bus bounced along the access road, slowing down as it reached the construction site.

Upon entering the warehouse, the new arrivals were greeted with cheers and pats on the back as they disembarked.

Their leader lifted his AK-47 in the air. "Allahu akbar! Allahu akbar!"

～

IN THE DISTANCE, and unknown to the bus driver, a McDonnell Douglas MD 500 Defender helicopter tracked the vehicle. Harry focused his binoculars on the cloud and spoke over the intercom. "Larry, send a secure text to Javier and let him know the terrorists are converging."

After Larry acknowledged the instruction, the pilot interrupted and pointed to his instruments. "We must refuel—now. We'll be back on station within an hour."

Harry gave a thumbs-up to the pilot, who swung the helicopter in a tight turn. *We'll be back.*

JAVIER SMILED when he received the message from Larry: *Twenty tangos converging at Acuña wind farm. Must refuel. Awaiting your arrival.* He turned to Mamba. "Put your foot down. The party's forming."

Mamba tapped the Nissan's horn, and stuck his hand out the window, waving the two-vehicle convoy forward.

Cursing his fat fingers, Javier typed a short response. *Cavalry arriving within the hour. Meet at designated rendezvous point. Time to end this.* He grabbed the panic bar as Mamba hit a massive pothole, sending the pickup toward the guardrail. "Do you mind staying on the road?"

Mamba laughed. "Sure thing, boss." He gestured with a thumb over his shoulder to the vehicle's cargo space. "Good thing we strapped everything down. Wouldn't want the gear to explode. That Mexican captain gave us plenty of firepower. Hope we get to use it."

"We will." Javier crossed his arms. "In addition to the observation chopper carrying Harry and Larry, Captain Hernández arranged for ten of his men to join us a couple of clicks from the target."

"Great odds—about two to one!" Mamba thumped the dash. "Let's get 'em!"

Javier gazed over the parched countryside. A variety of stunted trees and shrubs dotted the landscape, growing denser in areas bordering the scattered streams. He turned toward Mamba. "Shouldn't be long now—hope we're there before dusk settles in."

Mamba nodded as a helicopter passed overhead, descending toward a distant bluff. A second chopper followed. "Must be the cavalry. Isn't the trailing chopper an AH-64 Apache?"

"Yep. The Mexicans are going all out to help us." Javier chuckled. "Will definitely ruin someone's day."

Thirty minutes later, after providing the prearranged signal, the two Nissan pickups stopped next to a Panhard VBL command post. Two soldiers sat on top of the lightly-armored vehicle, one aiming an FN MAG multi-purpose machine gun toward the new arrivals.

When Javier stepped out of the pickup, a soldier approached and saluted. "Colonel Smith? I'm Lieutenant Benito de Santa Anna. Captain Hernández sends his greetings."

Javier returned the salute and shook hands. "Any relation to General Antonio López de Santa Anna?"

"A distant relative." The lieutenant grinned. "I believe our objective will be the terrorists' Alamo?"

"All being well. I suggest we attack just after midnight."

"Yes, sir. In that case, we will share our combat rations with you and your men."

AT THE APPOINTED TIME, connected via tactical comms to the Snakes, the pilots, and Lieutenant de Santa Anna, Javier gave the order to attack. The Apache fired four 70mm rockets at the unlit warehouse. Explosions sent pieces of the prefab roof into the air, followed by billowing clouds of dense smoke, outlined by the light of several fires.

Situated on a slight rise overlooking the compound, Javier focused his binoculars on the now-burning building and smiled. *Got 'em!*

The sound of the attacking forces' automatic weapons, nick-named Fire Snake, drowned out the intermittent return fire of a few AK-47s.

One terrorist, his clothing on fire, burst through a side door. His body jerked multiple times before collapsing to the ground. Foam dribbled from his mouth as blood saturated the ground.

The attack helicopter continued to encircle the perimeter, watching for anyone trying to escape.

Within fifteen minutes of the first rocket hitting the building, all resistance crumbled. Firing from within the warehouse stopped, and a white flag appeared through a hole one of the projectiles had punched in the wall.

The attacking force held their fire as the screams of dying men filled the air. Flames clawed toward the heavens as part of the roof collapsed. The stench of toxic materials, weapons fire, and several fires filled the air.

Two soldiers who had entered through the door after shooting the burning terrorist, rushed out, one carrying a package. After a brief word with their commander, they joined the other soldiers.

Lieutenant de Santa Anna rushed up to Javier, a briefcase in one hand. "Sir. You'll want this. One of my men took a quick look before handing it to me." He smiled. "Appears some of the terrorists planned to attack the real Alamo." He cast his gaze downward. "Unfortunately, they killed two of my men and wounded four others."

"I'm sorry for your loss, but they didn't die in vain." *At least we didn't lose too many. I hope the injured survive.* Javier clapped a massive paw on the lieutenant's shoulder. "Let's check for any signs of life and anything else of intelligence value. If possible, take photos of the faces of any bodies. But we must hurry before it's not safe to enter the building."

"Yes, sir. What should we do with survivors?"

"I'm more interested in the safety of our men than prisoners. If you meet any resistance, use your judgment."

40

P enny Lane
Guantanamo Bay, Cuba

LINTSTONE UNLOCKED the door to Olivia's cottage and stepped inside. As he scanned the living room looking for her handbag, she came out of the bathroom.

Olivia gasped and pulled the towel tighter as she stepped out of the bathroom. "What now?" Gaining her composure after being startled, she stomped her foot. "Is this how you get your kicks? If it's a naked woman you seek, try your mother's house. Don't you have anything better to do than scaring defenseless women?" She glared at him. "Not that you scare me."

"I suppose I have a distinct advantage at the moment." He leered, staring at her head and working his way down her athletic, bronzed legs. "Is there anything I can do for you?" He licked his lips. "Anything at all?"

Her intense gaze made him look away. "You're a lecherous

bastardo. Wait outside while I change." She stormed into the bedroom and slammed the door.

Lintstone laughed as he ignored her and grabbed a seat, continuing to scan the room. *Where is it?* Unsuccessful, he settled into one of the living room chairs and grabbed a magazine lying on the table while he waited.

Ten minutes later, Olivia returned, fully dressed in jeans and a thin green sweater. She stood in front of him, hands on her hips. "You didn't answer my question. What do you want?"

"Transfer a million dollars into this account." He slid over a slip of paper with numbers scribbled on it.

"What's this? Are you loco?" She dropped the paper on the floor. "How do I know you've done anything for me? Where's the proof?"

"I'll have proof soon, but I need more money for spreading the rumors." *No harm in taking more of her money—it's from illegal sources anyway.* He cleared his throat. "I've started the process, and I'm satisfied we will achieve our objectives." *At least mine, anyway.*

"If that's true, you owe me. Release me now. I want what you promised—access to the Afghan poppy fields. I also want to visit my new domain."

"Send my money, and I'll arrange for your visit to Afghanistan." Lintstone leered at her. "I'll need a day or so. Plenty of time to take care of other business."

Olivia sat in a chair across from him and opened her laptop. "I'll transfer your funds now." She rolled her eyes. "But don't get any ideas. Nothing else is available. When I land in Afghanistan, you can ask again, and I'll tell you what you have to do."

As Olivia watched a movie the following evening, a knock on the door interrupted her solitude. She stood and moved closer to the exit. "Who's there?"

"Ms. Moreno, I'm here to escort you to a plane. Mr. Lintstone sent me."

Olivia frowned but unlocked the door. "Not much notice. I must pack." *Why the rush?*

One of her regular guards waited on the porch. "Just got the call. The plane will be here in less than an hour."

"Very well." Olivia opened the door wider and stood aside. "Give me a few minutes. Take a seat."

When she was ready, she returned to the living room, a bag over her shoulder and pulling a wheeled suitcase.

The escort jumped to her feet and offered Olivia a phone. "Mr. Lintstone said to use this satellite phone when you want to talk with him. You must keep it powered up at all times in case he needs to speak with you."

She examined the ordinary-looking device and shrugged before shoving it into her bag. "I'm ready. Shall we go? You can bring my suitcase."

TWO DAYS LATER, after a series of stops for refueling, the aircraft landed at Kandahar International Airport in Afghanistan. Two armed security officials, dressed from head to toe in black, boarded the plane. After checking Olivia's documentation, they escorted her down the steps to a waiting SUV with blacked-out windows.

After they dumped her luggage in the back, one of them held a rear door open for her. He jumped in beside her while his partner climbed into the front passenger seat.

A brief check at a security gate and the vehicle pulled onto a two-lane road, heading west running away from the setting sun.

"Where are we going?" Olivia glanced out the window at the bleak scenery. Dry, rolling hills, dotted here and there with an occasional young boy trying to herd sheep toward grassy patches. *Have I made a mistake trusting Lintstone? Will he live up to his promise to reunite me with Maria and Silvina? If not, I'll hunt him down—he'll beg for mercy.*

The armed man sitting beside her gestured toward the west.

"We've been instructed to take you to one of the poppy fields in Helmand Province. We'll overnight at a compound outside the provincial capital, Lashkar Gah, since we never travel in the dark unless necessary. Our escort from Helmand will arrive in the morning."

"I see. Who will I be meeting with?"

"Mr. Lintstone arranged for you to meet one of the owners of the largest poppy field. I understand his name is Abdul Jaleel."

"Does this Abdul know I'm taking over?"

The man shrugged. "Too far above my pay grade. I just take clients where and when they need to be somewhere."

Olivia leaned her head against the door and closed her eyes. Before long, the rocking motion of the SUV lulled her to sleep.

WHERE AM I? Olivia woke with a start as the vehicle bounced through a series of potholes. She glanced outside. Red, orange, and purple streaks edged across the sky, chasing the golden orb as it disappeared over the horizon.

Her head whipped back and forth as she tried to determine their location, looking for anything that might serve as a landmark. She recoiled when a hand touched her arm.

"Relax." The guard gave a soft chuckle. "We're almost to Lashkar Gah. About ten minutes to your overnight stop."

"My overnight stop?" Olivia's eyes seemed to grow larger. "Aren't you staying, too?" *What's going on? Lintstone said the escort would remain with me at all times.*

The man shook his head. "After we drop you off, we have other business to attend to in the city. It'll be some time before we return this evening."

Turning into a street not much wider than the vehicle, they traveled between a row of high walls, numbers written on them in Roman numerals and Dari script.

The driver hit the horn, and a gate ahead on the right opened. He pulled through the opening and stopped in front of a two-story whitewashed building. An armed guard, his AK-47 pointed at the sky, approached the vehicle.

Olivia climbed out of the SUV and entered the aging house. After the escort deposited her luggage in what appeared to be a common room, an Afghan woman approached.

"Hello?" Olivia smiled. She glanced at the bare walls and the sparse, worn furniture.

"She doesn't speak much English, but she'll take care of you this evening." The guard headed toward the door. His hand on the knob, he stopped and turned around. "Remain inside at all times. Keep your phone handy. I'll give you a call if there is anything you need to be aware of before I return."

~

THE AFGHAN WOMAN led Olivia inside and took her to a rough-hewn table. After she was seated, the woman brought Olivia a plate of food and motioned for her to eat.

"Where's my knife and fork? Or a spoon?"

The woman gave a toothless grin and mimed lifting some of the goat and rice with her right hand and placing it in her mouth.

Olivia cringed. *How disgusting!* However, hunger soon overcame the lack of utensils, and she mimicked the woman, who began eating from her own plate. *Food's good, though.*

Her food finished, Olivia drank from a bottle of lukewarm water. Her eyes became heavy.

Before long, she leaned forward, head resting on her arms. *I'm so tired. Did the woman put something in the food to poison me?* Tears seeped from her weary eyes. *How are my babies?* Her eyelids closed, and she drifted into an uneasy sleep.

~

WHAM! Wham!

The building shook, and the shabby furniture bounced across the uneven wooden floor. Walls cracked as a hole large enough for a new door appeared.

Olivia screamed and scrambled under the table.

Wham!

A third explosion rocked the house.

Craack!

One end of the building tipped as a wall and corner gave way.

"*Yeeeah!*"

A blood-curdling scream filled the room as the roof collapsed, crushing the table.

And Olivia.

Seven thousand miles away, Lintstone stared at the live footage of the drone attack in Lashkar Gah being piped into his office. *Yes! One loose end tied up. I'll get Alonzo to send me more money, or I'll release the photos.*

His office door locked so no one could enter, Lintstone burst into laughter and clapped his hands. "After I bleed him dry, his body will be found. The autopsy will find he died using his own product."

41

H ospital Saint Marie
Monclova, Mexico

THE DOOR CREAKED OPEN, forced wide by a massive rainbow of red, orange, green, yellow, and various shades of blue. The vivid flowers appeared to float into the room, the aroma wafting through the air. They approached the bed and hovered.

A disembodied voice seemed to emanate from the arrangement. "A little help, please."

Samantha shook her head to break free of her trance and rushed forward. "Damn, Javier. Did you buy every flower in town?"

"Almost. I skipped some that make me sneeze." Together, they placed the flowers on a cart one of the nurses had deposited in the room earlier.

Javier stepped to the edge of the bed, a grin from ear to ear as he gazed at the occupant. "Hello, beautiful."

"With my black eyes and my head covered in a turban, I doubt I deserve your compliment." AJ laughed. "Perhaps it's time for you to retire or start wearing glasses."

"Who said it was a compliment?" He sat in the chair Samantha had pulled next to the bed for him. "My eyesight's good. I just had trouble remembering your name."

AJ chuckled. "What a charmer. I bet you say that to all the women you've dragged by the hair into your cave. How many times did you have to clobber them over the head with a club before they would stop fighting you?"

Javier shrugged. "Only the ones in the hospital—they needed cheering up." His hand snaked up the cover and gave a gentle squeeze to hers.

"I hope you're here to spring me from this prison." She flexed her back. "Everyone's been super helpful, but I'm itching to return to work."

"It's only been a few days." Javier glanced at Samantha. "Is she always this pushy?"

A smile etched across Samantha's face, but she didn't respond.

"Hey, guys. " AJ cocked her head. "Will someone fill me in on what's been going on?"

"First things first." Javier stood and stepped into the corridor, returning moments later, pushing a wheelchair. "I recall doing this in Panama."

"Yeah, people are going to start talking about me hanging around with you." AJ pointed at him. "You're bad luck."

"I guess so, but I mean well."

Samantha raised her iPad. "MacKenzie sent an update, but Javier and I thought you'd feel better getting on the plane first. When we're in the air, we'll give you a SITREP."

"I'm outnumbered. Let's get the paperwork done, or whatever they want so I can get out of here."

AFTER THE GULFSTREAM G650 leveled off, Javier unbuckled his seatbelt and went to the galley. He returned with three bottles of orange juice and handed one each to Samantha and AJ. Twisting off the cap of his bottle, he guzzled the cold drink before turning to AJ. "Time to put you in the picture. Do you want to begin with MacKenzie's email?"

AJ nodded and held her hand out for Javier's laptop.

To: Hunter, Cobra, Samantha

From: Fortress

Many congrats on a successful mission. Mexican authorities report a total of sixty-four terrorists killed. Twelve others were captured. We've agreed with Mexico taking credit for the operation, so no overt kudos to our people—job well done from on high.

Based on our calculations and the initial interrogation reports provided by the Mexicans, it's probable at least four terrorists escaped. Efforts will continue to identify and locate them.

Take the weekend off and see you bright and early Monday morning.

AJ handed the device back to Javier. "Well done, you. So, fill me in."

"Remember our contact, Captain Hernández? Appears he stepped well outside his authority, but in the end, his efforts made the difference. After our initial firefight near Múzquiz, two vehicles loaded with bad guys escaped. The Snakes and I gave chase."

"Do you mind?" He took AJ's unfinished juice and drained the bottle. He burped. "Ah."

AJ chuckled. "Pig."

"Javier grinned. As I said, we took off in pursuit. In the meantime, Harry and Larry called in a marker or two and arranged for surveillance from the Mexican Air Force. They tracked the escapees to a warehouse at a wind farm under construction near the border. Captain Hernández coordinated additional military support for us, including—get this—an Apache attack chopper." Javier shook his head. "You should have seen those guys blow the warehouse—wasn't much left."

"What about the Snakes?" AJ smiled as she placed a hand on Javier's arm.

"Viper, Mamba, and Rattler received minor injuries when the warehouse blew apart. Adder didn't participate in the warehouse attack because he had a bullet through his calf in our first attack, but he's going to be fine. Harry and Larry escaped unharmed. Everyone is back at their normal duties."

AJ frowned. "Are there any loose ends we need to worry about?"

"Yes. Olivia's daughters are still in El Paso." Samantha grinned. "If no one claims them, can I take them home with me?"

Javier and AJ chuckled. She turned to her friend. "Are you sure you want kids? Besides, we'll need to arrange for them to rejoin Olivia. What's her status? Last I remember I dropped her off at Penny Lane."

Samantha glanced at Javier. "The only thing MacKenzie mentioned about Olivia was Lintstone taking a personal interest in her situation."

AJ rolled her eyes and shook her head. "If anyone can screw things up, it's him. I'll sort Lintstone out on Monday—won't have him creating more problems for us." She yawned.

Javier glanced at his watch. "About three hours until we arrive at Andrews. Why not take a snooze? I'll wake you before we land."

AJ's eyes closed. "Good idea."

JAVIER GAVE AJ's shoulder a gentle nudge. "Time to wake up—we're starting our descent."

She stretched and glanced out the window. "Clear night—plenty of lights. What's next?"

"After we land, I'll take you home." Javier grinned. "If you're hungry, we can order a pizza or something."

"Ugh! Don't want pizza. How about a thick ribeye steak, baked potato, and salad?"

"Hmm. Does anyone deliver steak? If not, I guess we could stop somewhere before heading to Alexandria."

AJ nodded. "I know an excellent place in D.C., the Capital Grille. A bit out of our way, but worth it. Their steaks are to die for."

"Be right back." Javier headed to the restroom.

After their plane landed at Joint Base Andrews, a black stretch limo waited by their designated parking area. A driver wearing a dark suit and a chauffeur's cap leaned against the vehicle.

Samantha waved farewell to Javier and AJ and climbed in a waiting taxi.

"What's this?" AJ turned to Javier and smiled. "Expecting visitors?"

He shrugged. "Thought I'd surprise you. Since our vehicles aren't here, this was the next best thing." Javier spoke to the driver before climbing in after AJ.

They sat next to each other in silence as the vehicle whisked them into the city. Before long, the driver stopped in front of a restaurant on Pennsylvania Avenue and dashed inside.

AJ glanced at Javier, a puzzled expression on her face.

"Wait." Javier raised his brows.

Moments later, the driver returned, carrying a large parcel. After putting it on the front passenger seat, he climbed behind the wheel and departed.

"I know the staff quite well. Remember when I went to the restroom on the plane? I gave them a call and ordered dinner—all we had to do was pick it up."

When they arrived at AJ's condo, the driver carried the package inside for them.

AJ gestured toward the kitchen.

After he set the container on the island, he doffed his cap.

She opened her handbag. "How much do we owe you?"

The driver shook his head. "My family owns the restaurant. After Colonel Smith saved my life on one of our missions a couple of years ago, there's nothing we won't do for him. Enjoy your meal."

As soon as he left, AJ opened the box. "What are we eating?" She pulled out several containers and peeked inside. "Just what I asked for, plus two bottles of wine. Do you plan to get me drunk and have your way with me?" She gave him a coy glance and licked her lips.

Javier laughed and held out his arms. "We'll see how the evening goes. The possibilities are endless, and the weekend's ahead of us."

She walked into his embrace. "Promises, promises."

42

J's Condo
Old Town, Alexandria, Virginia

JAVIER SLAMMED his hand on the horn of his black GMC Yukon as a driver cut him off, almost clipping the front bumper. "How do you put up with the drivers here? We're gonna be late." He gestured at a vehicle he passed. "Look! She's putting on her makeup while driving!"

AJ laughed. "The Beltway chaos always gets me riled. One minute you're cruising at seventy miles an hour and the next you're crawling along the highway. Glad to see you're no different."

He gave her a sideways glance. "Unlike you, I'm kinda anal about being on time."

"Yeah, you have a tight ass." She cackled. "Don't worry, big boy. We're the golden children at the moment. Lintstone might bark a bit, but he'll be taking credit for our mission and using it to his advantage. He won't rock the boat—too much—if we're a bit late."

"He better not."

"C'mon, Javier. I can't wait to hear all about Lintstone's brilliant execution of our mission." *As if!*

MacKenzie and Makayla met AJ and Javier at the elevator. Once again, the twins were dressed alike—this time in yellow blouses and green slacks, with black shoes. After a hug for AJ and shaking hands with Javier, MacKenzie gave AJ a stern look. "Late again, boss. You'll upset Lintstone."

"Like I care." AJ screwed up her face in imitation of Lintstone before bursting into laughter.

Makayla struggled to contain a giggle. "Yeah. Maybe he'll blow a gasket. He could have a stroke or something, and it'll be all your fault."

AJ laughed. *I wish.*

They hurried along the corridor and entered a conference room. Nineteen chairs sat around the rectangular table. Downlights reflected off the polished surface.

Lintstone sat at the head, arms crossed, his forehead puckered. "Did that head wound affect your ability to tell time? Just because you were injured in the line of duty is no excuse to be late."

"Yes, sir." AJ took a chair as far from Lintstone as possible. *Asshole. The closest he got to being injured in the field was a paper cut.*

Javier took a seat next to her and placed a folder on the table.

"Report." Lintstone drummed his fingers on the table as he glanced at his watch.

AJ expelled her pent-up anger in a whoosh of breath. "As you're aware, the overall mission objective was to identify and disrupt Islamic State activities which could impact on the security of our southern border region. Thanks to assistance from the Mexican military, we achieved our goals. A secondary outcome of this operation resulted in the—"

"If the Mexicans hadn't stepped in, you would have failed."

She frowned at Lintstone's objection. *How'd he expect us to be successful without support? He's been watching too many Jack Ryan movies.* She ignored his comment, gave him a lackluster smile, and pressed on. "Through a new source within a drug cartel, we learned more about Islamic State's creation of terrorist training facilities in Colombia and Panama. Efforts are underway with local authorities to infiltrate these areas and ensure they're no longer operational."

"Who is this so-called source?" Lintstone glared at AJ. "You never mentioned him in any of your erratic and brief SITREPs. Why?"

Does he really think I'd tell him? "Protocol dictates we protect sensitive sources in communications, especially if their lives might be in danger. We—I felt this was the case in this situation. I can now reveal our source was Ramon Cristobal Alvarez, chief of security for the Moreno drug cartel." She glanced around the room. "He stumbled across a plot hatched by FARC commander Días, who was apparently supporting Islamic State in return for their assistance in removing the head of the Moreno Cartel."

"Where is this Ramon now?" Lintstone crossed his arms. "I want to meet him."

AJ struggled to keep her emotions in check. *Why would he want to talk with an asset?* "We don't know. He's missed several scheduled check-ins." She glanced around the table. "We also came across further details of a plot to eliminate Olivia Perfecta Moreno, the head of the drug cartel. Her husband kidnapped their children and then pretended to be distraught over their disappearance. Someone—we suspect Días—put out a contract on her. In order to keep Ramon supporting us, at his request, we took Olivia into protective custody. She's now at Penny Lane. Through human and electronic means, we identified where the children—Maria and Silvina—were being held and rescued them." She frowned. "Her husband, Pedro, also disappeared as has Días."

"Hmm." Lintstone's pursed his lips. "What you're telling me is way outside the parameters of your mission. You couldn't keep track of what was happening right in front of your face. We'll talk about this in private, but I dare say this was your last field assignment. I think you need a rest—spend time with your family and friends—if you have any. Your incompetence forced me to take control—"

"What?" AJ's eyes flared. "We always go where the intel takes us. You have no right—"

The double doors to the conference room burst open. A tall, silver-haired gentleman with chiseled features stood framed in the entrance. Two other men dressed in suits flanked him. Additional security officers wearing open shirts and sport coats blocked anyone from leaving the room. One of the officers closed the doors after everyone stepped inside.

"What is the meaning of this interruption?" Lintstone slammed a fist on the table as he focused on the new arrivals. "Oh. It's you—sorry, Director."

The director of the CIA spoke in measured tones as he waved the officers forward. "Arrest Lintstone for the murder of Olivia Moreno. Read—"

Almost everyone gasped.

AJ and Javier focused angry eyes on Lintstone's face.

Javier glanced at AJ. "What the hell?"

She shrugged, lips set in a grim line. *Olivia dead! Those poor girls! If he's guilty, I hope he gets what he deserves.*

The director waved toward Lintstone. "Read him his rights or whatever it is you do, but throw him out of my building. I won't tolerate any blatant rogues putting this agency in a negative light more than it already is."

Lintstone struggled against the security officers as they forced his arms behind his back, handcuffs locking into place around his wrists with a resounding click. "I'll bring you all down. You don't know what it's like to—"

"Get him out of here."

The officers dragged the resisting Lintstone from the room.

The director sat in Lintstone's vacated chair and gazed at the shocked expressions of the room's occupants. "Please continue."

"Yes, sir." AJ swallowed. "I was ending my wrap-up of our recent mission when you arrived. Do you want me to begin again?"

He shook his head. "Won't be necessary. Get on my calendar for later in the week. We need to talk about your operation and also your new role in this organization."

"My new role?" AJ's mouth hung open. "I wasn't aware I was going anywhere."

The director waved a hand toward the doors. "Appears I have a vacancy to fill. How does being responsible for all anti-terrorist operations in Latin America sound?"

"Uh, yes. Yes, sir." AJ's mouth twitched. She prevented herself from grinning. "What about Lintstone? What will happen to him?" *As if I care. Good riddance. She stole a glance at Javier, who sat grim-faced with his arms crossed.*

"At a minimum, he's going into enforced retirement. If he protests and wants the scandal to be open to public scrutiny, he'll face criminal charges of murder, misuse of government property, extortion, and money laundering to start with. I suspect we'll add to the list as we conduct our internal investigation. I've had a special security team monitoring him for months after some strange disappearances of funds under his control." The director stood and headed toward the door. When he reached AJ, he stopped and shook her hand. "Well done on a successful mission."

TEN DAYS LATER, AJ was sipping on an espresso as she read a report on the computer in her new office. *Hmmm. Something strange happening in Cuba—have to put the twins on it.* She typed a brief email and sent it to MacKenzie and Makayla.

Knock. Knock.

"Come in." AJ set her coffee on a red limestone coaster and stood when she recognized the visitor.

"Have a minute?" He held a piece of paper in his hand.

"Of course, Director. Is there a problem?"

"No, nothing to worry about. Thought you might like to see this press release before it's sent to the *Washington Post*." He handed her the notice.

Robert Lintstone, a senior CIA official, died suddenly at his home after a short illness. It's believed undiagnosed diabetes triggered a massive heart attack. His colleagues mourn his passing, with one stating, "He was an interesting character and will be sadly missed."

Lintstone is survived by his wife and twin boys, who were recently accepted at Georgetown University to study political science. A private memorial service will be held.

AJ handed the paper back to the director, her brows raised. "Sadly missed?"

He smiled. "Yep. Least we could do for his family."

"Who arranged this?"

The director raised a brow, a flicker of a smile on his face.

"Never mind—probably better not to know what really happened. I do have one question. I've never been able to figure out how you knew what Lintstone was up to with Olivia and her family. Who told you?" AJ stared into the director's face.

"I suppose you've earned the right to know." He sighed. "Many years ago, when I was a young field agent, my first posting was to Colombia. I was introduced to a young captain in the Colombia military—Bautista Santiago."

"The name seems familiar."

The director smiled. "It should. Bautista is now a colonel. His daughter is romantically linked with Alonzo Salvador, Olivia Moreno's son from her first marriage. When Lintstone threatened Alonzo, he happened to mention this to Bautista, who in turn, called me. I requested a quiet investigation—turns out it was justified, too."

"Thank you for sharing this with me, Director. My lips are sealed."

43

C IA Headquarters
Langley, Virginia

JAVIER STRODE along the corridor with a bouquet cradled in an arm. He paused outside a door to examine the brass nameplate and noticed a smudged fingerprint in a corner. He yanked a handkerchief from a pocket, wiped the blemish away, and knocked on the door.

"Come."

Javier stepped inside, strolled to AJ's desk, and handed her the flowers.

She set them down and rushed around the desk into his embrace.

"Javier! About time you showed up!" AJ gave him a peck on the cheek and waved him to a high-backed polished leather chair with brass tacks along the seams, taking one opposite him. "Coffee?"

At his nod, she pressed a button and requested two black coffees.

When her secretary came in, she handed mugs to AJ and Javier, closing the door on her way out of the office.

"Do you remember the photos taken by Lieutenant de Santa

Anna's men after the warehouse was blown up? MacKenzie and Makayla confirmed one of the Islamic State trainers named Michael was killed. No confirmation about the one called Alberto."

Javier grinned and sipped his drink. "Couldn't happen to a nicer scumbag. Maybe we got Alberto, too. So, how does it feel to move up in the world and oversee counter-terrorism operations in Latin America?"

AJ tasted her coffee and grimaced. "Not sure how long I'll be able to do this. I already miss the field, and it's only been two weeks."

"I understand what you mean." He set his cup and saucer on the side table. "Since being reassigned to the Pentagon, it's been nothing but pushing one pile of papers across the desk to make way for more." He shook his head. "Perhaps I'm not cut out for this."

"Same here, but what can we do?" AJ laughed. "The price we must pay for moving upward in our careers."

Javier rubbed his chin. "I've been thinking. Since I'm eligible to retire, perhaps it's time to do something else. Don't want to end my career as a rear-end paper pusher."

"Sounds pretty drastic. What would you do?"

"My time in the military has been the thrill of my life. Made loads of friends—and some enemies, too. However, I'm not ready to be put out to pasture, so I've been weighing up my options. If my retirement is approved, I'll go into business."

AJ laughed. "What type of business? Anything I might be interested in?"

Javier gestured around the room. "Would you really give this all up?"

"In a heartbeat. I'll stick around for a year, but if another position doesn't open up, it might be time to find something different."

"Are you sure? Don't you have some time yet before you're eligible to retire?"

"Yes, to both questions." AJ smiled. "However, when my parents passed away, I ended up with a small inheritance. I've never touched it, but it's sufficient to meet my needs for a few years without relying on a government pension."

Javier grinned. "Here's my idea. I talked to a couple of guys I've gotten to know over my career. They have a ton of experience, and they'll help me. I'm going to open a security and investigative agency, working mainly on overseas cases—if I can find enough jobs to keep us going. I already identified a couple of potential contracts, though once they're over, I worry we won't get enough work to keep us afloat."

"Really? Would there be room for me?" Dimples appeared in AJ's cheeks as a broad smile etched across her face.

"Of course—you're part of my plan. That is, if things don't work out for you here."

"Have you thought of a name for this wild idea?"

Javier nodded. "Remember Lintstone introduced me as Colonel Smith? It's not my real name."

"Oh, I figured." AJ chuckled. "As soon as Lintstone assigned us to work together, I had MacKenzie and Makayla check into your background. Where does Busch originate?"

"It's German. I was thinking of combining our last names. How does the Brusch Agency sound?" He stood and pulled AJ from her chair.

"Different." She smiled before he kissed her.

Six Months Later
San Antonio, Texas

Alonzo waved as the last vehicle from the moving company pulled out of the driveway of his new four-bedroom, two-story home in a secluded area of San Antonio. His smile faded as he turned around, gazing at the brown and yellow brick and stone facade. *If only Mamá were here to see this.* He shook his head, went inside, and headed to the kitchen.

He opened the fridge door and pulled out a pitcher of lemonade.

Filling three glasses, Alonzo placed them on a tray and followed the sounds of laughter and splashing water. He squinted as he stepped into the brilliant sunlight and sauntered to a wicker table nestled under the trees. "Maria! Silvina! Lemonade's ready."

The girls climbed out of the pool and rushed to the table.

Alonzo handed each of them a glass. "How's the water?"

"Fantastic!" Silvina glanced back toward the pool. "Alonzo, thanks for bringing us to your new home. With Mamá gone, we had nowhere to go."

He clasped her hand. "This is your home now. Once you are settled in, we'll get you registered for school. There's a great one nearby."

"What about Papá?" Maria's eyes widened. "Will he be able to find us here?"

"I hope he leaves us alone and never comes back!" Silvina's nostrils flared.

Alonzo shook his head. "You'll be safe here." *I'll protect them with my life.* "Finish your lemonade and get cleaned up. Our guests will be here in a couple of hours."

"Who's coming?" Silvina emptied her glass. "Do we have to dress up?" She frowned while Maria's face lit up.

"We'll need to create new rules. I suggest the first one is we will dress like our neighbors do and not try to impress anyone. Wear what you want, as long as it's clean." He chuckled. "As far as who's coming, it's a surprise, but you met them a couple of times."

Maria clapped her hands. "Good. I love surprises. But I want to wear one of my new dresses—the yellow one."

"Of course."

When the doorbell rang, Maria and Silvina raced to answer. Breathless, they grabbed the handle together and pulled. The girls squealed with delight when they realized why Alonzo had kept the identity of their guests a secret from them.

Colonel Santiago, his wife Sofia, and their daughter Gabriela wore beaming smiles as they waited to enter. He was dressed in a green sport shirt and matching trousers, while the women wore floral blouses and multi-colored skirts.

"Girls, please let our guests come in." Alonzo shook hands with the colonel and traded air kisses with Sofia and Gabriela. He also gave Gabriela's hand a quick and gentle squeeze.

The Santiagos stepped into the foyer and gazed at the vaulted ceilings, tiled floors, and terracotta and cream-colored walls.

"What a lovely home." Sofia nodded her approval. She turned to Gabriela, who smiled.

Colonel Santiago turned to Alonzo. "If I may be so bold, would it be possible for the girls to show my wife and daughter your home while we take care of some business? It should not take long, and then we can enjoy the rest of the weekend."

"Of course, Colonel. Girls, do you mind?"

Maria took Sofia's hand while Silvina took Gabriela's.

"We'll go upstairs first." Maria led the way.

Alonzo gave an open-handed gesture to the colonel and guided him toward the rear of the house. He stopped near a mini-bar. "Would you care for a drink, Colonel?"

"Yes. Whatever you are having. Also, let us not be so formal. At least for the weekend, please call me Bautista."

"Yes, sir—I mean, Bautista." Alonzo grabbed a bottle of rum from the bar and poured a generous serving in two glasses. "We'll relax on the veranda. With the sun dropping, it's cool enough to sit outside and enjoy the evening."

Once seated, they tapped glasses and took a sip of their Juan Santos twelve-year-old Colombian rum.

"Excellent choice, Alonzo." Bautista glanced around. "To business. First, I am sorry about your loss. While I disapproved of your mother's livelihood, I did admire her tenacity and beauty."

"Thank you. We miss her but are beginning to settle into our new life here. Once the girls start school, I'll begin my new job." Alonzo grinned. "I'll be an adviser to the DEA."

Bautista raised his glass in the air. "I am sure you will be a resourceful addition to their organization."

Alonzo acknowledged the compliment with a tilt of his head.

"I have four things for you. The Colombian government finally decided to do something about Días. They threw him in *La Modelo* Prison, and housed him with other FARC prisoners." He took another sip of his rum. "I received word before we departed for our flight—he is dead."

"Suicide or murder?"

"Does it really matter?"

"No, I suppose it doesn't. Any word about Pedro?"

"Number two on my list. His efforts to assume control of Los Urabeños met with stiff opposition. They decided reliving the past was more to their liking than trying to muscle into the current drug trade. His bullet-riddled body was found in the Doña Juana landfill."

"Good. After what he put Maria and Silvina through, they won't miss him, and neither will I."

"I spoke to a long-time friend about this Lintstone who tried to blackmail you. Nothing to worry about—he will not bother you again."

"Thank you, sir."

"That takes care of the unpleasant business." Bautista reached into a pocket and pulled out a small black box. He handed it to Alonzo. "Sofia and I would be honored if Gabriela accepts your proposal, you use this engagement ring. It belonged to Sofia's great-great-grandmother."

Alonzo opened the box and stared at an exquisite piece. Set in eighteen-carat yellow gold, a stunning rose cut diamond dominated the center of the ring. A double halo of antique diamonds surrounded the main gem, with additional diamonds set into the shank. "Colonel—Bautista. It's exquisite! Must be worth a fortune! I hope Gabriela will accept my proposal."

Bautista stood. He grasped Alonzo's left shoulder and clasped his right hand. "I am sure she will—welcome to the family."

~The End~

Dear Reader,

Thank you! I hope you've enjoyed reading this story as much as I did in creating it. If you did, I'd greatly appreciate it if you could take a minute or two to write a brief review on Amazon. It doesn't need to be long, but your feedback helps other readers and me.

Reviews are so important to all authors. For me, I don't have the benefit of being supported by one of the major New York publishers, nor can I afford to take out ads in the newspapers and on television. Your review helps to get the word out, not just on Amazon, but also through various social media outlets as I use these to create posts on Facebook, Twitter, and LinkedIn. If you are so inclined, you can jump to the appropriate page by clicking on one of the links below:

Amazon U.S. -

Amazon UK -

Amazon CA -

Amazon AU -

ALSO BY RANDALL KRZAK

If you enjoyed *Colombian Betrayal*, you might also enjoy reading my award-winning novels:

The Kurdish Connection

A semi-finalist in the 2018 Chanticleer International Book Awards (CIBAs) in the global thrillers category.

In their daily struggle for survival, Iraqi Kurdish scavengers uncover a cache of chemical weapons. They offer the weapons to fellow Kurdish rebels in Turkey and Syria to assist in their quest to free an imprisoned leader and create a unified homeland. After receiving a tip from an unlikely source, the newly formed Special Operations Bedlam team is called to arms!

Travel with Craig Cameron and his international team on their covert operation as they weave their way through war-torn regions seeking to locate and recover the weapons before they can be used to cause irreparable harm and instigate a world crisis.

The odds are stacked against them. Can they manage to keep their operation hidden and prevent further clashes before it's too late?

Amazon U.S. - https://amzn.to/2uue6Pl

Amazon UK - http://amzn.to/2lbM5H2

Amazon CA - https://amzn.to/2MA3lY2

Amazon AU - https://amzn.to/2EZ5m9U

DANGEROUS ALLIANCE

One of seven First in Category Winners in the 2018 CIBAs, global thrillers category.

United Nations' sanctions are crippling North Korea. China has turned her back on her malevolent partner. The North Korean military machine is crumbling, unable to function. Oil reserves are minimal and the government seeks new alliances.

Cargo and tourist ships are disappearing along the Somali and Kenyan coastline at an alarming rate. Speeches abound, but inaction emboldens Al-Shabaab to seek their next prize: Kenya. The terror organization controls land but requires weapons.

Bedlam Bravo team leader Colonel (Ret.) Trevor Franklin leads the small international team into East Africa. Tempers flare as the team is embroiled in a political quagmire. The axis must be stopped to avert an international crisis but at what cost?

Amazon U.S. - https://amzn.to/2Dop28e

Amazon UK - https://amzn.to/2PcXcCe

<u>Amazon CA</u> - https://amzn.to/2D77SuI

<u>Amazon AU</u> - https://amzn.to/2QlrpeG

CARNAGE IN SINGAPORE

A semi-finalist in the 2019 CIBAs , global thrillers category (as of January 26, 2020)

Terrorist groups such as Abu Sayyaf and Jemaah Islamiyah have flourished in recent years with new recruits joining them and ISIS-affiliates at an alarming rate. Blended operations by various Asian countries have forced the groups to work together to identify a new operational base.

They seek an island nation to call home, one where they can plot against countries who oppose their ideals. They found a target, a small nation-state, perfect for their needs: The Republic of Singapore.

Before anyone can respond, the ambassadors of the United States, Great Britain, and Australia are kidnapped from their residences in Singapore. Right index fingers of each victim are sent as a warning. Any attempt to recover the ambassadors will result in the removal of additional body parts.

Bedlam Charlie team leader, Evelyn Evinrude, leads the group to rescue the ambassadors and capture the local leaders of Abu Sayyaf and Jemaah Islamiyah. Can Bedlam succeed or will events escalate, resulting in more deaths?

Amazon U.S. - https://amzn.to/2MHoDS6

Amazon UK - https://amzn.to/2MIrXbk

Amazon CA - https://amzn.to/2YLgeiO

Amazon AU - https://amzn.to/2GNSyEt

Dangerous Alliance and *Carnage in Singapore* are also available for free if you're a member of Kindle Unlimited.

ABOUT THE AUTHOR

Randall Krzak is a U.S. Army veteran and retired senior civil servant, spending thirty years in Europe, Africa, Central America, and the Middle East. His residency abroad qualifies him to build rich worlds in his action-adventure novels and short stories. Familiar with customs, laws, and social norms, he promotes these to create authentic characters and scenery.

His first novel, *The Kurdish Connection*, was published in 2017, and the sequel, *Dangerous Alliance*, was released in November 2018. Both placed in the 2018 Global Thriller Book Awards sponsored by Chanticleer International Book Awards, with The *Kurdish Connection* finishing as a semi-finalist and Dangerous Alliance being selected as one of seven first in category winners. The third novel in the series, *Carnage in Singapore*, was released in August 2019, and is currently a semi-finalist in the 2019 Chanticleer International Book Awards. He also penned "A Dangerous Occupation," a winning entry in the August 2016 Wild Sound Writing and Film Festival Review short story category.

He holds a Bachelor of Science degree from the University of Maryland and a general Master in Business Administration (MBA) and a MBA with an emphasis in Strategic Focus, both from Heriot-Watt University, Edinburgh, Scotland. He currently resides with his wife, Sylvia, and six cats in Dunfermline, Scotland. He's originally from Michigan, while Sylvia is a proud Scot. In addition to writing, he enjoys hiking, reading, candle making, pyrography, and sightseeing.

Keep in touch with Randall on Facebook, Twitter, LinkedIn, or his website: http://www.randallkrzak

CONTINUE READING FOR AN EXCERPT OF
THE KURDISH CONNECTION

Halabja, Iraq
March 1988

Two weeks after the attack on Halabja, Dersim Razyana, an eighteen-year-old engineering student, returned from Beirut to the remains of his hometown—to bury his parents and two brothers.

His childhood friends, seventeen-year-old Ismet Timur and sixteen-year-old Hawre Vandad, were also victims of Saddam Hussein's regime. Ismet suffered horrendous burns over his face, upper body, and arms. His lungs seared by chemicals, Hawre became weak and developed a persistent cough.

Despite their injuries they numbered among the few survivors.

Halabja, a peaceful city of 70,000 inhabitants in Iraqi Kurdistan was surrounded by mountain ranges on three sides, the Sirwan River to the west, and less than ten miles from western Iran.

Forty-eight hours earlier, bombardments shattered the city's peace. Continuous pounding by Iraqi artillery reduced many homes to rubble and destroyed the infrastructure.

The earth shook with each barrage. The screams of the injured penetrated the putrid stench of the dead and acrid, billowing smoke.

Many suffocated in the toxic air. Cries of grief over the mangled bodies of loved ones rose everywhere.

Rocket and napalm attacks resumed on the third day, March 16, 1988. Fires raged out of control and residential areas collapsed. People hid in basements or crawled under teetering concrete slabs.

The softening of Halabja had ended.

That evening, sounds burst over the city—jet engines and strange whistling noises like metal falling to the ground. "Gas!" someone yelled. Others picked up on the warning and shouted at passersby. People panicked, trampling one another in vain to find safety.

An aroma, not unlike sweet apples, mixed with the pungent odor of rotten eggs spread across the city. Birds fell from the sky. Insects curled up and died. Cats, dogs, livestock, and then humans sank to the earth.

Waves of Iraqi aircraft flew over the doomed, dropping sarin, mustard gas, and other chemical agents.

Those fortunate enough to be outside the immediate blast area fled. If they owned a vehicle, they drove. If not, they ran. The nearby mountains provided temporary escape as refugees fled into Iran. Those who couldn't became statistics.

More than five thousand died that day, and during the following weeks and months, thousands more joined them due to secondary infections and lack of sustainable medical care.

After burying his family, Dersim sought out his friends. He searched everywhere but couldn't locate them.

"Check at the hospital." A masked worker paused his search through the rubble to speak with Dersim. "The authorities transported many injured people to Zakho."

Dersim made the trip to Zakho's hospital, arriving two days later. He spoke to several nurses, all too busy to waste time on a healthy person. A male aide recognized Dersim's frantic face as belonging to someone searching for relatives.

"Try room four. Many from Halabja are there." The stench reached Dersim before he entered. A room designed to hold ten patients held twice that number. He went from bed to bed, stopping at each one.

In the far corner, he spotted them, crammed into the same bed. They appeared to be asleep.

"Psst. Ismet. Hawre, it's me, Dersim."

Filthy bandages covered the injuries to Ismet's face and upper body. Hawre, whose face appeared almost normal, except for burns around his mouth, opened an eye. "Dersim." He pushed aside an oxygen mask and stretched a shaking hand out to his friend.

"Dersim. I ... knew you'd find ... us." "How's Ismet? He seems bad." "Yes." Hawre coughed several times before using the oxygen once more. "They keep him ... sedated. So he ... will heal."

"No more talking, my friend." Dersim grasped his arm and replaced the mask over Hawre's face. "Rest."

Hawre drifted off.

"Sleep, my friends. I'll be here for you."

As his friends dozed, Dersim's thoughts wandered.

What's our future? How'll we persevere?

~

Halabja, Iraq
Thursday, December 30, 2010

"You must swear by Allah never to say a word of what I'm going to tell you. If you promise, come to me. Now. At my house. Swear by Allah, or disaster might occur. This is the most important secret."

~

Dersim Razyana stretched his left hand toward the dun-colored rocks for balance as he inched around the exposed artillery shell. Once past, the breeze forced him to pull his tattered coat tighter around his body. Although bright and sunny, the morning wind carried a hint of rain from the nearby mountains.

He trudged through the soft sand caught in crevasses and climbed over a small ridge, an area without trees or any animals, yet only an hour's walk from his home. Dersim squeezed through the rusted barbed wire enclosing an abandoned military compound. Rows of derelict buildings stood like silent guards waiting for their leaders.

A once-impressive parade ground now housed the rusted hulks of forgotten vehicles. Miniature sand dunes stretched from the trucks, like fingers, with random shriveled weeds where some forgotten plants once achieved a foothold. Only the occasional call of a passing crow interrupted the silence.

"Come on, you two," Dersim said. He spoke in Sorani, a Kurdish dialect. "Don't take all day. There's scrap to salvage and sell."

Ismet Timur and Hawre Vandad, his friends for more than thirty years, stared at the shell. Streaked with rust, the shell was about seven inches in diameter, and at least two feet long. The men sidled by and joined Dersim.

Dressed in frayed clothes and wearing American-style baseball hats, they continued to move farther away. Of average height, the three men were wiry and strong despite their weathered appearance.

"Don't worry about the shell." Dersim raked his hands through his wavy black hair while he waited.

"Should we—" Hawre broke into a coughing fit. A gust of wind blew sand into his face. He took a piece of cloth from a pocket and wiped the grime away. "Should we try to remove it?"

"No. Through Allah's blessings, we've always returned home without injuries. I don't think any of us are reckless or desperate enough to tempt fate."

"Dersim's right. We don't need to risk our lives."

"Pray to Allah for more good fortune today to end the year." Hawre sank to his knees to offer a prayer before a convulsion ravaged his body.

They often traveled up to one hundred kilometers from Halabja searching for anything to salvage. The Iran-Iraq war had ended twenty-two years before but the once-fertile land yielded a meager living for the three scrap dealers. Together they spent many long days picking through the rubble of war-torn villages and the countryside, examining the insides of abandoned and derelict buildings.

Today, though, they continued to scavenge on a hillside east of Halabja, not far from the Iranian border. Dersim and Hawre loaded Dersim's dilapidated Turkish BMC truck with salvage they had identified during the previous three days. The truck sagged on broken springs. Cracks spider-webbed the windshield and the paintwork was so faded it became difficult to recognize any of the original colors. Dersim maintained the engine and other moving parts in superb working order, at least, when he obtained the necessary components.

Fifty yards away, Ismet screamed and waved his hands. Long-legged and built for running, he left the loading to the others. Dersim spotted Ismet, cringed, and ducked behind the truck.

"Hey!" Ismet whistled. "Dersim! You coward. Come here."

Dersim raised his head and scowled. "By the grace of Allah, don't yell! I thought someone was attacking us."

"Check this out. Wait 'til you see. I can't believe our luck." Ismet locked his hands behind his head and danced his version of the Kurdish Chapi. He pushed his left foot forward twice, stepped back twice on his right, while throwing his right hand upward, moving in a circle.

Dersim hurried to his friend, who stood with a broad smile on his dust-covered face near a collapsed wall by the hillside. The wall hid the entrance to a large cavern, and Ismet had dug around the opening, making a space big enough to squeeze through.

"What did you find?" Dersim bent down, pushing giant cobwebs aside for a better view. Through dark shadows, he made out a well-worn, dust-covered floor beneath stacks of crates.

"Ismet, go to the truck and make some torches. Use the oily rags in the back and grab a few pieces of wood."

Once Ismet returned, Dersim lit a torch, and they crawled inside.

"What did I say? I sensed we'd find treasure." Ismet whooped with delight.

Unlike many other areas they uncovered, concrete paved the massive grotto area. Dersim and Ismet walked between rows of crates stacked ceiling high, marveling at the potential value. Once they reached the end of the cave, Ismet spotted steps carved into the rock and lit another torch.

They descended a long flight of steps to a deep cellar. A hoard of military supplies stretched beyond the light of the torches. Their gaze fell on boxes of uniforms, boots, emergency food rations, tents, and medical supplies.

Ismet hoisted a small box of boots over his head, a grin still on his face. "We're rich, we're rich. Allah has blessed us."

"Let's check this out before you count your money." Dersim waved a hand in Ismet's face to bring him back to earth. "We've found other stockpiles suitable only for scrap."

"This must be one of Saddam's hidden bunkers. I can't believe our luck."

Hawre leaned against a pile of rubble to ease his stiff limbs, shuffled a foot in the sand, and kicked a few stones while he guarded the main entrance. A gust of wind blew grit into his face, which he cleaned with a dirty piece of cloth. "Allah has blessed us!" He overheard Ismet's muffled shout and entered the cave to join the others.

"Ismet, you and I'll sort through the items. Hawre, please go back outside and warn us if anyone comes near." *I hope he's a better watchman than he's a scavenger. I wonder if his illness is getting worse.*

Departing, Hawre launched into another coughing fit. He wiped his mouth with his rag. Before putting the cloth back in his pocket, he saw bloodstains, more than last time.

Four hours later, Dersim and Ismet completed their inventory of the cave. Dersim stretched his weary back. "How many uniforms?"

"I stopped counting when I reached one hundred." Dersim gasped. "What?" "Brand new. They're all from the Iraqi Army. At least two hundred pairs of boots, too."

"I found hundreds of boxed meals and many cases of bottled water." Dersim pointed down the corridor. "Must be at least fifty to seventy boxes of medical supplies."

"These items are worth a fortune! And we still must count the weapons."

Together they stacked the weapons. Ismet estimated at least fifty Kalashnikov AK-47 assault rifles and seventy-five Glock pistols. Dersim tallied the boxes of ammunition, one for each weapon, and over one hundred 7.62mm magazines.

Along one wall, hidden by a discarded tarp, they found another stack of wooden crates. Dersim pried open the first one with a small crowbar.

Crack!

The dry wood shattered as he forced the lid open, sending splinters and dust into the air. A damp odor wafted from the container. Moving aside an oily cloth, the contents appeared.

Grenades! What a find.

The squeak of nails forced out of their holes and labored breathing filled the air. An odor of mildew mixed with the tang of lubricants and aged pine made breathing difficult. When he finished, he counted ten crates filled with grenades, while another ten contained plastic explosives.

Ismet kept repeating, "We're rich," as he worked.

Dersim mumbled. "You realize we must keep this quiet? Control yourself and be careful where you wave your torch. You might set something on fire and blow us up."

Gravel trickled into the cave entrance and echoed throughout the chamber. The two men froze.

His heart racing, Dersim whispered, "What was that?"

Wide-eyed, Ismet shook his head.

The next sound, Hawre coughing, flooded Dersim with frustrated relief. "Hawre," he said. "Go back to your post. I told you before, pay attention. We don't want anyone to sneak up on us. You'll be able to view everything later."

Hawre shuffled back outside to the wall and sat down. He pulled his wooden prayer beads from a pocket and recited the ritual prayers of the Tasbih to praise and glorify Allah.

While Dersim opened the crates, Ismet found a large steel container secured by an old padlock. He forced the lock with a chisel and hammer from the truck and found six more boxes, each larger than those holding the grenades and explosives. A hand- painted Iraqi flag covered the side. Across the top, a single word written in Arabic script: DANGER. He called Dersim over.

Curious to find out what they contained, they opened the boxes, one at a time, using slow, controlled movements.

"Ismet, be careful with those tools."

Ismet reached down to pick up the pry bar and wrapped the end in a rag. "Sorry, Dersim."

Each box contained nine canisters, wrapped in protective padding. Dersim pulled one out. "Ever come across one of these before?"

Ismet shook his head and pulled another one from the protective covering.

Dersim peered at the faded writing on the canister he held. The mixture of letters and numbers meant nothing to him. He waved the canister at Ismet. "Do you understand what this is?"

Ismet pointed at the label. "Skull and crossbones mean one thing —danger."

Dersim nodded. "We must be careful. Come. Let's move the stuff to the front of the cave."

They made more than a dozen trips to move the treasure to the cave's entrance. During one trip, Dersim found Hawre asleep against the wall. "Hawre, wake up! We need you to pay attention."

He gave instructions to Ismet when he returned. "When you go outside, scout the area in case Hawre missed anyone trying to sneak up on us. I caught him sleeping."

Ismet came back a few minutes later. "I found Hawre bent over making a terrible hacking sound. Is he getting worse?"

"Perhaps. I told him to go back to the doctor, but he refused. No idea how much longer he'll be able to work with us."

Dersim made a decision once they placed the weapons and munitions by the opening.

"The truck isn't large enough to take everything in one trip. Let's take the weapons first because we'll receive more money for them. We'll leave everything else inside until we return. Hawre, you must remain to keep your eyes on things."

Exhausted from the exertion of hauling their hoard to the surface, Dersim and Ismet gulped water and took a short rest. Anxious to leave, they finished loading with a renewed sense of urgency before anyone spotted them.

Stashing their find on the truck, they concealed everything under a load of scrap metal. The two men covered the load with large beige tarps and tied them down with coarse ropes. Dersim walked around the vehicle, double-checking the ropes and glancing around, searching for trouble.

No one. Must be my nerves.

Hawre stayed behind to guard the remaining treasure. They waved to him as they departed on the dusty forty-minute journey to Dersim's walled compound on the western outskirts of Halabja. Other than a couple of donkey-drawn carts and some wild dogs, they controlled the road.

As they approached Dersim's property, an elderly man trudged along the edge of the road, struggling under a load of chopped branches tied together with a piece of rope. He set the load down and waved.

Dersim waved back and slowed to a stop. "Allo, Ahmed. How are you today?"

"Tired, Dersim, but still breathing. It appears you've done well."

He pointed at the covered load on the back of the truck. "What did you find?"

"The usual. Old tires, sheet metal, wooden crates. Even some copper."

"Good for you." The man bent down, grabbed his load, and pulled the rope over his shoulder. "Later. Tell Xalan I said hello."

"I'll do. May Allah watch over you."

Dersim nosed the vehicle ahead. Ismet jumped out of the cab and opened the gates, and Dersim pulled into his back yard. They unloaded the truck and covered the weapons with the tarps, weighting the edges down with chunks of concrete.

The men hurried back to the vehicle and returned to the compound. Collecting Hawre and the munitions, they drove back to Dersim's residence arriving as dusk fell. Two people stood by the pedestrian gate. As they drew closer, Dersim recognized them—nosy neighbors.

"Allo, Dersim. Where's Xalan? I came over an hour ago. No one answered. May I come inside and wait for her?"

"Allo, Rana. She took the children this afternoon to visit her parents. They'll be back tomorrow."

"Ah. Okay. Thank you." They headed toward their compound, glancing back at Dersim and the others as they did so.

When he pulled into the compound, he parked next to the house. "Let's move everything inside."

Dersim reset his simple but effective alarm system while the others hauled the stash into the house. Set four feet from the wall, Dersim maintained a rope-linked series of cans, half-filled with stones and broken glass. When disturbed, the contents rattled. During the still of the night, the disturbance couldn't be missed inside.

Dersim lifted a trap door hidden by a carpet under the sofa in the front room. "Hand the crates down."

The men worked together in silence. Noise not unlike the horn on a train shattered the night. The men froze.

The horn sounded again. A deep rumble shook the house.

"The guy lives down the street. He drives a big truck for a Zakho company." Dersim smiled, understanding the fear shown on Ismet and Hawre's faces. "Every time he's back he shows off."

By midnight, they secured the munitions in Dersim's bolthole, built to protect his family in an emergency. He set one of the unknown canisters aside. His cousin might understand the writing.

∼

The next morning, Dersim wrapped the canister in a blanket and went outside. He placed the package in the back of his truck and hid the bundle beneath scrap metal. There would likely be police or military checkpoints along the way.

He hopped into the truck and headed toward Erbil, the capital of Iraqi Kurdistan, where his cousin Egid lived. Now a pharmacist, Egid spent several years in the Iraqi military and might tell him about the canisters.

If the security people take the baksheesh, perhaps they won't inspect the cargo. Dersim hoped he brought enough money for bribes at checkpoints along the route.

As Dersim downshifted to climb the next steep part of the road, the engine groaned. His eyes scanned for potholes, and he swerved back and forth to miss the larger ones. The vehicle shuddered every time he misjudged. He uttered a brief prayer. "Tires don't puncture, brakes, don't fail."

Reaching the apex of the steep climb, he inched the vehicle along, past an occasional boulder hanging over the road. He began the treacherous downhill stretch toward Erbil.

The brakes squealed as Dersim tapped them to keep the vehicle under control. A large grinding noise came from the back—the scrap iron slid back and forth while he rocked the vehicle to avoid the largest potholes. At last, the road leveled out again, and he boosted his speed.

Dersim knew he was approaching Erbil by the familiar gray smog of wind-blown dust and ash from soft coal fires lingering over the city. He wrinkled his nose at the pungent stench and tasted the coal dust permeating the air.

He approached one of the permanent security checkpoints outside the city. A burly mustachioed guard dressed in a khaki uniform waved a red flag, signaling Dersim to stop. "Where are you going? What's in the back?"

"I'm taking this scrap metal to the market." "There's a fee for using this road."

Without a word Dersim handed over an envelope he prepared in advance. The guard grabbed the envelope, took a quick peek, and waved him along.

Dersim drove to the Erbil bus station and parked. He called his cousin when a pay phone became available.

"Egid, it's Dersim. How are you, Cousin? I hope all is well."

"Hello, what a surprise! Where are you?"

"I'm in Erbil with a load of scrap to sell. Do you mind if I stop by when I'm done?"

"Of course, happy to see you again. Come after I close for the evening. We can talk and not be interrupted." "Good. Until tonight." Dersim returned to his truck and drove to the junkyard to sell his salvaged metal.

When he arrived, Egid ushered him inside the store and closed the door. They went into the back room where Dersim unwrapped his prize.

Egid examined Dersim's bundle. "*Bxo*—shit! Where'd you find this canister? It's dangerous stuff!"

"I suppose. I spotted the skull and crossbones and was careful. What's inside? Fertilizer or poison? We found several of these and plan to sell them."

"I can't be sure, but—see these letters and numbers? They're chemical formulas. Based on what I can make out." Egid picked up the canister and studied the writing. "*Sagbab*—son of a dog! I think this contains a chemical agent used in Saddam's gas attack on Halabja."

Dersim's heart pounded, and his eyes grew wide as he stepped back from the table. He remembered returning to the village after the attack, finding his family—parents and two brothers—dead. His best friend, Ismet, scarred for life, his upper torso, arms and face disfigured. The stench of decaying bodies had overwhelmed him and the screams of the injured and those in mourning haunted him. He shook his head, trying to erase the memories while tears slipped down his face falling to the floor.

"Uh ... okay, thanks." Dersim paused, rubbing his chin. He let out a long sigh. "What do you think we should do? Perhaps we should take them back to the compound and bury them deep in the ground."

"Dispose of them. Don't mess with these canisters. Nothing good will come to you. *Dayk heez*—son of a bitch." Egid ground his teeth together and shook his head as he continued to inspect the canister.

Dersim witnessed the doubt in Egid's eyes. "You're right. They're too dangerous."

Dersim spent the evening with Egid. After a quiet meal, they retired early. Dersim tossed and turned throughout the evening. Visions of his parents and brothers swirled through his mind, tormenting him. At last, he fell into a restless sleep

The next morning, Dersim headed back to Halabja. Before departing, he wrapped the canister in heavy padding and secured the container in a sack of grain purchased with the money raised from selling the scrap.

Waving to Egid, he drove away, all thoughts on the previous two days and their unbelievable discovery. *Do I put the canisters back in the ground as I promised Egid? We might make good money for the metal, and not tell anyone what's inside.*

"Damn! What do I do?" Dersim slammed his hand on the steering wheel. "Think." *A lot of money to be made if we're smart. Do we keep the weapons and ammunition, and sell the other stuff?* "Allah, guide me!"

Dersim paid little attention during the return trip, rocking the truck back and forth as he dodged around the worse stretches of the road. His concentration centered on their find and the dilemma they now faced.

"That's it!" *Something I've always wanted to do. We can still raise money to feed our families. Perhaps ... we'll also help our people. Create our own destiny.*

Dersim went straight to the post office when he arrived in Halabja. He used the outside pay phone to call his cousin, Babir, in Zakho, to check if he'd a sufficient supply of goods for him to transport to Turkey to sell.

"Happy New Year, Babir!"

"The same to you, my brother."

"You won't believe what we've found."

"Tell me. What did you find?" "You must swear by Allah never to say a word of what I'm going to tell you. If you promise, come to me. Now. At my house."

"Why the mystery? Tell me!" "If you can't swear to Allah, disaster might occur."

"All right, Dersim, all right. I swear by Allah to keep what you say to myself. I'll come as soon as I can."

"This is the most important secret. Ever!"

Printed in Poland
by Amazon Fulfillment
Poland Sp. z o.o., Wrocław